An Image
in the Lake

A JOANNE KILBOURN MYSTERY

GAIL BOWEN

*An Image
in the Lake*

This book is also available as a Global Certified Accessible™ (GCA) ebook. ECW Press's ebooks are screen reader friendly and are built to meet the needs of those who are unable to read standard print due to blindness, low vision, dyslexia, or a physical disability.

Get the ebook free!*
*proof of purchase required

Purchase the print edition and receive the ebook free. For details, go to ecwpress.com/ebook.

LIBRARY AND ARCHIVES CANADA CATALOGUING IN PUBLICATION

Title: An image in the lake / Gail Bowen.

Names: Bowen, Gail, 1942- author.

Series: Bowen, Gail, 1942- Joanne Kilbourn mysteries; 20.

Description: Series statement: A Joanne Kilbourn mystery; 20 | Previously published in 2021.

Identifiers: Canadiana (print) Canadiana 20220213844

ISBN 978-1-77041-678-9 (softcover)

Classification: LCC PS8553.O8995 !43 2022 | DDC C813/.54—dc23

ALSO ISSUED AS:
ISBN 978-1-77041-613-0 (Hardcover)
ISBN 978-1-77305-830-6 (ePub)
ISBN 978-1-77305-831-3 (PDF)
ISBN 978-1-77305-832-0 (Kindle)

Published by ECW Press
665 Gerrard Street East
Toronto, Ontario, Canada M4M 1Y2
416-694-3348 / info@ecwpress.com

Cover design: Michel Vrana
Author photo: © Madeline Bowen-Diaz

The publication of *An Image in the Lake* has been funded in part by the Government of Canada. *Ce livre est financé en partie par le gouvernement du Canada.* We acknowledge the support of the Canada Council for the Arts. *Nous remercions le Conseil des arts du Canada de son soutien.* We acknowledge the support of the Ontario Arts Council (OAC), an agency of the Government of Ontario, which last year funded 1,965 individual artists and 1,152 organizations in 197 communities across Ontario for a total of $51.9 million. We also acknowledge the support of the Government of Ontario through Ontario Creates.

PRINTED AND BOUND IN CANADA

PRINTING: HOUGHTON BOSTON   5   4   3   2   1

For Jack David, Nathaniel Bowen and Ted Bowen,
with thanks for the gift of another very good year

CHARACTER GUIDE

JOANNE'S FAMILY

ZACK SHREVE: fifty-five, Joanne's second husband of seven years. Once a hard-driving, hard-drinking paraplegic trial lawyer who lived like an 18-year-old with a death wish, he fell in love with Joanne and decided to clean up his act.

TAYLOR LOVE-SHREVE: turning twenty-one, a gifted visual artist. Joanne adopted four-year-old Taylor when her mother, Sally Love, Joanne's half-sister died. Currently dating Vale Frazier.

MIEKA KILBOURN-DOWHANUIK: thirty-five, Joanne's eldest daughter. Married to Charlie Dowhanuik (second husband). Mother to Madeline (thirteen) and Lena (twelve) from her first marriage and soon-to-be new baby, Desmond Zackary Dowhanuik.

PETER KILBOURN: thirty-three, Joanne's son, married to Maisie. Peter and Maisie have twin boys, Colin and Charlie, turning four.

ANGUS KILBOURN: twenty-eight, Joanne's youngest son, a lawyer in the Calgary branch of Zack's law firm and a great admirer of his stepfather.

CHARLIE DOWHANUIK (CHARLIE D): thirty-five, Mieka's husband. Host of the hugely successful radio show, *Charlie D in the Morning*. It's a mix of in-depth interviews, fun interviews, music and Charlie D's riffs on life.

MAISIE CRAWFORD: thirty-three, Joanne's daughter-in-law, married to Peter. One of Zack's law partners and a killer in the courtroom.

ESME AND PANTERA: Joanne and Zack's dogs.

MEDIANATION-CONNECTED CHARACTERS

*Joanne and her family are connected to MediaNation through *Sisters and Strangers*.

THE SUMMER INTERNS
(STUDENTS FROM THE SCHOOL OF JOURNALISM)

AUSTIN BRINKMANN: twenty, member of the University Park Road Gang.

CLAY (EVANSON) FAIRBAIRN: nineteen, twenty soon, step-grandson of the CEO, Hugh Fairbairn. Adopted his step-grandfather's surname. Member of the University Park Road Gang.

RONAN "FARKY" FARQUHAR: twenty, member of the University Park Road Gang.

THALIA MONK / MORGAN: just turned twenty-one, daughter of Patti Morgan and Joseph Monk. Reverts to father's surname, becoming Thalia Monk after her brother's death. Member of the University Park Road Gang.

EMPLOYEES AND ASSOCIATES

AINSLEY BLAIR: midforties, director of *Sisters and Strangers*, long-time professional partner of Roy Brodnitz.

ALISON JANVIER: thirty-five, successful candidate in race to become leader of the political party that Joanne and Zack support.

ELLEN EXTON: midthirties, a MediaNation employee for eleven years. Worked her way to producer of the company's number one show. Devoted to her cats, Mary and Mr. Grant.

ETIENNE SIMARD: fifty-eight, actor in *Sisters and Strangers* (plays Izaak Levin).

GEORGIE SHEPHERD: forty-four, executive producer and co-writer on *Sisters and Strangers*.

HAL DUPUIS: forty-five, costume designer for *Sisters and Strangers*.

HARPER JANVIER: nineteen, Alison's son, excellent student with a promising future.

HUGH FAIRBAIRN: late sixties, Julie Evanson's third husband and Clay's devoted step-grandfather. CEO of MediaNation.

JARED DELIO: late thirties, previous host of the morning show. Fired after three women charged him with sexual harassment.

JILL OZIOWY: midfifties, worked her way to the top at MediaNation. Takes on Rosemary Morrissey's role to ensure a successful launch of the new season of programming. Ex-best friend of Jo. Former chief of staff and mistress of Ian Kilbourn and godmother to Jo's kids.

JOSEPH MONK: late forties, Thalia and Nicholas's father. Head of HR for MediaNation. Based in Toronto.

KAM CHAU: early thirties, associate producer for Charlie D; takes on executive producer role.

MARK EVANSON: thirty-five, wife Lori, dad Craig, former Member of the Legislative Assembly (MLA), son Clay (Fairbairn). Works at MediaNation as officer for visitor management.

MIKE BRAEDEN: late sixties, married to Patti Morgan, ex-football player. First wife Sylvie (d.).

NICHOLAS MONK (d.): Thalia's brother.

PATTI MORGAN: late forties, former host of *Sunny Side Up*. Mother to Thalia and Nicholas (d.), ex-wife to Joseph Monk. Married to Mike Braeden.

ROSEMARY MORRISSEY: late forties, former executive producer for programming at MediaNation.

VALE FRAZIER: twenty, actress in *Sisters and Strangers* (plays Sally Love) and Taylor's girlfriend.

CHAPTER ONE

As our Bouvier, our bullmastiff, and I set out for our morning run on August 29, the muggy heat that had shrouded our city for over three weeks showed no signs of abating. It was shortly after five, but the acrid scent of heat was already rising from the pavement, and mist was burning off Wascana Lake. The city was in for another scorcher, and Esme, Pantera and I were in for a short run. Even a twenty-minute jog was punishing. By the time we circled back to the Albert Street bridge, the dogs were shooting me baleful glances, and my hair, T-shirt and shorts were soaked. When the light changed, a beaver appeared on the other side of the bridge and, with stolid deliberation, began crossing the road towards us. Spotting a beaver usually sent the dogs into a state of high alert, but on that blistering Saturday, Esme and Pantera watched without interest, as the beaver ambled towards us, then scrambled down the creek bank to the shade and cool water.

"That's one smart critter," I said. "Let's follow his lead and head home."

My husband, Zack, was at the breakfast table checking his phone, but he turned his wheelchair to greet us. At the sight of me, his face creased in sympathy. "Whoa! Did someone turn a fire hose on you?"

"I wish someone had," I said. "I'm hitting the shower."

When I came back to the kitchen, the dogs were fed, watered and sprawled on the floor, and a bowl of strawberries, yogurt and granola was waiting for me.

My husband held out his arms. "Feel better?"

I bent to kiss his head. "Infinitely," I said. "And guess what? We met a beaver on the bridge."

Zack raised a quizzical eyebrow. "Is that supposed to be good luck?"

I pulled out my chair and sat down. "Beats me," I said, "but considering that I am no longer sweaty, our dogs are no longer panting and the man I love laid out the perfect breakfast for me, I would say that particular beaver brought me luck." I tasted a spoonful of parfait. "Mmm. Good. And bonus, our entire day is free of outside demands."

"So, what do you want to do with our freedom?"

"You said you need to catch up on your files, and I should pull some research together for the speech the new leader of our party is giving in Saskatoon next week."

Zack scowled. "All work and no play?"

"Nope. Just work first, and then chilled gazpacho, warm baguette, a glass of crisp Sauvignon Blanc and a long nap."

Zack grinned. "Sold, and thanks to our prescience, we don't have to brave the heat to get to work."

When we had converted our former junk room into a home office, I'd wondered how much time we would spend there. As it turned out, the answer was a lot. On New Year's Day, Zack and I celebrated our seventh wedding anniversary. Our gift to each other was an agreement to cut back on work and focus on time together.

Zack, a senior partner in his law firm, has since the beginning of the new year only gone into the Falconer Shreve offices three days a week, unless he's in a court. I'd spent much of my adult life either teaching political science at a university or as a jill-of-all-trades in political campaigns. I enjoyed the work, but Zack's and my wedding rings were inscribed with the words "A Deal's a Deal." We had agreed to step back, and we did.

That morning, Zack and I were just settling in when we heard our son-in-law's staccato knock and the front door opening. I had known Charlie Dowhanuik literally from the day he was born, and when he called out, "Anybody home?" my nerves twanged. Charlie's wife, our daughter Mieka, was eight-and-a-half-months pregnant, and within seconds, I was out of my chair and halfway down the hall. "News about Mieka?"

Charlie gave me a one-armed hug. "Mieka's fine. She's anxious to get our baby out in the world, but she's blooming.

Everything at our house is great, but something's come up at MediaNation I'd like to talk to the Big Man about."

Zack wheeled out into the hall. "And here I am," he said.

I turned to Charlie. "Should I make myself scarce?"

He shook his head. "No, it's not a legal problem — not yet at least. It's something else, and I value your opinion, Jo."

I gestured towards the open door behind Zack. "In that case, let's go into the office and make ourselves comfortable."

Charlie had inherited his mother's striking good looks — penetrating hazel eyes and coal-black wavy hair — but he was born with a port wine birthmark that covered half his face like a blood mask. Marnie had explored the medical possibilities available at the time, but until Charlie was well into his twenties, the blood mask remained. Ultimately, he underwent laser treatments that almost erased the birthmark, but a faint trace of the blood mask remained, as did Charlie's immense well of empathy for the outcast and the alienated.

He had been a wild child, a danger freak and a magnet for other kids. Marnie Dowhanuik's wry assessment that her son didn't have friends, he had fans, had proved to be prophetic.

For thirteen years Charlie has hosted a national radio call-in show on CVOX in Toronto. *The World According to Charlie D* was a blend of cool music, edgy riffs on life, careful listening and dogged efforts to convince callers that life was worth living.

Charlie D's audiences depended on him, and he depended on them. Had it not been for the #MeToo movement, Charlie would probably have spent the rest of his working life at CVOX. But as #MeToo raised public consciousness about sexual harassment in the workplace, a trio of brave women exposed the ugly private life of Jared Delio, the host of MediaNation's two-hour morning radio show, and the network was forced to act. Charlie D not only had a big on-air personality; he had a reputation of working well and respectfully with women, and he was a hometown boy.

The corporation had just acquired the old Nationtv building in Regina, and kicking off their retooled morning show from a new location was a shrewd publicity move. Someone with clout in management had heard good things about *The World According to Charlie D* and urged MediaNation's decision-makers to check out the show. They moved fast. The network needed a new broom to sweep away the ugly shards left by the precipitous fall from grace of their tarnished golden boy, and Charlie Dowhanuik was the perfect fit.

MediaNation signed him, and for the first time in years Charlie and Mieka were in the same city. The bond that had connected them since they were children deepened into love. Now Charlie was family, and that morning as he pulled out the chair beside me, Zack and I both leaned forward, ready to help.

"Start at the beginning," Zack said.

Charlie's smile was sardonic. "Good advice, except I'm not sure where the beginning is. All I know is that until late yesterday afternoon, everything at *Charlie D in the Morning* was normal. After the show was over at noon, my executive producer Ellen Exton, the production staff and I met to continue planning for Labour Day and beyond. During July and August we've been coasting on our 'best of' interviews, but Labour Day begins our new season, and we need to start strong."

"From what Mieka tells me, the show is flying high," I said.

"It is. Our audience is continuing to build, especially among our target demographic of listeners between twenty-five and fifty-four. Our podcasts are getting one hundred and eighty thousand downloads per episode. Four more stations in the U.S. have picked up *Charlie D in the Morning*, and the publicists of people with big names and big careers are lining up to book interviews for their clients.

"We're on a roll and we're all excited about what we're putting in place for the new season. There've been a few bumps along the way, but we've dealt with them. When the meeting yesterday ended, we wished each other a good weekend and went our separate ways."

"But something happened," Zack said.

Charlie D grimaced. "Boy, did it ever," he said. "At four o'clock yesterday Ellen phoned me, saying she'd just had a call from Joseph Monk, the head of Human Resources for MediaNation in Toronto. Monk told Ellen that a man who identified himself as a friend of Jared Delio's said Ellen had sent him sexually explicit videos. The man threatened to take the videos to a competing network unless MediaNation paid him a substantial sum of money for the Jared Delio Defence Fund."

Zack sneered and leaned back in his chair. "Is there really a Jared Delio Defence Fund?"

"Your guess is as good as mine," Charlie said. "But MediaNation was spooked. They gave Ellen an option. If she resigned and signed a non-disclosure agreement, the company would give her six months' salary and a glowing reference. Monk told Ellen the corporation believes that if she's no longer an employee of MediaNation, the extortionist will lose his bargaining chip and walk away."

"And if Ms. Exton refuses to resign, the corporation will fire her," Zack said, and his tone was scathing. "No six months' salary, no glowing reference. Nothing." He paused. "How long has Ellen Exton worked for MediaNation?"

"Eleven years," Charlie D said. A pen lay on the desk in front of him, and he gave it a spin. "She does a terrific job. She says MediaNation deserves the best, and that's what she delivers, even if it means working overtime or on holidays."

"How many videos are there?" I said.

"Just three — all of Ellen masturbating. According to her, they were pretty tame — nothing wild and wacky. The recipient was a man she'd met online."

"Had he reciprocated?" I said.

"No. Apparently, he promised to, but he never did." Clearly frustrated, Charlie picked up the pen and began thumbing the cap. "Ellen is unflappable. No matter what goes wrong, she's always in control, but when she called me, she was shattered — humiliated and furious at herself for being a fool and at MediaNation for cutting her loose."

Zack frowned. "I'm missing something," he said. "I don't mean to underestimate Ellen Exton's value or her contribution to the success of your show, but she's a behind-the-scenes person who lives in Regina. Why would anybody care about innocuous sex videos she sent to a man she met online?"

"Two words," Charlie D said. "Jared Delio. MediaNation really stepped on its joint there. When the first three women went public with their accounts of Delio's sexual aggression in the workplace, he denied everything. MediaNation defended him and defamed the women."

"Jared was a valuable property," I said, "and the women were dispensable. I remember reading the network's press release. It said the charges against Delio had been looked into internally, and there was nothing to substantiate them."

"And then Jared took to the air with his tearful monologue about how wounded he was to be lied about by colleagues he trusted and how grateful he was for the enduring faith of his listeners and his employers," Charlie said. "The sick thing is that Delio's behaviour was an open secret. The powers that be at MediaNation knew he was a sleaze, but he had the ratings, so . . ."

"Mieka and I took Madeleine and Lena to the protest outside the MediaNation building the day Jared had his on-air meltdown," I said. "It was bitterly cold, and no one from the corporation came out to speak to us, but we were determined. It wasn't long before we saw on social media that there were protests outside MediaNation stations across the country. That other women were coming forward with stories that supported the accounts the first three women gave."

"Jared was fired the next day, and a week later I was offered his job," Charlie D said. "The goddess Fortuna gave her wheel a random spin: I got the windfall, and Delio got the shaft."

Zack chuckled. "I suspect the MediaNation board laid a guiding hand on Fortuna's wheel to make sure they got the outcome they needed. Ana Sorenson, who started her career at Falconer Shreve, works at the same Toronto firm as Delio's first lawyer. After the Delio trial was over, Ana and I were hammering out an agreement on a case that involved both our firms. Ana has always been a sharer when it comes to scuttle-butt, and she passed along what she'd heard at the office."

"Is that ethical?" I said.

"The trial was over, and lawyers like to talk shop," Zack said. "Most of us see it as part of our ongoing education, and learning how Delio's lawyer handled his case was a master class in what not to do. Ana told me that when Delio's lawyer heard that three of his client's former colleagues were coming forward with charges that he had forced them to have sex with him and that the sex often became violent, he advised Delio to make a pre-emptive strike by handing management the material the women were about to make public."

I was dumbfounded. "What kind of lawyer would advise his client to do that?"

"A stupid one," Zack said. "He must have thought if Delio played show and tell, he'd get management on his side. To be fair, for a while it worked. Management shook hands on a confidentiality agreement not to release the material which, incidentally, included tapes Delio sent to the women describ-ing in graphic detail the sexual fantasies he wanted to act out with them."

I shuddered. "And he still walks among us."

"A chilling thought," Charlie said. "But thanks to Delio's public shaming, although he is walking among us, he is no longer respected, admired or rich."

"According to Ana, the day of the protests was Delio's day of reckoning," Zack said. "When management realized the wind had shifted, they breached the confidentiality agreement, released the material, including the tapes, and cited the salacious material as their reason for firing Delio."

"No honour among thieves," Charlie said.

"Are you surprised?" I said.

"No," Charlie said. "I checked Joseph Monk's biography online. He was head of HR at MediaNation when Delio was fired. In fact, he was probably the mastermind who engineered Delio's exit."

"Okay, I understand why MediaNation doesn't want the Delio case revisited," Zack said. "It was a black eye for them, but from what came out in court, Delio had a pattern of being sexually aggressive and violent with women, not just in the workplace, but also in his private life. Those are criminal offences. Ellen Exton's only offence is bad judgment."

Charlie D clasped his hands behind his neck and stretched his legs in front of him. "What do you think she should do?"

Zack drew a deep breath. "If you're asking me if Ms. Exton has a case for wrongful dismissal, I would say she does, and Falconer Shreve has a dozen skilled lawyers whose specialty is labour law. If you're asking if I think Ms. Exton should pursue a case of wrongful dismissal, the answer is no.

"By the time Delio's case came to trial, he'd fired his stupid lawyer and hired a primo lawyer who knows every trick in the book, has no problem getting blood on her hands and heads up her own boutique firm filled with the best and the brightest. Delio was found innocent not because he is innocent, but because he had the finest legal representation money could buy. The fees for that defence were through the roof. It will take him years to pay them off."

I could feel my bile rise. "So even though what happened to Ellen Exton is neither fair nor just, because MediaNation has deep pockets and endless time to watch the wheels of justice grind, she should just walk away. That is so wrong."

"Agreed," Zack said. "But that's the way the system works."

Charlie D ran his fingers through his hair. "Duly noted, but something about the way this whole thing went down has my spidey senses tingling. After Ellen called, I drove over to MediaNation. Ellen was downstairs boxing up her personal things beneath the watchful eyes of the corporation's officer for visitor management. Mark's a nice guy, and he seemed just as upset as she was. I asked Ellen what I could do to help. She said all she wanted was to get out of that building."

"Exactly the response MediaNation was counting on," Zack said. "Did the powers that be have any reason other than the extortion threat for wanting Ellen Exton out of there?"

Charlie's eyes flashed. "That's what I've been trying to figure out! Especially since our previous executive producer for programming left under circumstances that were unsettling, to say the least."

"Rosemary Morrissey is gone?" I asked. "She's been a fixture in that building since I was a political panellist on the old *Canada Tonight* show. She was so passionate about her work. I can't imagine her just walking away. What happened?"

Charlie made the lip zipping gesture. "Can't talk about it. Lawyers' orders. Our colleagues at MediaNation know that

Rosemary was not herself in the weeks before she left, but we don't know whether HR in Toronto put her on medical leave, she resigned or she was not so gently shoved out the door. It was all hush-hush, and it's supposed to remain that way."

"When did this happen?" I asked.

"End of June," Charlie said. "And no one — not even Ellen — has heard a word from Rosemary. She's always been a traveller, and money has never been a problem for her. The assumption is that she flew to a place as far away as possible from MediaNation, and she's staying there."

"But she and Ellen were close?" I said.

"As close as either of them got with anybody," Charlie D said. "Neither of them was gregarious. They were both movie lovers, and they were regulars at the film series at Central Library. As far as I know, that was the extent of their relationship."

"Still, Ellen must have been upset about Rosemary leaving," Zack said.

"She was." Charlie straightened. "Do you think there's a connection between Rosemary's exit and what happened with Ellen yesterday?"

Zack's gaze was penetrating. "If I knew more about the circumstances under which Ms. Morrissey left, I'd be better positioned to hazard a guess."

Charlie D drummed his fingers on the table. After a long moment of deliberation, he stopped drumming. "You're right," he said. "You should have the full picture. It's just that talking about what happened to Rosemary is a punch in the gut for me."

He hesitated, and when he continued, I could hear the sadness in his voice. "For lack of a better word, Rosemary deteriorated. She suffers from migraines. She told me once that she felt migraines inhabited her, the way viruses inhabit their hosts, and that even when a migraine ended, she knew the virus was still inside her, stealing what it needed from the host cells."

I shuddered. "Imagine living with that sword hanging over your head."

"Rosemary was a pro," Charlie said admiringly. "She accepted the migraines as part of her life and carried on. But that changed. On the May long weekend, Rosemary drove to her cottage at Katepwa. When she returned to work on Tuesday, she looked as if she'd been through hell. She said she'd suffered the worst migraine she'd ever experienced, and she was reeling from the after-effects.

"Everybody was sympathetic, and we were familiar with the pattern — we knew it was only a matter of time before Rosemary regained her strength. So, we all carried on as usual."

"But that didn't happen," Zack said.

Charlie's face darkened at the memory. "No, Rosemary didn't bounce back. She got worse. She had trouble focusing; she'd always been quick to size up a situation and make a decision, but she became indecisive, and she forgot things. Most significantly — she was making mistakes. Big ones. Rosemary had always been a perfectionist. Suddenly everything she touched went awry. At first, we covered for her and let it pass, but when the problems persisted and grew more serious, we had to face the fact that something was very wrong.

"Ellen was convinced that what Rosemary suffered on the long weekend at Katepwa was a stroke, not a migraine, but when she tried to convince Rosemary to see a specialist, Rosemary shut her down."

"MediaNation's a large company," Zack said. "You must have some form of workplace counselling service for employees."

"We do, and it's first rate. The company prides itself on its employee assistance program, but EAP can't help if an employee doesn't seek assistance."

"And Rosemary refused to seek help," I said.

"She said she no longer knew who to trust. We were at an impasse. Rosemary had become a liability, and something had to be done. MediaNation, like all the networks, is losing ground to streaming services. The fall schedule was our Hail Mary pass, and we couldn't afford to drop the ball. Rosemary had to go."

"So, how was the situation resolved?" I said.

Charlie let out a long breath. "In the worst possible way. Someone, I don't know who, reported Rosemary's condition to HR in Toronto. And that's when the shit hit the fan. At the beginning of July, everyone working on a project Rosemary was supervising received an email from Joseph Monk asking them to submit a frank assessment of Rosemary's ability to continue as executive producer for programming. The assessments were to be sent directly to him by the end of the week."

"Death by a thousand cuts," I said.

Charlie winced. "Death by a hundred and fifteen cuts. Only one hundred and fifteen of us reported directly to Rosemary, but she believed everybody in our unit was her friend, so one hundred and fifteen cuts did the job. The following Monday, Rosemary was not at work. Her office had been cleared out; she'd put her house and her cottage up for sale. The problem had disappeared." Charlie's voice was thick with self-disgust.

"Charlie, don't beat yourself up over this," I said. "I know you, and I know you did everything you could. You told us that when Rosemary failed to show up for work after the letters had been sent to HR in Toronto, the assumption was that she was travelling. I think that's a fair assumption."

"Travelling off the beaten path *is* one of Rosemary's passions," Charlie said. "She liked to search out lives that were being lived differently from her own. She was never a tourist; she always spent enough time to at least give her a real sense of what it was like living that person's life. She was never superficial. She read as much as she could about a people's history and cultural beliefs beforehand; experienced as much of their lives as she could when she lived with them. And then she kept up with them, learning everything she could from them even after she left."

"I remember talking to her after she'd just come back from Cambodia," I said. "She was wearing an exquisite Khmer golden silk tunic that she'd sewn herself. When she talked about the Cambodians who had welcomed her into their lives, she was like a schoolgirl."

Charlie's expression was hopeful. "So, you don't think she's reached a point of no return."

"I don't. A woman with that zest for living would not give up," I said. "Rosemary was at the centre of a perfect storm of agonizing pain, self-doubt, professional insecurity and what appeared to be betrayal by those who knew her best. Travel had always brought her release. It's been barely a month. My guess is that Rosemary has chosen to retreat, take stock, get the help she needs and restart. She'll come out of this stronger than ever."

"And Ellen?" Charlie said. "Jo, if you could have seen her yesterday in the MediaNation parking lot, you wouldn't have been confident of her future. She was at the point where Rosemary must have been when the axe dropped on her: broken, despairing and angry.

"After we'd loaded the boxes in the car, she said, 'I should go back and check to see if I left anything . . .' She started towards the building and then she just froze. I pivoted to see what she'd reacted to. There was nothing — just a summer intern heading home for the day.

"When I asked Ellen if she wanted me to go back to check her cubicle, she shook her head and slid into the passenger seat. We didn't exchange another word until we'd carried the boxes into her apartment. When we'd finished, she thanked me and walked me to the door."

"And have you heard from her since?" Zack said.

"No. I expected to hear from her last night, but nada. When I phoned her this morning, my call went straight to voicemail. I've texted but no response."

I touched his arm. "Charlie, you've done everything you can. The last three months must have been painful for everybody working in your unit. Two good people were treated abominably. Sadly, that is not unprecedented. Don't assume the burden for what happened. Let it go — at least for a while. If you can think of anything we can do, let us know."

"I can think of something," Zack said. "Instinct tells me there's more behind this than the videos Ellen Exton sent to Mr. X, but that aside, Ellen needs to open up to someone. Charlie, she obviously sees you as an ally and a friend, but you're also employed by the corporation that fired her. She may be concerned that she's made you vulnerable or that they'll put pressure on you to tell them what you know."

Charlie D's laugh was short and mirthless. "Which is nothing."

"Let's keep it that way," Zack said. "Could you text Ellen my contact information? Whatever's going on, she needs to talk it through, and as her lawyer, I could offer her a zone of privacy. And Charlie, let Ellen know this one is on the house."

"That's generous," Charlie D said.

"Nope. Just self-serving," Zack said. "After thirty years as a lawyer, I still believe in justice."

CHAPTER TWO

When Alison Janvier had announced she was running for leader of the political party Zack and I supported, we were both excited. At a time when politics was too often tawdry and fierce, Alison was a gift, a candidate whose shining idealism was tempered by an even-handed pragmatism. She had drawn together a coalition of progressive millennials, old-line supporters of the left and people who simply believed our province had lost its way. It was no small feat, but I was content to stand on the sidelines and cheer Alison on until the night two weeks before the leadership convention, when she made a throwaway comment that could have cost her the leadership.

A wildly successful political rally can induce a state of euphoria akin to a runner's high in a candidate. The rally that night in Moose Jaw had been a triumph for Alison. It was the first time she felt victory might truly be within her reach, and when a reporter asked her if it was time for someone like her to lead the party, she said, "Why not? We haven't had much luck with our string of old white guys."

Our daughter-in-law, Maisie, and Alison had been in the same year at the College of Law, and they'd both played lacrosse on the college team. Maisie was not political, but her loyalty to her former teammates was primal, so when Alison announced her candidacy, Maisie compiled a list of backers and went to work. Our daughter-in-law always played to win, and the number of memberships she sold was impressive.

She and Alison had chosen divergent career paths, but the campaign had brought them together, and Maisie was with Alison the night she made the "string of old white guys" comment. Recognizing that Alison's words might alienate a huge swath of voters who had previously been on her side, my daughter-in-law called us immediately. I told her to bring Alison to our place that night as soon as they were back in the city.

It was Zack's and my first meeting with Alison, and the circumstances were not ideal, but five minutes after we sat down together at the kitchen table, I understood why people responded so positively to her.

In person, Alison was striking rather than beautiful, a reed-slim thirty-five-year-old with shining blue-black hair anchored in a high ponytail, deep-set eyes so dark they were almost black and a generous mouth. Perhaps most importantly, she had what old-time politicos used to describe as the "royal jelly," that indefinable quality that separates truly exceptional political leaders from the pack. Informed, passionate and, until that night, disciplined about staying on message, Alison was a dream candidate. But she had blundered badly, and she knew it.

After Maisie introduced us, Alison didn't waste time on preamble. "My answer to that reporter was ageist, sexist and unbelievably stupid," she said. "How do I dig myself out?"

"The first step is to identify the problem, and you nailed that," Zack said. He wheeled closer to her. "I'm curious, Alison. Has all your experience with older white men been negative?"

Her head shake was vehement. "No. I have needed help to get where I am, and much of that help came from the kind of person who I so stupidly categorized and dismissed tonight. On our way here, I told Maisie about the significant role people like your friend Warren Weber have played in my life. Mr. Weber endowed a scholarship that made it possible for people like me from Northern Saskatchewan to study law or medicine and still spend summers at home working in the community."

When Zack asked Alison if he should call Warren, Alison didn't hesitate. She knew she needed his backing.

The next morning Alison made the media rounds, saying essentially what she'd said to Zack. Her apology was straightforward and heartfelt. Warren joined her on our province's most popular and controversial call-in show. Alison took a beating, but Warren's support was steadfast, and by the time the show ended, it was clear she had weathered the storm.

Two weeks later, she won the nomination, and I was once again writing speeches.

As a rule, I found writing speeches for Alison absorbing, but that morning distracted by Charlie's story about Ellen Exton, I couldn't seem to string two coherent thoughts together, and I was relieved when it was time for lunch.

Gazpacho is better the day after it's made, and as I broke off a piece of baguette and Zack handed me a glass of Sauvignon Blanc, I felt the tension of the morning lift. Our love-making after lunch was lazy and very nice, and afterwards I fell asleep curled up against my husband, feeling that all was right with the world.

We slept for over two hours and awoke to definitive signs of a change in the weather. The light in the room was shadowy, and Pantera, who feared storms and adored Zack, had slunk in and wedged himself against Zack's side of the bed.

The south wall of our bedroom overlooks the creek, and the original owners had installed double doors that opened onto a small flagstone patio. I slid out of bed, shrugged into my robe and stepped outside. Low dark clouds were rolling in, the temperature was dropping and the air was unnaturally still. "Something's coming our way," I said. "Come see for yourself."

Zack transferred his body from the bed to his chair, wheeled over to join me and tilted his head back to assess the situation. "We're in for a gully-washer," he said. "That is what Fred C. Harney would call a rat-coloured sky."

"Fred certainly had a way with words," I said.

"He did," Zack agreed. "I learned more about law and life the year I articled for him than I did in three years at the College of Law. And if Fred ever drew a sober breath, it wasn't in my presence."

"A sad life," I said.

Zack was meditative. "Fred didn't see it that way. He loved the law; he was one helluva lawyer, and he died the death trial lawyers dream of — a heart attack seconds after the jury came back with the verdict."

"Had he won his case?"

At that instant, a thunderclap split the stillness. Zack glanced up at the heavens. "Fred says the jury found his client innocent on all counts." He grinned. "Fred always had to have the last word."

When the rain began, Zack and I rushed inside and closed the patio doors. "Finally, a break in this weather," I said. "And just in time. A Real Prairie Picnic is scheduled for tomorrow afternoon. Asking people to turn up in the heat we've been having would have been unconscionable."

My phone rang. It was Charlie D. "Who do you hear from more often than me?" he said.

"Today, no one," I said, "but if you're calling with good news, bring it on."

"Well, I have news, but it's not good. I still haven't heard from Ellen. I keep telling myself it's been less than a day since Joseph Monk gave her the axe, and she needs time to regroup."

"How's that working for you?" I said.

"Not well," Charlie D said. "But I'm calling to ask a favour.

I just had a text from Monk telling me that our new executive producer for programming is arriving on the three thirty flight from Toronto, and suggesting that I pick her up and take her to MediaNation for a get-acquainted meeting."

"So, MediaNation has chosen somebody to take Rosemary's place," I said. "That has to be a relief for everybody. Do you know anything about the new hire?"

Charlie hesitated. "Rosemary's replacement is not a new hire," he said carefully. "She's been with the company for a while. She's walking into a mess, but she'll handle it."

"Good news," I said. "But you said you needed a favour."

"Right," he said. "Madeleine and Lena are at what was supposed to be a pool party, but given the weather, I imagine they're partying indoors. Whatever the case, I don't like leaving Mieka alone. Could you come over and keep your daughter company?"

"Of course," I said. "You do realize that Mieka will accuse me of hovering."

"Blame it on me," Charlie said. "I have broad shoulders. Jo, I'll try to keep this meeting short. With luck, I'll be home around five. Text me if anything comes up with Mieka or if Zack hears from Ellen."

"Everything's under control," I said. "Just focus on your meeting with the new producer."

Charlie's voice was deep and intimate. "I hope you and Zack know how grateful Mieka and I are to have you in our lives."

"We know, and that goes both ways. I've never seen Mieka happier than she's been since she married you." I swallowed hard. "This is turning into a Hallmark moment. We'd better end the call before the violins start."

When Mieka's first marriage ended, she moved back to Regina into the house where my first husband, Ian Kilbourn, and I had raised her and her brothers. Mieka was a single mother with two very young daughters and the new owner of a café play centre called UpSlideDown. Her plate was full. Redecorating was at the bottom of her to-do list and it had stayed there as she opened her second play centre and married Charlie. So, the house I walked into that afternoon was pretty much as it had been in all the years I had lived there: a welcoming place with a mix of some handsome pieces Ian and I had inherited and the comfortable, sturdy, family-friendly furniture we had purchased when the kids were little.

Mieka had trained as a caterer, and cooking was her go-to activity in times of stress — even on a summer day. When I arrived, she was in the kitchen wearing a sundress the colour of a cut peach and tidying up after making snickerdoodles. My daughter is one of those fortunate women who blossom in pregnancy, and that day with her fair hair bleached by sunshine and her skin, tanned and glowing, she was more beautiful than ever.

She raised an eyebrow when she saw me. "Let me guess. Charlie D sent you over to keep me from running outside and playing in traffic."

I hugged her. "Something like that."

"Perfect timing," she said. "There's iced tea in the fridge.

Sit down, and I'll get us some. The snickerdoodles will be ready in about thirty seconds."

"You sit," I said. "I'll get the tea and cookies."

Mieka lowered herself carefully into a chair and sighed contentedly. "Who knew sitting could be such a pleasure?"

I poured our tea, added a sprig of mint, took the cookies out of the oven and slid them onto the cooling rack.

Mieka eyed them hungrily. "Let's live dangerously and eat some of those while they're still hot," she said.

For a few moments we were silent, content to sip iced tea and nibble at snickerdoodles. "It doesn't get much better than this, does it?" I said.

Mieka shook her head. "Mum, do you remember that old TV ad where the mother tucks her kids in and goes outside and sits on the steps of her front porch?"

"I do," I said. "Her husband comes out and asks her if something's wrong. And she says, 'No, it's just that everything is so right.'"

Mieka's grey-green eyes shone with emotion. "That's exactly what I'm feeling, and, Mum, please hold back on your 'don't tempt the fates' glare. I just want you to know how happy I am."

My daughter's words meant the world to me. Mieka had known her share of pain: her father's death; the break-up of her first marriage; the challenges of starting her life again as a single parent with two very young daughters and new business; the end of a relationship with a decent but deeply troubled man with whom she hoped to spend the rest of her life; and — perhaps the cruellest cut of all — the revelation that the father she had idolized was a liar and a cheat.

I took her hands in mine. "Look at my face," I said. "Not a trace of my 'don't tempt the fates' glare. Mieka, no one could be happier for you than I am."

My daughter patted her abdomen. "I can't wait for this little dude to make his appearance."

I pricked up my ears. "Hey, did you just let it slip that the baby is a dude, not a dudette?"

My daughter slapped her forehead with the palm of her hand. "Pregnancy brain, and Charlie and I came so close to keeping it a secret," she said. "But yes, it's a boy, and his name will be Desmond after your father, and Zackary after Zack, who has been the best grandfather and stepfather the girls and I could have asked for."

"Zack will be touched. I am too, but won't Howard be hurt that his name's not included?"

"Charlie's relationship with his father is still a work in progress," Mieka said. "Des's surname will be Dowhanuik, so everybody will be happy."

"I certainly am," I said.

Mieka's phone rang. She saw the caller ID and frowned. "Sorry, Mum. There's a problem at UpSlideDown, and I have to deal with it."

"Why don't you take your phone into the living room, and let me clean up here?"

After I washed the cookie sheets and put our tea things in the dishwasher, I returned to the round maple table where Mieka and I had been sitting. It was my grandmother's, and

I'd spent hours there, planning and dreaming when I was pregnant with Mieka. The rain was beating steadily on the roof, and the world outside the kitchen window was grey. Not surprisingly, the memories flooded back. For many years after Ian died, I found comfort in remembering our life together — the years when he was the province's attorney general, and I was the woman behind the man, raising our children, writing speeches for him to deliver, roasting turkeys and hams for political dinners and handling the constituency work.

It wasn't the life I'd anticipated. When I met Ian in university, we believed we'd be like D.H. Lawrence's twin stars: separate and brilliant and eternal. As it turned out, Ian became the star, and I became the star-gazer, but it was a good life, and when Ian was killed on a snowy highway in the south-west of our province, I was devastated. For weeks, I was an automaton, dully and dutifully going through the motions of living. Mieka was fifteen, and every morning, I awoke to find her beside my bed, eyes anxious, asking me to get up and help her make breakfast for her brothers, so they could all go to school. That period was beyond terrible, but I pushed through because I had children and because I believed that our children and I had been the centre of Ian's life.

Fifteen years later, on my fifty-eighth birthday, Mieka, her brothers and I were presented with unassailable evidence that, from a time shortly before Mieka's birth until the day he died, Ian had been involved sexually with his chief of staff, Jill Oziowy. Jill and I were as close as sisters. She was godmother to our children, and they loved her. With Ian's encouragement, Jill had become part of our family.

The magnitude of their betrayal was overwhelming. For my adult children and me, it was as if we'd entered a parallel universe, a world that coexisted with the world we had known, but threw everything we believed our lives had been into question.

My older son, Peter, is the gentlest of my children, but after he learned about Ian and Jill, his bitterness frightened me. He was thirteen when Ian died — on the cusp of becoming a young man. When he learned about the affair, Pete told me that after Ian's death, the only way he could get to sleep was by remembering every moment he had spent with his dad. The revelation that Ian had been an adulterer tore Peter apart. Instead of the comfort of childhood memories, all he had were jagged, unanswerable questions about what his father and Jill were doing the hundreds of times Ian couldn't be with us because he had "urgent business" at the legislature. There was nothing I could do to lessen my son's pain because I was experiencing that pain myself.

I was relieved when Mieka returned from her phone call and drew me back into the present. "Disaster averted," she said. "The roof in the quiet play area is leaking, and the manager had to close UpSlideDown. I called Zack, and he said one of the big roofing companies is a Falconer Shreve client, and he'd have them send somebody over when the rain stops." She shook her head. "Mum, I don't know what we'd do without Zack. He is so supportive of us all."

"He knows what it's like to run a business when it's just getting established."

My daughter and I had another glass of tea and talked of the inconsequential matters mothers and daughters have talked about since the earth cooled. We were both surprised when Charlie texted to say he'd picked up the girls at their party, and they'd be home in ten minutes.

* * *

When Madeleine and Lena burst through the kitchen door, they were soaked to the skin and fizzing with excitement. The girls were twelve and eleven, respectively, and there had been boys at the pool party. According to Lena, they were goofy, but Madeleine said they were goofy in a nice way, and as soon as the rain started, the boys were really helpful carrying things inside.

"Boys have their uses," I said.

When Mieka caught my eye, her smile was impish. "Mimi's right. Having a boy around the house could be a lot of fun."

It had been a fine afternoon for everybody, and when I picked up the cookies Mieka had boxed for us, I was smiling.

The smile didn't last long. After the usual flurry of good-bye hugs, Charlie took an umbrella from the hall closet and said he'd walk me to my car. I assumed that once I was safe and dry in the Volvo, Charlie D would go back to the house; instead, he slid into the passenger seat. My body tightened. "Is there news about Ellen?" I said.

"No," he said. "That's gnawing at me, and now there's something else. Jo, there's no way to soften this blow. The new executive producer for programming is Jill Oziowy."

I was dumbfounded. "Charlie, this can't happen."

His gaze was level. "It's already happened. I did my best. Ten minutes after I left here this morning, Joseph Monk called with the announcement. Monk said that he, our CEO Hugh Fairbairn and Jill Oziowy had 'an intense meeting' immediately after MediaNation severed Ellen's connection with the corporation. Decisions had to be made, and they had to be made quickly."

"So the upshot of the intense meeting was to send Jill Oziowy to Regina to save the day."

My tone was waspish, but Charlie responded with quiet logic. "Jo, you're aware of the situation. The streaming services are clobbering us. Our strategy is counter-programming premised on the belief that there's an audience out there that's smart, curious and hungry for knowledge and a deeper understanding of what it means to be human. We're aiming high and it's a risk, but the pieces were falling into place until Rosemary Morrissey left. That's when Jill Oziowy stepped in. She was working from Toronto, but with Ellen Exton's help, Jill was able to manage the day-to-day decisions about the new programming."

"And yet they fired Ellen," I said. "This doesn't make any sense, Charlie."

"I agree, but ours is not to wonder why. Senior management has made its decision. After I talked to Monk, I called Hugh Fairbairn to plead our case. He invited me to come to his office. He was welcoming; he said he would hear me out, but the decision was made.

"Jill had been open about the affair she'd had with Ian and how devastated you and your children had been when you learned about it. Hugh offered to call you to apologize for any hurt Jill's presence in Regina would cause you and explain why her presence is necessary."

"I don't want Hugh Fairbairn's apologies or his explanations," I said, and my voice quivered with anger. "I just want Jill to go back to Toronto."

My son-in-law's dark honey voice was soothing. "I'm always on your side, Jo. You know that, but Hugh's reasons for wanting Jill here are sound."

"My reasons for not wanting her here are also sound. Two hours ago Mieka told me how happy she is because everything in her life is 'so good.' Learning about Ian's betrayal changed Mieka. She'd always seen the best in people, but for a long while after she learned about Ian and Jill, she was bitter and cynical. It hasn't been easy for her to regain the trust she lost, but for the girls' sake, she has. Mieka is finally back to being the woman she was. She doesn't need a reminder of how little Ian's family meant to him."

Charlie leaned back against the headrest and half closed his eyes. "I remember how Mieka worshipped her father," he said. "I never understood it. To me Ian was as self-centred and indifferent to his family as my father was. But in Mieka's eyes, Ian could do no wrong. The night she learned about the affair, she phoned me after the girls were in bed. She'd held it together for them, but when she called me, she was barely coherent. I was living in Toronto, but I offered to come to Regina. Mieka said she had to work this out on her own. After that, we talked almost every night."

"Did she talk about Ian and Jill with you?"

"No. We talked about old times and the twists and turns out lives had taken since I moved east. Somewhere along the line, we fell in love. When I was offered the job here, we had our happy ending." Charlie paused. "Jo, did you ever learn how Mieka found out about Ian and Jill?"

"I told her," I said. I drew in a deep breath. "It happened during Zack's campaign for mayor. Slater Doyle, the campaign manager for Zack's opponent, came into our headquarters with an old compact cassette player and an ultimatum. He said he had a number of audio tapes of Ian and Jill 'sampling the smorgasbord of sexual delights,' and if Zack didn't withdraw from the race, he'd make the tapes public."

"Audio tapes?" Charlie's brow furrowed. "Where the hell did they come from?"

"Ian's secretary, Valerie Smythe. Apparently, from the time I was pregnant with Mieka until Ian's death, covering for Jill and him was part of Valerie's job. She knew Ian's schedule, and her hobby was making tape recordings of Ian's speeches in the legislature or at public events. The temptation to record Ian's private utterances must have been irresistible. The affair lasted fifteen years. Slater Doyle had boxes of the tapes, neatly labelled with dates and times. I told Doyle the decision wasn't Zack's to make, it was mine, and I refused to give into black-mail. So Doyle turned the cassette player on — full volume — and played a tape of Ian urging Jill on as she fellated him. It was like being in the same room with them."

"How did Slater Doyle get the tapes?"

"Valerie Smythe gave them to him. She had testified against a client of Zack's and according to her, after Zack tore her apart on the witness stand, she had a breakdown, and she was never able to get a decent job again."

Charlie narrowed his eyes, reading my expression. "Are you all right, Jo?"

"No, but you asked how Mieka found out about Ian and Jill, and this is part of the story. There was a rally at the Pile O' Bones Club a couple of hours after Slater's big announcement. It was my birthday, so after the speeches and hoopla, my family gathered around me onstage so everybody could sing 'Happy Birthday' and the grandchildren could help me blow out the candles on the cake. As soon as we got off stage, I took Mieka and her brothers back to the green room and told them about the tapes. It was the worst moment of my life."

Charlie's eyes were filled with pain. "Jo, I'm so sorry."

"Me too, and it gets worse. Doyle delivered a box of the tapes to Mieka's house. The tapes were all identified by date, time and location. Mieka was able to match one of Ian and Jill's quickies with the night of her farewell ceremony from grade eight. After the ceremony there was a bonfire and a barbecue for the grade eights and their parents. Ian had to skip it because he said Howard needed him at the legislature. When Mieka played the tape, she heard her father tell Jill that he couldn't get through the night without being inside her."

For a long while Charlie D and I were silent, watching the rain pelt the sunroof, absorbed in our own thoughts. Finally, I turned to look through the side window. Across the street, the neighbourhood's gentle eccentric, Ruby Mullins, and her dog were out for their afternoon walk. Today they wore matching tartan slickers.

I touched Charlie D's arm and pointed. "Rain or shine, Ruby and Sparky never miss a day. The first time I saw those two I was pregnant with Mieka," I said.

"Thirty-five years ago," Charlie D said. "So, the dog you saw that day must have been the original Sparky."

"It was," I said. "And this is number three. Ruby likes the name, and she says all her dogs have liked it too."

"Proof once again that whether or not it is clear to us, the universe is unfolding as it should," Charlie said.

"That quote was your father's kryptonite," I said. "Whenever he exploded because one of our policies was, in his words, 'going tits up in the ditch,' your mother would smile sweetly, quote those lines from 'Desiderata' and walk away."

"It always drove him crazy," Charlie said, and we both smiled.

Memories of Marnie always drew Charlie and me close. "We're going to get through this," I said. "I guess I should start by listening to Hugh Fairbairn's argument for having Jill in town."

Charlie leaned in. "Do you know Hugh?"

"I've never met him. All I know about him is that he's Julie Evanson's third husband. Her first two husbands were principled, kind and gentle, and Julie walked all over them."

"She won't walk all over Hugh Fairbairn. He's a hard-ass."

"He may have a soft side. He did offer to apologize to me about any hurt Jill's presence in Regina would cause our family."

"He did, but only because you were a hurdle he had to clear. Other people's emotions don't matter to Hugh. That's not necessarily a character defect for a CEO. He's taken a big gamble with the fall programming, and he wants to win. Hugh believes Jill is the only person who's aware of exactly where each of our new programs stands. She knows what's been done, what still needs to be done and she knows how to make it happen. Kickoff is Labour Day — nine days from now. Hugh says we need someone who can get us out of the gate, and Jill is that person."

"That makes sense," I said. "And since *Sisters and Strangers* is the story of my childhood and adolescence, our family has a stake in this too."

"Hugh is aware of that, and he raised another point that he felt would resonate with you and with Mieka. If MediaNation's fall programming tanks, the jobs of the people in our unit will be on the line, and that will just be the beginning. Most of our programming comes from production companies, and if the new season fails, the production companies working with us will take a hit. Careers will be derailed, and jobs will be lost." He paused. "I don't think we have a choice. Do you?"

"No. So, fill me in. I know you and Jill had a meeting. How did that go?"

"Professionally, it was great. We went to the MediaNation cafeteria. More accurately, we went outside the MediaNation cafeteria, so Jill could smoke."

"I thought she'd quit."

"Apparently not. Anyway, it's Saturday, so there weren't many people around, and we were able to talk freely. She's aware of the morale problem, and she shares my opinion that everything that's gone wrong can be traced back to what happened with Rosemary Morrissey.

"Jill was in Nunavut when the Morrissey fiasco occurred. She was appalled not just at what happened to Rosemary, but also at Joseph Monk's tactics. Jill said she tore a strip off Monk, but he claims he had no recourse. She's tried to track Rosemary down, but so far no luck. She didn't know much about the situation with Ellen — just that it happened — but she does want to be kept apprised of developments."

"Jill won't let what happened to Rosemary and Ellen be swept under the carpet," I said. "That's another plus for having her in Regina." I glanced past Charlie D's shoulder. "Mieka's at the living room window. She'll be worrying."

"I'll go inside in a minute."

"If you're planning to plead Jill's case with Mieka, Pete, Angus and me, you might as well go inside now." I started the car. "Are you familiar with the old saying, 'What the axe forgets, the tree remembers'?"

Charlie D shook his head. "No, but I get what you're saying."

"Good, because every time Jill and my husband checked into a motel or had a quickie at the office, they took an axe to our family. Seemingly, they were oblivious to the damage they were doing, but we've had to live with those cuts."

Charlie D shifted his position to face me. "And despite all the cuts, the tree is still growing, Jo. Everyone in our family has a good life and a bright future."

"And you think Jill doesn't."

He nodded. "My experience at CVOX taught me to really listen to what a person says or doesn't say. As long as Jill and I were talking shop, she was fine, but I noticed that she kept checking the time. I asked if I was keeping her from something. She said no, but she was concerned that she was keeping me away from Mieka and the girls. I was getting anxious about that myself, so I picked up on the cue and offered to drive her to her hotel."

"Where's she staying?"

Charlie D grimaced. "She's staying with my father."

"With Howard?" My sigh seemed to come from deep within me. "Just when I thought the situation couldn't get worse."

"The arrangement makes sense — at least on a practical level. Jill suddenly needed a place to live, and Howard's leaving for Toronto on Labour Day. He'll be gone until December, when the class he's teaching finishes, so his condo will be empty in the meantime."

"I'm sure Howard sees this as a golden opportunity to bring Jill back into our lives. In the days after we learned about the affair, Howard was relentless in trying to get me to forgive Jill." I could feel the beginnings of a headache and I rubbed my temples. "Jill and I did manage to patch together a reconciliation of sorts, but I was relieved when she moved to Toronto, and it was finally over."

"It isn't over for Jill," Charlie said. "Howard wasn't home when I took Jill to his condo. She knew where he'd left the key, so I helped her carry her bags inside and said goodbye. When I turned to leave, she stepped in front of me. We were so close our faces were almost touching. She said, 'Two months, Charlie D. That's all I'm asking. I know that Joanne and her family don't want me here, but two months will let me give the new slate of programming a solid start, and if

I'm lucky, it will give me a chance to recover at least a part of what I've lost. I'm trying to be realistic. I've been seeing a therapist, and I've faced the fact that I will never again be a part of the lives of Joanne and her children."

"Charlie, if Jill has accepted the fact that things between us will never be the way they were, what is she hoping to recover?"

He paused to consider it. "Her self-respect. Jill said the therapist has helped her understand that she seeks out relationships with men who will hurt her because she believes she deserves to be hurt."

"That's a first step, and it's a good one," I said. "After Ian died, I spent years watching Jill squander her emotional capital through entanglements with 'bad boys,' as she called them. It puzzled me; it made me angry and it worried me sick. Jill is smart, attractive and giving, but she always chose men who hurt her, and hurt her badly. As soon as I heard Slater Doyle's tapes, I understood everything. For fifteen years, Jill was Ian's mistress. Somehow she was able to delude herself into believing that what she and Ian were doing didn't affect our family. After he died, she saw what his death did to us. It was a massive betrayal, and Jill saw it through the prism of Catholic guilt. She told me once that a Catholic education is like stigmata — perpetually suppurating. That's not true, but it was Jill's perception."

"So, Jill's 'bad boys' were a way to expiate her sins?"

"I guess so. Charlie, where do Mieka, Pete, Angus and me fit into this?"

"Jill wants you to give her a chance."

"And what did you say?"

"I said exactly what you would have said if you'd seen Jill's face."

"You told her you'd try," I said.

"And I will. All I'm asking is that you keep an open mind." Charlie gave me a crooked smile, then leaned across and kissed my cheek. "You and Mieka are strong, and you're fair. You'll do the right thing." With that, he jumped out of the car and ran up the driveway. I waited till he was dry and inside, before I headed home to a night filled with memories and unanswerable questions.

CHAPTER THREE

Zack was waiting at the door with a martini. I placed the box of snickerdoodles on the cobbler's bench in the entryway, removed my raincoat, took the martini glass from Zack and sipped deeply. "Transcendent," I said. "But aren't you supposed to be decked out in nothing but Saran Wrap when you welcome me home?"

Zack turned his wheelchair towards the kitchen. "Remind me where we keep it."

"Not necessary," I said. "The image of you swaddled in Saran will be enough."

"Good. Then let's take our drinks into the family room, watch the weather and be grateful we're inside."

Like our bedroom, the family room overlooks the creek, and for a few moments Zack and I sat hand in hand, absorbed by the ferocity of the storm. A finger of lightning flashed from sky to earth, throwing into sharp relief the struggle of the creek bank's saplings to withstand the lashing wind.

"If it's this bad so close to the centre of the city, it must be wicked in those new developments in the north end," Zack said.

Zack knew me well. When I didn't pick up on the subject of the storm's effect on the city, he realized I needed time to gather my thoughts. Being close to Zack always centred me. He's a handsome man, strong featured with a broad forehead, penetrating green eyes and a generous sensuous mouth. The familiar woody-citrusy scent of his aftershave was calming, and it wasn't long before I was ready to plunge in.

"Jill Oziowy is back in town," I said. "She's MediaNation's new executive producer in charge of programming, so she'll be based in Regina."

"That sounds as if she's here to stay," Zack said.

"According to Charlie, the first order of business will be restoring a sense of camaraderie among the members of their unit. Jill's apparently plugged into the Rosemary Morrissey situation, so she'll be a real asset at raising morale."

"I haven't heard from Ellen Exton yet. Jill might be in a position to help straighten that out."

"It's still early, but Jill has asked to be kept in the loop about Ellen, so that's good news. Charlie says that fine-tuning programs to ensure they're running smoothly will take at least two months. He also says that whether Jill stays here permanently will be up to the kids and me."

Zack sipped his martini. "Do you want to talk about it?"

"No," I said. "But I should, because Charlie said we're going to have to find a way to go forward that works for us all — at least for the next two months."

"Isn't the simplest way to go forward just to have Jill return to Toronto and do what needs to be done from there?" Zack said.

"That was my first thought too," I said. "But according to Charlie, the situation at MediaNation is grave, and Jill needs to be on-site."

"We've had a few situations like that at Falconer Shreve, and they do require steady hands on the tiller until the crisis has passed. I imagine Jill will be so focused on work that you and the kids won't know she's in town."

"That's not the way Jill sees it," I said. As I related our son-in-law's assessment of Jill's state of mind, Zack's eyes never left my face.

When I finished, he said, "Charlie's right, Jo. Knowing how much Jill is counting on this chance to make amends, you won't walk away. Mieka and Pete are going to have to come to their own decisions about how to deal with the situation, but they're smart enough to realize that they have futures filled with possibilities, and Jill has nothing but a shred of hope. They won't take that from her."

"I'll talk to them tomorrow, and Zack, I feel good about this decision. When I went to the studio to tape the interview with Charlie D about *Sisters and Strangers*, seeing how the old Nationtv building was coming back to life warmed my heart.

For almost a decade, the place was all but deserted, and it was great to see people working in that beautiful space again."

"My partners and I were invited to a holiday shindig in that building — that must have been in the mid-'80s. We were drumming up clients, and there was free booze, so the event was a magnet for a start-up law firm like ours. The event was held in the galleria and it was a knockout: three storeys high with glass walls, terrazzo floors and this towering Christmas tree.

"We'd just moved into our office over the company that made dentures, and we were excited about having an entire floor to ourselves. I remember the five of us gazing at that glittering two-storey tree and realizing we had a long way to go."

"And you got there," I said. "Falconer Shreve now occupies the top three floors in a glass tower that it owns."

A shadow of grief passed over my husband's face. "And because someone hated Falconer Shreve's founding partners enough to kill three of us, I'm the only partner still alive to see our shining offices."

I moved behind Zack's chair and reached down to embrace him. "You, Blake, Delia, Chris and Kevin had twenty-five great years together."

"It wasn't enough," Zack said. He cleared his throat. "But focusing on what might have been is pointless. Let's talk about the future. Tell me more about the resurrection of MediaNation."

I gave Zack a quick hug and went back to my place beside him. "The day Charlie and I had lunch, we ate in what was

once the Nationtv cafeteria, but is now the MediaNation cafeteria. It's as gorgeous as ever."

"I've never been in it," Zack said. "Whenever I had an
interview, I just went straight to the elevator and downstairs."

"We can remedy that," I said. "When the leaves turn,
I'll take you to MediaNation for breakfast. The cafeteria has
killer cinnamon buns; a sensational view of the park; and on
the east wall, a Victor Cicansky ceramic called *The Garden
Fence* that's a real stunner. Sixty feet of bright ceramic vegetables and flowers peeking out through the slats of a fence. I
used to take Madeleine there for tea when she was younger.
She always insisted on sitting at a table near the sunflowers."

As always when we talked about the grandchildren, Zack's
face grew soft. "I suspect Lena chose a table near the vegetables. Remember all those weird vegetables she used to draw?"

"Every vegetable had a face," I said. "And now we'll be
able to revisit *The Garden Fence* with the girls and their baby
brother. It's nice to see that space come alive again. When
Nationtv hit bottom, the cafeteria turned into a morgue.
They cut back on food services and finally eliminated them
altogether. At the end there were just machines with soft
drinks, chips and candy bars. Nobody sat at the tables; they
took whatever they'd purchased downstairs to their desks.

"The day Charlie and I had lunch, it was like old times.
The cafeteria offered a full menu, and people were sitting
at the tables again, chatting and eating. Charlie wanted to
talk about MediaNation's promotion plans for *Sisters and
Strangers*. He's seen some of the clips they're going to be

using. He says they're powerful, but he was concerned they might be too close to the bone for me."

"Are you worried about that?" Zack said.

"No," I said. "I was as involved as I needed to be with the production, and we've seen the director's cut. It's terrific, and I'm glad an audience will get to see the series. I told Charlie D that revisiting the past had been painful, and I was ready to let go of *Sisters and Strangers*. The issue was settled, so we moved onto other subjects."

"And moving on yet again," Zack said. "Taylor called when you were at Mieka's."

"How did she sound?"

"Terrific. She was in the Great Hall of the Museum of Anthropology at UBC."

"All those carvings and sculptures from the West Coast Indigenous Peoples — Taylor must have been in her element."

"She was. Apparently, she's bought what she describes as a 'serious' camera, and she's enthusiastic about the stills she's been taking. She knows how much I love that eagle carving she and the other kids and grandkids gave me for my birthday, and she thought I could go over her photos and pick out some I'd like framed for my office."

"It sounds as if our daughter might be over whatever was troubling her," I said. "I'm relieved. This is the first serious relationship for both Vale and Taylor, and they've had a slew of adjustments to make. They're both at pivotal points in their careers. Vale's role as Sally Love in *Sisters and Strangers* is attracting a lot of media attention, and she's putting in twelve-hour days on the set of her new movie. Taylor has a show at the Seibel Gallery in November, and she's alone in a hotel room 1,743 kilometres from her studio. Not ideal circumstances for two young women starting a life together."

"Not ideal at all," Zack said. "But she really did sound like herself today, so let's follow the old adage, 'Never trouble trouble until trouble troubles you.' Cross our fingers, and hope for the best."

CHAPTER FOUR

When we awoke Sunday morning, it was clear that Mother Nature had cut the organizers of a Real Prairie Picnic a break. The day was picnic perfect.

The event was being held on farmland forty kilometres north of Regina. Madeleine and Lena were coming with us, and when they asked Zack if we could put down the top of his convertible, they didn't have to ask twice. It was definitely a top-down kind of day.

The big prairie sky was brilliantly blue; the temperature had dropped to a balmy 23 degrees Celsius and the breeze was gentle. Fields with crops that in late May were the colour of a new fern and by harvest had turned to beaten gold were now stripped bare, ready for spring seeding when the cycle would begin again.

Not far outside the city the acrid smell of smoke drifted towards us. When we spotted a fire that appeared to be out of control in a field west of the highway, Madeleine was anxious. "Mimi, should we call 911?"

"No. This year the grain crops were heavy, so a lot of straw was left behind. That farmer's burning off the straw to get the fields ready for next year. I'm sure he's keeping a close eye on it."

"You grew up in Toronto," Lena said. "How do you know stuff like that?"

"Because when your Uncle Howard was premier of the province, I spent a lot of time in areas like this asking people to vote for us. I always hated knocking on doors, but I liked talking to people and listening to what they had to say."

"I like talking to people too," Lena said. "But I'm not really good at listening."

"Next time someone is talking to Granddad, watch how he listens," I said, glancing at Zack. "He's one of the best listeners I know."

Lena chortled. "Mimi, listening is just sitting there, doing nothing. Nobody can be good at that."

"Your grandfather is. He gives people a chance to say what they need to say, and because he doesn't interrupt, people tell him things that really matter to them."

"Maybe I'll try that," Lena said.

This time it was Madeleine's turn to chortle.

The storm that hit Regina the night before had not travelled north, and the grid road that led to the farm where the picnic was taking place was dry as the proverbial bone.

During our half-hour drive, I had checked both my phone and Zack's several times. When we turned into the farmyard, I handed Zack's phone to him. "No word from Ellen," I said.

He frowned. "It's been almost forty-eight hours."

"She may just be lying low," I said. "On Friday afternoon, Ellen was executive producer of a successful radio show, a goal she'd been working towards for eleven years, and now her dream job has been taken from her. She may be just taking time to process what happened and figure out her next move."

"Do you really believe that?" Zack said.

I touched his hand. "We live in hope."

The fields of summer fallow the owner of the farm had designated for parking were already almost filled, and the line of cars coming down the hill for the picnic showed no sign of abating. Zack was adamant about not using his disabled parking permit, but when I reminded him that if Mieka went into labour, we'd want to get back to the city ASAP, he grumbled and pulled into one of the three remaining parking spaces for the disabled.

The homespun charm of the event advertised as a Real Prairie Picnic sanded the rough edges off one of the underlying goals of the event. After eight years of witnessing the rudderless incompetence, dirty deals and scandals of the government in power, the public was ready for a change.

Our party's chances of winning the next election were good, and the fight for the leadership had been intense. Many of our sitting members of the Legislature (MLAs) believed their turn to lead the party had come and that Alison Janvier was an outsider. She had announced her candidacy early, and by the time her rivals started taking her seriously, Alison had already gained traction among potential supporters.

The grassroots organization behind Alison's candidacy had been determined and energetic, and she proved herself to be a tough, tireless and engaging campaigner. It had taken three ballots, but Alison had won decisively. Now it was time to soothe the men and women she'd defeated and bring them onside.

I'd been to a hundred political picnics like the one we walked into that day, but the folksy appeal of softball games, horseshoe pits, booths selling corn on the cob, pie by the slice and lemonade made from scratch never failed to seduce me. With the unerring radar of preteens, two of Madeleine and Lena's friends from school appeared and asked the girls to join a selfie scavenger hunt — a scavenger hunt for our times where kids took pictures of themselves with the objects they had to find.

Lena's eyes were huge and her tone, plaintive. "Can we? Maddy and I were sure this picnic was going to be dorky, but a selfie scavenger hunt will be cool."

"And we can get a really good start," Maddy said. "Alison Janvier's over there, and she's on our list. Please, Mimi."

"Here's my phone," I said. "Have fun and meet us in an hour at the barbecue chicken place."

Madeleine gave the area a quick once-over. "Where's the chicken place?"

"Sniff the air, and follow your nose," I said.

Zack watched as the girls zeroed in on Alison. "Let's go

over and get a photo of the ladies with our next premier," he said.

"The girls are already taking a selfie with our next premier," I said.

"Then let's take a selfie with our next premier," he said.

"You win," I said. "But I get to delete the photo if it's terrible."

When Alison Janvier spotted us, she waved, and after the girls took their photo and sprinted off in search of the next item on their list, Ali walked over to meet us. She was wearing green runners, white shorts and one of the new campaign T-shirts. Her blue-black hair was knotted in a chignon at the nape of her neck, and her eyes, black as obsidian, were bright. She was ebullient. "I love all this," she said, extending her arms as if to embrace the entire picnic.

"A happy warrior," Zack said. "The campaign must be going well."

"It is," she said. "There are at least a hundred and fifty selfies of scavenger hunters and supporters and me floating around here."

"Better you than me," I said. "I've always hated having my picture taken."

"So have I," Ali said. "But Peggy Kreviazuk says that selfies are manna from heaven for candidates. Supporters show them to their friends and families; the talk turns to politics, and if we're lucky, the votes come to us."

Zack chuckled. "Peggy Kreviazuk knows how to keep a campaign team on its toes."

"We're lucky to have her," Ali said.

"We are," I agreed. "Now you'd better get back to work. You have our votes, and I'm sure there are at least a hundred more people here today keen to have a selfie taken with you."

Ali grinned. "Peggy says the first two rules of politics are never pass up a chance to make contact with a voter or visit the bathroom."

"More wise words," Zack said. He turned to me. "So, what's your pleasure? Slo-pitch? Horseshoes? Looks like they're getting together a game of ultimate Frisbee over there."

"It does," I agreed. "It also looks as if everyone signing up for the teams is under the age of thirty. Let's get a glass of lemonade and do something dorky."

Peggy Kreviazuk was on duty at the lemonade stand, and as always, she was a cheerful sight. Her dandelion fluff of white hair shot out like a halo around a face tanned by a summer of devoted gardening. She was wearing one of the T-shirts we'd ordered for Alison's volunteers and supporters to sport during the upcoming election campaign.

"I love the shirt," I said. "I saw the design, but this is the first time I've seen the real thing. It's perfect."

Peggy raised an eyebrow. "It took us long enough to decide on the design."

"Reaching agreement in a coalition is always tricky," Zack said. "Especially among groups who have a contentious history."

"The people in Alison's coalition certainly share a contentious history," I said. "Plenty of battle scars in our group. Everybody at our first meeting self-identified as politically progressive, but our politics ranged from slightly left of centre to Marxist, and it wasn't long before the recriminations started. We were headed for yet another donnybrook when Peggy saved the day."

Zack turned his attention to Peggy. "So, what did you do?"

Peggy's voice was still girlishly breathy. "Nothing of consequence," she said. "I asked those who'd supported a cause or a candidate who'd been defeated to raise their hands. Of course, we had all lost most of our campaigns. Then I asked those who wanted Alison Janvier to be our next premier to raise their hands. When there was a sea of hands, I said it appeared that we were all on the same side, so we should get started.

"We decided to go back to the roots of the party when it was the CCF — the Co-operative Commonwealth Federation," Peggy continued. "Our campaign's colours would be those of the old CCF — green with a yellow maple leaf and a green banner bearing the motto you used for your mayoral campaign, Zack: 'Enough for All.' Hence the shirt design. Today's the first day they're available. There are stands selling them at the entrance, by the stage where the program will take place and at the exit."

"We'll make sure we get one for everybody," I said. "Including Mieka and Charlie D's baby, who's due on Labour Day."

Peggy's smile was wide. "Perfect — the day that celebrates the worker. Now let me treat you and Zack to a glass of lemonade. I made it myself and it's the real McCoy. I must have juiced two hundred lemons yesterday."

"You're a better woman than I am," I said.

"Not true," she said. "And I had company. Alison's son came over to my house and squeezed along with me."

"I'd forgotten Alison had a child," I said.

"She does, and he's a very interesting young man. We had a fine time. I told him about being jailed for joining the Mohawk protestors blocking access to the land that had been taken from them to expand a golf course, and Harper told me about a pilot program to deal with suicide among young Indigenous men that he and his grandparents have introduced in a community north of La Ronge."

The name Harper piqued my curiosity. "Do you know if Harper is named after Elijah Harper?"

Peggy's face lit with pleasure. "Good for you, Jo. Not many people would have picked up on that."

"I was teaching classes in Canadian politics when the to-ing and fro-ing about the Meech Lake Accord was going on," I said. "It was a dramatic time."

"And a tense one," Peggy said. "I remember all the provinces had to ratify the accord by midnight on June 23. Among other omissions, the accord ignored Indigenous rights. When Elijah Harper stood in the Manitoba Legislature, raised his eagle feather and began speaking, the clock was ticking. Elijah spoke very softly and very slowly, and midnight came and went."

"The accord was never ratified," I said. "Elijah Harper became the face of all those who had opposed it. Alison chose a fine name for her son."

"And Harper is already proving himself worthy of his name.

He just finished his second year of political studies at the University of Saskatchewan, and he did brilliantly."

I was taken aback. "How old is he?"

"Nineteen," Peggy said. "And Alison is thirty-five, but that's her story to tell or not tell."

Thirsty people began appearing, so Zack turned his wheelchair. "Seems the reputation of your real McCoy lemonade has spread, Peggy. Time for Jo and me to make way for the paying customers."

Peggy laughed and then extended her arms first to Zack and then to me. "The struggle continues, Joanne," she said. It was her standard farewell to me, and I gave her my standard response. "And so do we," I said.

As soon as Zack and I were out of earshot, he said, "That was enlightening. We learned that Alison has a nineteen-year-old son, and that Peggy was jailed during the Oka Crisis of 1990. She must have been at least sixty."

"She was sixty-two," I said. "But she felt strongly about the issue, so she went to Quebec and stayed at the blockade for over a month."

Zack shook his head in amazement. "You prairie women are a hardy breed," Zack said.

"We have to be," I said.

* * *

I'm not a fan of crowds, but that afternoon, being surrounded by people enjoying a late summer day buoyed my spirits. Many of the faces I saw were familiar — I didn't remember all their names, but for years we had been part of the same community. We'd attended the same party potlucks, rallies and fundraisers. We'd passed around the Colonel Sanders bucket for donations at the end of gatherings. We'd shared bad coffee and war stories in campaign offices. We were what Howard Dowhanuik called the "foot soldiers": loyal, reliable and irreplaceable. We were the stalwarts, the ones who renewed our party memberships without being reminded, brought Tupperware containers of egg salad sandwiches to meetings without being asked, tore the party apart at conventions and defended it to the death over the back fence.

It was an intense life, and it had been mine for almost three decades. The reasons I had drifted from involvement in provincial politics could be summed up in three words: I'd had enough. But that day as Zack and I watched the smoke waft from the barbecues where a man from the poultry association was broiling quarter chickens, as he or another member of his family had at our party's picnics for as long as I could remember, a sense of homecoming washed over me.

"Are you in the mood for chicken?" Zack said.

"Always," I said. "And the lineup is still short." We'd just started towards the picnic tables set out for the chicken man's customers, when Mark and Lori Evanson approached us. Mark was pushing a baby in a stroller. The encounter was, as New York Yankees catcher Yogi Berra famously remarked, "déjà vu all over again." One of the last times I'd seen the Evansons, Mark had been pushing a stroller.

He had been nineteen then, a solid good-looking young man with a solid good-looking three-year-old son squirming to get free of the stroller. The baby's mother, Lori, had been at Mark's side. At nineteen, she had the beauty of a teen magazine cover girl: shoulder-length dark blond hair, peaches-and-cream complexion, blue-green eyes, pert nose and perfect rosebud lips.

It was sixteen years since I'd seen the Evansons. They were now thirty-five, and yet they seemed not to have aged at all. When Lori recognized me, she clapped her hands together in delight. Her voice was sweet and lilting. "Oh, Mrs. Kilbourn, this is the best surprise. I've hoped and hoped that we would see you one day, and now, here you are." She looked at Zack with frank curiosity. "And you're?" Her brow furrowed in concentration as she worked through the possibilities of Zack's relationship with me. Then, as suddenly as they had appeared, the furrows vanished. The problem was solved. "Why, you must be Mrs. Kilbourn's friend," Lori said, and her tone was triumphant.

Zack's correction was gentle. "I'm Joanne's husband, Zack Shreve," he said.

Mark extended his hand to Zack. "Well, congratulations, Mr. Shreve. Mrs. Kilbourn has always been a very good friend to us."

"I hope we can all be good friends now," Zack said.

I crouched in front of the baby in the stroller and looked up at Lori. "Is this little guy yours?" I asked.

A shadow crossed Lori's face. "No, Clay is our only child." She brightened. "But Andy is family."

"Andy is my dad and stepmum's baby," Mark said. "They have three children together: Gabriela is sixteen, Craig Junior is fourteen and Andy is twenty-two months."

The name evoked memories of another Andy — one who had been dear to me and to many in our party. "Is he named after Andy Boychuk?"

Mark nodded. "He is. My dad said Andy Boychuk was a decent man."

"He was," I said. "And he would have been very proud to have this handsome boy as his namesake."

"This Andy was a surprise," Lori whispered.

I stood. "My youngest was a surprise too," I whispered, "but a nice one." The sun was full on Lori's face, but even in that unsparing light, she had the dewy freshness of a girl. As they had been sixteen years earlier, Lori's wide, innocent eyes were carefully made up — peach eyeshadow blended into mauve and then a soft smudge of grey eyeliner beneath her lower lashes. Clearly she had found the look that worked for her and stuck with it.

"I'm so glad we ran into you today," I said. "You both look great. Life is obviously treating you well."

"It is," Lori said. Her voice was as musical as a wind chime. "We don't live in Wolf River anymore. We live in Lumsden. It's thirty-three kilometres from Regina."

When Lori didn't elaborate, Mark provided the context. "Seven years ago, my stepmother, Manda, inherited her father's house in Lumsden. It's a big, beautiful house. Manda and my dad said the house was big enough for all of us, and it would be good for everybody if we moved in. So, we had a family meeting, and we moved in."

"And it's worked for your family and Craig and Manda's," I said.

Lori cast her husband an anxious glance. Obviously there was a piece of information that was Mark's to deliver. His gaze was steady. "Mrs. Kilbourn, I believe God moves in mysterious ways, and that sometimes we see through a glass darkly."

A prairie picnic seemed an unlikely setting for an existential discussion. A group of boys to our left was having a contest to determine who could spit a watermelon seed the farthest. A woman next to them was selling chances on a star quilt glowing with the colours of sunset. Next to her, children not much older than Andy Evanson were crawling and climbing through an obstacle course. Andy had spotted them and was struggling to get free of his stroller. Lori reached down, released him and murmured, "Hang on, buddy. That's where we're going next."

When he was certain Lori's assurance satisfied Andy, Mark began what was clearly a narrative he had delivered often. "Wolf River Bible College grade school is a wonderful God-centred community of people who share the same beliefs," he said. "It had been the right place for Lori and me, but it was never the right place for Clay.

"Our son had questions that Lori and I couldn't answer. Clay never fit in, and he didn't believe what the teachers tried to teach him. He started asking questions, and when the other students told him the teachers were right and he was bearing false witness, Clay started acting out. Lori and I tried to talk to him, but he wouldn't listen. Clay said he was smart enough to find his own answers."

Lori nodded emphatically. "And Mr. and Mrs. Shreve, Clay is smart. He's like Mark's mother — very smart. We bought him a copy of the *New World Translation of the Holy Scriptures*, so he could find his own answers. We paid extra to have his name, Clay Thomas Evanson, embossed on the leather cover in gold. That book of the Holy Scriptures was beautiful, but Clay wouldn't even open it." Lori's lovely blue-green eyes filled with tears. "Mrs. Kilbourn, do you remember me telling you that we chose Clay's name from Isaiah 64:8? 'But now, O Lord, You are our Father; we are the clay, and You are our potter; and we are the work of Your hand.' Mark and I tried. We did our very best. So did Clay's teachers. So did everyone else in the community. But no matter how hard we tried, Clay would not be shaped."

Mark swallowed hard. "Finally, the principal of the school called Lori and me in and said that it would be better for everyone if we found another school for Clay."

The story seemed to be moving inexorably towards tragedy. Zack's eyes were downcast, and my chest was growing tight. Lori picked up on our concern. "Don't be worried," she said. "God had a plan."

Mark picked up the narrative. "Mrs. Kilbourn, do you remember my mother, Julie?"

"I do indeed," I said. Julie Evanson had been a thorn in the side of everyone who knew her. "I heard she remarried," I said.

"She did, and the man she married is an important person with important friends who all have cottages up north at Emma Lake. My mother really loves Clay and so does her husband. Clay was never happy in Wolf River, especially not in the summer. He didn't have friends, and there was nothing for him to do. When Clay was seven, my mother and her husband started taking him to their cottage for the summer. He was happy with them, and when we told my mother and her husband about Clay's problem at school, they said they were planning to move back to Regina, and he could live with them and finish school there. So, that's what he did."

"Clay just finished his second year at the School of Journalism," Lori said. "We're very proud of him. He has a job at MediaNation, and he might be here today. Mark and I are hoping we'll see him."

Mark put his arm around Lori's shoulders. "I think my dad knew Lori and I would be lonely without Clay, so that's why he suggested we move in with their family. My mother's husband got me a really good job, and Manda and Lori opened up a preschool together in our house."

"It's called Just Beginning," Lori said, and her eyes were shining again. "I love the name, because it's kind of the way it's been for Mark and me and Clay and everybody. We're all just beginning."

Mark's gaze at Lori was adoring. "That's exactly right," he said. "We are all just beginning."

Lori handed Andy to her husband and came over to Zack and me. "I'm just going to hug you both," she said. Lori's arms were warm; her hair smelled of sunshine and summer, and her voice was gentle. "God bless," she said.

Zack and I watched as Andy Evanson ran off to join the kids on the obstacle course. Hand in hand, Lori and Mark ran after the little boy.

Zack took one look at my face and moved his chair closer. "Are you okay?"

"No," I said. "Lori and Mark are such innocents and they wanted so little from life."

"That son of theirs sounds like a real piece of work," Zack said.

"The last time I saw Clay he was wearing a Mr. Pumpkin Halloween suit and twirling around in front of a mirror laughing at his reflection," I said. "He was about three, and I'd bought the Mr. Pumpkin costume on impulse — it was very cute and it was half price. When I gave it to Lori, she was beside herself with joy."

"What went wrong there?"

"I don't know," I said. "I was only there for the beginning of the story. Mark is the same age as Mieka. All the wives of the MLAs seemed to have babies within a year or so of one another, so there were plenty of birthday parties and trips to the park and get-togethers over coffee. We all thought our kids were special, but Julie Evanson was obsessed with making Mark the best and the brightest. She centred her life on her son: instructing him, challenging him, urging him to reach for the top."

"And Mark turned out to be average," Zack said.

"Actually a little below average," I said. "As soon as Julie faced the truth that Mark would never excel at anything, she turned away. It was as if he had ceased to exist for her."

More than a few of Zack's legal colleagues referred to him as the "Prince of Darkness," but my husband had a soft spot for children, and Julie's rejection of her son touched him. "How could anyone do that to a young boy?" he said. "Was Mark's father in the picture?"

"He was. Craig Evanson is a good man and he did his best to fill the void, but he was an MLA for a Regina riding, and that meant that in addition to his work in the legislature, he had to be present at every Robbie Burns dinner, fiftieth wedding anniversary and high school graduation in the constituency. His schedule didn't leave much time for parenting. Anyway, somewhere along the line, Mark connected with a group of kids from Wolf River Bible College. At sixteen he was born again, and at seventeen he became a husband and not long after that a father."

"To a son who, as soon as he was old enough to see the lay of the land, abandoned his parents and moved onto greener pastures," Zack said.

"It *is* an ugly picture," I said. "But I'm trying to see this from Clay's perspective. The teachings of Wolf River Bible College are fundamentalist. They believe in a literal interpretation of the Bible and its events. If Clay is as smart and persistent as his parents say he is, he must have found the atmosphere at Wolf River stifling."

"I'm sure he did, but from what Mark said, he and Lori tried to do what they believed was best for their son. They deserve a place in his life."

"They do," I agreed. "But Clay is young. Maybe given time, he'll work that out for himself." I checked my watch. "Madeleine and Lena are going to be arriving any minute, so we'd better stake out a claim on a picnic table."

CHAPTER FIVE

The entertainment and Alison Janvier's speech were scheduled to start at five o'clock. Many of those attending the picnic were people who, like Peggy Kreviazuk, had been party supporters for decades; many were millennials with young kids, and the organizers had wisely decided to keep the program short and the speeches to a minimum. The picnic coordinators aimed to have everyone fed, fired up and on their way by 6 p.m.

As people gathered in front of the temporary stage at the north end of the field, it was obvious the organizers' decision had been a smart one. The mood was mellow, but after a day of eating, drinking and playing under the prairie sun, people were ready to pack it in.

When I led Madeleine and Lena past the crowds to a shady spot beside the stage, Lena's look was questioning. "How come we never sit out front like everybody else?"

"Just habit," I said. "Political people always sit by the side in case something goes wrong."

"Then they can help," Lena said sagely. "Okay, Madeleine and I will spread out our blanket here." She turned her attention to Zack. "Do you ever think you're lucky because you always have your own chair?"

Zack was pensive. "You know, I've never thought of it that way, but I guess I am lucky."

"And Lena and I are lucky," Madeleine said. "Our team placed second in the selfie scavenger hunt. We won these cool 'Alison Janvier' T-shirts, and we learned to play Bocce."

"And Maddy and I beat you at horseshoes," Lena said.

"Not by much," Zack said. "And Mimi and I watched a slo-pitch game."

"How could just watching be fun?"

"Because there was a man there selling chili dogs and root beer," I said.

"That makes sense," Lena said. Suddenly something in the distance caught her attention and she leapt to her feet. "Look! Uncle Pete, Aunt Maisie and the twins are here."

"So they are," I said. "And right on time."

Charlie and Colin were almost four, and they were handsome boys. They had inherited their mother's copper curls and gold-flecked brown eyes, but the perfect oval shape of their faces, their sculptured features and their sensitive mouths were the legacy of the Kilbourn males. Like their parents and their cousins, the twins were wearing the forest-green shirts that were popping up all over the picnic grounds like mushrooms after a three-day rain.

I crouched down to talk to the boys. "So, did you have fun?" I asked.

"We threw a ball. We climbed and we crawled through something," Charlie said.

"And we ran and got these." Colin held out the bright yellow ribbon attached to his shirt.

I looked at it closely. "Wow," I said. "A ribbon for participation."

Zack gave me a sidelong look. "I told you our grandsons were law-school material."

Maisie, an accomplished trial lawyer, rolled her eyes. "Granddad's right," she said. "Just show up at the College of Law, participate for three years and they'll give you your J.D. Easy-peasy."

"Mummy won Lego," Charlie said.

"And just like that, the subject changes," I said.

"Nope," Peter said. "The subject is family triumphs, and Charlie's right on topic. Maisie guessed there were eight hundred and seventeen pieces of giant Lego in a toy box and her estimate was right on the nose."

"We get to take the Lego home," Colin said.

"Congratulations all around," I said.

Maisie glanced at her husband. "We're a lucky family," she said.

Pete's arm was around Maisie's shoulders, and he drew her close. "Very lucky," he said.

The first two years of their marriage had been troubled: Maisie's twin sister, Lee, had died tragically; beaten down by sorrow, Maisie and Peter decided to move to the family farm and continue Lee's heritage poultry breeding program.

Like many decisions made by those mired in grief, the move had been a mistake. Maisie loved her husband and her children, but she was passionate about the law, and she was frank about admitting that she felt most fully alive when she was trying a case.

Their farm was an hour's drive from Regina — not a long distance, but the work of trial lawyers is gruelling, and by the time Maisie returned to the farm at night, she was exhausted and preoccupied. Ours is a close family, but there was nothing any of us could do but watch helplessly as the cracks in Pete and Maisie's young marriage deepened. Their estrangement had reached the crisis point, and Maisie and Pete realized that the only way to keep their family whole was to sell the farm.

The move back to the city had been painful for both of them, but it saved their marriage, On that late afternoon, I could see the confusion and fatigue that had knifed their faces for far too long had disappeared. Experiencing an old-time prairie picnic was a simple pleasure but a deep one, and as Synergy, the wildly energetic, multi-talented group of ten kids from an inner-city high school burst on stage to warm up the audience before Alison's speech, Maisie's eyes were bright. "This political thing can really be kick-ass," she said.

Inspired by the U.K. group Stomp, Synergy used innovative choreography, drum-line precision and brooms, metal garbage cans and oil barrels to create a dazzling eight-minute celebration of the noises we usually try to block out of our lives. Their performance received a standing ovation, and when Alison came onstage, the audience, already on its feet, went wild. She embraced each member of the group before moving to the podium and leaning into the mic to address the crowd.

Alison had the gift essential in every successful politician: she could make even a stock speech sound intimate and fresh. "In the past year I've come to know the members of Synergy," she began. "Their backgrounds are diverse and their stories, very different, but they share a common goal: to show our community that by working together, using the ordinary things at hand, we can create something that is more than the sum of its parts. We can create something amazing.

"I see plenty of our campaign T-shirts in the audience. I also see plenty of shirts that are not in our campaign's colours. That doesn't matter. What matters is knowing that the issues confronting us are urgent: effective policies to combat human-caused climate change; investment in our infrastructure; retraining workers to give them the skills they need to get decent jobs in a rapidly changing job market; first-rate affordable child care; schools that meet the needs of all our children. The list is daunting, but together we have hammered out precise, practical policies to meet the needs of all our citizens.

"We have learned to work alongside people whose political beliefs do not always align exactly with our own, but we have identified our common destination, and we agree that to reach that destination, there will be times when we have to paddle a little on the left, and times when we have to paddle a little on the right. All that matters is that we get there."

It was a short speech, and it contained nothing that Alison Janvier hadn't said scores of times before, but it worked. When Alison's speech ended, as it always did with J.S. Woodworth's haunting words, "What we desire for ourselves, we wish for all," the crowd's roar was full-throated.

It was the perfect ending to a perfect day, but there was a coda that resonated deeply with many of us. If Synergy had been a gift to the millennials, the man who came on stage wearing battered workboots and strumming the opening chords of "The Farmer's Song" was a tip of the cap to those whose work for social justice spanned decades.

The man onstage, fumbling a little as he adjusted the microphone, was not Murray McLauchlan, but McLauchlan's tribute to all the unrecognized dusty old farmers out working their fields had long been an anthem at our party's events. As Peter, Maisie, Zack, the girls, the twins and I hummed or sang the song that had been so much a part of our history, I felt the sting of tears. When Lena eyed me with concern, I tried a smile and turned to focus on the grove of poplars edging the field. Their leaves were turning, and the late summer light caught them, warming them to the colour of amber. It was a golden moment, but as the poet said, "Nothing gold can stay."

Tall, burly and assured, Howard Dowhanuik stood out in a crowd, and I always brightened when I caught sight of him. But that day as he moved towards us, my breath caught, because Howard wasn't alone. Jill Oziowy was with him.

Oblivious to the fact that he was about to drop a grenade in our midst, Howard gave our family his quick, well-practised public smile and turned his attention to our candidate. Ali had joined in singing the final verse of "The Farmer's Song." "God, she's good. She'll go the distance," he said. His voice was deep and assured, the voice of a man accustomed to being listened to. "Something came up, so Jill and I are late. How did Ali's speech go over?"

"You're the éminence grise," Zack said. "You heard the crowd. They loved her."

Howard nodded. "It sounded that way," he said. "But a smart éminence grise always seeks a second opinion."

The relationship between my husband and my long-time friend had not always been cordial, but that afternoon, there was real affection in their comradely exchange. And that was a boon, because warmth was suddenly in short supply in our small group. Seconds earlier, we had been exuberant. Now our granddaughters, and Pete and Maisie were silent, their faces impassive. When Colin and Charlie began looking uneasy, Maisie and Peter each picked up one of their sons.

Finally, Jill took a tentative step towards Madeleine and Lena. "You've both grown so much," she said. "Maddy, will you be in grade eight this year? And Lena, are you heading into grade seven?" When the girls didn't respond, Jill tried a smile. "That must be exciting," she said.

Madeleine and Lena hadn't seen Jill in three years, and they were at a loss about what to do. Lena eyed me beseechingly. "Mimi . . ."

"The first day back to school is always an adventure," I said, "and the girls are excited. But Ali's about to make her exit, so it's time for us to go back to the city."

"What the hell," Howard said. "Jill and I just got here. We haven't had a chance to talk yet."

Now the singalong was over, and people were clapping and calling Ali's name in a ragged chorus. "Ali! Ali! Ali!" The event had been a triumph, but an old political friend once warned me that when a campaign appears to be going too well, somewhere there's a dragon crawling out of its lair, heading towards your candidate with bedlam on its mind.

Our dragon wasted no time making its appearance. Alison may have been a political novice, but she could judge when applause had reached its peak. When she was handed a John Deere cap, she donned it, waved one last time to the crowd and started towards the back of the stage. What happened next was a blur. There was a tangle of wire cables on the floor. Alison did a quick check to make sure her path was clear, then someone in the crowd called out to her and she turned towards them. When Alison's attention shifted, a young blond man in a spiffy golf shirt leaned against the edge of the stage and pushed the tangle of cables into her path. When Alison turned in the direction that would take her off stage, her foot caught on the wires, and she fell forward. It was a hard fall, and for a few agonizing seconds, she was motionless.

Maisie handed Colin to Zack and pushed herself onto the stage and knelt beside Alison, murmuring her name. The man in the golf shirt pulled out his phone and started taking pictures of Alison lying face down on the stage. Jill had her phone out too, but her camera was pointed at the man, and she was moving towards him. I followed close behind.

When she was close enough to be heard, Jill said, "Delete that video," and her tone was flinty. As soon as I saw the young man's face, I knew he was Clay Evanson. His likeness to his mother was remarkable, but where Lori's face radiated innocence, her son's face was dark with arrogance and anger. He had a press pass on a lanyard around his neck. He grabbed the pass and flashed it at Jill. "I'm a journalist with MediaNation," he said.

"That's a coincidence," Jill said, pulling her photo ID out of her purse and waving it at Clay. "I work for MediaNation too. Delete the video."

Clay Evanson held his press pass closer to Jill. "Read the name of this ID."

Jill glanced at the name and shrugged. "I heard you had a summer internship here, Clay. Those internships are a great opportunity for professionals to assess what an intern could bring to our profession. Our CEO would be very disappointed to see that video of you deliberately obstructing Alison Janvier's path, so you could create a clip that shows her falling flat on her face."

Clay was sputtering. "Hugh Fairbairn is the CEO, and he's also my grandfather. I could have you fired."

Jill may have had a history of choosing deeply flawed men as romantic partners, but she recognized a prick when she saw one, and she made short work of diminishing Clay Fairbairn. "Hugh and I go way back," she said. "He's a pragmatist. He would never fire a colleague for showing him that one of his budding journalists needs a refresher course in ethics. Do yourself a favour — delete that video."

Clay's peaches-and-cream complexion was mottled by anger. "You really are a cunt," he said.

"Strike three," Jill said, and she touched her phone's keypad. "Time to let Hugh see you in action."

Clay's mouth twisted. "Don't," he said. He tapped his keypad. "There. It's deleted. Now you delete yours."

Jill was derisive. "No way," she said. "First rule of journalism: Preserve the evidence."

Clay reached out to grab Jill's phone.

Zack wheeled his chair to Jill's side. "I don't know what your game is, Mr. Fairbairn, but I'm a lawyer, and you should be aware of the fact that if Alison Janvier sustained a serious injury because of that fall, you'll be up on charges. What Ms. Oziowy has on her camera is evidence of what might well turn out to be a criminal act. The law takes a dim view of people who destroy evidence."

Clay spat out the word "cunt" again, then stalked off.

"A limited vocabulary," Jill said mildly. "He'll have to work on that."

Howard took her arm. "I think Jo and her family can handle this. There are a couple of people I'd like you to meet." He gave me a quick peck on the cheek and pointed to the stage. A crowd had gathered around Alison. Howard was clearly concerned, but he was also aware he was exacerbating the situation. "Call me later and let me know what's happening?"

"Of course," I said.

Pete's expression was grave. "Sports have taught me

enough about concussions and possible concussions to know that Ali needs watching tonight. Maisie and I will take her back to our place."

"Do you want us to keep the boys for a sleepover?" I asked.

Pete shook his head. "That's a tempting offer," he said. "And I'm grateful, but the boys need to know what's going on. And if they're with us, we can tell them."

"Good parenting," I said. "If you need help later, let us know."

Maisie had made her way to the edge of the stage, and she jumped down. "Luckily a doctor was sitting close to the front and he's checking Ali out. He believes the injuries are not serious, and Ali says she's taken harder hits in lacrosse, but they agree that she should be watched tonight." She turned to Peter. "I volunteered."

"That's exactly what I would have done," Pete said. "Time for Charlie, Colin and me to head out." He gave his wife a quick hug and scooped Colin from Zack's knee. "The boys and I will bring the car around to the exit so Ali won't have far to walk."

"I'll let Ali and the doctor know the plan," Maisie said. She turned to Zack and me. "I'm glad you two were here. I always feel stronger when you're around." And with that, our daughter-in-law climbed back onto the stage and disappeared into the crowd.

"That was intense," I said.

"It was," Zack agreed. "Clay Evanson Fairbairn appears to have travelled a long way from that sweet little boy in the pumpkin suit you remembered."

"I wonder what happened," I said.

"Clay's keeping his eyes on the prize," Zack said. "He dropped his parents' surname, he dropped his parents and he turned into an asshole."

"Succinct but accurate," I said. "I just wish it didn't have to be that way. Zack, I'd like to talk to Jill for a minute. Can you take the girls to the car? I'll meet you there."

Zack held out his arms, and I leaned in. "You always know what I need," I said.

Howard was talking to a young couple wearing the campaign shirts, and Jill was standing a few feet away from them checking her phone. Thirty-five years earlier when I met her, Jill had untamed shoulder-length carrot-red hair, freckles, shining eyes and an open smile. Her hair was now a fashionable shade of burgundy, styled in a severe, side-parted gamine cut that set off her extraordinary tawny eyes. When I approached her, her smile was guarded.

"I wanted to thank you," I said. "Do you have any idea what that was about?"

Jill put away her phone and turned to face me. Her gaze was steady. "I've been trying to figure that out," she said. "I'm sure Charlie D explained why I'm here. We've lost two key employees under disturbing circumstances; we're under the gun as far as time for introducing the new season is concerned, and morale is terrible."

"Charlie is very concerned about Ellen Exton," I said. "He told me about how HR in Toronto had handled Rosemary's situation. Forcing her colleagues to send individual written reports on her ability to do her job was cruel and stupid."

"Cruel and stupid pretty much sums up Joseph Monk's skill set," Jill said. "Those individual assessments he insisted on have left everyone feeling like Judas."

"I'm sure you're right," I said, "but I don't believe what Clay Fairbairn did this afternoon was a result of tensions in the workplace. I was watching his face. He didn't hesitate for a millisecond before he pushed those wires into Alison Janvier's path. She could have been badly hurt, but all that mattered to him was getting a photo of her being humiliated."

Jill raised an artfully shaped eyebrow. "So, you think I should follow up on this? See what I can dig up?"

"No. I think you should let it go. Summer's over. Clay will be going back to the School of Journalism. His step-grandfather is your friend and your boss. Don't get in the middle of this, Jill. In fact, you'd be smart to give Clay a wide berth. I have a bad feeling about him, and I don't want to see you hurt."

Jill's smile was weary. "You say that as if you actually care."

"That's because I do care," I said. "Do you still have the same phone number?"

She nodded. "I wanted to make sure you could get in touch if you felt like talking."

The girls were quiet as we started back to the city. Finally, I broke the silence. "Do you have any questions about what happened?"

"Granddad talked to us about it on the way back to the car," Madeleine said. "He told us that the name of the blond man with the camera was Clay Fairbairn, and that he wanted to get a video of Ali that would make her look weak."

"Grandad also told us that Jill did the right thing when she made him delete the video."

"She did," I agreed. "Jill realized that Clay Fairbairn deliberately set out to hurt Ali, and she stepped in to keep Clay from hurting Ali even more."

Madeleine was pensive. "Was what Jill did today enough to make up for the mistake she made before she went away?"

"How much did your mum tell you about that?"

"Not much. Just that Jill made a bad mistake and it hurt our family. Will what she did today be enough to make things right?"

"I don't know," I said, "but it could be a start."

CHAPTER SIX

Monday morning, when the dogs and I returned from our run, Charlie and Zack were in the kitchen having coffee. Zack was dressed for the office in a lightweight mochaccino suit, and Charlie was dressed for radio in blue jeans and a T-shirt bearing a photo of a heartbreakingly young Chet Baker holding his trumpet. While Zack fed the dogs, Charlie D filled a mug and handed it to me.

"Glad you're home, Jo," he said. "I have to get to work, but I wanted to give you both an update — such as it is — on Ellen Exton. Kam Chau called me just before I left the house this morning. Kam's been the associate producer of our show since it started, and he's taking over Ellen's job. He's smart, and he knows what he's doing, so the transition will be smooth.

"Kam's usually a no-drama guy but when he called, he was keyed up. He's been out of town, so he didn't learn Ellen had been fired until last night. As soon as he heard the news, he tried to contact her. No luck. He called some of the other people on our production team. Still nada, so he called Ellen's parents in Saskatoon. They hadn't heard from their daughter since Thursday, and they hit the panic button."

"Understandably," I said.

"Kam tried to reassure them, but he's concerned too. Ellen is a cat owner, and when she's out of town, Kam takes care of Ellen's cats. He has the keys to her house, and this morning on his way to work he stopped by her place. When there was no answer at the door, Kam let himself in. He called me from there, and he's convinced something has happened to Ellen. The house was in good order, but the cats' water and food dishes were empty, and they were frantic."

"Cats are pretty self-sufficient, aren't they?" Zack said. "If Ellen needed to get away for a while and she left them food and water, wouldn't they be okay for a couple of days?"

"As a general rule, they would, but as Kam pointed out, everyone who knows Ellen knows she would never leave Mary and Mr. Grant overnight without having someone check on them."

Zack's eyes widened. "The cats are named Mary and Mr. Grant?"

"Mary and Mr. Grant are characters in an old sitcom," I said.

"Ellen told me that when she was growing up in Saskatoon, she taped *The Mary Tyler Moore Show*, and she watched every episode so often, she had the characters' lines memorized," Charlie D said tightly. "Mary Richards, the lead character, was Ellen's role model, a single woman working as a producer in a TV station."

Zack was pensive. "Ellen is an adult, and she's only been out of touch since Friday, but people's patterns of behaviour matter. If everyone who knows Ellen agrees that she'd never leave Mary and Mr. Grant unattended, that's a red flag. I'll call Debbie Haczkewicz. She's head of Major Crimes. She's sharp. When we fill her in about Ellen's devotion to her cats and give her a timeline, she'll take this seriously."

Alerting Debbie Haczkewicz to the situation was the right move, but my heart sank as Zack made the call. I liked and respected Debbie. She was smart, she was fair, and she and Zack were close. At a function honouring Zack, Debbie said that police officers and trial lawyers are like the orca and the great white shark, natural enemies, but that she and Zack had learned to cherish the times when they were able to swim side by side. Debbie's involvement meant that Ellen Exton's disappearance could no longer be explained away. Debbie, like Zack, was dogged. She would not give up until she'd learned the truth about what happened to Ellen Exton, and I knew Zack would be beside her all the way. The stillness my husband and I longed for would have to wait.

* * *

For all of us Zack's health was a huge concern, but it was one about which we seldom talked. Paraplegia complicates everything, including the working of internal organs, the blood's ability to flow without clotting and the skin's ability to heal. As a paraplegic Zack was vulnerable to respiratory ailments, renal failure, pulmonary embolisms and septicemia.

I worried about every detail of Zack's life and I worried about letting him know how much I worried. As a trial lawyer, his hours and stress level were horrific.

One of the features that drew us to the house on the creek was that it had an indoor pool. Taylor and I were both enthusiastic swimmers, and after spending eighteen hours a day in a wheelchair, Zack needed exercise to give his cardiovascular system a workout, help control the leg spasms that harassed him and just relax.

The original owners of our house had installed the pool for therapeutic reasons, and the area surrounding it had been antiseptic and depressing. One wall was glass, but Taylor had filled the other three with a mural depicting an underwater scene of swimmers — human, finned and crustacean — that pulsed with movement and colour.

The explosion that had rocked our house six years earlier had destroyed the beautiful room. The contractors restoring the house had replaced the pool and the area was once again functional, but the walls were once again bare and antiseptic. Our lives were busy and restoring the pool to its former glory was low on our list of priorities. After Taylor and Vale had moved into a place of their own, decorating the pool area drifted even lower on the priority list.

But Zack was having leg spasms; his blood pressure was

too high, and the cold weather was on its way. It was time to make the pool area inviting once again.

We'd hired the workers, chosen a soft grey shade called Metropolitan for the walls and complementary porcelain tile for the flooring. I'd hit the late summer sales for poolside furniture and tropical plants. The plan was to have the workers start on Monday. The foreperson estimated ours was a three-day job, so we could have the furniture and plants delivered Thursday and all would be in place by the weekend.

However, once again, Robbie Burns's tart observation that "The best laid schemes o' Mice an' Men / Gang aft agley" was proven true. Just after Zack left the house for an appointment downtown, Dawn McCudden, the foreperson of the crew, called. One of her workers had broken his leg over the weekend and was in traction. Dawn had found someone to take his place, but the new person couldn't start until later in the month.

When she was a teenager, Mieka had a skiing accident that landed her at Regina General in traction for ten days, so I was empathetic. After I assured Dawn that the delay would not inconvenience us, I went outside to tackle a task I'd been avoiding: deciding what to do with our garden.

We'd been at the lake for most of August and despite my sporadic forays against the weeds and the best efforts of my neighbours, the heat had taken its toll. I had moved the planters of herbs into the cool of the mudroom and they were thriving, but except for the marigolds, which my late friend Hilda McCourt prized for their great life lesson — "they're blooming when you put them in and blooming when you pull them out" — our zinnias and asters, the normally hardy prides of the late summer garden, were beyond resuscitation.

I picked up a basket and wandered through the vegetables, rescuing survivors: a hidden cuke, six green onions, a handful of late lettuce and, unsurprisingly, a zucchini. Encouraged, I picked up another basket and began pulling the carrots, beets and onions. Clearing a garden was a task I could handle, and energized, I decided to continue harvesting the rows of root vegetables. When I finished, I was sweaty, dirty and satisfied.

I was stretching to get out the kinks, when Julie Evanson Gallagher Fairbairn appeared around the corner of the house. When she saw me, Julie gave me an assessing gaze and cooed, "I've caught you at a bad time."

"Not at all," I said. "What can I do for you, Julie?"

As always, Julie was immaculate. Her silver hair fell smoothly from a centre part to a point just below her cheekbone. She was wearing a filmy lilac blouse and matching slacks and carrying the distinctive pink and white striped box of Gâteau des Rois, our city's finest patisserie. She held the box out to me with a dimpled smile. "Peace offering," she said. "We share thirty-five years of history, Joanne — not all of it good. I knew a phone call wouldn't be enough. We had to meet face to face."

"And here we are," I said. "Face to face. You're welcome to come inside for tea, Julie, but if you're here because of the incident with your grandson, Clay, yesterday afternoon at the picnic, you're wasting those fancy pastries. Take them to Jill Oziowy. She's the person who has what you want."

Julie made a moue of disgust. "I'm not going to ask for anything from that woman. You talk to her."

"It's not my concern. To be blunt, it's not your concern either. This is between Clay and Jill. They work for the same company."

"The company of which my husband, Hugh, is CEO," Julie said.

"Then it's a work problem," I said. "Let the three of them deal with it."

"Clay doesn't want his grandfather to see that tape. He's nineteen years old, and you know how nineteen-year-olds are, Joanne. They make mistakes. He tried to apologize to Jill, but she wouldn't hear him out."

"Julie, Clay did not try to apologize to Jill. The first word that came out of his mouth when Jill refused to give in to his demands was 'cunt.'"

Julie's reaction was visceral. She gasped. "My grandson would never use that word."

"I was there, Julie, and that is the word Clay used. Zack there too, and as a lawyer, he advised Jill not to delete her recording because if Alison Janvier's injuries were serious, Clay would be up on charges, and it would be evidence."

Julie stiffened. "Clay has already determined that Ms. Janvier has recovered from her little tumble." That hurdle cleared, Julie forged ahead with an appeal to my better self. "Joanne, you and I were never close, but after Reid died, you were kind."

Her reference to Reid Gallagher was a deft touch, but my better self always seemed to vanish when Julie appeared. "I liked and respected Reid," I said. "I wanted to give his colleagues at the School of Journalism a chance to honour Reid's memory, and I knew you needed help. This situation is completely different.

"Julie, when your grandson saw that Alison Janvier had been distracted, he deliberately pushed an obstacle in her path, so she would trip. After she fell and was lying flat on her face, he turned his camera on her. It was a malicious act, and it could have had serious repercussions."

"You don't know the whole story, Joanne. Clay suffered a disappointment yesterday. He was wounded and he lashed out. I want to show our grandson that Hugh and I are on his side."

"If you really want to show Clay that you and your husband are on his side, you should sit down with him and make him see that what he did wasn't journalism; it was a crime. And you should urge him to start making amends by apologizing to Alison Janvier."

Julie's response was withering. "If I followed your advice, Clay's career would be over before it began. I'll find a way around this. Not everyone is as moralistic as you are, Joanne."

It was a stinging exit line, and having delivered it, Julie strode off, stopping only to drop the pastry box on our picnic table.

A peace offering from Gâteau des Rois deserved a better fate. I picked up the box, went inside, called Mieka and invited myself to tea.

Mieka answered after the first ring. "Telepathy," she said.

"The nursery is finally Desmond-ready, and I was hoping you'd be able to come over."

"I'll be there in twenty minutes, and I'm bringing a treat."

* * *

Mieka was waiting in a rocker on the front porch when I arrived. When she spotted the patisserie box, she rubbed her hands together in glee. "Gâteau des Rois," she said. "Pretty upscale for a nursery viewing."

"I'm regifting and I'll tell you all about it, but first, let's look at Des's room."

Mieka extended her arms, so I could help her out of the rocker. Her face was pink with excitement. "Maddy and Lena spent hours choosing exactly the right colour and theme, and we did the rest together. The girls and I put on the finishing touches this morning before I dropped them off at day camp."

When we reached the second floor, Mieka linked her arm with mine. "Close your eyes, and I'll tell you when you can open them." She led me down the hall and into the room that had served as the nursery for Mieka, her brothers and her daughters. "You can look now," she said.

"Wow! This is a lot to take in," I said. "It's spectacular." Indeed it was. The walls of the room were the velvety blue of the sky on a clear night, and they were covered in patterns of stars. "The zodiac constellations," I said. "And the sun at the centre."

My daughter was beaming. "Madeleine found the original design online and printed off the description so we could memorize it and be knowledgeable when we were showing off the nursery. You're our first customer."

Mieka took a deep breath. "What Des will be looking at are 'constellations lying on the circular path of the ecliptic. As seen from Earth, the Sun appears to pass through these constellations over the course of the year, and that path is called the ecliptic. The twelve constellations in the zodiac family can all be seen along the ecliptic.'"

"And they're labelled, so when he's older Des can learn to read their names." I pointed them out. "Aries, Taurus, Gemini, Cancer, Leo, Virgo — that will be Des's sign — Libra, Scorpio, Sagittarius, Capricorn, Aquarius and Pisces." I turned to my daughter. "This is perfect," I said.

Mieka was beaming. "Charlie, the girls and I think so."

"Taylor will love this," I said. "So will Zack. But she's in Vancouver, and he can't do stairs, so it's smartphone time — not the optimal solution, but as Hilda McCourt always said, 'Needs must.'" I took my phone out and began snapping away. Two minutes after I sent Zack and Taylor the photos of the zodiac constellations; the beautiful white crib, dresser and changing table; the maple rocking chair and the hooked blue and white rug on the hardwood floor, Taylor sent a one-word text: "Stellar!" Zack had also limited himself to a single word: "Grateful!"

* * *

When we sat down for tea, Mieka cast an appraising eye at the pastries. "That's quite a spread," she said. "Chocolate

eclairs, rhubarb and custard slices, raspberry and white chocolate macaroons and your favourite lemon slices. Julie must
have had a large favour in mind."

"She did," I said. Mieka listened with interest as I told
her about meeting up with the Evansons at the picnic. Craig
Evanson had been an MLA during the years our party had
been in power, and Mark was the same age as Mieka. They'd
grown up together, and when I told Mieka that Clay had cut
himself off from his parents, her eyes filled.

"Hormones," she said, wiping her tears with a napkin.
"But Mark really has had some tough breaks. First, that
witch of a mother. She was always at Mark to be the best.
He was a lovely kid, and he tried so hard to please her,
but it was never enough. Then she just turned her back on
him. It must have been devastating, but Mark never com-
plained. He was a sweetheart."

"So is Mark's wife, Lori," I said. "Those two had so much
love to offer a child."

"And they ended up with the bad seed," Mieka said. "The
girls told us about that stunt Clay Evanson pulled with the
cables and wires lying on the stage. What he did was just
plain cruel."

"I suspect Clay simply saw it as taking advantage of an
opportunity to make Alison Janvier look weak. Incidentally,
his name now is Clay Fairbairn. Somewhere along the line,
he dropped the Evanson and adopted his step-grandfather's
surname."

"Sounds like his grandmother has taught him well,"
Mieka said.

"And he's learning all the wrong lessons. I advised Julie not to sweep what Clay did under the carpet — to help him see that what he did was wrong and make amends. I suggested that apologizing to Alison Janvier might be a good place to start."

Mieka raised her eyebrows. "How did that go over?"

"Julie said if she heeded my advice, Clay's career would be finished before it began. She said she'd find a way around the problem because not everyone is as moralistic as I am."

Mieka wiped a smear of chocolate from her upper lip. "Mum, do you remember that horrible little kid who ruined Peter's sixth birthday party?"

I winced at the memory. "I do. Of all the birthday parties we've had in this house, that was the worst. The boy's name was Everett, and his parents made a point of telling me that they didn't believe in 'caging a child's spirit.' All the other parents just dropped their kids off, but Everett's parents stayed. Whenever Everett didn't get his way, he screamed or had a tantrum, and his parents never moved a muscle."

"Everett and his parents were the last ones to leave," Mieka said. "When they finally left, Pete said, 'Everett's parents need to talk to Everett,' and then he just wandered off."

My daughter and I both smiled at the memory. "That's a classic Pete story," Mieka said, "and somebody should tell it to Julie Evanson before it's too late."

"Maybe it already is too late," I said, and it seemed the words had formed themselves.

* * *

That night, after we'd cleared away the dinner dishes, Zack and I took our tea out to the patio overlooking the creek. The days were getting shorter. That evening the sun would set at a quarter to eight. It was a pretty night, still, and except for birdsong and the occasional plash of a beaver sliding into the water, it was quiet.

Zack closed his eyes and leaned his head back against his chair's headrest. "We need more of this, Jo."

I touched his hand. "More stillness in our lives? I'm for that."

"I am too," Zack said. For a blissful few minutes we *were* still, but it wasn't long until Zack opened his eyes and straightened. "Hey, I almost forgot to tell you — Annie and Warren Weber dropped by this afternoon. Warren wants the four of us to get together at the Scarth Club for lunch any day this week that works for us. Apparently, the club has a new chef, and the food is not only edible, it's delicious."

"That is definitely something to look forward to," I said. "We could have lunch with the Webers and then head to the lake later in the afternoon and start the weekend early."

"I'll call Warren and tell him we're on for Wednesday," Zack said.

In a perfect world my husband and I would have continued to sit in the gloaming, hand in hand, chatting quietly about our lunch with the Webers and the changes in the Scarth Club, until it grew dark, but the world was not perfect.

When Zack wheeled his chair closer to mine, I knew he'd decided it was time to talk about Ellen Exton.

"It's been seventy-two hours, Jo," he said, "and we still know nothing. This morning after Charlie's show, he and I went to the cop shop to talk to Debbie directly. Charlie D was exactly the right person to make the report because he was close to Ellen and he was able to give Debbie a very complete picture of Ellen's life, including her state of mind in the hours before she dropped out of sight.

"Late this afternoon, Debbie called my office with a progress report. The police are doing everything they're supposed to do. They've gone through Ellen's apartment and through her car which, incidentally, was in the garage adjoining her house. There was a note in Ellen's handwriting affixed to the fridge door with a magnet. One sentence: "It's not enough!" The last two words were heavily underscored."

My throat tightened. "Do the police think it's a suicide note?"

"They're considering that possibility," Zack said, "but if so, where's the body? And once again, what about the cats? No matter how desperate Ellen was, from what Charlie says, she would not have made her final exit, until she'd found a home for Mary and Mr. Grant."

Esme, always attuned to my moods, lay her head on my lap. I scratched her head and murmured, "Best dog ever." Pantera grunted and moved closer to Zack.

"It gets worse," Zack said. "Ellen's parents have come down from Saskatoon. They're distraught, of course, but when they were interviewed, they were able to give Debbie a thorough account of Ellen's educational and employment history. Ellen spent at least one weekend a month in Saskatoon, and her parents gave the police the contact information for their daughter's friends there. She's an only child, and they're a close family. Anyway, the police have current photos of her and a detailed physical description. They're interviewing Ellen's colleagues at MediaNation, and they've put Ellen's photo and physical description on social media as a missing persons case."

"So, everything that can be done is being done," I said.

"Yeah," Zack said. "But it's being done seventy-two hours too late."

CHAPTER SEVEN

When Zack came to pick me up for lunch with the Webers on Wednesday, he was wearing the golf shirt and casual slacks he'd been wearing when he left for a morning meeting at a client's home.

"Aren't you going to change?" I said.

"I thought you liked this shirt?"

"I love that shirt — pomegranate is a great colour for you, but the Scarth Club has a jacket and tie rule."

"Not anymore," Zack said airily. "The times, they are a changin'."

"I didn't think the times would ever change for the Scarth Club," I said. "It wasn't that long ago that the only woman who'd ever been inside the building was a lady of the evening whose client died while they were making whoopie in one of the rooms upstairs."

"That was at least a century ago," Zack said. "The club has moved on. Women are welcome, guys don't have to wear a coat and tie, and the building has been renovated."

I groaned. "They haven't ripped out all that beautiful cherrywood, have they?"

"No. All that beautiful cherrywood is still there. The focus was on the kitchen, which had last been 'modernized' in 1952; there's a new menu, and . . . Do you remember that old cricket pitch the club had out back?"

"I do," I said. "Gone with the wind?"

"Gone and replaced with raised beds, where the new chef is growing herbs and vegetables. The Webers have arranged for us to have lunch on the patio, because Warren knew you'd be interested in the gardens. He's also sending his driver to pick us up, so we can enjoy one of the club's famous old-fashioneds."

"Warren thinks of everything,"

"He does indeed," Zack said. When our doorbell rang, my husband gave me a Cheshire cat grin. "Warren's driver. And he's right on time."

* * *

The club manager greeted us warmly. "There are many changes, and you'll be among the first to see them. Our official opening is on Labour Day, but Mr. and Mrs. Weber have been generous supporters of our remodelling, and this week we've opened our doors to club members eager to show their friends what we now have to offer. The Webers are waiting for you on the patio."

Warren and Annie Weber were a head-turning couple. Warren was eighty, an attractive six-footer with an enviable head of thick snowy hair, an always meticulously trimmed moustache and a level, steely gaze. The Webers were partial to outfits in complementary hues. That afternoon, Annie, a thirty-year-old blond, with a heart-shaped face and eyes as steely as her husband's, was wearing a periwinkle cotton sundress. Warren's slacks were dazzlingly white and his long-sleeve polo shirt was periwinkle. The gossips had a field day when the Webers married. Before her marriage, the bride had managed a biker bar called Wheelz, and the groom was the sole owner of a very profitable farm machinery company. But the cynics were wrong. Warren and Annie were a love match, one of the happiest couples we knew.

They both rose when they saw us. After a round of embraces, we took our places at the lunch table.

"I'm so glad we're able to eat outside," Annie said. "A perfect summer day, dear friends and a menu offering food that hasn't been sitting in a steam table since seven in the morning. What more could we ask for?"

The server arrived with the menus and announced the special for the day: coho salmon flown in from the Queen Charlottes that morning, served with lemon, tarragon and garlic sauce, a wild rice salad and grilled asparagus. He added that if we so chose, we could watch as our salmon was barbecued. We all ordered the salmon and our drinks: the Scarth Club's storied old-fashioneds for Zack, Warren and me, and a lemonade Shirley Temple with extra maraschino cherries for

Annie who had broken up enough fights at Wheelz to see the wisdom of sobriety.

Lunch was a happy affair. The meal was excellent, and listening to the chef explain how he grilled salmon to the perfect degree of doneness was a lesson I needed to learn. Our conversation was light-hearted. Annie was eager to see pictures of Des's nursery, and Zack and I were eager to see photos of the lakefront room the Webers had built at their place across the lake from us at Lawyers Bay.

We decided against dessert, but when Warren said he had something to discuss with us, we asked the server to bring us a pot of Earl Grey. As soon as Warren poured our tea, he waded in. "Hugh Fairbairn asked me to talk to you about MediaNation. His father and I were friends, and since Alistair died, Hugh and I have had some dealings. At any rate, when the son of a friend asks . . ."

"No need to explain, Warren," Zack said. "You've been there often enough for Joanne and me."

"Thank you," Warren said. "Context first. When Media-Nation purchased Nationtv last year, there were no shock waves. Everybody knew the federal government loathed Nationtv, but although they slashed Nationtv's budget every year, the feds still had taxpayers' money going to a public corporation. It was a political albatross with their supporters, so when MediaNation offered to remove the albatross, the federal government jumped."

Zack chuckled. "I imagine a lot of Hugh's shareholders were ready to jump too. More than a few people I know thought he'd bought a pig in a poke. Of course, when *Charlie D in the Morning* started to gain traction, the naysayers took another look at the pig."

"Having *Charlie D in the Morning* produced here was certainly a gamble," I said, "but it turned out to be a gift not just for our family, but also for the city. As our son-in-law reminded me recently, MediaNation has created a number of well-paying jobs with promising futures."

"It has indeed," Warren said. "And the VP who suggested that Charlie D replace Jared Delio in a show produced in Regina was not shy about taking credit for the show's success, because it gave her the opportunity to make the case for some bold new programming."

Warren turned to his wife. "Annie has stock in MediaNation, and she has some interesting news about her fellow and sister stockholders' reception to the fall schedule."

Annie flashed her husband a quick smile, then shifted her position so she could face Zack and me. "As you know the new slate of shows is being presented to the public as programming to 'expand the mind and feed the spirit.' Half of us are enthusiastic about the programming and the branding; the other half are vehemently opposed to what they brand 'back from the future' programming."

"To be fair, what MediaNation is proposing does sound very much like what the old Nationtv did in the '60s and '70s," I said.

Warren's deep bourbon-cured bass was gentle. "Annie was born in 1990." He turned to his wife. "You'll have to take

Joanne's word for it, my love. Nationtv's programming back then was remarkable."

"What MediaNation will be offering is remarkable too," Annie said. "News in depth, presented honestly and without bias. Hugh Fairbairn says that one of the reasons that *Charlie D in the Morning* is having such success with American audiences is that Charlie D gives every guest a fair and honest interview. He does his research and then he allows his guests, no matter what their political stripe or beliefs, to tell their story without 'gotcha' questions or loaded language. And that's why podcasts of Charlie D's interviews average one hundred and eighty thousand downloads per episode.

"There will be a weekly show on politics focused not just on developments in the last twenty-four hours, but also on discussions about what politics has become and what it has the potential to be — no raised voices, just careful listening and thoughtful responses. And there will be a weekly program that explores issues from a spiritual and ethical perspective."

"Like the old Roy Bonisteel program *Man Alive*," I said. "We live in turbulent times. We could use a program like *Man Alive*."

Annie dimpled. "That's exactly what Warren said. And there will be programming where performers and creators with diverse backgrounds talk about the role played in our lives by music, literature, visual arts and dance. The idea is to open the audience's minds to the ways in which a culture's arts reflect the universal experiences we all face: from cradle to grave."

Zack nodded approvingly. "A nod to that old Italian proverb: 'At the end of the game, the king and the pawn go back into the same box.'"

"Always a timely reminder," I said. "And I like the whole concept behind this programming. But Warren, why did Hugh want you to talk to us about this?"

Suddenly the penny dropped. "Because he's aware of the situation between Jill Oziowy and me," I said.

"He didn't hear it from us," Annie said. "His wife, Julie, told him." She shuddered. "I can put up with Hugh, but that wife of his really grinds my gears."

"Mine too," I said.

"I'm not surprised," Annie said. "Anyway, when Hugh broached the subject with Jill Oziowy, Jill was frank about her betrayal of you and your children. She told him that if her presence in Regina is going to pour salt in your wounds, she's willing to be replaced."

"Charlie and I talked about this," I said. "He believes that Jill staying on at MediaNation here is the best option for all of us, and I agree. There'll be some rough patches, but if we acknowledge that the best path for us all is to work through the problems, we'll get there."

"Hugh will be relieved to hear this," Annie said.

"It's the right thing to do," I said. "Not just for MediaNation, but also for Jill. She has always believed the public deserves programming that offers something more substantial than water-skiing squirrels. She fought her battles and lost most of them, but she never gave up."

Warren drew a deep breath and slowly exhaled. "Joanne,

you won't regret your decision." The corners of his mouth twitched. "Now I think Annie and I would like to hear more about that squirrel."

"Years ago, Jill was working for Nationtv here in Regina. She'd produced a show about how smaller cottages where generations of families had spent their summers were being crowded out by massive summer homes owned by people who seldom used them. I saw a rough cut of the program, and it was beautifully done. Jill had created a perfect balance between the human story of the loss people felt when cottages that had been in their family for three generations were threatened, and larger questions about our values as a community and the use of lakefront land.

"It was first-rate programming," I said. "But a wunderkind in Toronto saw a preview of the show and called Jill to tell her to cut her piece by seven minutes because he'd heard of a man with a cottage on Long Lake who had taught a squirrel to water-ski."

Warren raised his eyebrows. "Did Ms. Oziowy cut the piece?"

"No," I said. "She told the wunderkind he could stick the squirrel's water skis up his patoot."

Annie groaned. "I hope this story has a happy ending."

"It does," I said. "The wunderkind backed down. Jill's cottage program was shown without editing and was enthusiastically received."

"What about the squirrel?" Annie asked.

"Still water-skiing," I said. "Every summer our local TV news does a five-minute feature on him."

"A great story from a cherished friend," Warren said. "Annie and I are looking forward to sharing many more hours like these with you two."

Warren had called to let his driver know we were ready to leave, and we'd meet him at the entrance. As we moved from the patio through the main dining room, we were still buoyant. With its gleaming cherrywood walls, large windows framing outside greenery, well-spaced tables and wall sconces shedding gentle light, the dining room was a welcoming place.

Most notably, while the menu had been revamped, the ambience was old school. On special occasions, there was a string quartet, but the unspoken rule was no music. The club's manager took pride in the fact the only sources of sound in the dining room were the pleasingly modulated voices of guests and servers, and the clinking of glasses and cutlery. Her guests liked it that way, and she respected her guests' wishes.

We were halfway across the room when Annie plucked Warren's sleeve. "Mike Braeden and Patti Morgan are at that table by the window. The young woman with them must be Patti's daughter. We should go over and say hello."

"It's always good to see Mike," Zack said.

Mike Braeden was a wide receiver with the Saskatchewan Roughriders in 1989 when they won the Grey Cup. He was agile and fast on the field and smart enough off the field to earn an MBA from Queen's and build a successful business career. After his first wife died, Mike married Patti Morgan, the fortyish former host of a local morning TV show. Rumour had it that the marriage was not a happy one, but that day as Mike, Patti and the young woman Annie presumed was

Patti's daughter sat together at lunch, it seemed that, for the time being at least, all was well.

The illusion was short-lived. When three male servers in the smart, black-on-black Scarth Club uniforms emerged from the kitchen with a birthday cake alight with candles and approached the Braeden table singing "Happy Birthday," the young woman at the table leapt to her feet and in a low angry voice began berating Patti Morgan. "You knew I didn't want this — no candles, no cake. When are you going to get this through your empty head? My brother is dead. There will never again be anything to celebrate. Weren't you listening when I read that poem at the birthday boy's funeral? 'Nothing now can ever come to any good.' That's what the poet says, and that's the reality, Patti. Live with it!"

Tears streaming down her cheeks, she ran towards the club's entrance. Patti Morgan rose and tried to follow her daughter. Disoriented and unsteady, she'd walked only a few feet before she stumbled, fell against a table where a family was having lunch and sank to the floor.

Mike Braeden stood immediately and started towards his wife, but Annie Weber was quick off the mark. She raised her arm and stopped him. "I've got this, Mike," she said. Within seconds, Annie had crouched beside Patti, clasped her firmly around the chest and raised her to her feet.

"I'll call a cab," Mike said.

Annie shook her head. "Our driver's out front. I'll get Patti home and then come back."

Like many whose path has been smoothed by solid decisions, Mike Braeden was a confident person, but at that moment he was clearly at a loss. Annie picked up on his uncertainty. "Trust me, Mike. Patti will be better with me."

Mike lowered his head. "You're probably right," he said. "At least she likes you." His voice was gentle, flat and unhurried — a prairie voice, accustomed to accepting facts, however harsh.

His bleak words were followed by a long silence that seemed to freeze us all in place, as we watched Annie shepherd Patti outside. When, finally, Mike made his way to the table that Patti had fallen against, Warren followed. The club manager was already there. The conversation was brief but cordial, and when Mike and Warren rejoined us, Mike seemed to have regained command of himself and the situation.

"The people at the table were very kind," he said. He squared his shoulders. "Now I should get back to the house and see if there's anything I can do. Joanne and Zack, it's always good to see you. I'm sorry the circumstances weren't more pleasant. Warren, thanks for being here, and please thank Annie. Once again, she's been a friend when we needed one."

After we mumbled our reassurances and goodbyes, a server came over and handed Mike a gift bag filled with unopened presents. Mike thanked the server, turned and walked away: a big man with the shambling gait of an athlete whose body had taken a beating, holding a pink and silver party bag and facing an uncertain future.

When Mike Braeden disappeared through the entrance doors, Warren sighed heavily. "Let's wait for Annie in the portrait gallery where we can have some privacy."

Warren's choice was a wise one. The gallery with its por-traits of all the men who had served as the club's presidents, had a wistful early twentieth-century charm, and the words carved into the mantel above the fireplace always touched me: "They builded better than they knew." It was a comforting room, and as we followed Warren to a conversational grouping of leather chairs in the far corner, I knew we were in need of comfort.

We didn't talk about the painful scene we'd just witnessed. The memory was too fresh. So we settled on a topic that absorbed us all: dogs. Annie and Warren had decided it was time to share their lives with a dog. We were exploring breed possibilities when Annie texted to say that the Braedens' housekeeper was with Patti, that all appeared to be fine and that Annie was on her way back to the club.

After Warren relayed Patti's message. He seemed weary. "Mike doesn't deserve this."

"No," I said. "He doesn't."

Zack cocked his head. "I didn't realize you knew Mike Braeden, Jo."

"I don't know him well," I said, "but at last year's Falconer Shreve holiday party, he did something that has stayed with me. Patti had had too much to drink. Not many people were dancing, but Patti was. She was wearing a very revealing dress, and somehow, one of her breasts slipped out. I was only a few metres away. I went over to see if I could help, but Mike Braden was already handling the situation.

"He'd taken off his dinner jacket and draped it around his wife's shoulders. He told her it was time for them to leave. When she started to put up a fight, I introduced myself to Patti and asked her to come to the lobby with me to see the hotel's Christmas decorations. While Patti and I were look-ing at the Victorian village, Mike Braeden got their coats from the cloak room. He and I helped Patti into her coat; he thanked me and they left."

Zack was pensive. "No matter what the circumstance, Mike is always a gentleman."

"There's not much gallantry in the world," I said, "but what Mike Braeden did that night was gallant."

"It was," Zack said. "Anytime I've seen Mike since that night, he's been alone. He always asks to be remembered to Joanne, and I always ask him to give Patti our best. I didn't realize until today that he had a stepdaughter. I gather that relationship is not bringing anyone much joy."

"It isn't," Warren said. "Mike has been my friend for over forty years. We've celebrated good fortune together, and we've comforted each other in times of loss. Sylvie, his first wife, was the love of Mike's life. They were unable to have a child together, so they committed themselves to ensuring that all our city's children felt they were part of a community that valued them."

"Sylvie was an extraordinary woman," I said. "She and I both volunteered at April's Place, Mieka's café play centre, in the downtown core. Sylvie was never Lady Bountiful, drop-ping in once every six weeks, perfectly coiffed and manicured, so she could post photos of herself serving lunch to inner city kids on her social media accounts. She was always ready to roll up her sleeves, wash pots and pans, scrub the floor in the boot room or clean up and comfort kids who'd peed their pants.

And even at the end, when she must have been suffering terribly, she never lost her sense of humour."

"Sylvie left a very generous bequest to April's Place," Zack said. "Mieka has a framed photo of her in the quiet play area. She's hung it low enough for the kids to see so she can tell them about Sylvie."

"Apparently, Mike Braeden drops by April's Place every so often to see how things are going," I said. "Mieka says Mike's really tickled when one of the kids asks about 'the lady in the picture.'"

"Sylvie's death was devastating for Mike," Warren said. "But he carried on. He stayed in the house on University Park Road that they'd shared for forty-three years. He continued to drive to his office every morning at eight o'clock. He'd always returned home for lunch with Sylvie, but when she was no longer there, he began having lunch at the Scarth Club with whatever old friends were around that day. He continued his philanthropic work, and he continued to attend Knox-Met United because it was a downtown church that welcomed all."

"Did he ever talk about his marriage to Patti Morgan?" Zack asked.

Warren frowned. "Annie's closer to that situation than I am. Let's wait till she joins us to talk about that."

It wasn't long till Annie arrived, breathless but with reassuring news. Annie and Halima, the housekeeper who had been employed and depended upon by the Braedens for over twenty years, were friends. Halima was a nervous driver, and she and Annie grocery-shopped together. Halima was the soul of discretion, but when Patti's angry outbursts began erupting, she had asked for Annie's advice. Annie had suggested that Halima simply trust her instincts. Halima had, and she had become expert at calming Patti when she was having what Halima referred to as "a time of storm." That afternoon, she had drawn a warm, lavender-scented bath for Patti.

"When I left," Annie said, "Patti was in the tub, sipping camomile tea, and Halima was sitting close by in a rocker singing what sounded like a lullaby. Mike was just pulling into the driveway, so everything was under control."

"What about Patti's daughter?" Warren said.

Annie shrugged. "I don't know. I was afraid if I mentioned her, I'd upset Patti, so I didn't say anything. It's a complicated relationship. Mike is strong, but he really took on a lot when he married Patti."

Warren took his wife's hand. "The Shreves asked if Mike had ever talked to me about his second marriage. I told them I thought you might have more insight into that subject than I do."

For a few seconds, Annie was silent, seemingly gathering her thoughts. Finally, she began. "Around Easter, there was an incident at a planning meeting for the Chris Altieri dinner. Patti had volunteered to be on the committee, but she never showed up for any of the meetings. That afternoon she came late, and she'd been drinking. When we'd handled all the items on the agenda, and people started to leave, Patti had difficulty walking. I took her keys, told her I'd drive her home and call our driver to pick me up at their place.

"It was raining, so when we got to the Braedens' house, I made sure Patti was safely inside and then I waited for our driver in the front hall. Patti offered me a drink. I thanked her and said no, but she refused to take no for an answer.

"She came over, grabbed my hands and said we needed to talk because we had so much in common. In her words, we were 'two peas in a pod' — two women in their prime who'd married old men for their money and got what they deserved."

Annie's voice had been strong and controlled when she described the scene between her and Patti Morgan, but as she looked at her husband, she faltered. "I love you so much," she said softly. "You're the best thing that ever happened to me. I hope you know that."

"I do," Warren said. The moment was intimate, and Zack and I both averted our eyes.

Annie turned back to us. "I was furious," she said. "Managing Wheelz taught me how to handle insults from drunks, and I knew Warren would want me to take the high road, so I tried. I told Patti that she was married to a fine man and that her life with Mike Braeden might not be the life she'd dreamed of, but it was the life she had. Then I told her that she, her daughter and Mike should sit down and talk until they'd come to an agreement about how they could make their family work.

"The word 'family' set her off. Patti was in pretty much the same state that afternoon as she was today. She wasn't making much sense, but I could piece together some of what she said. She said she had no family because Nicholas, her 'glowing child' had been 'ripped away' from her. I didn't understand what she meant by 'ripped away,' so I said I was sorry to hear about her son, but that she still had a daughter.

"Big mistake. I'd poured kerosene on a long-smouldering fire. Patti believes that somehow Thalia supplanted her in Nicholas's life; in Patti's words, Thalia 'led Nicholas astray' and caused his death."

"How did Nicholas die?" I said.

Annie's lips were tight. "Suicide. It was four, maybe five years ago. Patti says she'll never recover from his death, and from what we witnessed today, it appears her daughter will never recover either."

Zack's gaze was probing. "What was that travesty of a celebration about anyway?"

"Nicholas and Thalia shared a birthday," Annie said.

"They're twins?"

"No," Annie said. "Nicholas was a year older than Thalia. They just happened to be born on the same day."

I was incredulous. "So, Patti threw a party to celebrate the birth of her dead son and torture her living daughter? She must have known that luncheon would be agonizing for both Thalia and her."

"And for Mike Braeden," Zack said. "Mike was the one left to pick up the pieces today."

"It won't be the first time," Warren said. "Nor will it be the last. But Zack, I'm grateful that you and Joanne were here today. Not just because of our lunch together, but also because the four of us have now seen first-hand what Mike, Patti and Thalia are going through. They're going to need help. Without even asking I know you'll be there, and that's a great comfort for Annie and me."

* * *

By the time the Webers' driver dropped us at home, it was close to three, so our plan to leave for the lake in the early afternoon was scuttled. Our exposure to the pain-filled lives of Mike Braeden, Patti Morgan and her daughter had been sobering. The prospect of loading up the dogs and the car, driving to Lawyers Bay and unloading, getting settled in and starting dinner had lost its appeal, and we decided, instead, on a quiet afternoon on the patio reading and catching up on unfinished business. I'd just finished the last chapter of Jennifer Egan's *Manhattan Beach* and was revelling in the deep satisfaction of a well-written novel, when my phone rang.

I checked the caller ID, then turned my phone towards Zack. When he saw Jill Oziowy's name, he mouthed "good luck" and wheeled into the house.

Jill's voice was tentative. "Is this a bad time?"

"No. I'm doing absolutely nothing."

"Lucky you," she said. "Something of interest just popped up on my newsfeed. Are you familiar with the Lee Gowan Prize?"

"I am. It's a big deal — fifty thousand dollars to an emerging writer under the age of thirty who's written a non-fiction piece on something in politics, popular culture or community activism that the writer feels will be transformative. One of the three judges has to be an academic, and I was a judge one year. It was a challenging job. There had been some winnowing by the time the final crop got to us, but we still had to consider over fifty submissions, and they were all first-rate. It was tough to choose a winner."

"Well, this year's winner is Harper Janvier, Alison's son."

"The Janvier family will be thrilled, and they won't have to worry about charges of favouritism because the submissions are blind — no names, just numbers. Jill, is this news embargoed or can I tell Maisie?"

"It is embargoed, but the Lee Gowan committee will be announcing the winner at a snazzy brunch in Toronto this Friday, so you can certainly tell Maisie. And there's something else: Clay Fairbairn was on the short list for the prize."

"That explains something his grandmother said to me the day after the picnic. Julie brought me a box of pastries from Gâteau des Rois and urged me to get you to destroy the video of Alison's 'little tumble.' She explained that Clay was upset because he'd suffered a disappointment."

Jill's tone was withering. "Poor baby. And Julie believes I should destroy evidence of her little snowflake working off his disappointment by an act that threatened the health of another human being."

"Yes, and when I turned her down, she called me moralistic, said she'd find another way to handle the problem and stomped off."

"She should handle the problem by talking it over with Clay's grandfather," Jill said.

"That's what I think too, because what Clay did was not

child's play. Are you close enough to Hugh Fairbairn to talk to him about this?"

"I am. But Hugh has a blind spot when it comes to his grandson. Our friendship means a great deal to both Hugh and me. I don't want to risk it."

"I understand. I'd find it difficult to be grateful to someone who decided to deliver a few home truths to me about one of my one kids."

"I'm not closing the door, Jo. I just want to make certain that telling Hugh is worth the risk."

* * *

When Zack returned with our drinks, I took mine gratefully. "Just after the nick of time," I said.

"Bad news?"

"No, just a puzzle piece I wish I hadn't been handed."

Zack sipped his martini. "So, what's the puzzle piece?"

When I told him about Harper Janvier winning the award Clay believed should have been his, Zack was sanguine. "So, that was Clay's motivation. I was watching his face when he pushed that tangle of wires into Alison's path. He was smirking."

"The stunt he pulled was payback," I said. "Lori and Mark are such gentle souls. Knowing what their son has become would break their hearts."

Zack looked as troubled as I felt. "I'm certain this was not an isolated incident," he said. "The alacrity with which Clay moved when the opportunity presented itself and his lack of remorse afterwards point to an unsettling possibility."

"That Clay's behaviour is pathological," I said. "I asked Jill if she and Hugh Fairbairn were close enough for her to talk to him about his grandson. She said they were, but that Hugh had a blind spot when it came to Clay, and she didn't want to risk their friendship."

"Not discussing the possibility that Clay may have serious mental health issues raises other risks," Zack said flatly.

"So, what do we do?"

Zack drained his glass. "We don't do anything — we're not in a position to. We don't know Hugh Fairbairn. You and Julie have a history, but she's already made her stand on the issue clear, and she will not welcome an overture from you."

"No, Julie and I slammed that door shut the day after the picnic. That leaves Clay's parents. Mark and Lori would do anything in their power to save their son, but Clay and his grandparents have cut them out of his life."

Zack turned his chair towards the house. "We're pretty well stymied. The next move is up to Clay. All we can do is keep our eyes on him. If he stays on the straight and narrow, all will be well."

"And if he doesn't . . ."

Zack shrugged. "We'll jump off that bridge when we come to it."

CHAPTER EIGHT

At eight o'clock Thursday morning, Zack and I were sitting on our sunny patio, with our dogs flattened beside us, drinking coffee, listening to the murmur of the creek and reading — the poster couple for gracious retirement living.

After listening to me wax ecstatic about Rex Stout's *Nero Wolfe* series, my husband had begun reading the novels at the beginning of summer and quickly became a fan. To see Zack in his wheelchair reading Rex Stout, stopping only to give Pantera the occasional head scratch, was to witness true happiness. My husband's pleasure doubled when, as was often the case, he was able to share a passage with me.

He was reading *The Final Deduction*, and from his chortles and grunts of approval, I knew it wouldn't be long before he peered at me over his reading glasses to signal that he was in a sharing mood.

"You'll like this," he said. Zack has an actor's voice, musical and expressive, and even when he read *The Pigeon Finds a Hot Dog* to our granddaughters, he had his audience sitting on the edge of their chairs. But Zack had a particular affinity for Archie Goodwin, and when he read a paragraph of Archie's narrative, I was immediately transported to the old brownstone on West Thirty-Fifth Street. That morning as Zack cleared his throat and began, I kicked back and enjoyed the performance.

> At the dinner table, in between bits of deviled grilled lamb kidneys with a sauce he and Fritz had invented, he explained why it was that all you needed to know about any human society was what they ate. If you knew what they ate you could deduce everything else — culture, philosophy, morals, politics, everything. I enjoyed it because the kidneys were tender and tasty, and that sauce is one of Fritz's best, but I wondered how you would make out if you tried to deduce everything about Wolfe by knowing what he had eaten in the past ten years. I decided you would deduce that he was dead.

The passage was vintage Archie, and we were savouring the moment when my phone rang.

It was Maisie extending an invitation we couldn't refuse. "Your birthday present for the twins is being delivered this morning," she said. "Pete and I are taking the boys over to Mieka and Charlie D's to keep them out of harm's way till the workers are finished putting up what they are referring to reverently as the Rocky Mountain Play Structure and Clubhouse. Pete and I thought you might want to be here when Charlie and Colin see their gift for the first time."

"Wild horses couldn't keep us away," I said. "What time should we be there?"

"The Rocky Mountain Play Structure and Clubhouse should be ready to rock by eleven. When you get here, just come through the side gate, and we'll meet you in the backyard. Nobody wants to waste a day like today waiting around inside."

The twins and I share a September 29 birthday, so our gift was twenty-six days early, but as Zack pointed out, the early delivery meant Charlie and Colin would have twenty-six extra days of good weather in which to have fun, and Zack would have twenty-six extra days in which to watch them.

When they'd moved back to Regina, Peter and Maisie bought the lovely old Tudor house that once belonged to Zack's late law partner Blake Falconer, his wife Lily and their daughter Gracie. Zack's partners at Falconer Shreve had been like family to him. When I married Zack and he adopted Taylor, she and I joined that family.

It had been a soft landing for Taylor. Like Isobel Wainberg and Gracie Falconer, Taylor was an only child, and Isobel and Gracie were just a year older than she was. All three attended Luther College High School, so the gravitational force of the world of girls had pulled Isobel, Gracie and Taylor inexorably towards one another's lives, and the Falconers, the Wainbergs, and Zack and I had come to know one another's homes well.

Lily Falconer was a perfectionist, and the landscaping of the Falconer home had reflected her passion for order. The lawns were always manicured, the three Monet lily ponds offered guests serenity and the gardens were an ever-changing showcase for the delights of the earth. From the moment the first snowdrop raised its milky white head till frost claimed the last Michaelmas daisy, Lily's gardens were breathtaking.

The backyard that Zack and I entered that day was a far cry from Lily's Arcadia. Peter, Maisie and the twins were a busy family, and they needed a space where they could throw a ball around and have fun.

The lily ponds had been drained and converted into a triple sandbox that was home to an impressive collection of Tonka construction vehicles. Tricycles and scooters had mastered the intricacies of the winding garden paths. And now there was a new wonder.

When it came to finding exactly the right birthday gifts for the people he loved, my husband was indefatigable. It had taken many hours and reserves of patience Zack didn't often draw upon, but finally he found exactly what he had been searching for, and now the holy grail of playsets was firmly in place in the Crawford-Kilbourn backyard.

We'd barely had time to catch our breath before the new owners of the Rocky Mountain Play Structure and Clubhouse, their parents and their cousins arrived. As always, Colin and Charlie burst through the side gate and barrelled into the backyard, but the new addition that confronted them stopped them in their tracks.

Even Madeleine and Lena were taken aback. "That is *awesome*," Lena said, and for once her sister did not chide her for overusing the word. Understandably. Because with its swings, slides, climbing wall, monkey bars, tunnels, ropes and clubhouse, the Rocky Mountain was indeed awesome.

When instead of racing to explore the new wonder, Charlie and Colin seemed rooted on the spot, Pete went to them. "Don't you guys want to check out your birthday present?"

Colin looked wary. "It's too big."

"It's about the same size as the play structure in the park, and you two are on that all the time," Pete said

"It's too big for a present," Charlie added helpfully.

"It's from Mimi and your granddad," Pete said. "There are two of them and two of you, so it's really like four presents rolled into one."

The twins' ability to communicate wordlessly always dazzled me. Without exchanging so much as a wink or a nudge, the decision was made and the boys streaked towards their four-in-one birthday present. Within seconds Colin and Charlie were halfway up the climbing ropes. The new owners of the Rocky Mountain Play Structure and Clubhouse had taken possession.

Maisie draped an arm around her husband's shoulder. "Nice math there, Dad."

Pete's grin was sheepish. "It worked," he said. "Now who's for pizza?"

We all placed our orders, and Pete called the Copper Kettle. When he announced the pizza would be delivered in thirty minutes, Maisie turned to Madeleine and Lena. "Plenty of time for you two to give each other that back-to-school pedicure we talked about. You know where everything is. Go for it."

"Maddy and I are going to paint our toenails in the school colours: navy blue and yellow," Lena said. "We already asked Mum. She said it's fine, but toenails only."

With nothing more weighty on our minds than waiting for the pizza man, Maisie, Peter, Zack and I settled back to watch the boys do what kids do best: stretch their muscles and their imaginations. Our conversation was easy and aimless until Maisie introduced a topic that caught Zack's attention and mine.

Our daughter-in-law had been sitting on the edge of a lounge chair, both eyes on her sons, gauging their ability to handle the new challenge. Like their mother, Colin and Charlie were natural athletes. When Maisie had assured herself that the boys were in command of the situation, she swivelled to face us. "That was an inspired gift. Well done, grandparents." She paused. "Change of topic. Did you two happen to catch *Quinlan Live* this morning?"

"No," I said. "Zack was reading *The Final Deduction* to me."

Maisie's laugh was wry. "Sounds like more fun than *Quinlan Live* was today. Alison was Jack Quinlan's guest. Call-in shows are always a landmine, but everything was going well until a caller asked Alison why she chose not to have an abortion when she became pregnant at sixteen."

Zack leaned forward. "Is the fact that Alison had a child when she was sixteen common knowledge?"

"Yes and no," Maisie said. "Alison has always been public about the fact that she has a son. Her parents raised him in La Ronge until Alison graduated from law school, but Harper has always known Alison is his mother." Maisie tented her fingers and flexed them for a few seconds. "What is not common knowledge is the fact that Harper was conceived after his mother was raped."

Zack scowled. "Her assailant was never charged?"

"Alison was ashamed, and she didn't tell anyone about the assault," Maisie said. "By the time she discovered she was pregnant, the man who raped her had left La Ronge. He was her grade eleven history teacher. It was the end of the school year, and he packed up his things, drove off and was never heard from again.

"Ozzie and Ruth Janvier never pressed Alison about the circumstances surrounding her pregnancy. They simply said they would support whatever decision she made about her future."

"That's a big decision for a sixteen-year-old," I said.

Pete's voice was gentle. "Not the approach you would have taken if it had been Mieka?"

"I honestly don't know," I said. "By the time Mieka was sixteen, life had dealt her some punishing blows. Your father's death and then — you remember how it was, Peter — in the months after Ian's death I wasn't the person I'd been before. By the time, Mieka was sixteen, she'd taken on a heavy load of responsibilities, and she'd handled them well. I knew how strong she was, and I trusted her judgment. That said, I'm glad I never had to make the decision that Alison's parents faced, but I hope I would have done what they did."

"Ozzie and Ruth are remarkable people," Maisie said. "They're both community organizers. When we were in law school, Alison went back to La Ronge every summer; she would work with them and be with Harper. She really loves that boy."

"Understandably," I said. "And yesterday Jill Oziowy told me Alison now has another reason to be proud of Harper. The announcement hasn't been made yet, but Harper Janvier is the winner of this year's Lee Gowan Emerging Writer Award."

Maisie's eyes widened. "Wow. That is major. Ali must be having a tough time keeping that under her toque."

"I'm sure she is," Zack said. "But there's a dark side to Harper's win. Clay Fairbairn was on the Lee Gowan short list, and he did not take his loss well."

Pete's expression changed rapidly from confusion to disgust. "That's unbelievable. Clay loses out on a prize, so he attacks the mother of the guy who won."

"That does strain credulity," Zack said. "But it seems to be the case. Clay's grandmother paid a call on your mother the day after the picnic. She said Clay had suffered a disappointment and 'acted out.' We didn't learn what the disappointment was until yesterday."

Maisie turned to Pete. "Do you think it's possible Clay Fairbairn is connected somehow with the weird questions that have been cropping up in Alison's Q&As?"

"Given what we've just heard about how Clay's mind works, I guess it's conceivable," Pete said. He turned to Zack and me. "In the past week, during the Q&As after Alison's speeches, someone has asked a series of identical questions. They all centre on Alison's decision not to terminate her pregnancy when she was sixteen. The questions posed by that caller to *Quinlan Live* this morning followed the pattern."

I felt a lash of unease. "If the questions are always the same, they must be coming from a single source. Jill said the official announcement about the Lee Gowan Award will be made at a gala brunch tomorrow in Toronto. Seeing Harper publicly honoured will be another blow for Clay. He might be making a pre-emptive strike by attempting to get under Alison's skin."

Maisie ran her fingers through her thick springy curls. "Alison's strong, but she's not bulletproof, and she is vulnerable through Harper. Alison's told him that his father never knew about her pregnancy, and that when he moved away at the end of the school year, she thought making a clean break with him was best for everyone."

"The truth, but not the whole truth," Zack said. "I imagine Harper has always just assumed that his father was a student. But with their opening salvo, the questioners let Ali know they have intimate knowledge of her history. Maisie, how many times has this happened?"

"Five counting this morning," Maisie said. "The first time was at an open forum at the university and the questions have been posed at every event since."

Zack narrowed his eyes. "Do the questioners come from a specific demographic?"

"Alison says it's hard to tell. She thinks they're all male, but she's not even sure of that. They all wore sunglasses, jeans and ball caps, visors forward so their faces were partially obscured."

"Jeans, sunglasses and ball caps are pretty much the go-to outfit for eighty percent of our city's population," I said. "Was there anything distinguishing about their voices?"

"Yes," Maisie said. "And here's the zinger. They all spoke slowly and precisely as if they were working from a script and had been coached about how to say their lines."

"So, a single source is providing them with questions that put Ali's past right out there," I said.

Zack scowled. "And throwing her off her game by forcing her to wonder how much else they know. When's Alison's next speech?"

"Tonight," Maisie said. "It's at a symposium on women's rights. I'm planning to go, and I'll have my phone at the ready."

"Good," Zack said. "When the abortion question comes up, have Alison ask the questioner to meet her privately after the session to discuss the issue further."

"Do you think the questioner will show up later?" I said.

"Not a chance," Zack said. "My guess is that as soon as Alison challenges the questioner to meet her privately, they will beat a hasty retreat."

Maisie smiled. "And I will follow whoever it is out of the venue and ask them to choose a time and place where Alison can discuss the matter one-on-one. And I'll take their picture."

"No flies on you," Zack said. "Being followed will spook them, and having their picture taken will knock them off base. While they're squirming, move in close and see what you can get out of them."

Maisie's gold-flecked eyes were sparkling. "I am so looking forward to this."

Zack grinned. "Yeah, it's always fun when you get a chance to play by the other guy's rules."

* * *

As soon as we got back from Pete and Maisie's, I called Jill. "There's something weird going on in Alison's campaign. Have you got time to talk?"

Jill's voice was strained. "Not really. Can you run the highlights by me and fill me in later?"

"Of course."

I gave Jill the condensed version of what we'd learned about the oddly staged questioning at Ali's recent events and about Maisie's plan of attack for Ali's next Q&A. When Jill didn't respond, and the silence between us became awkward, I said, "So what do you think?"

Jill was clearly preoccupied. "I'm not sure. Jo, can we discuss this later? There's something I need to talk to you about, but I don't want to do it here at the office. I'm just on my way out to a meeting. It shouldn't last more than an hour. Would it be all right if I dropped by your house later?"

* * *

It was close to one thirty when Jill arrived. Zack and I had eaten our share of pizza at Pete and Maisie's, so neither of us was hungry, but I wanted Jill to feel welcome. So I'd taken a tray with Boursin au poivre, a bowl of B.C. cherries and a baguette to the back patio, and Zack had opened a bottle of Riesling. When Jill arrived, I led her to the patio where Zack was already pouring the wine.

No one suggested a toast, so Jill set her laptop on the table, opened it, took a large sip of her drink, thanked us for our hospitality and plunged in. "Two hours ago, I received a text with a link to a video that the writer of the text noted was 'of interest.' I went to the link and watched a video of Vale Frazier having intercourse with Etienne Simard." Jill's tawny eyes met mine. "I know that your daughter and Vale Frazier are in a relationship, and I thought if Taylor wasn't already aware of the video, she should know that it's online. Do you want me to bring up the link?"

Zack's jaw tightened, and he turned to me. "Jo?"

"You always say it's better to know than not know. We should see what our daughter's going to see. Jill, if you wouldn't mind . . ."

Jill nodded, and the screen filled with images of the young woman we had come to think of as a daughter having sex with the actor I'd been introduced to at the wrap party for *Sisters and Strangers* the previous November. I had been charmed by Etienne Simard, as three generations of Quebec women had been charmed. He was not much taller than me — probably around five nine, actor fit, very slim, with carefully tousled silver hair, knowing grey eyes and uncommonly expressive features. Identifying the source of his compelling charm was difficult, but the charisma was definitely there.

By a circumstance none of us could have foreseen, I had become involved in writing the script for *Sisters and Strangers*. Unravelling the intertwined fates of the Ellard and Love families had been an essential but painful exercise. Digging up facts that had been hidden in obscurity for years had revealed ugly truths about the forces that shaped me. After one particularly gruelling writing session, I told Zack I felt flayed, as if I was watching my own autopsy. The day the script was locked, I walked away from the production studios, grateful for what I had learned and relieved that my excavation of the past was over.

Except for Vale and Rosamond Burke, the renowned British actor whom I had come to like and respect when she was filming in Regina a year earlier, I knew the principals in the cast of *Sisters and Strangers* only in passing. The producer had sent me headshots and résumés of the actors being cast, but still raw from my experience co-writing the script, I simply glanced at them and slid them back in the envelopes in which they'd arrived. I'd questioned none of the casting choices except that of Etienne Simard for the role of Izaak Levin. Simard's easy charm and whimsically flirtatious smile seemed wrong for the man I'd known as a young girl, and connected with again when Sally and I reunited in the months before her death and his.

By the age of thirty, Izaak Levin had established himself as one of the most influential visual art critics of the mid-twentieth century. Much sought after as a speaker and lecturer, he too seemed destined for a charmed future, but when Nina Love handed over her fifteen-year-old daughter to him, Izaak Levin's fate was tragically altered. Sally became his reason for being and, until the day he died, his life was driven by the dark disruptive power of his love for her.

Etienne Simard, a man who, seemingly without effort, caused hearts to flutter and sailed through life with the wind at his back seemed a poor choice for the role of Izaak, but I misjudged Simard's gifts as an actor.

I had always believed that the relationship between Izaak and Sally was symbiotic, but until I saw the scenes between Etienne and Vale, I had never understood that the unbreakable bond between Sally and Isaak was fuelled by the simplest of human emotions: need and love. Over the years the needs changed as did their casual sexual liaisons, but Izaak and Sally's love remained constant and undiminished.

The soul-baring physical and emotional intimacy in the scenes between Vale and Etienne was powerful, and as we watched, Zack covered my hand with his. His face was impassive, but the vein in his neck was pulsing rhythmically. As soon as the video ended, Zack picked up his phone. "I'm calling Taylor," he said. Jill turned off her laptop, and we waited. "Straight to voicemail," Zack said finally.

"This isn't what we thought it was at first," I said. "It's an outtake of a scene the director, Ainsley Blair, discarded because she felt it made the character Vale is playing seem unsympathetic. The other writer and I disagreed with Ainsley's decision."

Jill was shocked. "Why would you disagree? I never knew Sally Love, but she was fifteen years old. Her relationship with Levin was not only illegal; it was immoral."

"Towards the end of her life, Sally talked a great deal about her relationship with Izaak," I said. "Sally was always clear on one point: she initiated the sexual relationship with him. She was not the victim; she was the instigator. I supported including the scene we just watched because it shows how desperately Sally needed Izaak. He was the only protection she had against Nina, and Sally used the most powerful weapon she had to make Izaak let her stay."

Jill slumped. "Her sexuality. What a world we live in. Ainsley Blair was wrong. That scene was an essential part of Sally's story."

"Fair enough," Zack said. "But how the hell did it end up online?"

"I don't know," Jill said. "*Sisters and Strangers* is the flagship for MediaNation's new drama programming. That should have been kept under lock and key, but we live in the digital age. Piracy's easy."

Zack rubbed the bridge of his nose, always a sign that he was perplexed. "So we're back at the old legal question: cui bono? Who profits?"

"That video's already gone viral. Some enterprising publicist at MediaNation may have decided it was a way to get the drums beating before *Sisters and Strangers* premieres."

Jill's headshake was vehement. "Hugh Fairbairn would never consent to a stunt like that."

"Would he have seen the outtake?" Zack said.

Jill nodded. "From what I heard, Hugh was very hands-on about *Sisters and Strangers*. If there was a dispute between the director and the writers about the impact of the scene between Sally and Izaak, I'm certain Hugh would have watched both versions and weighed in."

"So, we're back to square one," Zack said.

At that point, my phone rang. I glanced at caller ID. "It's Taylor."

Jill smeared Boursin on a piece of baguette, popped three cherries on top and finished her wine. "Lunch," she said. "I can let myself out. Jo, when the dust clears we can talk about what's going on with Ali's campaign. Meanwhile, call if there's anything I can help with."

Zack touched her arm. "Thanks for coming over."

I answered my phone, and when I greeted our daughter, I amazed myself by sounding close to normal.

"Just checking in," Taylor said.

"Your dad's here," I said. "Okay if I put you on speaker-phone?"

Taylor laughed. "That goes without saying. How are you doing, Dad?"

"Couldn't be better now that I'm talking to you."

"Same here," Taylor said. "Any news about Mieka and the baby?"

"Still waiting," I said.

"I'm so excited about that little guy," Taylor said. "So what's going on with you two?"

Zack looked at me questioningly, and I nodded. "Taylor, we can talk about that later, but there's something else we need to discuss," Zack said. "It concerns Vale."

Taylor didn't respond. As the silence between our daughter and us lengthened, the anxiety in Zack's eyes mirrored my own. When she finally spoke, Taylor's voice was small and strained. "If it's about the video of Vale with Etienne Simard, I've already seen it."

"You do realize it's an outtake of a scene Ainsley Blair decided to cut."

"Yes," Taylor said. "Vale and I talked about whether or not Ainsley should use that scene. Sally was my birth mother, so at least I was useful to Vale for information like that."

Taylor's comment was harsh, and I didn't follow up on it. I tried to move along. "Since we've established that the video is just an outtake, I guess we should focus on the real question. Taylor, do you have any idea about who might have posted it?"

"Someone who wants to hurt me," Taylor said.

My stomach clenched. "Taylor, has the video going viral affected your relationship with Vale?"

Our daughter's laugh was uncharacteristically bitter. "Oh, it affected it," she said. "Big time. She and I are finished. You were right about the video being an outtake, but Vale and Etienne Simard did have an affair. It started when *Sisters and Strangers* was shooting in Regina." Taylor's voice was shaking. "Vale and I were starting our life together in our new home. I thought we were two people who loved each other enough to make a commitment."

A blow to Taylor was a blow to Zack, and his face crumpled. "Taylor, why don't you come home for a few days?" he said. "Give yourself some time to breathe and think things through."

"I'm way ahead of you, Dad," she said. "I was calling to tell you that I flew in yesterday, Gracie Falconer picked me up at the airport and we came straight to Lawyers Bay. I wanted to let you know that I'm all right."

"Are you?" Zack said.

"Not yet," Taylor said. "But I will be. Last night, I curled up in my old bed with my cats, and we all had a good night's sleep."

"You brought the cats back with you?" I said.

"Yes, I wanted them with me. Jo, I'm not here to process what happened, I know what happened, and Vale and I are no longer a couple. Saying that is hard, but it's the truth." She paused, and when she continued, she tried for a light note. "As Dad always says, the only thing worse than knowing is not knowing."

Zack and I both flinched. I swallowed hard. "He's right about that," I said. "Taylor, you know that if your father and I could carry this pain for you, we would."

"I know that, and I'm grateful. And when I go into Eeyore mode as Gracie calls it, she reminds me of how much I have to be grateful for, and it's a lot."

"You do have a lot to be grateful for. We all do. I'm so glad Gracie's there with you. Taylor, your dad and I were planning to drive to Lawyers Bay tomorrow morning, but if you need us now, we can be there in an hour."

"No. I want you to come, just not yet. Everything happened so quickly. I'm not second-guessing my decision. I just need time to regroup. Could you come tomorrow after lunch?"

"Tomorrow after lunch will be fine," Zack said. "Taylor, we love you so much."

"I love you too, but I'm going to hang up now because if I start blubbering, you'll be so worried about me, you won't sleep, and I'll be so worried about you being worried, I won't sleep either. See you tomorrow, and could you please stop by Pawsitively Purrfect on your way? I forgot to bring cat food. My guys like the canned tuna we have, but it's not all that great for them."

"Your mum and I are on it, Taylor. Tell Bruce, Benny and Bob Marley that all will be well."

"They're cats, Dad, and cats are born knowing all will be well." Taylor laughed softly. "I'm starting to believe they're right. This morning, after breakfast, Gracie and I walked around the shoreline, checking the inuksuit that she and Isobel and I built a hundred years ago. Every stone was still in place, exactly where we put it. I'm exactly where I should be too."

When Taylor broke the connection, Zack moved his chair close to me. "How are you doing?"

"I feel as if I've been body-slammed."

"So do I, and Jo, it's not just that our daughter's had her heart broken. That's bad enough, but what happened with that footage is another loose end. From what Jill said, the production company would have kept that video secure."

"She also pointed out that we live in a technological age, and that piracy is not unheard of."

"But who's the pirate? Corporate espionage is a possibility, but not a likely one. A rival network or streaming service would have had nothing to gain by posting that video. The public's appetite for prurience is insatiable, and that outtake will draw an audience to *Sisters and Strangers*. I think the targeting is personal. When we asked Taylor who she thought posted the video, she said 'someone who wanted to hurt me.'"

"Zack, I know we're biased because we're Taylor's parents, but she's never been a person who made enemies. High school is a landmine for many girls — cliques, rivalries, rumours, jealousies — but Taylor never elicited animosity. I know lawyers believe the question *cui bono* is key in determining who might have committed a crime, but I can't think of anyone who would have had something to gain from hurting our daughter."

"Okay, let's cast the net wider. Etienne Simard and Vale are the actors in the video. But when we saw the rough cuts for *Sisters and Strangers*, you said that for both Simard and Vale, those would be breakout roles. It would have been pointless for either of them to post the video, and I can't see what someone who had it in for either of them would gain."

"Hurting Taylor," I said. "So, we're back to that again."

Zack rubbed his temples. "So, another loose end, and 'it's the loose ends of our lives that hang us.' Jo, there are already too many loose ends here: Rosemary Morrissey's disintegration and dismissal. Ellen Exton's firing and inexplicable disappearance. The crap that's going on at Ali's appearances.

And that enigmatic note on Ellen's refrigerator door saying, 'It's not enough.'"

"All the incidents are connected somehow to MediaNation," I said. "Do you think it's possible Ellen Exton discovered who was doing the targeting?"

"I think it's more than possible," Zack said. "I also think the odds of Ellen turning up safe and sound are negligible. Debbie Haczkewicz isn't talking, but I'm certain that's what she believes too. The last time I talked to her, she said Major Crimes has theories but no hard evidence."

"And that's exactly what we have: a theory without proof." I took his hand. "So, where do we go from here?"

"Back to the patio," Zack said. "You hate wasting food, and I hate wasting booze, so let's do the right thing and polish off the Boursin, those succulent B.C. cherries and the overpriced Riesling."

CHAPTER NINE

The next morning when the dogs and I came home from our run, Zack was sitting at the kitchen table checking his messages. I was surprised to see him. Since we were driving to Lawyers Bay after lunch, he was only working a half day, but determined to make the most of his time, he'd scheduled a breakfast meeting with a client and a partners' meeting that would last till noon.

When he saw Pantera, Esme and me, he smiled. "Just in the nick of time," he said. "I was afraid I was going to have to leave you a message. Maisie called. There's a new development."

"Let me get these guys off their leashes and fill me in," I said.

As soon as he was leash-less, Pantera lumbered over to Zack and rubbed himself against Zack's leg. It was molting season, and from the knee down, Zack's pant leg was instantly covered with bullmastiff hair. Zack rubbed Pantera's head and said, "Good boy."

When I pulled a chair up to the table, Zack began. "Last night Ali took part in that symposium on women's rights. When the abortion question was raised, Ali gave her standard answer: that she supported a woman's right to choose, and that whatever choice the woman made should be supported by the law and respected by the community. She then suggested that after the symposium, she and the questioner meet privately to discuss the matter further."

"All according to plan," I said.

"Yep. And also according to *our* plan, the questioner hightailed it, but Maisie was right on his heels." Zack shook his head admiringly. "Our daughter-in-law is definitely a force to be reckoned with. Anyway, before the guy escaped, Maisie had grabbed his ball cap and his sunglasses and taken three close-ups of his face with her phone."

"I don't suppose the man in Maisie's photos was our pal, Clay Fairbairn?"

"No, but he did call Maisie a cunt, so he and Clay must have attended the same finishing school," Zack said. He held his arms out for a hug. "Time for me to hit the road, but maybe give Jill a call about this. She's been part of this since she forced Clay to delete the photos he took of Ali after he engineered her fall at the Real Prairie Picnic. We should keep her in the loop."

When I called, Jill was at her desk at MediaNation. She picked up on the first ring, but asked me to wait to talk until she closed her office door, so we could talk privately and without interruption.

I hesitated before telling Jill that Harper Janvier had been conceived when Ali was raped, but I knew that fact was part of the story, and I was certain Jill would keep the information confidential. I finished by telling Jill that, like Clay Fairbairn, the mystery questioner had called the woman who confronted him a cunt, and that Zack said the men's shared fondness for the word suggested that Clay and the questioner had attended the same finishing school. We both laughed, but when Jill responded to my description of the encounter, her voice was tense.

"Remember those stories Mieka loved so much about the twelve little girls who lived in the old house in Paris that was covered in vines?"

"Ludwig Bemelmans's *Madeline* books — I think I can still recite every word of those books by heart."

"So can I," Jill said. "The scene that's been gnawing at me lately comes in the middle of the night when Miss Clavel turns on the light and says, 'Something is not right.' Jo, I keep coming back to Clay Fairbairn. We've drawn a straight line between Harper Janvier winning the prize Clay thought should be his and his attempt to hurt Harper's mother. Do you believe that was an isolated incident?"

"I don't," I said. "I'm sure there's more. Have you heard of any problems Clay's had at work?"

"No, but that doesn't mean anything. In theory, summer interns shadow people who are doing the work they hope to do someday. There is some of that, but primarily interns do whatever needs to be done to lighten the load of the full-time employees. Their duties are not onerous. They spend most of their time on research for the people they're shadowing — nothing heavy, just monitoring what's coming down the pike in entertainment and politics, gathering background material on guests and checking social media to see what's trending. It's a nice summer gig. These interns are twenty years old, and they're being paid to do what they'd be doing anyway."

"But Clay fits in," I said. "There's no evidence of friction with his colleagues?"

"I'm not in a position to judge," Jill said. "I arrived here when the interns' tenures were just about over, and not surprisingly, Clay's been avoiding me since our confrontation at the picnic. But I was curious about Clay's ability to play well with others, so I talked to Kam Chau. He was here when they arrived in May. Kam said this year's crop of interns are particularly tight. Apparently, they all attended the same high school. Actually I think it's the school Taylor went to."

"Luther College High School," I said.

"Right. Jo, I didn't want to pry, but now that the subject's come up. How's Taylor doing?"

"She's struggling. Taylor really believed she had found Ms. Right — that she and Vale belonged together, so this has been hard on her."

"She's a fine young woman, and she didn't deserve to have her private life exposed so brutally."

"Agreed," I said. "And Rosemary Morrissey didn't deserve to have a hellish ending to a distinguished career, and Ellen Exton didn't deserve to lose her job and perhaps her life for a lapse of judgment. Jill, after we talked to Taylor, Zack and I tried to come up with a factor that connects the troubling occurrences at MediaNation this summer . . . and we came up empty."

"Keep trying, Jill said. "Because my spidey senses tell me there's something."

After the call ended, my body felt heavy, weighed down by the burden of unanswered questions, but as I turned on the shower and stepped in, I knew I had to shelve that particular burden. In a few hours Zack and I would be with our daughter, and she deserved our full attention. Twenty minutes later, dressed and ready for what came next, I turned my attention to the happy chore of grocery shopping for a holiday weekend that suddenly included Taylor and Gracie.

* * *

After I'd stocked up on food and liquor, I headed for my last stop, Pawsitively Purrfect where, thanks to Taylor's patronage, I was welcomed royally. From the time she was six and decided it was her civic duty to feed the feral cats in the warehouse district during the winter, up to and including her years as a cat owner, Taylor had been a fixture at Pawsitively Purrfect, and the owners were so delighted to hear that she was back in Regina that they gave me brightly wrapped gift bags of treats for all three of Taylor's cats.

Cat food was not my forte, but I was doing my best, and I was pondering the list of ingredients in Kitty Kaviar when a compact, lightly muscled man with a smoothly planed face appeared at my side and tapped my arm. "You're Joanne Shreve," he said.

"I am, and you're . . . ?"

"Kam Chau," he said. "Charlie D's producer. I saw you squinting at the list of ingredients on that can as if it were written in Cyrillic. Charlie tells me you're a dog person, and I wondered if I could help."

I handed him the can. "Is this any good?"

Without comment, Kam placed the Kitty Kaviar back on the shelf. "If you tell me something about the cat you're buying this for, I'll have an idea about what might work."

"There are three cats, and they belong to our daughter. They all just seemed to come our way, so I don't know much about their history. We're not sure of their ages, but they're all fully grown, and Taylor makes certain they're healthy and pampered."

"Another reason for me to hold your daughter in high regard," Kam said. "Charlie has shown me photos of some of Taylor's art. It's impressive, but I thought she was in Vancouver."

"She was, but she's spending some time at our cottage on Lawyers Bay. It was a last-minute visit, so she asked us if we could pick up some provisions from Pawsitively Purrfect."

"Got it," Kam said. He took my shopping basket, started up the aisle and I followed along behind him. He was a decisive shopper with an easy manner, and it was fun to watch him make his selections.

"This should take care of Taylor's cats for a while," Kam said, "but I have a suggestion. I make the food for my cats. It's easy, it's cheap, and it's better for them. I can recommend a book that Taylor will find helpful if you think she'll be interested."

"She'll be interested," I said. "Thank you."

"My pleasure," he said.

Kam helped me carry my purchase to the car, but when he started to say goodbye, I stopped him. "There's a coffee place two doors down from here. If you have time, I'd like to ask you about the summer interns. My treat, and the sky's the limit."

Kam smiled. "Count me in," he said. "But Dutch treat because half an hour ago something came across my desk that I could use a second opinion on."

"Dutch it is," I said. There was no lineup at Brewed Awakening. Kam and I placed our orders, and when they were ready, we each paid for our choice, split the tip and headed for a booth at the back.

After we'd settled in, Kam said. "Okay if I start?" When I nodded, he began. "All our summer interns are required to write an exit letter."

"Summarizing the pros and cons of their work experience?"

"Right. In other years, we've received four individual letters, detailing four different working experiences. This summer's interns submitted four copies of a single letter signed by them all. When I read what they'd written, I felt sick. That letter is a poisoned arrow."

"Aimed at whom?"

"Rosemary Morrissey," Kam said. He slid his tablet across the table at me. "Read it, and tell me what you think."

We are all honour students entering our second year of B.A. studies at the University of Regina School of Journalism. Aware of the ambitious slate of programming MediaNation was undertaking, we anticipated that our internships would give us the chance to grow both professionally and personally.

We were excited to be part of the MediaNation team, but as it turned out, there was no place for us on that team.

We have chosen to write our exit letter collectively rather than individually because if MediaNation is to learn from our experience, it must understand that the problems we dealt with are systemic and that solving them will require an examination of the protocols that govern the rights and responsibilities of the summer interns it employs.

On May 4, our first day at MediaNation, the senior executive tasked with mentoring the interns publicly cautioned one of us against reading the philosophy book she was carrying. In the senior executive's words, "the ideas expressed in the book required a discernment beyond [the intern's] level of understanding."

When the intern approached a permanent staff member and explained that the senior executive had publicly scorned the intern's level of intelligence without ever having exchanged a word with her, the permanent staff member urged her to ignore the slight. He said that the senior executive was under a great deal of stress, and it would be in everyone's best interests if the intern kept silent about the incident. We interpreted his words as a clear warning to us to remain silent about questions or concerns. We were powerless.

In the period between May 19, the day we returned to work after the May long weekend and the Canada Day weekend, the atmosphere in our workplace grew steadily worse.

The senior executive charged with launching the new season and with "mentoring" us was clearly unstable. Frequently, she was unable to remember either the decisions she'd made or the names of the staff members she'd assigned to carry out those decisions. Her allies attempted to cover for her, and when her errors and omissions became too numerous to paper over, they heaped the blame on the interns.

Later the senior executive suffered a major mental breakdown and left her position at MediaNation, but the damage had been done, and the problems remained.

Had we been made aware of the executive's disintegrating mental faculties, we might have worked with permanent staff to deal with their colleague's emotional problems. We were never told anything. We were shut out, and we struggled.

Had our roles and responsibilities as interns been articulated, we could have worked to fulfill them, but we were never given even a minimal job description. We had hoped that our work at MediaNation would give us the opportunity to form relationships with colleagues that would deepen our understanding of the calling we shared. However, because of the corporation's internal tensions we were uneasy about reaching out to staff.

To say that we are disappointed with our experience this summer would be an understatement. We were given a unique opportunity, and we failed to make the most of it. That said, we do not believe the fault was wholly or even largely our own.

We recommend that, in future, protocols are in place for interns who have concerns and that members of permanent staff with whom they can speak frankly be identified.

We send this letter without prejudice and with the hope that no other group of interns will feel the disappointment and disillusionment we feel as our tenure as summer interns ends.

I slid Cam's tablet back to him. "That is one deadly letter," I said. "It puts the interns squarely on the side of the angels, shames MediaNation and hammers the final nail into Rosemary Morrissey's coffin. How widely was it distributed?"

"To every member of our unit."

"The unit that Rosemary supervised. Has there been any response from HR in Toronto yet?"

"Nothing so far," Kam said. "But there'll be something. It's established corporate policy to answer a letter of complaint from employees. The company has to show they respect the people who work for them enough to find out exactly what happened."

"That's a sound policy," I said.

"It is," Kam agreed. "Except in this case, there's nothing to find out. The people involved, and that includes me, know exactly what happened."

"Can you talk about it?"

"With you, yes. But the facts do not reflect well on Rosemary, so I hope HR in Toronto doesn't dig too deeply. I've tried to pinpoint exactly when Rosemary's behaviour became erratic." For at least a minute, Kam was silent, watching the pattern the tip of his spoon made as he drew it through the hearts the barista had created on the surface of his latte. Finally, he raised his eyes and met my gaze. "The confrontation between Rosemary and the intern with the book occurred the day after the interns arrived. The intern was Thalia Monk."

The image of the shattered girl fleeing her birthday celebration at the Scarth Club flashed through my mind. "Thalia Monk is Patti Morgan's daughter?"

"Yes, and I was the staff member Thalia came to when she felt slighted by Rosemary's dismissal. I produced the final year of Patti's show, so Thalia knew I was aware of how close she and her late brother were, and she thought I would be on her side. I was, and I still am. But I'm also still baffled by the fact that Rosemary accosted Thalia about the book. Rosemary knew that *Thus Spake Zarathustra* had a special significance for Thalia. Patti told her that Nicholas had introduced his sister to Nietzsche's writings, and they had discussed his work together."

"I thought Nicholas was seventeen when he committed suicide?"

"He was, and Thalia was sixteen, but they were both brilliant and they were attracted to Nietzsche's concept of the Übermensch."

"The idea of a superior being who believes there are no moral truths, so the Übermensch is free to create their own morality. That is certainly part of what Nietzsche wrote, but . . ."

"A little knowledge is a dangerous thing," Kam said. "My father was a scholar. He quoted those words many times to the arrogant kid I was when I was growing up. I haven't studied *Thus Spake Zarathustra*, but I am aware of its complexity and I understand why Rosemary might be concerned about Thalia embracing it."

Kam's smile was guilty. "I had to spend an afternoon with Herr Doktor Google before I understood the Übermensch concept. There were three people in the room when the incident occurred, and I talked to each of them separately.

All three not only corroborated Thalia's story, but also they expressed surprise that Rosemary would have directed such a gratuitous insult at Patti's daughter because Patti and Rosemary had always been close."

"That surprises me," I said. "I don't know either of them well, but Patti and Rosemary strike me as being very different women."

"They are, but Rosemary took Patti under her wing when she was signed to host *Sunny Side Up*, and Patti had always looked up to her. Whatever Rosemary's motivation, the after-effects of the book incident were devastating. When I told Thalia it would be best for everyone if she simply let the matter drop, I was thinking of her as well as of Rosemary. Nicholas's death is still a raw wound for Thalia. I thought revisiting the memories of what the book had meant to them both would be painful for her, but as the exit letter makes clear, the interns interpreted my advice as a warning. The next morning all four interns were carrying a copy of *Thus Spake Zarathustra*."

"In solidarity with Thalia," I said.

"That's not how Rosemary saw it. She saw it as a declaration of war, and from that day on, the situation grew steadily worse. Everyone, including me, did their best to give the interns the guidance they needed, but Rosemary regarded any attempt to reach out to the interns as siding with the enemy."

I leaned forward. "Charlie said morale at MediaNation had reached rock bottom, but now that the interns are going back at school, the tensions should lessen."

Kam drained his cup. "No, the internships last two semesters. The students go back to the J school after Christmas. Our interns are all still in Saskatchewan. Two are in Saskatoon, and Thalia and Clay Fairbairn are still at MediaNation Regina."

"Nepotism?"

"I'm sure nepotism was part of it, but despite all the hand-wringing in the exit letter, both Thalia and Clay did outstanding work while they were here. Thalia's working on a promising feature for *Charlie D in the Morning*, and Clay is doing the editing. She and Clay could both end up being real assets to the company."

"Time will tell," I said. "Kam, I'm glad we ran into each other. I was curious about the relationship among the interns, and now I have a clearer picture."

"Talking about the situation helped me too." Kam pushed his chair back from the table. "Time to move along," he said. "I should get back to work. After all, I have three cats to feed." The words were light-hearted, but Kam's voice was heavy.

"How are Mary and Mr. Grant doing?"

"Fine, I think. They're eating; they're active; they've made peace with Feng."

I smiled. "I'm assuming Feng is your cat."

As he whipped out his phone, Kam's expression was boyish. "I just happen to have two or three hundred photos of her, but here's one I took last night."

Feng was a strikingly regal looking cat with a distinctly reddish brown coat. "I've never seen a cat with that colouring," I said. "Her coat is gorgeous."

"The colour of a maple leaf in autumn," Kam said. "Hence the name 'Feng' which means 'maple' in Chinese. Here's a photo of her with Mary and Mr. Grant. It's not easy to get three cats in the same picture, but I thought if I heard from Ellen, she'd want to know that Mary and Mr. Grant are well taken care of."

I picked up our empty cups. "I'm worried. Do you believe you'll hear from Ellen?"

Kam met my eyes. "No, but as long as there's no evidence to the contrary, there's hope. Right?"

"Right," I said. "Kam, let's stay in touch."

As soon as I returned home, I phoned Jill Oziowy. When I received her voice message, I left a message of my own. "No need to get back to me. Roseanne Roseannadanna was right. It's always something. If this particular something turns out to be significant, I'll call you."

CHAPTER TEN

I didn't talk to Jill until the day after Labour Day. By then Zack and I were back in the city with Taylor and Gracie. Our time at the lake with the young women had been restorative for us all. Zack and I had agreed to let Taylor choose the moment when she was ready to talk about Vale. Surprisingly, the subject of the break-up did not hang heavy in the air. The bonds between our family and the families of Zack's law partners were strong, and Gracie's presence made it easy for us to embrace the comfortable pattern of the summer weekends we had shared with the Falconers.

Seven years earlier, my friend Kevin Hynd had invited my family to stay in his cottage at Lawyers Bay for the summer. It was a summer that changed my life and the lives of my children. I met Zack at the Falconer Shreve Canada Day party, and by the end of the summer we knew we belonged together. That Canada Day had proved fateful for Taylor too. She met Gracie Falconer and Isobel Wainberg, the daughters of two of Zack's law partners. The five partners all had cottages on the horseshoe of land around Lawyers Bay, and from that summer on, our families were inextricably linked.

Gracie and Isobel were a year older than Taylor but they attended the same schools, and the three girls quickly became inseparable. When our daughter called to tell us she'd left Vale, but that Gracie was with her at the lake, relief had washed over me. Big-boned, red-haired, freckled and blessed with a winning smile, a great free throw and a caring heart, Gracie was exactly the comforting presence Taylor needed.

Gracie too was at a point of change in her life. Without drama or explanation, Gracie had completed her pre-med at Notre Dame and returned home to enrol in the College of Medicine at the University of Saskatchewan. It was the university where her father had met Zack and the other three young students who sardonically referred to themselves as the Winners' Circle and who became law partners and remained close friends throughout their lives. Zack was the last living member of the Winners' Circle, and he was taking immense pleasure in Gracie's decision to attend their alma mater.

That weekend the four of us fell into the easy rhythm of our accustomed pattern at the lake: swimming, canoeing and wandering with the dogs along the shore of Lawyers Bay. We watched all three of the *Godfather* movies and agreed that while *The Godfather Part III* was okay, it did not meet the standards of its predecessors. We played cutthroat games of Monopoly Deal, talked about politics, Notre Dame's football prospects for the season ahead and perused Taylor's photographs of the Haida carvings at the Museum of Anthropology at UBC, so Zack could choose the ones he wanted framed for his law office. It was all very low-key but there was one unsettling moment. It came when Gracie and Taylor were looking at photos of the twins and their new play structure on Zack's tablet.

Listening to the young women, heads together, laughing softly at the photos, evoked memories of the countless times Gracie, Isobel and Taylor, as close as triplets, sat planning, chatting and sharing the experiences of being girls on the path to womanhood. The memory was soothing, but suddenly Gracie shot to her feet, strode across the room and handed Zack his tablet. "Why do you have this picture of Farky Farquhar?" she asked.

"Maisie sent it," Zack said. "Do you know that guy?"

Taylor joined us. "Farky is a nickname. His real name is Ronan Farquhar, and he was in Gracie and Isobel's class at Luther, a year ahead of me. Gracie and Isobel told me to steer clear of him, and I did."

Gracie rolled her eyes. "That didn't stop him from asking you to grad."

"I couldn't believe he asked me," Taylor said. "I'd never really talked to any of them."

"Any of whom?" Zack said.

"Farky's group — the University Park Road Gang, three boys, including him, and one girl. They all hung out together."

"They didn't just 'hang out' together," Gracie said. "They were glued to each other. Clay Fairbairn referred to their group as a 'cohort.'"

Zack narrowed his eyes "As in the cohorts of warriors in the Roman army?"

"I guess," Gracie said, and her tone was withering. "Clay Fairbairn said they were a 'band of warriors' — kid stuff," she said.

I felt my nerves twang. "Clay Fairbairn is part of the cohort?"

"He considers himself their leader," Gracie said. "Farky, Clay, Austin and Thalia, the brains of the group. Taylor, remember that rumour the cohort started about you after you turned down Ronan Farquhar's invitation to grad?"

The look Taylor shot her friend would have curdled milk. "That's ancient history," she said. "Nobody cares about that."

"I care about it," Zack said mildly. "How come we never heard about this before, and what was the rumour?"

Taylor was clearly exasperated. "A member of the cohort told everybody that I was frigid, and that you and Jo had sent me to at least five psychiatrists, but none of them was able to cure me. End of story. Why did Maisie send you a picture of Ronan?"

"Because your pal, Ronan, attempted to disrupt Alison Janvier's presentation at a symposium."

Taylor rolled her eyes. "That's exactly the kind of stupid thing Farky would do. I hope Maisie nailed him."

"She did," Zack said.

"Good," Gracie said. "But tell Maisie to watch her back."

"Do you think Ronan might retaliate?"

"I don't know," Gracie said. "But there was an aura around that group — a darkness. I'm not into that weird woo-woo stuff, but when the four of them were together, they emanated bad energy. You could feel it."

"Did you know that Thalia Morgan had a brother who committed suicide when she was sixteen?" I asked.

"No." Gracie paused. "I wonder if that's why Thalia started Luther in February. It's unusual for a student to start that late in the year, and we all wondered. By grade eleven, most of the cliques are firmly in place, and Thalia was so alone. I felt sorry for her, but she was unapproachable. Some kids are really into emo — they wear black slim fit jeans and black T-shirts, and that's cool, but Thalia's emo look was way off the charts: ankle-length black dress, black boots and she always wore this weird amulet necklace. We thought she was just a drama queen, but in retrospect, I guess she was in mourning for her dead brother." Gracie was clearly exasperated with herself. "Why are we always so shitty to each other?"

"That's a question for the ages," I said. "But Gracie, Thalia obviously moved on. The girl in the cohort that you and Taylor remember was not a girl to be pitied."

"No, she was not," Gracie said. "Starting after the February break meant Thalia had missed over half the school year, but she didn't fall behind. She did brilliantly. My grades were always good, but Thalia left me in the dust."

"And she continued to do well academically," I said.

"Oh yeah," Gracie said. "She's absolutely brilliant. And by the time we started grade eleven, Thalia was no longer a loner. She was a different girl. She'd hooked up with the University Park Road Gang."

"But she was fine with that?" Zack asked.

"More than fine," Gracie said. "She was definitely in control."

Zack winced, and I noticed his right leg had extended itself and started to spasm. For Zack, these involuntary muscle spasms were an annoying but harmless side effect of life in a wheelchair. Other paraplegics had far more serious problems with spasms, but despite their often inconvenient timing, Zack's spasms brought a bonus by helping strengthen the muscle tone in his legs. Zack usually handled the spasms himself, but Taylor was quick off the mark. She placed both hands under her father's knee and swung his foot back on the foot-plate of his chair. When his foot continued to bounce, Taylor pressed down on it, stretching his heel and tendon until the foot grew still.

When the spasm was over, Zack gave Taylor a quick grateful smile and carried on talking to Gracie. "When you referred to the boys from University Park Road as a 'gang,'" Zack said, "were you suggesting they were troublemakers?"

"No, far from it," Gracie said. "They were leftovers — nerds without friends. But after they formed the cohort, the University Park Road boys were nerds no more. They became super-confident, got great haircuts and started dressing like CEOs."

"Do you think Thalia was responsible for the transformation?" I said.

"Probably," Gracie said. "I know she got them all reading *Thus Spake Zarathustra.*"

"Thalia had them reading Nietzsche in grade eleven?" I said. "That's amazing. What's even more amazing is that the members of Thalia's group are entering their second year at the School of Journalism and *Thus Spake Zarathustra* still seems to be their bible."

Gracie's eyes widened. "Now that *is* bizarre," she said.

"Anything else we should know?" Zack said.

"I can't think of anything," Gracie said, "but I'll let you know if I do."

"Thanks," Zack said. "This has been really helpful. I hope you know how happy we are that you've been here for Taylor when she needs you."

"I'm happy too," Gracie said. "And you know something else I'm happy about? The condo is universal design. Totally accessible for the guy who's been like a father to me since my dad died."

Zack swallowed hard. "Time to move along. Now who's up for Monopoly Deal? I haven't won a single game this weekend, and I deserve a chance to redeem myself."

* * *

We didn't talk about the end of Taylor and Vale's relationship until after dinner on Sunday. Peter and Maisie had given Zack a rotisserie barbecue for his birthday, and it had supplanted the deep fryer as his treasured culinary toy.

Before we left the city for the weekend, I had splurged and bought Taylor's favourite, a rolled prime rib, so Zack spent a happy late afternoon reading *Homicide Trinity*, with Pantera at his side, both watching the prime rib turn, spitting fat on the coals and filling the air with the melt-in-your-mouth scent of succulent beef.

Our Sunday dinner celebrated the glories of early September. That afternoon we'd driven over to Standing Buffalo where a farmer, who had known Gracie since she was knee-high to a grasshopper, let us pick corn and choose vegetables for a salad. After we'd eaten, we pulled our chaise longues into a space on the west side of the lawn, where the last sunlight of day was pooling.

Our mood was mellow. Simply being together again was sublime, but the slight chill in the air was a reminder that change was on its way. "A week from now I'll be walking into the College of Medicine in Saskatoon," Gracie said. "Ever since I explained to my Notre Dame coach why I was coming back to Saskatchewan to finish my degree, I've wondered how I'd feel when it suddenly became real. I was still wondering when Taylor called and asked me to pick her up at the airport. Since then I've felt that every step I'm making is the right one."

Zack and I were silent. We knew this was Taylor's moment to choose, and Zack wheeled his chair closer to mine.

"As soon as the plane touched down and I saw that big prairie sky and Gracie waiting for me, I knew I was where I belonged," Taylor said. "Maybe not forever, but for now." Her dark eyes searched her father's face and mine. "I really am all right. I hope you could see that this weekend."

"We did," Zack said. "Jo says you're sad but hopeful."

Gracie flashed me a victory sign. "Jo, the mood-reader, nails it again. 'Sad but hopeful.'" She gave our daughter a wry smile. "That's you, Taylor, but with the emphasis on the hopeful. Now, I'm going to leave you three to talk this through."

Gracie bent to kiss Zack on the head. "Sleep well," she said to us. "Taylor's in good hands."

Taylor shifted on her chair to face us. For a minute or two she was silent, gathering her thoughts. Finally, she said, "Jo, do you remember telling me about that friend of yours who married her college sweetheart, and when the marriage ended, she travelled back to every place they'd lived to see if she could understand when their relationship had started to unravel?"

"I do," I said. "It seemed a strange journey to me, but she said she needed to hear the click of closure."

Taylor's smile was rueful. "Vale telling me that she and Etienne Simard had an affair was definitely my click of closure. Figuring out when our relationship started to unravel isn't easy. It happened so gradually that I think neither of us really noticed.

"When we moved to Vancouver, the only apartment we could get was across the city from where Vale's movie was being shot. She was working twelve-hour days, so it made sense for her just to stay where she was working. One day it struck me that Vale and I were leading separate lives. I guess I thought we'd deal with it when the movie was finished, but when that video went viral, it pretty well blew that plan out of the water."

"It was a painful way to find out," Zack said.

Taylor's voice was weary. "Actually I'd seen the outtake months ago when there was a question about whether or not to use it. I was in favour of including it, because the insight it gave into Sally and Izaak's relationship was the truth."

"Taylor, I'm still not getting this," I said. "If you knew the video was just an outtake, why was it a problem?"

"Because after the video went online, I had a text from a blocked number calling themselves 'a concerned friend' and suggesting I ask Vale when her affair with Etienne Simard began."

"And you did," I said.

"I was certain she'd say there'd never been anything real between them," Taylor said, and her eyes filled. "But she told me the truth. She said they started having sex when they were shooting in Regina in November. That was when she and I moved into our first real home together. I thought it was perfect. I thought we were perfect."

Seeing our daughter alone in her confusion and grief was heartbreaking, and Zack and I both started towards her. Taylor raised both hands, palms out, to stop us. "Let me finish. I have to get this out. Vale says the sex had nothing to do with her feelings for me. She says she and Etienne knew that they weren't getting the balance between Sally and Izaak right."

"And the only way they could get it right was by having sex," Zack said, and he made no attempt to hide his disdain.

"Vale said it meant no more to her than going to a voice coach to work on an accent or sitting in makeup for three hours every day for *The Happiest Girl*, where her character is an old woman looking back on her life."

"But it meant more to you," Zack said.

Taylor nodded numbly. "I thought Vale and I truly knew each other — in every possible way. But she couldn't have known anything about me if she thought I'd see her having sex with someone else as just part of her job."

I leaned towards her. "Do you think there's a way you could work this through?"

"No. When we quarrelled we both said hurtful things, but what we said was true. Vale said she loved me, but what mattered most to her would always be her work. As soon as she said that, I realized that was true for me too. While we were in Vancouver, I didn't make art — nothing, not even a sketch. I wasn't a recluse. I saw the city, walked on the beach, went to galleries, had coffee with people, but I didn't make art. I still don't understand why. It was as if my life was on hold. I couldn't keep living like that." She shrugged and tried a smile. "Sally's genes, I guess. And now here I am."

I moved towards her, then hesitated.

She stood and held out her arms. "It's okay. Now I'm ready for that hug."

CHAPTER ELEVEN

Zack and I slept well that night. The knowledge that our daughter was two cottages away with her cats and one of her closest friends as company was a powerful antidote to an evening of disquieting revelations.

Zack's and my morning walk with the dogs along the shoreline was shot through with shared memories of our daughter and Vale. The two women had met briefly backstage in New York City when we saw Vale's performance in *The Happiest Girl*, but their first meaningful encounter came at the after-party for the dancers who'd been part of a gala celebrating a local patron of the arts. I'd been asleep when Taylor returned, but Zack had been waiting up, and the next morning at breakfast he reported that Taylor was incandescent as she described her evening. Apparently, she and Vale Frazier had bundled up and spent the evening on one of the penthouse balconies overlooking the city and all its Christmas lights and, in our daughter's breathless words, "talking about everything." Vale had introduced our daughter to the work of Joseph Campbell, the professor of comparative mythology and comparative religions who wrote *The Hero with a Thousand Faces*. It was heady stuff, and in the ensuing days and weeks, Taylor introduced Vale to a world where families ate meals together, shared stories of their day and where, as Taylor had once exploded in exasperation, "there was always somebody with you whether you wanted them with you or not."

Vale and Taylor were both twenty, and neither had been in a serious relationship before. They moved into their relationship cautiously because, as Taylor explained when she told us that she and Vale were in love, they knew that bringing two lives together in the right way would involve careful planning.

For Zack and me there were many shining memories of their time together. Taylor and Vale, tanned and ebullient, decked out in red and white ready to wave the flag at Falconer Shreve's annual Canada Day party. Their quiet pride as they showed us through the condo that would be their first home together. The river of photos they sent us of their fairy-tale Christmas in London with the legendary actor Rosamond Burke. The small gestures of tenderness between them that said what words could not.

As we headed back to the cottage, Zack was silent, and I knew he was brooding. "They had everything going for them," he said. "All that promise. And then . . ." He snapped his fingers. "It's over."

My phone rang. I checked caller ID and squeezed Zack's shoulder. "It's our son-in-law," I said. "And guess what? Something else is just beginning." I turned on the speakerphone.

Charlie was jubilant. "Guess who's here?" When we heard the lusty cry of Desmond Zackary Dowhanuik, Zack and I both sighed deeply with relief.

"Everything went well?" I asked.

"Everything went brilliantly. Mieka was stupendous, and Des already scored ten out of ten on his Apgar test."

Zack was clearly baffled. "What's an Apgar test?"

"It's a test performed when babies are one minute old to see how well they made it through the birth process," Charlie said. "They repeat the test when the babies are five minutes old to see how well they're doing in the world outside their mother's womb. Not many babies score ten out of ten."

"Five minutes old, and Des is already at the top of his class," Zack said.

Charlie's laugh was self-deprecating. "You're mocking me," he said. "But I can take it because I've just been part of the most amazing experiences anyone's ever had. I can hardly wait till we do it again."

Mieka's groan was audible, and Charlie's contrition was instant. "I should probably let Mieka talk," he said.

"Just after the nick of time," I said, and we both laughed.

* * *

We decided that Mieka, Charlie and Des needed some family time together before we visited, so it was six thirty that evening when Madeleine, Lena, Zack and I arrived on the second floor of the Regina General Hospital. My memories of the Mother Baby Unit were not all gilt-edged.

Madeleine had been eighteen months old when Lena was born. To prepare her daughter for the birth, Mieka read her all the right books and did all the right things. She talked daily to Madeleine about the child who would be joining their family. She helped Maddy choose welcome-to-the-world books for herself and for her new sibling, and when she left for the hospital, Mieka gave Maddy her favourite red cashmere scarf so Maddy would know her mother was coming home.

As we drove to Regina General on the day Lena was born, Madeleine was quiet. Taylor, who was then nine and a half, tried but failed to engage Maddy in the clapping game that was her current favourite. In the elevator, Maddy held tightly to the gift-wrapped copy of *Goodnight Moon* she'd chosen for her new sister. There was no reason to anticipate trouble, but a storm was brewing.

As she approached her mother's hospital bed, Madeleine was tentative but when she spotted the baby in her mother's arms, she growled — a low guttural, feral sound that seemed to come from the depths of her being. Then she grasped me behind the knees and began to sob; within seconds, Mieka was sobbing too. "I've never seen Maddy like this," she said. "We're breaking her heart."

I scooped Madeleine up and held her close. "She'll be fine," I said. "But I think we need to go home. We all love you, and we all love Lena." At the sound of her sister's name,

Madeleine stiffened. "I'll call you later," I said. "Mieka, this will work out."

And it did. We never paid a return visit to the hospital, but the afternoon Mieka and Lena came home, Maddy, Taylor and I set the table with Mieka's best linen tea cloth, the delicate china cups and dessert plates reserved for special occasions and a platter of the lace cookies Mieka adored. We were ready, but when I heard the car in the driveway, my nerves tightened.

Mieka came through the door alone, went straight to Madeleine and, murmuring endearments, wrapped her older daughter in her arms. When finally they broke apart, both mother and daughter were beaming. "Daddy's waiting in the car," Mieka said. "Are you ready for him to bring Lena in?"

"I'm ready now," Madeleine said. And on that enigmatic note, the page was turned.

* * *

The scene today couldn't have been more different, and as Madeleine and Lena walked, hand in hand, into Mieka's hospital room to meet the newest member of their family, I felt a frisson of joy. The bliss continued. Mieka was holding Des, and she zeroed in on Zack. "This boy needs his grandfather," she said. "He weighs a shade over ten pounds. I just fed him, so he's down for the count."

Zack wheeled to Mieka's bedside and held out his arms. Madeleine and Lena positioned themselves on either side of Zack's chair, and I moved closer. Des snuggled right in, the picture of contentment. He was a handsome, long-limbed baby with white blond hair, fair skin and a large and expressive mouth. "He's perfect," Zack said finally. "Well done, you two."

"All praise gratefully accepted," Charlie said. "And you're right. He is perfect. And so far, he seems to have an even temperament. He sleeps. He gazes. He eats. He sleeps."

"No diaper change in there?" I asked.

Charlie raised an eyebrow. "Des is impressive in that area too. But enough said. What's happening in the big world?"

Zack pulled out his tablet and began showing photos of the twins on the play structure, until Lena called a halt and suggested it was time for Mieka to see their two-tone toenails. Mieka was enthusiastic, but I noticed she was flagging.

"I think the new mother needs some sleep."

"Good call," Mieka said. "And since Des is my roommate, I'll be lucky if I log a solid three hours."

I leaned over for a last look. "It's hard to say goodbye to this little guy."

"He's easy to love," Mieka said. "He's so good, and he really is beautiful. Charlie and I have been trying to figure out who he takes after."

"I can answer that," I said. "He looks like Desmond Love. Your son's likeness to my father and your grandfather is pretty stunning. I have some pictures of him when he was a little boy. I'll bring them along tomorrow."

Mieka sighed. "It's amazing to think that our son looks like the grandfather I never knew."

"If we're lucky, he'll have your grandfather's talent," Charlie said.

Lena's look was quizzical. "Whose talent do Maddy and I have?"

"Desmond Love was your great-grandfather too," Charlie said. "You could have inherited that talent."

Madeleine groaned. "Did you see the picture Lena and I drew for our new brother? He can probably do better than that already."

"Well, your great-grandfather loved to swim, and you two are great swimmers," I said. "And you're both optimists. You believe everything will work out for the best. Des believed that too."

"You and your brother all have some amazing genes going for you," Zack said. "So, don't sweat it. Just kick back and wait to be surprised."

"Words to live by," I said. "Now we really better get a move on. Tomorrow's the first day of school, and we still have baths and hair washing on the agenda. Mieka, I know the girls' outfits are in their overnight bags, and I know their school supplies are in their backpacks. I'll send you the first day of school photo, so you know they didn't go off wearing their PJ bottoms and a party dress."

Mieka rolled her eyes. "The way Taylor did when she was in grade one."

"When it comes to fashion, Taylor has always been her own woman," I said. "Speaking of Taylor, she's very excited about this little guy. She and Gracie Falconer are at the lake, but I'm sure she'll be here as soon as visiting hours start tomorrow."

"So, Vale's still working in Vancouver," Mieka said.

Zack was smooth. "Yep, Vale is still in Vancouver, but Taylor and Gracie are having fun catching up. Now it's time for us to say our goodbyes."

After Charlie D pried Des out of Zack's firm grip, we headed out. As the girls danced down the hall to the elevator, I turned to Zack. "Nice catch on Mieka's reference to Vale's whereabouts," I said.

"Mieka and Charlie will find out soon enough, and they deserve a day without complications."

"I could use one of those myself," I said. With that, we joined the girls to wait for the elevator that would carry us down to the hospital's main floor and back to the complex and uncertain world.

* * *

Tuesday morning the girls' high spirits were intoxicating as they spooned their bowls of junk cereal — a traditional first day of school breakfast since Mieka was in kindergarten — and rattled on about new teachers and old friends. Zack and I were content to sit back and breathe in the joy. We watched from the front porch as Madeleine and Lena boarded their school bus. However, as the school bus turned the corner and disappeared from view, I felt the pang of loss. After I closed the door, Zack gave me a searching look. "Carousel of time spinning too fast?" he asked.

I nodded. "It seems like only yesterday Madeleine was climbing onto that bus for her first day at École St. Pius X, and now it's her last year."

"Hey, next year, we'll be watching Charlie and Colin climb on that bus and in five years it will be Desmond Zackary Dowhanuik's turn."

"You really are a good guy," I said. "Not many grandfathers would turn down a chance to have breakfast with a retiring Supreme Court justice just to see his granddaughters off to their first day of school."

"The breakfast for retiring Justice Wayne Wren is being held at the Scarth Club, and Lucky Charms with Magical Unicorns are not on the menu," Zack said. "I checked. Besides, Wayne and I have known each other since law school. Our friendship had to be shelved for the twenty-five years he was on the court and I was practising law, but now that he's retiring, we're planning to have a drink together and make up for lost time."

"That might take more than one drink," I said. "Why don't you and Wayne go out to the lake while the weather is still nice? Have a barbecue and stay the night."

"Now that is a great idea. Wayne's keen to meet you."

"I'm keen to meet him too," I said, "but the reunion should be for just the two of you. When life settles down, we'll invite Wayne for dinner here."

"He'll get a kick out of that," Zack said. "Wayne's finding it hard to get his head around the idea that after forty-eight years living life on the edge, I've become a family man. So what's on your agenda for the day?"

"I'm going to dig up those photos of Desmond Love when he was a boy, and then I'm going to Gale's Florist to buy gerbera daisies for Mieka — half rosy orange; half vibrant pink, her favourites. Then I'm going to the Mother Baby Unit again to visit Desmond Zackary Dowhanuik and his mum."

Zack's smile was wide. "Just hearing that name makes me proud."

"That's exactly the reaction Mieka and Charlie D were hoping for," I said. "Anyway, before I go to Regina General, I'm going to call Jill to learn if Ronan Farquhar is one of the summer interns. Gracie said the members of Clay's little group are glued together, so it's possible Ronan followed Clay to MediaNation."

Zack's smile vanished. "This whole 'cohort' business creeps me out," he said. "Gracie dismissed Clay's 'band of warriors' as kid stuff, but what Clay Fairbairn and Ronan Farquhar are doing is not kid stuff."

"It wasn't," I said. "And I have a sinking feeling that what we actually know of Clay and Ronan's actions is just the tip of the iceberg."

"Let's hope you're wrong," Zack said. "I'm going to be stuck in meetings all morning, but when I get out, I'll call you. Give Desmond Zackary and his parents a hug from me."

* * *

As soon as Zack left, I called Jill. As I relayed Maisie's description of her encounter with Ronan Farquhar at the symposium, Jill listened without interruption, but when she confirmed that Ronan Farquhar was one of MediaNation's summer interns, her voice was tight. "Jo, do you have any idea what all this means?"

"Not yet, but Maisie sent us the three good photos she got of Ronan's face before he took off. They were on Zack's tablet. Taylor and her friend Gracie Falconer were looking at pictures of the twins when the photos of Ronan Farquhar appeared. Gracie recognized him immediately. He was in her year at Luther.

"Gracie didn't have much to do with Ronan, but what she knew about Ronan's connection with Clay Fairbairn and his 'cohort' of four is disturbing." When I passed along Clay Fairbairn's description of his cohort as a "band of warriors," Jill's excitement was palpable in her voice.

"Two questions," she said. "How are you going to handle this? And what can I do to help?"

"Maisie was involved in both the incident with Alison at the picnic and the confrontation with Ronan at the symposium. I'll run what you just told me by her and get back to you."

"I'll be here." Jill paused. "Jo, journalists get an adrenaline rush when they sense a real red meat story. Usually it's a blast, but I have a bad feeling about this."

"Maisie and I do too," I said. "The possibility that what we know about the cohort is just the beginning is alarming. Is Ronan at work today?"

"Actually, he just walked by my office. Do you want me to make sure he stays at the office?"

"I do. If Maisie can get away, I know she'll want to see him. I'll get back to you as soon as I know if she's free."

* * *

When Maisie picked up, there was an edge to her voice. "Everything okay with Mieka and the baby?" she said.

"Everything's fine on the home front, and through either a stroke of luck or cosmic justice, I learned the identity of your runaway. His name is Ronan Farquhar and he's an intern at MediaNation. If you can get away from Falconer Shreve, Jill Oziowy will keep Ronan there so you can talk to him."

Maisie was exuberant. "Booyah. I can return Ronan's ball cap and sunglasses, and after he has expressed his gratitude, he and I can chat. So he's a summer intern. Just like Clay Fairbairn." Maisie's tone was sardonic. "I'll bet you a box of Timbits they're bosom buddies."

"I have inside information, so it wouldn't be a fair bet," I said. After I delivered a précis of Clay and Ronan's shared history, Maisie was quick off the mark. "I have forty-five minutes till my next appointment — more than enough time to do my good deed for the day and be back at the office for my client. Come with me. If Ronan decides to run again, you can grab him. I'll pick you up in ten minutes."

"I'll let Jill know we're on our way."

As we sprinted up the stairs to MediaNation, Maisie and I were in Thelma and Louise mode, but my heart sank when we entered the foyer and I saw Mark Evanson sitting behind the circular sign-in desk where visitors waited for the person who would shepherd them to their destination on the lower level. At the picnic, Mark had said that Hugh Fairbairn had arranged for him to have a really good job. Seemingly, being MediaNation's officer for visitor management was just the ticket.

Mark's face lit up when he saw me. "This is such a nice surprise, Mrs. Kilbourn — but your name is now Mrs. Shreve. I wrote your new name down as soon as Lori and Andy and I got home from the picnic."

"Thanks for remembering," I said. "But I wish you and Lori would just call me Joanne."

"Lori will be so excited to hear that," Mark said. "You're one of her favourites."

"I'm very fond of you both too," I said. "Now let me introduce you to our daughter-in-law, Maisie. She's married to Peter."

"I remember Peter," Mark said. "He was always kind."

"He still is," Maisie said, extending her hand. "I'm very pleased to meet you, Mark."

"And I'm pleased to meet you, Maisie. Now please tell me who you're here to see, and I'll call them."

"We're here for Jill Oziowy."

Mark picked up his phone, pressed a button and turned back to us. "She'll be right up."

"Thanks," I said. "Maisie and I will wait for Jill over there by the door."

As soon as we were out of earshot, I turned to Maisie. "Mark Evanson is Clay's father," I said. "I didn't realize that he worked at MediaNation until now."

Maisie's face was troubled. "Damn it. Why does there always have to be collateral damage?"

"It's the way of the world," I said. "And it sucks, but Jill's coming. Let's do what we came to do and hope that Clay isn't in this too deep."

Jill's tawny eyes were bright with anticipation. She might have been apprehensive, but a red meat story is a red meat story, and Jill was a journalist. "Ronan's in the conference room. He doesn't know you're here, so it will be an ambush," she said. "Shall I vamoose?"

Maisie shook her head. "No. You're Ronan's boss. He needs to know that he screwed up big time."

* * *

The MediaNation open-concept office was a maze of cubicles and a conference room with three glass walls. Ronan was slouched in a chair at the head of the table, chuckling at something on his phone screen. When we entered the room, he jumped to his feet, looked around desperately and, realizing that Maisie was standing in front of the only exit, mumbled the word "cunt."

"There's that word again," Maisie said. "Ronan, did you know the origin of the word 'cunt' goes back to 1500 BC and the ancient Aryans? It's always been a powerful word because it refers to the sacred place within which life is created."

Ronan Farquhar had sandy hair, round blue eyes, a snub freckled nose and the sulky cupid's mouth of a spoiled child. He was visibly shaken. "What the hell are you talking about?"

"I'm talking about you, Ronan. I know that you began your life in your mother's cunt, and that you are now part of a cohort with four members: Clay, Austin, Thalia and you."

As Maisie recited the names, Ronan grew so pale that the freckles on his face appeared to be painted on, like a doll's, but he remained defiant. "So I have friends. Do you have a problem with that?"

"Not at all," Maisie said. "It's commendable that your 'band of warriors' has stayed close since you were in high school. Someone who knew you then said that it was as if the four of you were glued together."

"I need to get out of here," Ronan said. "I'm in the middle of something important."

"Whatever you're working on can wait," Jill said evenly. "Maisie is a top tier lawyer, but she was willing to take time out of her busy day just to talk to you."

"I only have one question," Maisie said, "and if you tell the truth, you can be back at your important work in a flash. Why have you and the other members of your cohort been asking Alison Janvier about her decision not to have an abortion?"

"It speaks to her character," Ronan said. He tried a smirk. "May I go now?"

"No, because that's not the truth." Maisie turned to me. "Joanne, tell Ronan what we've learned."

I was taken aback. What we had was flimsy — a tissue of conjectures — but Maisie had passed the ball to me, so I ran with it. "There were loose ends," I said. "When we started tying them together, we realized that the actions you and the other members of your cohort have taken against Alison Janvier began after Alison's son, Harper Janvier, won the Lee Gowan Emerging Writer Award. Clay Fairbairn felt he should have won the award, and your group chose to humili-ate Alison and her son by shining a spotlight on her decision not to have an abortion. It was payback, but karma caught up with you. Jill Oziowy's camera caught Clay pushing the tangle of wires into Alison's path so she'd trip, and the night of the symposium, Maisie took photos of you before you could flee. We've only scratched the surface of your history with the band of warriors, but we're going to keep digging." It was a shot in the dark, but when Ronan flinched, I knew we'd hit the target.

Maisie handed Ronan his ball cap and sunglasses. "We're through here," she said. "At least for today. But Ronan, be aware that if you and your merry band of pranksters so much as enter a room where Alison is speaking, we'll share what we know with the people you'll need as references when you're seeking permanent employment. One more thing. As Joanne said, you're not free of us yet. We're going to keep questioning people who know you and scrutinizing your past activities until we have a complete picture of what you've been up to. We're looking for the cohort's master plan, and I assure you, we're going to find it."

Ronan seemed frozen in place. Maisie rapped him smartly on the arm. "You may go now," she said. And he did — quickly.

I waited until I was sure Ronan wasn't loitering outside before I turned to my daughter-in-law. "That was a gamble."

Maisie shrugged. "Ronan took the bait. That's all that counts."

"Do you believe we've heard the last of the cohort?" Jill said.

Maisie's headshake was vehement. "Not a chance. Aesop was right. What's bred in the bone will stick to the flesh. If

Clay Fairbairn really is a sociopath, he'll already be planning his next move, but the news that we're onto him should at least slow him down."

"For everyone's sake, let's hope it stops him in his tracks," I said. "Jill, you're the one closest to the action. If your spidey senses start tingling, don't try to handle the situation alone. Call Maisie or Charlie or Zack or me. We're all in this together."

Maisie raised an eyebrow. "Kumbaya time?" she said, and her tone was flinty.

Jill's eyes met mine. "Let's not push it," she said. "Just hearing the words 'We're all in this together' made my day."

* * *

When Maisie and I came back upstairs, Mark Evanson was still at his desk, and Maisie and I went over to say goodbye to him. He was surprisingly touched. "Not many people take the time to say goodbye. I guess they're just busy thinking about where they're going next."

"You'll be interested in the next place I'm going," I said. "Do you remember Peter's sister, Mieka?"

Mark nodded. "She was always nice too. Does she have a family of her own now?"

"She does," I said. "Did you know she's married to Charlie D?"

"No. Charlie D and I usually just talk about the weather or football. I can't wait to tell Lori about Charlie D and Mieka."

"And there's more news," I said. "Charlie D and Mieka have two daughters who are almost finished grade school and a baby boy who's just a day old. His name is Desmond, and he's a big guy. He weighed a little over ten pounds when he was born."

Mark was beaming. "Clay weighed seven pounds, two ounces, and he was so beautiful — just like Lori." A shadow crossed Mark's face. "But that was a long time ago. Thank you both for stopping by to talk to me."

"You're welcome," Maisie said. "Mark, I'm glad I met you."

Mark's smile was winning. "I'm glad I met you too, Maisie. Joanne has always been a good friend to us. Lori is going to be really excited when I tell her that I had a real visit with you both."

Maisie was silent and stone-faced as we walked towards her Lexus. As soon as we were in the car I snapped on my seat belt, but Maisie didn't move. Finally, she closed her eyes, rested her forehead on the steering wheel and said, "Why don't the sweet and decent ones ever catch a break?" Then she took a deep breath, straightened and turned towards me. "Well?"

"Mark thinks he has caught a break," I said. "He has Lori and he has his memory of that newborn boy who weighed seven pounds, two ounces and was so beautiful."

My daughter-in-law and I didn't exchange another word till we pulled up in front of our house.

"That was excruciating," I said.

"It was." Maisie's voice was heavy with pain, but her eyes were fiery. "We have to see this through, Joanne. Lawyers know you get what you settle for, and we can't settle for less than the truth. Someone in that cohort is a sociopath. We don't know the extent of what they've done so far, but we do know they're not finished. They have to be stopped."

* * *

After I took off my jacket, I caught a glimpse of myself in the hall mirror: pale and haggard. I was in no shape to visit Mieka and our new grandson. I had hoped Zack and I would have our first swim in the newly renovated pool together, but my need for renewal was urgent.

I went to the mudroom and opened what my husband referred to as "the trunk of retired bathing suits." Every year I started summer with a new bathing suit and demoted the previous year's suit to backup status. The suits were all pretty much the same: cleanly cut from durable material and unadorned — suits for a serious swimmer. The previous year's suit was forest green, and as I pulled it on, I felt my nerves unknot.

My swimming style is orthodox: smooth, straight-armed, deep catch strokes; rhythmical rotations of the core with each stroke and bilateral breathing — inhaling on the right for one length of the pool and on the left for the next. It's not a joy to behold, but it works for me. Half an hour after I dove in, I felt like myself again. I showered, dressed, stopped at Gale's Florist to buy Mieka's gerberas, and as I walked down the hall to join my daughter and my new grandson, there was a bounce in my step.

Mieka and Desmond's room was a bower of blooms. Vases of gladioli, the showgirls of the garden, vied for pride of place

with elaborate arrangements, bright with blue ribbons, boo-
ties and streamers declaring *It's a Boy!* Mieka was sitting in a
chair by the window with Des's crib beside her. "Wow. Talk
about coals to Newcastle," I said, handing her our bouquet
of gerberas.

"Charlie says the room looks like a Mafia funeral, but the
gerberas are special, because they're from you and Zack, and
you know they're my favourites."

"Where did all these flowers come from?"

"Some of them are from people Charlie and I actually
know, but most of them are from fans of his show and people from Zack's law firm and friends of yours. I've asked the
volunteers to give the overflow to people who might enjoy
them." Mieka caught my look. "And yes, Mum, I'm keeping
the cards so I can send thank-you notes."

"That's my girl," I said. "How are you and Des doing?"

"We have a perfect relationship," she said. "I have plenty
of milk, and he's a hungry guy, so we're both happy."

I picked up my messenger bag, took out a very old photo
album and handed it to my daughter. "All the photos in this
are of your grandfather. He's not much older than Des in the
first ones and the pictures continue till he starts kindergarten.
And be warned — that's only the first album."

When Mieka smiled and opened the album, and I scooped
up the baby. He was still sleeping, so I was free to gaze and
marvel.

"The resemblance between Des and my grandfather
is uncanny," Mieka said, her voice low. "I wish I'd paid
more attention when we studied genetics and heredity in

biology." She turned the page to a large studio portrait and held it up so I could see. "Desmond Love is six months old here," she said. "He's so joyful; it's impossible not to smile when you look at this picture."

"When I was growing up, I used to love just being in the same room with Des," I said. "He had such a passion for living. When I close my eyes, I can still see him running down the hill from the cottage onto the dock and diving into the lake. He never hesitated." I gazed at the baby in my arms. "Zack has that same passion for living," I said. "I have a feeling Desmond Zackary, like his two namesakes, will embrace everything life has to offer and seize the day."

"Speaking of seizing the day," Mieka said, "Charlie and I are thinking about having Des baptized at Thanksgiving."

"The timing is right," I said. "Des is already a big boy, but in a month, we'll still be able to squeeze him into the Crawford family baptismal gown."

"Not the Kilbourn family baptismal gown?"

'No. I decided it was time to put the Kilbourn baptismal gown away."

My daughter's grey-green eyes met mine. "That was the right decision," she said.

"Good. In that case, why don't you and Charlie talk to Dean Mike at the cathedral, and we can start planning?" Des was stirring. He opened his eyes, looked at me and, realizing that I was not the person he needed to meet his needs, hollered. I handed him to Mieka. "You're being summoned," I said. "Time for me to get the girls from school. I'll have them call you to tell you how their days went, and then the ladies and I will visit the Fafard cows."

Mieka beamed. "You remembered."

"Hey, it's a tradition, and as Taylor says, this family has traditions for everything. Now, I really better get a move on."

The Fafard cows — half-sized bronze sculptures of a bull, cow and calf grazing on a landscaped urban meadow in front of the MacKenzie Art Gallery — are one of Regina's quiet treasures, and Mieka had made them part of her daughters' back-to-school tradition. The photos of Madeleine and Lena standing beside the bronze animals — Potter, Valadon and Teevo — told a wordless story of the girls' physical and emotional growth.

As kindergarteners they had embraced the animals. In later years, they made goofy faces or struck poses, but on that crayon-bright September day they simply admired the perfect lines and gentle expressions of the sculptured animals that were a philanthropic couple's gift to the city.

* * *

Zack arrived home at five thirty, looking weary. "Long day?" I said.

"It was," he said. "But I'm home now."

"Perfect timing," I said. "Because there's a pitcher of martinis in the fridge, a pan of eggplant parmigiana in the oven and two young women with school news to report, waiting for you on the patio."

The evening was mercifully uncomplicated, and after Madeleine and Lena had showered, FaceTimed with Mieka, Charlie and Des, and laid out their clothes for the next day, Zack and I tucked them in, looked longingly at our own bedroom and agreed that tonight was a double massage night.

Not long after Zack and I were married, we hit upon the idea of nightly massages. We were deeply in love, but the simple intimacies of normal domestic life weren't simple for us. Nightly massages gave us both pleasure, relaxed us and gave me a chance to check Zack's skin for the warning signs of pressure ulcers that, if left untended, could kill him.

That night as I squeezed the massage oil into my hand and began kneading the knotted muscles of Zack's shoulders, he groaned with pleasure. "Remind me. Why did we stop doing this?"

"Well, for most of August, we were at the lake, swimming every day, playing with the grandkids and being as carefree as any sentient being can expect to be." I began working on the area at the top of Zack's spine. "I could bounce a dime off these muscles," I said. "I take it your day was not free of care."

"Nope, it was shitty," Zack said cheerfully. "But it's over. Tell me about your day."

"Let's see. At supper, you heard the highlights of my visit to Des and Mieka, and of the girls' first day back at École Pius X. But I haven't told you about seeing our daughter-in-law in action today. She's impressive. She's also merciless."

"Maisie's not merciless, Jo," Zack said. "She's just a good lawyer who knows she can't pull back until she's absolutely certain she's won her case. She understands that her client's future is in her hands, and she can't leave anything to chance. Nice lawyers back away too soon and lose cases they shouldn't lose. Maisie doesn't quit pummelling until she's sure the job is done, and she wins."

I poured more oil into my hand and began to rub the base of Zack's spine. Pushing his weight in a wheelchair sixteen hours a day built muscle, and Zack's upper body was powerful, but his lower spine was incredibly vulnerable. The sight of the patchwork of scars that marked successive failed attempts to restore his ability to walk made my heart ache. I was gentle when I smoothed oil on his scars, but because Zack had no feeling there, he never knew.

"I hope Maisie won this morning," I said.

Zack turned to look over his shoulder at me. "Whoa," he said. "Can you roll the tape back for me? I obviously missed something. Were you at the courthouse today?"

"No. I was at MediaNation."

Zack was rapt as I described our meeting with Ronan Farquhar. When I finished, Zack took a deep breath and exhaled slowly. "Do you remember Ned Osler?"

"Of course. He had the most immaculate manners. Whenever we had dinner at his apartment in the Balfour, he always had a note hand-delivered to me the next day, thanking me for the pleasure of my company and mentioning a detail of the evening that had brought him special delight. Ned was a gentleman of the old school."

"He was also one hell of a lawyer," Zack said. "He cautioned me more than once against acting impetuously. He'd say, 'Think twice before you poke a hive, because once you've poked it, all hell will break loose.' It was a valuable lesson."

"Do you think Maisie and I went too far today?"

"We'll know soon enough," Zack said. "Take off your nightie and hand me the massage oil. It's your turn now."

CHAPTER TWELVE

The days ahead were a time of passages. Mieka and Desmond came home from the hospital, and the Kilbourn-Dowhanuiks embarked on life as a family of five. On TV, commercials featuring scrubbed kids with new backpacks and spotless sneakers gave way to ads featuring snaggle-toothed witches and leering pumpkins. Back to School was yesterday's story; Halloween was on its way. I packed away the pastel sundresses, shirts, shorts and casual wear in our closets and replaced them with turtlenecks, cardigans, dress slacks and, in Zack's case, three-piece suits in the deep rich hues of autumn. On our shoe racks, the sandals, slaps and slip-ons of summer ceded space to the serious, sensible shoes of people who lived serious, sensible lives.

Gracie moved into her apartment in Saskatoon and began classes at the College of Medicine, while Taylor stayed at

Lawyers Bay making art and meditating on Joseph Campbell's teaching that "we must be willing to let go of the life we planned in order to have the life that is waiting for us." Both Taylor and the young woman who introduced her to Joseph Campbell's work were letting go of the life they'd planned together, and going separately into the lives that were waiting for them. And, oblivious, the carousel's painted ponies pranced on.

The police investigating Ellen Exton's disappearance were diligent but frustrated. Almost three weeks had passed since Ellen walked out of MediaNation for the last time, and the investigation had turned up nothing. On a brighter note, Maisie's ambush of Ronan Farquhar had apparently done the job. The cohort's staged abortion questions had ceased, and although we suspected dark clouds were looming, we were grateful for the respite.

Thursday, September 17 was a splendid fall day. The sky was indigo, the air was clear, the sun was bright and the leaves were turning. Zack joined Pantera, Esme and me for our morning run, and as soon as we got home, Zack and I showered, dressed and headed for MediaNation's cafeteria and their peerless cinnamon buns. We found a table by the window, and when we looked out and saw four deer in perfect stillness walking on the leaf-strewn grass we reached out and touched each other's hand.

The cinnamon buns were sweet, soft and sticky, and Zack and I were considering the wisdom of splitting a third bun when Jill Oziowy, carrying a cup of coffee, approached our table. Jill was the epitome of fall chic: black leggings, a rust tunic top and beige suede boots. "You look terrific," I said.

"Value Village just got their fall line in," Jill said drily. "And thanks for the compliment, but what we need to talk about is not fashion-related. I hate to interrupt, but this won't take long."

"You're not interrupting," I said. "We're having a lazy day. Come join us."

"I'd love too, but I can't stay," Jill said. "A passel of people who believe they're important are waiting in the conference room downstairs."

"Let the passel wait. The three of us are here now," Zack said. "Strike while the iron's hot."

"Fair enough," Jill said. "*Sisters and Strangers* has been testing phenomenally well with audiences; the critics are creaming their jeans about it, and the whiz kids downstairs see themselves as potential partners for expanding the series."

Zack shook his head in disgust. "Here's an idea," he said. "Why don't the whiz kids arrange a meeting with the person who owns the rights to the series and her lawyer, who by happy chance is also the lawyer for the company that produced the series?"

Jill's smile was faint. "I suggested that very thing, and they suggested I make a priority of smoothing the way for a meeting between them and you and Jo."

Zack gave me a sidelong glance. "How do you feel about that?"

"Baffled," I said. "Haven't the people downstairs seen the final episode of *Sisters and Strangers*? Sally dies, and Joanne adopts Taylor — not a lot of room for expansion there."

"They're thinking of a movie, like the one that was made after *Downton Abbey* ended," Jill said.

"*Downton Abbey* is a story made up by a screenwriter," I said. "*Sisters and Strangers* is the story of a part of my life. I'm glad the series was made, and I'm proud of the production, but watching *Sisters and Strangers* come to life was like being flayed. Once was enough."

"I get that," Jill said. "But the movers and shakers downstairs won't. However, we'll jump off that bridge when we come to it. There's something else."

"There always is," Zack said, and his tone was one of weary resignation.

"Because of the positive response to previews of the series, MediaNation is prepared to pull out all the stops for the promotion campaign."

"I thought they already had," I said. "Zack and I don't turn on the TV often, but every time we do, it seems there's a promo for *Sisters and Strangers*. Madeleine and Lena, who don't know that the relationship between Vale and Taylor is over, bring us every magazine that has a cover story about Vale and the series. We're building quite a collection."

Jill took a deep breath. "And there's the rub," she said. "The publicity department at MediaNation has studied the reviews and the audience reaction statistics. They believe Vale Frazier will be a magnet for viewers. All the U.S. talk shows have expressed interest in having her appear. The movie

Vale's been working on in Vancouver has just wrapped, and MediaNation is booking her on all the U.S. talk shows that have expressed an interest."

"I don't see the problem," I said. "Vale's articulate; she spent hours talking with me about understanding Sally Love, and her performance is brilliant. She'll have no problem handling herself in an interview."

Jill was watching our faces closely. "Publicity has decided it will be good if Vale Frazier and Etienne Simard appear together for interviews. The rationale is that both are still relatively unknown, but the chemistry between them is good . . ."

"And if a potential viewer wants a peek at that chemistry, a video of Vale and Simard having raunchy sex together is just a click away," Zack said.

Jill kept her voice even. "I'm sure that was a factor in the decision," she said. "I tried to convince them to let Vale be interviewed solo, but apparently the joint interviews are already being publicized." She stood. "The only option now seems to be to prepare Taylor. I'm so sorry this is happening. I know it's pouring salt in Taylor's wound."

"When are these joint appearances going to start?" Zack said.

"This weekend. The series begins airing on September 25, so from now until at least the last episode of the series is shown, you can expect saturation coverage. I'll send you the schedule of the Vale-Simard interviews when it's finalized."

"I'm glad you told us," I said. "Forewarned is forearmed."

"And our daughter does not deserve another ambush," Zack said; his jaw was clenched tight.

* * *

After Jill left, Zack and I needed time to regain our equilibrium, and we both turned to the window to gaze out at the park. The deer had disappeared and with them the magic of the day. "We should go out to the lake," Zack said, finally.

"I agree," I said, "but not yet. Zack, we have to tread gently. Our daughter needs time and space to process everything that's happened. According to Jill, the interviews won't start till the weekend. Let's give Taylor another day to work through what's already happened before we pile this on her."

"Do you think the person who posted the outtake of Vale and Etienne Simard online was aware of how much pain that video would cause our daughter?"

"Taylor thought they knew what they were doing. And now that initial hurt is going to be compounded," I said. "I think we can help Taylor most if we're not hovering, but she knows we're there when she wants us."

Suddenly our lazy day had a chores list. If Zack was taking Friday off, there was a legal brief he had to work on, and I had to finish writing an article for a Festschrift honouring Howard Dowhanuik on his eightieth birthday in November. Worthy endeavours both, but the brief and the article would have to wait. Zack and I had a new grandson, and visiting Desmond Zackary took precedence over everything,

An hour later, when we left Mieka's, our phones were filled with photos and neither of us could stop smiling. I drove Zack downtown to the office and then went home to change for Soup and Bannock with Alison Janvier, an event being held at the Racette-Hunter Community Centre.

Along with Zack's law partner and our close friend Margot Hunter, Elder Ernest Beauvais and a score of others, Zack and I had been committed to making Racette-Hunter a reality.

The Centre, deep in the heart of one of our city's poorest and most crime-ridden neighbourhoods, had been the dream of Margot's late husband, Leland Hunter. Leland saw the centre as a place that would offer child care, recreational facilities, and programming and training for those who needed a second chance. The statistics for the number of students who, having completed courses that prepared them for employment, found jobs and continued to be employed were not overwhelmingly positive, but as we all pointed out, behind each number was a life that was no longer being wasted.

The Racette-Hunter Community Centre was an ideal venue for Alison to share her belief that the only way to elect a government committed to making our province work for all its citizens was for all its citizens to become politically involved. Voter turnout in North Central Regina was historically low and that had to change if its people were to have a voice in the government of our province.

Soup and Bannock with Alison Janvier had been the brainchild of Peggy Kreviazuk and Elder Ernest Beauvais, and it was an unqualified success. The prospect of eating hamburger stew and fry bread with friends and neighbours on a brisk but sunny day was a powerful lure, and the grassy area behind the centre was bright with quilts where families sat chatting and listening to a quartet of talented teenagers play songs about heartbreaks at the powwow, the amazing longevity of rez dogs and the blood-curdling power of the cannibalistic evil spirit Wendigo.

When I spied Elder Beauvais and Peggy Kreviazuk sharing a quilt, I knew I'd found my luncheon companions. After we'd greeted each other, Peggy patted the spot beside her on the quilt. "This is reserved for you," she said.

"Let's save the conversation till Joanne gets back with her meal," Ernest said. "We're a hungry crowd, and that hamburger stew is the best I've ever tasted."

Peggy looked at Ernest fondly. "You always say that."

Ernest, a retired iron worker, was a bear of a man, tall and large-featured, with a booming laugh that seemed to come from somewhere deep within him. "That's because it's always true," he said. "The best hamburger stew is always the one right in front of you."

"I'll ponder that while I'm standing in the lunch line," I said. I handed him my phone. "Meanwhile, you and Peggy can check out these photos of the newest member of our family, Desmond Zackary Dowhanuik, who arrived as scheduled on Labour Day."

Ernest beamed. "A young man who knows the importance of showing up on time. He'll do well in this life."

* * *

Ernest's assessment of the hamburger stew was right on the money. So was my choice of luncheon companions. A seemingly endless stream of visitors stopped by our quilt to say hello. Ernest and Peggy warmly welcomed all comers and then, seemingly without effort, steered the conversation to the role each member of the community needed to play if Alison Janvier were to become premier. After I wrote down their contact information, the callers invariably left with a big smile and a yellow and green "Ali" button.

It was time well spent, but I had an article to finish, and I was on my feet and ready to leave when Alison and a tall good-looking young man with copper skin, very white teeth and thick black hair worn in a traditional braid joined us. Both Alison and the young man were dressed casually, and in her cranberry pullover, form-fitting skinny jeans and multi-coloured sneakers, Alison was the embodiment of a leader who could get the job done. I'd worked for candidates with the brains and vision to lead a province, but whose uneasiness with the public was perceived as arrogance. An extrovert of modest intelligence with the ability to truly connect with voters would beat the smart introvert every time, but Alison was the whole package. That day, surrounded by people with concerns she understood and questions she could answer, she was in her element. She was doing something she loved and was good at, and as I watched her in action, I felt a frisson of excitement. It was possible that we might just win this one.

Alison's face lit up when she saw me. "Joanne, I'm so glad you're here. I wanted my son, Harper, to meet you."

Harper extended his hand. "My mother has been singing your praises, Ms. Shreve."

"Please. It's Joanne, and I've heard your wonderful news, Harper. Congratulations on winning the Lee Gowan Award!"

Harper rewarded me with a smile that was both shy and endearing. "I was totally zapped when I heard that I'd won. The award ceremony is in Toronto in November, and it's a big deal. I'm wearing my great grandfather's Métis sash. I'm pretty zapped about that too."

"I'm sure your whole family is."

"They are, and you know something else really special happened today. A courier came to my mum's apartment with a letter for me from Clay Fairbairn. He was one of the other people on the short list. He congratulated me on winning the award — which was cool, but what was really cool was receiving an actual letter. Nobody does that anymore, and it meant a lot to me. It also made me realize that maybe I should start writing letters to people when something special happens in their lives."

Alison squeezed her son's arm and turned to Ernest, Peggy and me. "I told you my son was a keeper," she said.

Like every young man whose doting mother has just publicly praised him, Harper rolled his eyes and muttered an exasperated "Mum."

It was a nice moment. "Your mother has every reason to be proud," I said. "Now, it's time for me to move along. We're going to the lake for the weekend, and there are always last-minute things to tend to. Congratulations again on the award, Harper."

Ernest raised one of his big hands, palm out in a halt gesture. "Harper, I would like to congratulate you too, but

I don't know what the Lee Gowan Award is. Can you fill me in?"

Seemingly from out of nowhere, a very slight and strikingly attractive young woman with fine features, white blond hair and a porcelain complexion appeared. Harper grinned when he saw her. "Hey Thalia, I was hoping you'd be here today."

"I knew you'd be here," she said. "And it seems I've arrived just in time." Given her diminutive size, Thalia's voice, deep and husky, was a surprise. "If Harper answers Elder Beauvais's question, he'll minimize his accomplishment. I'm from MediaNation, and Harper and I have already done an in-depth interview about the piece that won him the Lee Gowan." She held her hand out to Ernest Beauvais, and he rose to his feet to take it. "I promise you'll get the straight goods from me, Elder Beauvais," she said. "My name is Thalia Monk."

I was gobsmacked, and I blurted out what was on my mind. "I thought your surname was Morgan, like your mother's."

"I've reverted to my birth name." Thalia's eyes — cobalt blue and piercing — met mine. "And yes, my father is Joseph Monk. He works for MediaNation in Toronto. And you're Joanne Shreve, Jill Oziowy's friend."

Thalia's pivot to return her focus to Ernest meant her back was to me, and that was clearly her intent. Her tone as she addressed Ernest was deferential. "Elder Beauvais, may I join you and your friend on your quilt?"

Ernest was clearly charmed. "Of course," he said.

Thalia held out her hand to Harper, "Why don't you join us?" she said. "After all, you are the man of the hour."

Flushed with pleasure, Harper joined Thalia. I moved close to Alison. "That young woman knows how to take control," I said.

"She does indeed," Alison said, and she gestured for me to follow her to a spot that was out of earshot. "The courier who came to our place this morning brought a letter from Clay Fairbairn for *me* too."

"That's a shocker," I said. "What did he want?"

"Forgiveness," she said. "He explained that when he learned Harper had won the award, he was disappointed and he acted badly. He apologized for creating a situation that put me in danger. He said the incident had been a wake-up call for him. He was grateful that I hadn't been hurt, and he wanted me to know that something positive came out of what happened that day. Clay says he's been seeing a counsellor; he's cut himself off from the group with whom he'd always associated, and he's promised his grandparents he'll do everything he can to become a better man."

"Do you believe him?" I said.

"I want to," Alison said.

"So do I," I said.

Ali's dark eyes were troubled. "Maisie says that Jill Oziowy believes Clay is a sociopath."

"She does. Zack believes that too. Jill has had personal experiences with two men who were sociopaths, and Zack has had several as clients. Clay displays some troubling signs, and I'm sure Jill and Zack would advise you to be cautious about accepting Clay's letter as a genuine expression of his feelings."

"So, I shouldn't regard what he's written as the truth."

"I think you should regard what Clay wrote as the truth as he sees it," I said. "And who knows? If you accept his apology and offer support for his efforts to become a better man, you might tip the balance."

"Or Clay might have the last laugh and show my letter to the members of the cohort as proof that when it comes to manipulation, he is the master."

"Can you live with that possibility?" I said.

Ali's smile was sad and knowing. "Sure," she said. "I can live with being a laughingstock. What I can't live with is the possibility that I shut the door on someone who asked for my forgiveness."

"I needed to hear that," I said. "Zack always says I have a sunny view of human nature, but events lately have eclipsed my sunny view. I've become less trusting. I'm uneasy about the interview Thalia did with Harper. Could you make certain to get a copy of it before it's aired?"

"Consider it done," Alison said briskly. "I may have my Pollyanna moments, but I'm not stupid."

* * *

Alison was quick off the mark. When I checked my phone after dinner, I saw that she'd sent the MP3 file of Thalia's interview with Harper. Zack and I had planned a quiet evening, and when we'd cleared away the dinner dishes, we turned on the fireplace in the family room and sat down to listen to the interview.

It was a compelling piece, and Thalia Monk was a superb interviewer. Her deep throaty voice drew the listener into the small and intimate circle that seemed to enclose Thalia and her subject as they talked. She began by congratulating Harper Janvier on winning the Lee Gowan Award for his article on the disproportionately high rate of suicide of boys between the ages of ten and nineteen and of young men in their twenties.

When Thalia asked him to talk a little about what had drawn him to explore this subject, Harper paused before answering. "The pain," he said simply. "I saw it and I felt it in my own community. At first, my focus was on Indigenous boys and young men, but as I broadened my research, I saw that the statistics for suicide among non-Indigenous boys and young men were also disproportionately high, and that the risk factor for both groups was the same. These boys and young men shared the perception that they were facing a world that did not have a place for them."

"You gave your article the title 'Are We the Rabbits of *Watership Down?*'" Thalia said. "Could you explain why you made that choice?"

"Sure. I read *Watership Down* when I was a kid, and it stayed with me. The novel was written by Richard Adams and it follows a small group of rabbits seeking a place to establish a new haven after their home is destroyed." Harper stopped. "Have you read it, Thalia?"

"No," she said. "Until now I'd never even heard of it."

"I'll lend you my copy," Harper said. "Then we can talk about it together."

From that point on, the interview moved with the easy fluidity of a dance between a man and woman who wordlessly anticipated and responded to each other's thoughts.

When Harper explained that the rabbits encounter dangers along the way, and when one of their number dies, the survivors disappear into their burrows without acknowledging the death, Thalia's intake of breath was audible.

"They pretend nothing happened," she said, "and that's what we're doing with the boys and young men who commit suicide. When they cry for help, we disappear into our own lives and don't acknowledge what's happened. And your article is a challenge to us all to acknowledge the pain so many young men are feeling and reach out to them."

"Right," Harper said. "I wanted to shine a light on the need to talk about what is happening and explore the strategies that had been proposed for helping them find an answer to the questions that haunt them: 'Who am I really? Where do I fit in?'"

It was a compelling piece, and Zack and I were floating ideas about how to meet Harper's challenge when his phone rang. He took the call outside in the hall. When he returned fifteen minutes later, the creases that bracketed his mouth like parentheses had deepened — a sure sign he was confronting trouble.

"From the look on your face, I'm guessing we're going to shelve our discussion of Harper's article," I said.

"Yeah." From his laconic reply, I knew Zack's attention was elsewhere. "That was Warren on the phone. Mike Braeden's at the Webers' house. His wife attacked him."

After the drama at the Scarth Club dining room, I shouldn't have been surprised, but I found I was. "Patti attacked him physically? I can't believe it."

"According to Warren, Patti accused Mike of searching through her private papers. When Mike told her he had no idea what she was talking about, she lost it. She was holding a bottle of liquor. When Mike tried to take it from her, she smashed it and came at his face with the broken edge of the bottle. Mike was bleeding profusely and in no condition to drive, so he called the Webers. They live just a few doors from Mike on University Park Road, so they took him to Emergency. He's patched up and back at their place now, but Warren felt Mike needed to talk to a lawyer."

"And you're it."

"Looks like. Anyway, I should get going."

"I'll keep the bed warm."

Zack wheeled his chair closer and held out his arms to me. "Something to look forward to," he said.

* * *

For people like me, who have lived in Regina for much of their adult life, many street names convey information about the socio-economic status of those who live on them. Zack's reference to University Park Road conjured images of large, carefully landscaped homes with the close-to-the-ground profile and wide-open layouts of the ranch houses popular in the mid-twentieth century. Zack and I had been guests at parties or dinners in many of those homes, including the Webers', and my memories of the neighbourhood were pleasant, but as I turned down our bed, I thought of what Zack was facing and felt a coldness in the pit of my stomach.

It was half past ten when I heard the front door open and the swoosh of the wheels of Zack's chair as he came down the hall to our bedroom.

When he saw me sitting in the rocking chair by the window reading, Zack drew a deep breath and exhaled slowly. "I'm glad you're still up, because there's a cross-current in the Braeden case that's going to keep me awake. Talking it through might help."

"While you get ready for bed, I'll get us both a drink," I said. "Tea or something stronger?"

"Something stronger," Zack said. "Two fingers of bourbon neat, but you have slender fingers, so make that three."

Readying himself for bed was not a simple process for my husband, so I let out the dogs for a quick run around the yard and set the table for breakfast before I poured the drinks. When I returned to our room, Zack was in his robe waiting by the window. I handed Zack his drink and settled into the rocking chair with mine.

Zack took a large sip of bourbon and groaned with contentment. "That's soothing, thanks."

"You're welcome. Start when you're ready."

"I wasn't prepared for how bad Mike's face was. Patti did a real number on him. Luckily, she missed his eyes. Warren's going to help him check out plastic surgeons tomorrow."

"Mike must be in a great deal of pain."

Zack nodded. "He's an athlete, and athletes learn to play through pain, but it must hurt like hell. They gave him something at the hospital, but the opioid crisis has put the fear of God in everybody, so Mike's doctors haven't given him any heavy duty stuff."

"How are his spirits?"

"He's stoic, and Annie has done wonders with him already. By the time I got there, she'd managed to get Mike showered and into a clean robe and slippers, and she was at the mall getting him the toiletries and clothes he'd need in the immediate future."

"Annie's amazing," I said. "She never backs down from a challenge, and she never misses a beat. Managing a biker bar obviously builds character. So, what's next?"

Zack sipped his drink. "That's where the complications begin. Mike doesn't want the police involved. His only concern is Patti's daughter. He says he's never seen a human being suffer the way Thalia has suffered. He married Patti because he thought he could give Thalia some stability in her life."

"Did he manage to connect with Thalia?"

"No, Mike said the damage that had been done to her was irreparable."

"Does he know the source of the damage?"

"Mike knew that Thalia's brother committed suicide, but she refused to talk about his death. Mike said Thalia never mentioned Nicholas by name, but she wore a lock of his hair in an amulet around her neck."

"A grief amulet," I said. "People used to wear those, gen-erations ago. That's heartbreaking."

"And Mike is determined to protect her at any cost," Zack said.

"That means not involving the police," I said. "But Mike can't ignore what happened tonight."

"No. Having his wife attempt to tear off his face with a broken liquor bottle was definitely a tipping point." My hus-band's tone was ineffably weary. "Mike asked me to arrange an appointment for him with one of the firm's divorce law-yers, and I'll do that. I also took pictures of Mike's injuries and his discharge papers from the hospital. And I filmed him telling me exactly what happened and Warren explaining his role in the evening's events."

"Pretty much what the police would have done if they'd been involved," I said.

Zack nodded. "Pretty much. Also pretty much what Mike's lawyer will need if Ms. Morgan contests the divorce."

"So, that's it for tonight?"

"That was it for Warren and me. But after Annie came home, she went down the street to see how Patti was doing and to learn if the housekeeper knew where Thalia was."

"And the housekeeper was willing to talk to Annie?"

"Halima and Annie are friends," Zack said. "Halima's teaching Annie how to weave, and she's very fond of Mike, so she was glad she could be of help tonight."

"So, what's the situation at the Braedens?"

"Thalia arrived home an hour ago, and by that time Halima had the house straightened up, and Patti was in bed, asleep or whatever passes for sleep for that poor woman. Halima told Thalia there'd been some 'angry words' between her mother and Mike. As soon as Thalia heard that Mike was fine and staying at the Webers', she made a phone call, packed an overnight bag and said she'd be staying overnight at a friend's."

"No questions about her mother?"

"Not a one." Zack furrowed his brow. "Jo, what's your take on Thalia?"

"To paraphrase Churchill on Russia, Thalia Monk is a riddle, wrapped in a mystery, inside an enigma. She's a complex young woman who carries the key to everything she is in the grief amulet that contains a lock of her dead brother's hair."

"That day at the Scarth Club we had a glimpse of the pain she lives with," Zack said. "It's hard to reconcile that broken child we saw with the poised and polished interviewer we just heard on the tape with Harper. Discussing the tragedy of young men who see suicide as their only escape must have been excruciating for Thalia, but she never faltered. She's learned to keep her demons under control." He drained his glass. "That's no small accomplishment. Mike Braeden recognizes that. My guess is that's why he hung on so long to an empty marriage."

"When it came to helping a troubled child, his first wife was as dogged as Mike. That's why Mieka has Sylvie Braeden's photograph where kids can see it at April's Place. Sylvie always gravitated towards helping the child who wasn't easy to love — the one with attitude, or with a chip on their shoulder the size of a boulder. There are plenty of kids like

that at April's Place, and Mieka sometimes uses Sylvie's picture as a way to reach those kids.

"Sylvie was realistic; she accepted the fact that for every
step forward, there would be two steps back. And, of course,
most of the time there isn't a Hallmark ending; the damage is
too great. But Sylvie always stayed the course. She said, 'No
matter what happens in the future, those children will always
remember there was someone who never gave up on them.'"

CHAPTER THIRTEEN

The next morning, Zack had just left for an appointment with his barber when Alison Janvier called. "Is there a time today when you and I can talk?"

"How about right now?" I said. "Zack's getting a haircut, and we're packed and ready to go to the lake when he gets home."

"I'll be there in ten minutes," Ali said. "Jo, I know you're trying to get out of town, but I need your advice."

"Come ahead," I said, but I had to admit that I was surprised. I was still writing the occasional speech for Alison, but I had slipped quietly and gratefully into the role of consultant. Realizing that working on his mother's campaign for premier would give him a unique perspective on our province's political life, Harper was not returning to university until after Christmas. Alison was comfortable delivering her stump speech. It was always well received, and Harper was proving to be a gifted and efficient researcher, providing the information about specific communities that his mother needed to respond knowledgeably during her Q&A sessions.

I was still contemplating situations in which Alison might need my help when she arrived. She didn't drink tea or coffee and she turned down my offer of water, so the two of us went to the kitchen, pulled up chairs and got right to it.

Alison usually wore her shoulder-length hair in a ponytail or low chignon, but that morning her shiny, thick, black hair was loose and still damp from the shower. With her forearms resting in front of her, hands clasped, on the butcher block table, she looked like a schoolgirl poised to deliver a report. "Thalia Monk stayed at our place last night," she said. "Her mother has emotional problems, and apparently she had a breakdown. Thalia said their housekeeper assured her the situation was in hand, and that her stepfather was staying with friends, so Thalia packed her bag and came to our place."

"I didn't realize she and Harper were that close," I said.

Alison's expression was impassive, but when she spoke, her tone was chilly. "Neither did I, but preparing for the interview seems to have brought them together. Thalia said she's been thinking about moving out of the Braeden home for a while, and last night convinced her it was time to look for her own place. Apparently, she has friends she can stay with until she finds what she needs."

"But she didn't stay with those friends last night."

Alison raised an eyebrow. "No, Thalia chose Harper. She said her closest friends are the sons of friends of her stepfather, and she didn't want to place Mike Braeden in an awkward situation."

"Ali, are you concerned about the relationship between Harper and Thalia?"

"I am, but that's not why I'm here. Harper's always been astute at reading people, so I'm trusting him."

"You're a good mother," I said. "And a wise one. So, what do you need my advice about?"

"Thalia's come up with an idea she believes has merit, and she may be right. She's spoken to the producer of Charlie D's program, and he's supporting her idea. For the past week or so, I've been handing the microphone to Harper after the Q&A, so he can thank the audience and invite them to join our campaign. Thalia's been attending our events, and she's noticed the stacks of sign-up sheets Harper collects after every appearance. She says Harper's smart, attractive and effective, and he's offering millennials who are tired of being dismissed as the 'me, me, me' generation an appealing example of an alternate way of life.

"Thalia's written up a proposal for a podcast series produced by millennials featuring millennials committed to civic and political engagement. Ginny Monaghan is running as an independent in Saskatoon Fairview and both her daughters are working on her campaign. Thalia's already spoken to Emma and Chloe Monaghan, and they're in. Clay Fairbairn has approached Patrick Sinclair whose mother is running for the Saskatchewan Party in Swift Current, and he's keen on the idea."

"Sounds like it's a *fait accompli*," I said.

"Why do you think Thalia made certain she had commitments from the other two campaigns before she came to me?"

"Easy-peasy," I said. "Harper's the one Thalia's after, and she wanted to put you in a position where you had to say yes."

"And that's where I am."

"You've been painted into a corner," I said. "I just wish I understood what was going on."

"Only one way to find out," Ali said. She opened her crossbody bag, removed her phone, tapped in a message and then turned to me. "I just told Thalia I need twenty-four hours to think through the proposal before I give her an answer."

"But you have already decided," I said.

"Of course. My only option is to say yes, but now Thalia has twenty-four hours to second-guess herself." Ali's lips curled in private amusement. "And I have twenty-four hours to watch the paint dry."

* * *

When Zack returned from the barbershop, his mood was mellow. "Second best thing to do on a Friday morning."

"It was worth the effort. You're gorgeous."

My husband's smile was almost bashful. "Guido gives his customers first-class treatment: quality haircut and a hot lather, straight-razor shave."

I rubbed my cheek against Zack's. "So smooth, and you smell like somebody I'd like to get closer to."

"Clubman talc on my neck and Bay Rum aftershave."

"I haven't made our bed yet," I said.

"Do you want a hand?"

"A hand would be a very good start," I said. "I'll go down and fluff the pillows."

* * *

I waited until we were at the turnoff to Lawyers Bay before I mentioned Alison Janvier's visit that morning. Traffic was light, and warmed by the afterglow of good sex, it was a treat simply to listen to Oscar Peterson and savour the vibrant golds and blues that saturate the Saskatchewan landscape in mid-September.

When I described Thalia's proposal for the millennial podcast, Zack was unconcerned. "Let's not overthink this," he said. "The most obvious interpretation of Thalia's plotting is that she's attracted to Harper, and she wants to create a situation that keeps them in close proximity." He gave me a sidelong glance. "That said, Alison's strategy of delaying the announcement of her decision for twenty-four hours was a smooth move. Thalia should know that Alison is aware that she's being played."

When we left the house, I'd texted Taylor to let her know we were on our way, but I gave her the option of catching up with us later in the day if she was working. She'd texted back, "Good call," so I was surprised when she met us at the gate to our property, hopped in the back seat with the dogs and said, "Floor it, Dad." She helped us carry in and put away the groceries, praised the teeter-totter for the twins that I'd scored at a garage sale and then made us tea.

The day was overcast, but it was still pleasant enough to have our tea on the deck, so we sat outside, enjoying the quiet and the sight of the dogs reveling in their no-leash freedom. An idyllic scene, but there was tension in the air as we waited for Taylor to mention Vale. Finally, Zack took the proverbial bull by the horns. "How was your week, Taylor?"

Surprisingly, Taylor answered with a smile. Her smile was like Sally's — broad and generous but always tempered by a flicker of mockery that played across her lips. "To quote you, Dad, 'The week was shitty, but I'm still here.'"

"And your mum and I are grateful for that," Zack said. "Are you ready to talk about it?"

"I think I am," she said. "So much has happened since I left Vancouver, but I've finally made some tentative plans about what comes next for me, and I'd like your opinion."

"Whenever you're ready," Zack said.

Taylor took a deep breath. "On Tuesday, my old pal 'Concerned Friend' sent me a copy of Vale and Etienne Simard's travel schedule for *Sisters and Strangers*. Concerned Friend included a list of the hotels where they'd be staying 'in case I wanted to pay them a surprise visit.'"

Zack's eyes were blazing and he moved his chair closer to our daughter as if to protect her. "How the hell would someone get hold of that information?"

"That's a question worth asking," I said. "I'll have to check with Jill about this, but I suspect the hotel information would be kept pretty much in-house."

"Jo's right, Dad. The people who arrange the tours try to limit the number of people who know where the actors are staying. When I travelled with Vale for *The Happiest Girl* tour, we were told we shouldn't give anyone the names of our hotels. And every time Vale left the hotel, there would be a publicist with her to make sure that she arrived for her interviews safely and on time. Our relationship may be over, but I do care about Vale. She'll be protected. And now that Vale and I are no longer together, my private life will be private again. No one will care about where I am or what I do. The only story the tabloids can print about Vale and me now is that we are no longer a couple."

I felt the first fingers of a headache. "And Vale has accepted this?"

"Yes, because she had to. Concerned Friend's last communication was the push I needed to tell Vale what I needed to tell her. She'd called and texted dozens of times after I left Vancouver, but I never responded because I was afraid that when I heard her voice, I'd cave."

"But you did call Vale," Zack said.

Taylor hesitated before she answered. When the colour rose from her neck to her cheeks, it was clear she was embarrassed about what she was about to say. "No, Dad, nothing as simple and sensible as a phone call for me. I took the high drama route. I hopped in the car and drove straight to our condo on Dewdney. Gracie wanted to come with me, but I knew I had to be alone to do what needed to be done. Most of my luggage was still in Vancouver, so I packed my stuff in some big green garbage bags and hauled them to the front door. Then I piled all Vale's things on the bed in the guest room, called the cleaning service we used and told them to send someone over ASAP. I asked them to put everything on the guest room bed in mailing boxes, and I'd call them later with an address. Then I lugged the garbage bags out to the hall and locked the door to Vale's and my first and last home together."

For a few seconds, the pain of the memory stopped Taylor, but she carried on. "By the time I got to my car, the heaviness that had been pressing down on me since Vale told me about her relationship with Etienne had lifted. I was ready to pick up the phone and call Vale, and I did."

"And you're all right," Zack said.

Taylor's dark eyes darted from Zack to me and then back to her dad. "Yes, I'm all right. As it turns out, Concerned Friend did me a favour. I'm free at last." She paused. "Now if it's okay with you, I'm going to my studio to make some art."

"It's more than okay," I said. "But before you get back to work, give your old parents a hug."

We said our goodbyes, then Zack and I watched until our daughter disappeared inside the studio we'd built for her when we married. "Is it too early for a sigh of relief about her plans for the foreseeable future?" he said.

"No, Taylor's decision to make a clean break with Vale seems to have been the right move for her. But Zack, there's so much that's not right here. Taylor says Concerned Friend did her a favour by sending her Vale and Etienne Simard's itinerary, but she knows as well as we do that was not the intent. Twice someone has sent Taylor information about Vale that they knew would hurt her. It has to be someone she knows. I'll check with Jill about those travel schedules."

"So, another link to MediaNation," Zack said. "Ellen Exton, Rosemary Morrissey, Patti Morgan, Clay Fairbairn, Ronan Farquhar, Thalia Monk — and now Concerned Friend." He shrugged. "But it's just a list of names unless we can connect the dots."

"And the dots don't appear to have a pattern — at least not one I can see," I said. "Ellen and Rosemary have disappeared; Patti Morgan seems to have withdrawn into her own private hell; Maisie put the fear of God into Ronan Farquhar; and I'm sure that by now the band of warriors knows we're watching them. Clay Fairbairn has, at least in theory, severed himself from the cohort and is working with Thalia Monk on a podcast project about millennials that will draw new listeners to MediaNation and give Thalia and him an impressive credit on their résumés."

Zack raised an eyebrow. "So, we're going to operate on the 'Move along. There's nothing to see here' strategy?"

"No," I said. "I'm sure there's plenty to see. We just can't see it yet."

"So, we sit back and wait for the Rosetta stone that will answer all our questions?" Zack's headshake was vehement. "Jo, we both know that time is not on our side. We have to do something."

"Agreed," I said. "Any ideas about what we do?"

Zack leaned forward. "Just one. Let's go for broke: poke the hive and hope that all hell will break loose."

As it turned out, it was Jill Oziowy who poked the hive. When I called to ask her about the distribution of the list of tour hotels, I got her voicemail. She returned my call almost immediately. "I was just about to call you," she said, and her voice was tight. "Something's come up that Kam Chau and I would like to talk to you and Zack about."

"We're at the lake, but we'll be back on Monday," I said. "Can it wait?"

"No, Jo, if you don't mind, Kam and I will come out there. Kam's in a production meeting with Charlie D, but it should be over soon. We can be at Lawyers Bay in an hour."

"Come ahead," I said. "We'll have a late lunch."

"Don't worry about feeding us," Jill said. "We'll grab something from the cafeteria and eat in the car."

All morning, the weather had been hazy, but just as Jill and Kam pulled up at the gate to Lawyers Bay, the clouds lifted and the air cleared. When it came to omens, I had schooled myself to ignore the bad and seize the good. For me, the fact that the lake was suddenly sun-splashed, and the world around us once again appeared in sharp focus were signs that we were on the right track.

Like Zack and me, Jill and Kam wore hiking boots, blue jeans and pullovers in the warm, turning-leaf shades of autumn. This was Zack and Kam's first meeting, and Kam won my husband over with his first words. After giving the landscape an assessing one-eighty, he said, "This is my dream."

Zack's expression was pensive. "You know, Kam, I owned this place for over twenty years without giving it a second thought. It was just a place to come if my partners and I needed to get away from the office. Then I married Joanne, and it was as if I suddenly saw this place for the first time."

Zack and I exchanged a quick, affectionate glance and then Zack wheeled over to Kam. "But this isn't about my shock of recognition. This is about making you welcome. Are you up for an abbreviated grand tour?"

"Lead the way," Kam said.

Jill touched Zack's arm. "If you don't mind, I'll take a rain check. Jo and I have some catching up to do."

"Understood," Zack said.

Jill and I watched in silence as the two men disappeared into the russet and amber foliage of the Amur maples. "People are full of surprises," she said. "Kam never struck me as a country living kind of guy. But he and I both needed to get away. We're hoping distance will bring clarity." Jill shivered and hugged herself.

"It's getting chilly," I said. "Let's go inside, find some comfy chairs and make a pot of tea — my grandmother's panacea for all life's problems."

The house was invitingly warm, and as we had so often over the years, Jill and I headed for the kitchen. I filled the kettle, and Jill wandered over to the refrigerator to check out the latest photos of the grandkids on the fridge door. She took a long moment looking at them, and when she sat down at the table, there was sadness in her eyes.

"I remember when Madeleine was born," Jill said. "And now she's in grade eight, the *crème de la crème* of Pius X."

I smiled. "I was thinking something along those lines myself this morning. In grade three Madeleine developed a passion for limousines. She drew endless pictures of them, and when Zack let it slip that he'd actually ridden in a few limos, she pleaded with him for details. Kids usually blow through phases, but Madeleine has always been resolute. Zack was impressed. A few days before Madeleine's birthday, he asked Mieka what she thought of us hiring a limo for an hour to pick up Madeleine, Lena and some of their school friends, drive them past the legislature, through Wascana Park and then home.

"Mieka thought it was a great idea, so we hired the limo. Zack says it's the best eighty bucks we ever spent, and he's right. When that long white Lincoln pulled into the parking area at Pius, the kids swarmed it. Mieka, Zack and I were there for the big moment. The driver approached Madeleine, doffed his cap and said, 'Happy Birthday, Miss.' She turned to us, and her eyes were like saucers. 'When I saw this limousine, I never thought it would be for me. I was sure it would be for one of the grade eights.'"

Jill's smile was rueful. "And now Madeleine's a member of the elite."

"She is indeed." I paused. "Jill, how are things with you?"

"As far as work is concerned, all is well. The new programming is rolling out smoothly, and the response to it has been even better than we'd hoped for. My colleagues are no longer so tense that their shoulders are permanently hunched at ear level, and morale is definitely on the uptick."

"And personally?"

Jill shrugged. "Personally, I'm finally facing the fact that I inflicted some wounds on your family that will never heal. I've decided to go back to Toronto at Thanksgiving. I'm having dinner with Hugh Fairbairn tonight, and I'll tell him then." The room was warm, but Jill shivered. A shawl was hanging on a hook by the back door. I went over, took down the shawl and draped it over Jill's shoulders. She pulled it tight. "Did Mieka tell you she and I ran into each other at MediaNation yesterday?"

The kettle whistled. Grateful for the chance to delay answering Jill's question, I took the kettle off the burner, warmed the teapot, measured the tea and poured in the boiling water. Then I arranged the tea things on a tray and carried the tray back to the table. When I sat down opposite her, Jill's gaze was questioning.

"Mieka didn't mention running into you," I said. "But with the new baby and getting the girls back into the school routine, her plate has been full. We haven't had time for a real talk. Was there a problem?"

Jill shook her head wearily. "No blows were exchanged," she said. "In retrospect, that might have been easier. The encounter didn't last much more than a minute, but it was long enough to convince me that Mieka will never let me into her life again."

"What happened?"

"Nothing really," Jill said. "I had an outside appointment and when I came upstairs and walked into the galleria, Mieka was at the reception desk with our officer of visitor relations, Mark Evanson. Mark was holding your new grandson, and he and Mieka were laughing. I had a flashback to seeing the two of them together at political events when they were kids. It was a nice moment, and I was just about to sneak out the front door when Mieka spotted me.

"Jo, she froze. I was her godmother; I taught her how to tie her shoelaces. I played endless games of Crazy Eights with her when she had the flu. When she and her first serious boyfriend broke up, we split a tub of Ben & Jerry's Cherry Garcia and listened to 'A Rainy Night in Soho' by the Pogues at least fifty times. Mieka had been one of the best parts of my life, and now even seeing me turns her to stone."

"I'm so sorry."

"I brought it on myself," Jill said. "That's what the nuns always told us." Jill's expression was part wry, part defiant. "And it gets worse. Mark Evanson is a truly nice guy, but he's not quick. He misread the situation. When Mieka froze, Mark assumed the problem was that she didn't remember me. He was so relieved that he'd actually solved the problem that he was grinning from ear to ear. He said, 'Mieka, this is Jill Oziowy. She was your dad's chief of staff when he was attorney general.' When Mieka mumbled something about remembering me, Mark turned to me. 'Jill, I bet you'd like to hold Ian Kilbourn's grandson,' and then he tried to hand Desmond to me."

My heart sank. There were no words, and I didn't even try. Jill soldiered on. "Mieka was not about to let me anywhere near her new son. She took the baby from Mark and said, 'We all think of my stepfather, Zack Shreve, as Desmond's grandfather. This little guy's full name is Desmond Zackary Dowhanuik. Charlie D and I named our son after three people our son can be proud of.'"

There was no masking the pain in Jill's voice. Nothing I could say would allay it, so I did what generations of women faced with a heartbreaking situation had done. I picked up the teapot and poured.

When she lifted her cup, Jill's expression was dubious. "Do you really think this will help?" she said.

"It should," I said. "It's your old favourite, Constant Comment."

Jill took a sip and her eyes widened. "I'd forgotten how good this is." She swallowed hard. "I'm glad you remembered."

We finished our tea in silence, and then I refilled our cups. "Jill, I'm guessing your encounter with Mieka tipped the scales and that's why you've decided to leave Regina at Thanksgiving. But that's too soon. Thanksgiving is just a few weeks away."

Jill's sigh came from the depth of her body. "No use prolonging the agony," she said.

"I think you should give the situation more time," I said. "At least until Christmas. Howard's in Toronto teaching until then, so the condo's all yours. You're enjoying your work. You have nothing to lose by staying, and if you walk away at Thanksgiving, you'll always wonder if things might have been different. Jill, I know my daughter. You said she was one of the best parts of your life. You were one of the best parts of Mieka's life too. She needs you as much as you need her. Stick around."

"Are you sure about this, Jo?"

"I am. When you told me about Mieka turning to stone when she saw you, I realized that, for all our sakes, we have to keep trying." I reached over and touched her hand. "It was my Saul on the road to Damascus moment."

Jill's half smile was mocking, but her extraordinary tawny eyes were filled with hope. "You saw the light?" she said.

"Something like that. Jill, we all have to move on. It's been almost twenty years since Ian died. The Kilbourn family that you knew — Ian, me, Mieka, Peter and Angus — doesn't exist anymore. We've grown older, we've added new people to our family and we've all changed."

"Even Angus?" Jill said.

I laughed. "No, Angus is still Angus. He loves working at the Calgary office of Falconer Shreve; hiking, skiing and going for beer on the Red Mile with the other associates after Stampeders' games."

"Life has always been a cabaret for Angus," Jill said fondly.

"It has," I agreed. "But at his request, Angus is coming back to work in the firm's Regina office. His first love, Leah Drache, is moving back here to practise medicine." I'd been watching Jill's face carefully, and I was almost certain she was wavering. I waited a long moment. "Jill, why don't you stay in town long enough to see if Angus's first love turns out to be the one?"

"Are you sure?"

"I am," I said. "There'll be some rough patches along the way, but I'll be there."

Jill set a soft hand on my shoulder. "Thank you," she said. "I'll stay."

We cleared away the tea things and the next time we looked out the window the men had returned. They were in the driveway peering at the engine of Kam's Chrysler hybrid: Zack's expression was as intense as that of a person who had just discovered the one true faith, and Kam's face shone with the bliss of a zealot who had just snagged a convert.

When they finally came in, they carried with them the bracing scent of fresh cold air and more information about real-time power readings, pre-programmed charging and the efficiency coaching tool than I was able to process.

Finally, they wound down. "Time to deal with the issue at hand," Zack said. "Before we begin, can I get anyone anything? If you're up for a beer, Joanne and I discovered a very nice local lager."

"Sounds good," Kam said.

Jill and I exchanged a look. "Jill and I've been hitting the Constant Comment pretty hard," I said. "I think we'll pass."

When the four of us had settled at the partners' table, Zack leaned forward. "We're here to piece together the information we have, so we can figure out what the hell is going on. Kam, do you want to get us started?"

"Sure." Kam took a sip from his glass and gave a quiet sign of satisfaction. "Patti Morgan came to my office this morning. The fact that she was even in the building was unusual. The cancellation of *Sunny Side Up* had been difficult for her. She understood that the network needed a stronger local lead-in to the news hour they'd scheduled, but *Sunny Side Up* had been her life.

"The parting was amicable, but as far as I know, Patti hadn't been at MediaNation since the farewell show. This morning she was only in the building for a few minutes, but that was long enough for me to realize that she needed help. Patti was raging. Her words came in a torrent, and they made no sense. She said, 'Don't believe anything anybody tells you about my son. Don't let them taint his memory. He was perfect in every way.'

"Patti's arms were flailing, and I was afraid she was going to hurt herself, so I took hold of her wrists. I tried to reason with her. I told her that no one was going to say anything, that Nicholas had been gone for years and that what happened was in the past.

"She wrenched away from me. She was sobbing. 'People always leave something behind,' she said. 'Mike Braeden has been trying to force me to see a therapist. Those people can give you drugs that make you tell secrets. Every time I leave the house, Mike goes through my personal things searching for ugly lies about my son that he can give to a therapist to use against me.'"

"What did you do?" Zack asked.

"I tried to reason with Patti. When that failed, I tried to soothe her, but she was unreachable. Finally, she just turned and ran up the stairs that lead to the main entrance. That's when I went to Jill."

"I'd just ended a call from a source telling me that last night Mike Braeden ended up in Emergency after he'd been attacked with a broken bottle," Jill said. "Our source said she'd overheard Mike asking the admitting nurse not to call the police because it was a 'family matter.'"

"After Jill related what the source told her, she and I agreed it would be wrong not to warn Mike that Patti was out of control. We tried his home and office — Mike wasn't there, but I spoke to his executive assistant. I explained the situation and she said that you were Mike's lawyer, and that you could get a message to him if you felt it was necessary."

Zack nodded. "That was sound advice. Had Ms. Morgan been drinking when she came to your office?"

"I don't think so. Patti has suffered so much. Everyone who knows her was hoping that she'd find peace when she married Mike Braeden. And for a while, it seemed she had. Then just before Christmas last year, something happened. Rosemary noticed the change in Patti too, and she asked me if Patti had mentioned anything to me about a family problem. When I said no, she thanked me and walked away. In the next few months, Rosemary came to me several times to ask if Patti had spoken to me about the difficulties she was experiencing. I hadn't seen Patti in weeks, but by that point, I'd heard enough about her risky behaviours to be concerned. I suggested we talk to Patti's husband about professional help for her. Rosemary said she wasn't sure that was wise, but she'd consider it. She never mentioned the idea again. Then after the May long weekend, Rosemary's behaviour started to deteriorate, and MediaNation had a far more pressing problem.

"The morning after Rosemary left the building for the last time, I discovered this under a script on my desk." Kam removed a torn piece of paper from his laptop case and placed it on the partners' table.

My husband reached over, smoothed the paper and read aloud the words handwritten in black ink: "I am warning you not to be fooled. This person is young, charismatic, narcissistic and capable of . . ." Zack narrowed his eyes. "Kam,

I'm assuming that whatever came before and after those words had been torn off when you found the paper. Is this Rosemary Morrissey's handwriting?"

"Yes. She always used a fountain pen and black ink, but her handwriting was like Rosemary herself — strong, distinctive and controlled. This is almost a scribble, but there's no doubt in my mind that she wrote it and that she tore this section from a larger piece of writing."

Zack leaned back in his chair. "A letter to you, but she decided against sending the entire letter, so she just ripped off the part that mattered — the warning. Kam, did you show this to anyone else?"

"No. Not until today." Kam gestured towards the fragment of paper on the work table. "Look at it. A few scribbled words written by someone who removed the words that completed her thought because she didn't trust what she was thinking. At the time, this scrap of paper just seemed to be further proof that Rosemary was *non compos mentis*, and her reputation was already in shreds."

"The interns' exit letter certainly points to the fact that Rosemary had an enemy," I said. "Her suspicion that something was very wrong seems to be well founded."

Kam shook his head. "Except there's nothing in the exit letter that isn't factual. The three people who were in the room when Rosemary criticized Thalia for reading Nietzsche believed Rosemary was simply trying to protect Thalia. Thalia felt Rosemary's comment was gratuitous and condescending. Clearly, the interpretations of the four people, including Thalia, who heard what Rosemary said, differ, but they agree on the words she used. And Thalia's account of the words I used when she reported on her encounter with Rosemary is factually true, but she and I perceived the exchange differently. I saw my advice as an attempt to soothe troubled waters; Thalia saw it as a warning that she and the other interns should keep their complaints to themselves."

Zack placed his forefinger on the fragment of paper on the work table. "Once again, it's a matter of interpretation," he said. "And, squaring the circle, it takes us back to the question of whether the person who wrote this warning was of sound mind. And the only person who can answer that is Ms. Morrissey."

"Who has seemingly disappeared," Kam said. "Rosemary's colleagues — and that includes me — dropped the ball on that one. When the days turned to weeks, and we still hadn't heard from Rosemary, we should have followed up, but we didn't. Rosemary had frequently travelled to places most of us couldn't identify on a map, and she wasn't a fan of sharing her life on social media, so we assumed that she was simply doing what she'd done before. Of course, that meant brushing away an inconvenient fact. In the past, Rosemary believed we were her friends and on her last day at MediaNation, she had learned that we had all written letters that betrayed her."

"From what I've been told, the rationale for writing the letters was compelling," Zack said. "MediaNation was gambling heavily on the new season, and, for reasons no one could comprehend, Rosemary was screwing up. She was a burden the corporation could no longer afford to carry, and they felt it was time to cut their losses. All the head of HR at MediaNation was asking you to do was to tell the truth."

"And the truth destroyed a gifted woman who was suffering a health crisis," Kam said.

Zack wheeled his chair over to Kam and, in a gesture he seldom made with anyone outside the family, he put his arm around Kam's shoulder. "Don't beat yourself up over this. You and your colleagues did what most of us do when we're offered the easy way out of a situation in which we know we behaved badly. Now, let's finish our beer and go out and look at that hybrid of yours. I still have some questions that I'd like answered."

Jill and I went to the door with the men and watched as they ran appreciative hands over the Chrysler's shining flanks and chatted.

"We're witnessing what appears to be the beginning of a friendship," I said.

"And you and I have taken the first steps towards resurrecting a friendship that I thought had ended," Jill said quietly. "Despite everything, it's been a very good afternoon."

"It has," I agreed, "and I wish we could just bask in the glow. But, Jill, there is something else."

My account of Concerned Friend's communications with Taylor was delivered in broad brush strokes, but Jill was quick to see the picture. "You're wondering whether the fact that Concerned Friend had access to Vale's publicity itinerary suggests that they have a connection with MediaNation. I would say that's a strong possibility. The information about hotel accommodations is distributed sparingly. Hotels don't want their lobbies filled with fans and paparazzi, and there are always security concerns."

"Any ideas about the identity of Concerned Friend?" I said.

"That message Rosemary left on Kam's desk is significant," Jill said. "Despite their betrayal, Rosemary cared about the people in her unit. She wrote that message as a warning. At the last moment, she might have lost her nerve and ripped off the specifics. But she left enough of the message to alert her colleagues to the fact that they were facing danger."

"The exit letter was presented as a collective effort, but Kam is sure Thalia Monk was the driving force behind it. Do you believe that Thalia was also the danger Rosemary felt compelled to warn her colleagues about?"

"I think we have to face the fact that's a distinct possibility," Jill said tightly. "And ridding ourselves of Thalia will not be a simple matter."

"Because her parents are Patti Morgan and Joseph Monk," I said.

"Patti's too mired in her own misery to do much of anything," Jill said. "Over the years, Joseph Monk has formed some powerful alliances at MediaNation, but Thalia is her own winning lottery ticket. She's pitched a project that Hugh Fairbairn is very keen on."

"The millennials on millennials project," I said.

Jill's eyes widened. "That's supposed to be under wraps. How did you hear about it?"

"Alison Janvier came to our place this morning to talk about it."

"Then you know all the pieces are in place except for Harper Janvier's involvement," Jill said. "It's a good gig for him. Why did Alison throw up a roadblock?"

As I described Thalia's strategy for ensuring that she and Harper would be a team, Jill was first curious and then amused. "Thalia really is daddy's little girl," she said. "Joseph knows how to move the pieces around the board too, but it sounds like little Thalia may have met her match. She was not happy about having to wait twenty-four hours for Harper's decision. Neither was Clay Fairbairn. He was afraid Harper was going to deep-six the project, and he went straight to his grandfather. When we were on the way out here, Hugh called to ask me if I knew anyone who could talk to Harper. I said that Harper was nineteen years old, and he would not take kindly to being pressured."

"And he accepted that? From what I've heard, Hugh Fairbairn is not a man who takes no for an answer."

"He trusts my judgment, Jo. Hugh and I have always been fond of each other, but working together on this new programming has been exciting for us both and it's drawn us together."

Jill spotted the concern in my eyes. "We really are just friends. I won't lie to you. The attraction has always been there, but Hugh would never do anything that would jeopardize his relationship with his grandson."

"Where does Julie fit in?"

"Hugh never talks about Julie. Clay is another matter. He loves that boy, and he worries about him. Hugh sees this millennial project as something that could earn Clay the approval he so desperately seeks. And Hugh believes that Thalia — brilliant, creative, committed — could help Clay become the man he has the potential to be."

"Jill, if Hugh loves Clay that much, you should find a way of convincing him that Clay doesn't need Thalia Monk. Thalia will always overshadow anyone with whom she works. That's not a value judgment; it's simply a fact. If Clay handled the production of the podcast on one of the other campaigns, he'd be the golden boy, and he would be the one positioned to expand the millennials on millennials concept in new directions."

Jill slumped. "You're right, of course, and I'll try. But Hugh is convinced Thalia is the one 'capable of bringing Clay into himself.' And as much as Hugh respects me, he'll have questions that I can't answer. Jo, we have no proof that Thalia has done anything wrong. All we have is a scrap of paper that appears to have been written by Rosemary Morrissey to her colleagues, warning them that somebody is capable of something. We're the ones who are filling in the blanks. Hugh won't buy that." Jill took both my hands in hers. "But I do. Watch your back, Jo, and pass the warning along to the people who need to know."

CHAPTER FOURTEEN

Zack and I followed Kam and Jill outside to say our good-byes and watched until Kam's Chrysler passed through the security gates and headed for the highway. When it was out of sight, I turned to my husband. "So, is there a hybrid in our future?"

"That's a decision we'll make together," Zack said. "And it will be a relief to have something positive to focus on."

"I take it that when you and Kam took your walk in the woods, you talked about more than the pleasures of country living."

Zack nodded. "We did. But the first order of business is to call Warren, so he can alert Mike Braeden to the fact that Patti Morgan continues to be in a very dark place and that Kam believes she poses a threat."

Zack placed his call, and when it appeared that he and Warren were going to talk for a while, I went to the kitchen and rummaged around in the freezer for something quick, tasty and easy for dinner. No luck. The coupon drawer was more fertile ground. On the very top of the pile was a flyer for a new East Indian restaurant in Fort Qu'Appelle that reputedly made dumplings to die for, and — bingo — they delivered.

I'd just opened up my laptop to order online when Zack wheeled in.

"Warren's glad we gave him the heads-up about Patti, because when Lyn Goldman, the lawyer Mike hired for his divorce, met with Patti, she came away shaken. Not much shakes Lyn, but in her opinion, Patti's a loose cannon. When Lyn learned that Mike was staying at the Webers', two doors down from the house he owns but where Patti lives, she was not happy. Mike is now staying at the Marriott."

"So many lives turned upside down," I said. "It's eerie."

Zack raised his eyebrows. "What's even more eerie is the fact that all these lives are connected to MediaNation. Kam Chau says that every time he gets home after work and sees Ellen's cats waiting, it's a reminder that she isn't coming back. The uncertainty is getting to him, Jo. Kam's a level-headed guy, but he's convinced himself that Thalia is somehow connected to everything that's going on."

"Kam's not alone," I said, "Jill believes that too, but as she correctly points out, we're the ones who are filling in the blanks. I'm going to call Taylor and ask her to come by when she has a moment. She may remember something more about Thalia."

By the time Taylor picked up, her phone had rung so often I was prepared to leave a message. She was clearly distracted. "Sorry, I was working, and you know how spacey I can get."

"Come over to the house when you're through. No rush. It can wait."

"I was just about to take a break," she said, "but I'm spattered in paint, and I'm a hazard to furniture. Could you come to my studio? We can sit outside."

When Taylor had been away, Zack and I had had no reason to go to her studio, and I'd forgotten how inviting its small flagstone patio was. A few years earlier, at summer's end, Taylor had rescued two Muskoka chairs left on the roadside. She sanded the chairs and painted them in neon colours. When Zack saw them, he'd been delighted. "Add a few parrots and you'll have Margaritaville," he said. The Jimmy Buffett reference blew right past our daughter, but when Zack showed her images of Margaritaville on his phone, Taylor added the parrots.

She was sprawled on one of the Margaritaville chairs when we arrived, but she leapt up to give us careful paint-free hugs.

"Okay if we stay out here?" she said. "I've been inside for hours and the sun feels so good."

"It does," I said. "Taylor, Jill Oziowy and Kam Chau, Charlie D's producer, just left. They're curious about Thalia Monk, and we wondered if you'd remembered anything else about her."

Our daughter shrugged. "Pretty much just what Gracie and I told you. I always said hi to Thalia in the hall, but after the cohort started that rumour about my tragic frigidity, I decided Thalia wasn't exactly BFF material."

"I get that," I said.

"I knew you would," she said. "I'll text Gracie and ask her to call. There's something I wanted to talk to her about anyway."

When her phone buzzed, Taylor checked the text. "Gracie's in class," she said, "but she'll be out in ten minutes and she'll call then. Can I hang out with you guys for a while?"

"As far as I'm concerned," Zack said, "you can hang out with us till doomsday."

"I'm not making my doomsday plans yet," Taylor said, "but I have made some decisions about where I'll be in the immediate future."

Zack turned his wheelchair to face her. "We're all ears," he said.

As she rubbed at a spot of turquoise paint on the back of her right hand, Taylor's expression was thoughtful. "I don't want to travel," she said, "at least for a while. I'm tired of living out of suitcases, and I need time to make art. For me, that means settling down. I want to stay in Saskatchewan. All the people I love are here, and I need you guys. But I also need distance because I have some growing to do.

"So, here's my plan. I'm going to stay at Lawyers Bay till Thanksgiving, and after that I'm moving to Saskatoon. Gracie has a condo on the riverbank, and she says she needs a housemate." Taylor dimpled. "She doesn't, of course, but that's Gracie. She's always there when I need her, and she knows I need her now.

"The location is perfect. Gracie says when she squints, she can see Sally's old studio across the river. And by a stroke of serendipity, the studio is now permanently vacant. The university has ended its artist in residence program — 'budgetary restraints.' Anyway, the studio is now mine to sell or use."

"And you want to use it," I said.

"I do," Taylor said. "When my relationship with Vale fell apart, I wondered how I'd ever put the pieces of my life together again. And now . . ."

"And now the pieces are falling into place," Zack said. "As a client of mine used to say, 'I've been ciphering out your words.'"

"And what have you concluded?"

"The only way I could be happier with your decision is if you moved in next door to us," he said. "But I can live with this. It will take fifteen minutes to get to the airport from Gracie's condo; the flight from Saskatoon to Regina takes forty-five minutes, and we live ten minutes from the airport. Allowing for traffic, you and Gracie are an hour and a half away."

Taylor went to her father, stood behind his chair and kissed the top of his head. "You're taking this like a champ, Dad. I'm proud of you."

We were all still laughing when the phone rang. It was Gracie. Taylor picked up. "I'm with Jo and my dad," she said. "Can I put you on speakerphone?"

The moment Gracie heard that Taylor was about to become her housemate, she let out a whoop of joy, and for the next five minutes she and Taylor rattled on happily about the adventures awaiting them in the Bridge City.

When they were barely out of their teens, both young women had suffered punishing blows, and it was a joy to once again hear effervescence in their voices as they talked about the future.

"Time to focus," Gracie said briskly. "Taylor's voice message said you have some questions I might be able to help with."

My account of my meeting with Alison Janvier that morning was brief, but Gracie picked up on the fact that Alison and I both felt that Thalia Monk had manipulated the podcast proposal so that Alison's only option was agreeing to an arrangement that would have Harper working closely with Thalia.

"And Ms. Janvier is concerned that her son and Thalia might develop a personal relationship," Gracie said. "From what I've seen and heard of Thalia, Harper's mother has every reason to be concerned."

"Anything else we should know?" Zack said.

Gracie paused to consider. "I'm pretty certain I told you everything I knew that day Taylor and I found the photo of Farky Farquhar on your phone," she said finally. "I wish I could be of more help."

"Talking to you always helps," Zack said. "Gracie, I hope you know how happy we are that you and Taylor will be housemates."

"I'm happy too," Gracie said. "And I know how happy my Dad would be to know I won't be alone anymore."

Zack flinched at the reference to Blake Falconer's death,

but he continued. "Gracie, I've known you since the day you were born, and you never disappoint."

"That's good to hear. My dad was always my one-man cheering section," Gracie said. Her voice caught. "I miss him so much."

"So do I," Zack said.

It was a tender moment, and after the call ended, the three of us remained silent. The deaths of Zack's law partners were still an open wound for him, and Taylor and I had learned that the only way to reach Zack was to push forward. That day, Taylor took charge. "I'm in need of some time with Desmond and his sisters," she said. "How would you feel about me inviting Charlie, Mieka and their kids out here for lunch on Sunday? I'll be the host, and I'll handle everything myself."

"I think that's a terrific idea," I said. "Zack?"

Zack managed a smile. "Sure, let's do it."

"That's settled, then," Taylor said. "Back to work for me."

* * *

In the way of weekend weather in cottage country, on Saturday, the day upon which we had virtually no plans, the sun shone; the breeze was gentle, and the sky was clear. Zack spent Saturday morning indoors at the partners' table, working on a file that was proving troublesome, and Taylor and I drove into Fort Qu'Appelle to shop at the farmers' market for Sunday lunch.

I'd lost count of the number of times I'd taken first my children and later our grandchildren to farmers' markets. The pleasure of watching young faces as they discovered the earthly delights of the garden, the orchard, the kitchen and the smokehouse never diminished. But the joy I felt that morning as Taylor and I wandered from stand to stand heaped with vegetables, so fresh they still carried the scent of earth, and freshly picked fruit, vibrant with ripe beauty, was of a special order. I'd believed moments like this with our younger daughter were a thing of the past, and as I watched Taylor select the homemade borscht, pierogi, golubtsi and sausage that were on our menu, I couldn't stop smiling.

Taylor felt my joy. "There really is something special about markets," she said. "When Vale and I were with Rosamond Burke in London last Christmas, she took us to her favourites. They were amazing. The one at London Bridge had stalls all along the banks of the Thames. At night the stalls were lit, and their light reflected in the river. Leicester Square had a Ferris wheel, and after dark, the view from the top at was unbelievable." Taylor's eyes were dancing. "Borough Market had mulled cider and gingerbread and choirs singing holiday songs. Apple Market, which is near Covent Garden, had all these great shops: antiques, artwork, jewellery. I did most of my Christmas shopping there. I bought . . ." She paused at a memory and then hurried on. "I bought some bracelets there. After we'd seen Covent Garden, we went next door to the Royal Opera House to see *The Nutcracker*."

"Do you remember going to *The Nutcracker* here when you were six?" I said. "You and I found the perfect poufy dress, and every morning you put stickers on the kitchen calendar, counting off the days."

Taylor's brow wrinkled. "I don't remember seeing *The Nutcracker* at all."

"Well, we didn't stay long," I said.

"Why not?"

"At first, everything was fine — better than fine. I'd splurged on the seats, so you were able to see the orchestra. You waved at one of the French horn players, and when he waved back, you were beside yourself. Then the lights went down, the music started, the curtains went up and we were at the Stahlbaums' Christmas Eve party. It was a sparkling production, and when you saw the tree and the lights and the dancers, you leaned forward in your seat, and I leaned back in mine and then you crawled up on my knee and threw up."

"I didn't."

"You did. The people sitting around us were not impressed."

Taylor groaned. "You must have wanted to die."

"Pretty much, but I bundled you up, barf and all, took you home and gave you a bath."

"Was I sick?"

"No, you were perfectly fine — just excited, but I stayed in bed with you in case you were upset. You were smiling when you fell asleep, and that smile is one of my best Christmas memories."

Taylor set the shopping bags filled with our purchases on the ground and put her arms around me. "I love you so much, Jo."

"I love you too."

We were both teary, and we stood in the middle of the aisle between the stalls, embracing and snuffling until Taylor murmured, "We'd better break this up. We're starting to draw a crowd." With that, we picked up our groceries, walked to our car and headed for home.

* * *

Sunday morning I awoke to the staccato patter of rain on the roof. I slid out of bed, stepped over Esme, shrugged into my robe and walked to the patio doors. When I peered through the rain-spattered glass, I saw that the sky was the colour of pewter. "This rain is not going to let up," I said.

Zack pushed himself up to a sitting position. "So, we don't get to take the grandkids for a boat ride around the lake?"

"Seemingly not," I said. "But Des is a week old. He'll handle it. Besides, it's never too early to learn that the best laid schemes of mice and men *gang aft agley*."

The rain continued unabated, but we pushed on, and by the time Mieka, Charlie and the family arrived, the borscht was simmering, the golubtsi and sausage were in the oven, the pierogi were ready to boil and we were ready to party.

Taylor had chosen the russet earthenware dishes that we used every day in the fall, but set against the red-gold woven placemats she'd unearthed from the bottom of a cedar chest, the old dishes suddenly seemed to be making a statement. As we were leaving the market, Taylor had purchased sunflowers from a woman who'd sold everything except the strays in her bucket. The woman was eager to head home, so her sunflowers were now arranged in a glossy redware pitcher on the partners' table.

It was always a joy to see Mieka, Charlie and the grand-children, but as we sat down to our Ukrainian feast, the mood was restrained. We all praised the praiseworthy food and ate heartily, but except for Desmond, who cooed and gurgled contentedly, the Kilbourn-Dowhanuiks seemed preoccupied.

When we were cleaning up, I learned the sources of the preoccupation. After we'd started the dishwasher, Taylor took me aside. "Madeleine and Lena saw a picture of Vale with Etienne Simard on the cover of one of those magazines at the supermarket checkout. The banner on the cover said 'Switching Teams? Vale's New Lover.'"

I muttered Zack's favourite curse word. "Are the girls upset?"

"They are," Taylor said. "And they have questions. If you don't need me for anything here, I'm going to take Maddy and Lena over to my place, so we can talk this through."

"Are you ready for that?"

My daughter's smile was rueful. "No, but Madeleine and Lena are ready for answers."

Mieka and I handed the girls their slickers and wellies, and watched as they raced across the lawns to the cottage that Kevin Hynd had deeded to Taylor shortly before his death.

Zack and his law partners always referred to their places on Lawyers Bay as "cottages," but they were not cottages. They were spacious, architect-designed, handsomely appointed dwellings that could be lived in year-round. The cottage

Taylor now owned had been built by Kevin's parents in the mid-1950s. It was a solidly built log cabin with a screened porch, a living room, a large kitchen, where the family had taken their meals, three small bedrooms and a bathroom with a flush toilet and a shower but no tub. It was a true cottage, and Taylor loved it as much as I did.

As soon as the girls were inside, Mieka turned to me. "Mum, I've asked Charlie to tell Zack that I need some time alone with you. There's something we should talk about."

* * *

Mieka and I sat in the matching club chairs flanking the fireplace in the family room. Zack and I had chosen the chairs because they're upholstered in Zack's favourite colour (red) and because, although Zack seldom leaves his wheelchair during the day, he's insistent about our family and guests being made comfortable. That afternoon Mieka was far from comfortable. Her body was tense and her expression uneasy. "Have you talked to Jill lately?" she said.

I nodded. "She and Kam Chau, Charlie's producer, came out here Friday afternoon. There was a situation at MediaNation that she and Kam were concerned about."

"Did she tell you about our disastrous encounter at MediaNation?" When I nodded, Mieka slumped. "I feel terrible about what happened, Mum. No excuses. I just freaked. I was picking up Charlie because we were taking his father to the airport, and we wanted Howard to have some time with Des before he left for Toronto."

"That's understandable. Howard's going to be teaching for the next three months; babies go through some major changes in three months."

"It's not that simple," Mieka said. "Charlie's relationship with his father is still uneasy, and Howard hasn't exactly thrown himself into the grandfather role. I was .hoping spending time with Des might stir Howard's grandparental feelings and that he and Charlie might finally start to bond. That's where my mind was and then — out of nowhere — there was Jill, and I froze."

"Jill told me that Mark Evanson thought you'd forgotten who Jill was, and he tried to smooth over the awkward moment by reminding you that Jill was Ian's chief of staff."

"Mark didn't stop there. He was holding Des and when Mark said he knew Jill would want to hold Ian Kilbourn's grandson, I went ballistic. I ripped Des out of his arms before Jill could touch him. Mum, I'll never forget Jill's face. I might as well have plunged a knife into her heart."

"Jill doesn't blame you, Mieka."

My daughter's grey-green eyes met mine. "I blame me," she said, and her voice was heavy.

"I thought you might. You're a good person, Mieka. I don't remember ever seeing you intentionally hurt someone."

"I hurt Jill."

"Are you still that angry at her?"

"No. When we found out what she and Ian did, thinking about it made me sick. I hated them both. I threw out every picture I had of either of them."

"So did I."

"That doesn't sound like you, Mum."

"I didn't feel like me. But, Mieka, it's been almost twenty years since Ian died, and so much has changed. I adopted Taylor. I married Zack. I watched you and your brothers grow into fine people who make good decisions about their lives."

"There've been a lot of changes in my life too," Mieka said, "and most of what's happened has been better than anything I could have hoped for: giving birth to the girls and watching them grow up, marrying Charlie, giving birth to Des, being there for everything we've shared with you, Zack, Pete and Angus. My life is full. I don't have room to carry the pain of what happened years ago."

"Jill is still carrying that pain, Mieka. For the past three years, her life has been defined by her guilt about what she did to our family and her fear that she can never repair the breach between us. On Thursday, Jill told me that she's finally faced the fact that she will never be part of our lives, and she's leaving Regina at Thanksgiving."

"Because of what I did," Mieka said miserably. She was silent for a long while. "Mum, you know that if I had a chance to undo that, I would."

"Do you want that chance?"

"Yes, but if I had it, I don't know what I'd do with it. When I was young, I loved Jill. I can't remember when she wasn't part of my life."

"She was your godmother."

"She was more than that. She was a friend who was always there for me, and she always knew what I needed. When

Brent Nichols broke up with me, I thought my life was over. You were in Weyburn with Pete and Angus for a hockey tournament, so I called Jill. She came over with a tub of Ben & Jerry's Cherry Garcia and she and I talked for hours."

"And while you talked, you listened to 'A Rainy Night in Soho' by the Pogues at least fifty times," I said.

"Jill told you that?"

"She did. When she was here on Friday, she also told me you were one of the best parts of her life."

"And now that part is gone because she had an affair with my father and I couldn't forgive her." Mieka drew a deep breath. "Mum, I don't know what to do."

"I don't either, but I came across something that might help. Hang tight. I won't be long."

My laptop was in the kitchen. So were Zack, Charlie and Des. Charlie was slouched in his chair with his long legs extended. Des's cradle was positioned close to Zack's wheelchair, and Zack was rocking it. The world outside was grey and stormy, but the overhead light in the kitchen enclosed the two men and the baby in a pool of warm light. It was a comforting scene.

I went over to check on Desmond. He was fast asleep. I squeezed my husband's shoulder. "They say the hand that rocks the cradle rules the world," I said.

Zack grinned. "At this moment, that is exactly how I feel," he said.

"Hold on to that vibe," I said. When I picked up my laptop from the table by the back door, Charlie tensed. "Is everything okay with you and Mieka?'

"Yes," I said. "I think we've just about finished what we had to do."

When she saw my laptop, Mieka raised an eyebrow. "Puppy videos to strengthen my resolve?"

"I'm saving the puppy videos till later," I said. "But bring your chair closer; this is worth watching too." I turned on my laptop and pulled up the page I had bookmarked. "Not long ago, I came upon the word 'Kintsugi' in something I was reading," I said. "When I searched it, this picture of a ceramic bowl with irregular gold stripes came up. I learned that in Japanese Kintsugi means 'golden scar,' and the gold stripes are the bowl's 'scars.' Kintsugi is a Japanese art form that consists of filling the cracks of broken objects with gold. You can read the article for yourself, but the philosophy behind the art form stuck with me. In our culture if we break something, we're angry and frustrated, and we throw out the pieces. But the Japanese believe that all the pieces are part of a whole and they belong together.

"The teacher who coached our basketball team at Bishop Lambeth's used to say, 'Behind every scar, there's a story.' I don't imagine Miss Talbot ever studied Japanese art, but I think that's the principle behind Kintsugi too. Kintsugi reminds us that instead of being hidden, the broken parts of us should be known and recognized because they make us the people we are."

As I related what I had learned, Mieka's gaze remained fixed on the picture of the shallow green bowl with the gold stripes. When I moved to turn off the laptop, she stopped me. "Just one more minute, please," she said. "I have an idea, but

I need a little more time with that bowl to make sure I'm on the right track."

I sat back in my chair. "I'm not going anywhere."

For a long while, I watched the embers in the fireplace and hoped.

Finally, my daughter turned to me. "Could you send this link to me, Mum? I'm not making any promises, but I think the story behind this bowl may give Jill and me a place to start." She stood and came over to me. "Let's save the puppy videos for next time. I have a lot to think about right now."

"I'll send Jill's contact information along with the link," I said. "Just in case."

When we returned to the kitchen, Charlie leapt to his feet to Mieka. "Everything okay?"

Mieka slid her arm around her husband's waist. "We're on the right track," she said.

"Good. Now, I hate to cut the visit short, but I think we should get back to the city. That rain is not going to let up, and I know the road from here to the highway has been improved, but I don't want to push our luck."

Mieka went to the cradle and picked up Des. "I'm going to take this guy into the family room and feed him. Mum, would you mind calling Taylor and letting her know that we're going to be leaving soon? I know Maddy and Lena will want to give you and Zack a hug."

By the time Taylor arrived with the girls, Des was fed and bundled into his hooded bunting, and Mieka and Charlie had donned their rainwear. I could tell from the girls' faces that their talk with Taylor had gone well. The awkwardness had given way to exuberance. There were plans to be made: Thanksgiving all together and visits with Taylor and Gracie in Saskatoon.

After we'd waved off the Kilbourn-Dowhanuiks, Taylor drew a deep breath and exhaled. "That was an intense afternoon. I told Maddy and Lena that nothing was off the table. They could ask me anything, and I would answer every question honestly."

Zack gave our daughter a mock scowl. "You do realize you should never have made that offer without having a lawyer by your side."

Taylor laughed. "I'll take you along next time, Dad. It was pretty brutal. The girls weren't brutal. They were very tender with me. In fact, our whole time together was very warm and comforting. I put on the wood stove, and we sat on the couch together. Maddy was on one side of me, Lena was on the other, and we talked about everything: love, sex, why being faithful mattered, why trust was important and some other subjects the ladies might wish remain private. Finally, Madeleine and Lena both asked me two of the questions I've been asking myself. Would Vale and I ever be a couple again? Would I ever fall in love again? Answering those questions honestly wasn't easy, but I did it, and I'm glad."

"I'm glad too," I said. "Madeleine and Lena look up to you. They're on the cusp of young womanhood and having a frank talk with you about who to love and how to love is something they'll remember."

"It's something I'll remember too," Taylor said. "Can I stay here and eat leftovers with you? I'm bushed. Madeleine and Lena asked all the right questions, but after coming up with all those honest answers, I'm in need of something more substantial than a can of cold pork and beans."

Zack held out his arms to her. "You've come to the right place. The grub's good, the price is right and although the help tends to hover, they mean well."

CHAPTER FIFTEEN

Zack and I had started our day in a particularly pleasant way, and as I left to take Pantera and Esme for their morning run, Zack was in the shower singing "Ring of Fire." The path to the lake was muddy, so the dogs and I stayed on the grass, circling the cottages, the gazebo on the point and the woods. The run was far from strenuous; the air was fresh with the scent of wet grass and evergreens; the sun was bright; and I arrived home in a mellow mood.

Zack was sitting at the kitchen table checking his phone. He was dressed for the office, and he was clearly preoccupied. The dogs' water dishes were filled, so I poured Zack and me a glass of orange juice. "What's with the lawyer suit?" I said.

"Warren Weber called a few minutes ago. Patti Morgan is dead. They don't know exactly when she died. The best guess seems to be early this morning."

I took a sip of juice. "It's hard to know what to say. Patti was going through hell. Was it suicide?"

Zack sighed. "As cruel as this sounds, I wish it were that simple. Mike Braeden discovered Patti's body. He'd arranged with their housekeeper, Halima, to pick up his winter clothing this morning. The clothing was in the front hall, packed and ready for pick up, but the box where Mike kept cufflinks and memorabilia was on his dresser.

"Halima had left a note for him on the table in the front hall where the Braedens kept mail. She said she had a doctor's appointment and she'd called upstairs when she arrived, but Patti hadn't responded, so Halima assumed she was still sleeping. She told Mike that Patti took pills to help her sleep, and she was certain he could pick up the jewellery box without awakening her."

"So, Mike went upstairs," I said.

Zack nodded. "He found Patti lying face down on the bed. He tried CPR, but when that didn't work, he called Warren Weber. Warren called 911. Warren's there with Mike now. As is Debbie Haczkewicz, and my presence has been requested."

If the head of Major Crimes was on the scene, the case was heavy stuff, and high stakes meant more stress and punishing hours. I leaned forward. "Do you have to take this on?" I said. "We promised we were going to cut back."

"That's why I called Maisie just before you got in and asked her to meet me at the Braeden home. If the need arises, Maisie will take the lead, and I'll be second chair."

"You won't mind that?"

"Not at all. Maisie has been second chair for me a half-dozen times, and I've been second chair for her once. We work well together, and I value life with you too much to do anything that might cut it short."

"That's exactly what I needed to hear," I said. "Give me ten minutes to get dressed and load the dogs into the car, and I'll drive you to University Park Road."

* * *

The road to the highway was not in bad shape, but it required focus, so Zack and I remained silent until we turned onto the highway.

"I know you can't say much, but if you want to talk, I'm here."

Zack patted my leg. "I appreciate that. I also appreciate the fact that at the end of the day, you'll be there, and I won't have to be alone with my thoughts."

"Is there something particular that's worrying you?"

"No. When Warren called, he was pretty close-mouthed — understandably, because I'm sure he was surrounded by members of Regina's finest. It's nothing concrete, Jo. Just a nagging sense that there's more trouble ahead."

"We're the only ones on the highway." I tried a joke. "Want me to hang a U-ey? We could be back in Lawyers Bay in fifteen minutes?"

Zack's smile was weary. "If I had three wishes, that would be all of them," he said, "but duty calls."

Police cars blocked off the area in front of the Braeden house, so I had to drop off Zack. I watched as he made his way through the gauntlet of police officers, and when the front door was opened, my husband turned and waved to me. The house was not accessible, and I winced as two brawny police officers picked up Zack's chair and carried him inside. I knew that an already bad day had just become worse for him.

Zack called around noon with an update. He and Maisie were going back to Falconer Shreve to make some decisions about how best to proceed, and he would be home for dinner at the regular time. That left me with an afternoon free to tackle a task I'd been putting off. I'd harvested the root vegetables, but I still hadn't cleared off the vegetable garden.

I donned my gardening gloves and floppy sun hat, took a wheelbarrow and rake from the garage and went to the backyard to check the damage. As I'd anticipated, the vegetable garden was a mess of dead and dying plants. Cleaning away the debris was therapeutic, and when the beds were clear, I wheeled out two bags of compost and mulch. I was contemplating my next task when just as she had three weeks earlier, Julie Evanson Gallagher Fairbairn appeared around the corner of the house.

I wiped my forehead with the back of my hand. "We have to stop meeting like this, Julie."

"I rang your doorbell repeatedly, but no one answered."

"That's because there is no one in the house."

"I'm not in the mood for banter, Joanne. I need to talk to you."

"Fair enough. I was just about to take a break. Zack and I were at the lake, and the patio furniture is still in the garage, but we can sit at the picnic bench."

We took our places directly across from each other and, at close range, I noticed there was something different about Julie. In the thirty-five years I'd known her, I'd seldom seen her less than immaculate. But that morning the silver hair that always fell smoothly from its central part to Julie's mid-cheek was dishevelled, and her makeup had been hastily applied.

However, the differences in Julie went beyond the cosmetic. Over the years, storms might have lashed her psyche, but Julie had never dropped her mask of steely control. That afternoon she seemed lost, and despite our rocky history, I reached out to her. "Has something happened, Julie?"

It wasn't easy for Julie to open up. For a long while, she hesitated, biting her lip. "It's Clay," she said finally. "I'm losing him." After that, the words poured. "That girl has him wrapped around her little finger. I need an ally, and I know I have one in you. Thalia told Clay you don't like her, that you tried to convince Alison Janvier to reject the podcast she and Clay are working on together."

"That's not true, Julie."

She batted a dismissive hand in my direction. "I don't give a damn if you did or did not. That's the least of my worries. This morning I heard Thalia's voice in Clay's bedroom, and I walked in on them.

"Clay and I argued. We've never argued. There's been no reason to, and now . . . He said terrible things, vile things, and all the time he was castigating me, that slut lay in his bed with the covers pulled aside, so I could see that she was half-naked. When I told her to put on some clothes and get out, Clay grabbed my arm and pulled me into the hall.

"He's such a handsome boy, but he was so angry I could barely recognize him. I told Clay that Thalia was just using him, manipulating him the way she manipulates all of them. I said that she used her body to keep them all in line.

"And then . . . and then, Joanne, my grandson said, 'You have no idea what you're talking about.' Julie's eyes grew wide with disbelief. "And he slapped me across the face." Julie's hand moved towards her cheek. She touched it, tentatively at first and then she pressed hard and began rubbing it. She continued numbly pressing against it until the tears came.

Julie was pale and shaking. I was afraid she was sliding into shock. I got up and put my arms around her shoulder. "Come inside with me. You're cold. I can put on the fireplace and give you some blankets."

Docile as a child, she followed me inside. I turned on the fireplace and pulled a chair close to it. Then I wrapped her in blankets. The tea I gave her was milky and very sweet. She drank it quickly and then held her cup out for more. For a few moments we sat side by side watching the fire. Gradually Julie's breathing became more regular and her body relaxed.

Finally, she turned to me. "What should I do, Joanne?"

"Did Clay offer any explanation for why Thalia was in his bed?"

"He tried. He said Thalia texted him around five o'clock this morning. She was out for her morning run in Wascana Park and a man started following her. He tried to attack her, but she managed to get away. Thalia told Clay where she was, and he picked her up and brought her home. He suggested she stay in the guest room, but she was afraid to be alone."

"Did they report the attack to the police?"

"She wouldn't let him. When Clay said that, I told him I didn't believe a word of Thalia's story, and he shouldn't either. Clay said he believed her because she'd never lied to him."

"Had the man touched her?"

"According to Thalia, he tried. He ran past her and then jumped in front of her, blocking her way. The man grabbed at that necklace she always wore and said something about dragging her into the bushes. She pulled away and the necklace broke. Clay said Thalia was devastated over losing the necklace. Apparently, it had some significance for her."

"Was your husband there when the argument with Clay happened?"

"No, Hugh was already at the office."

"Julie, you asked what you should do. You're not going to like what I say, but I think you should call Hugh and the two of you can work this out together. You've raised Clay and you both love him. In my opinion, the best thing to do is sit down with Clay and Thalia, and hear them out."

"Do you believe her story, Joanne?"

"I do, because I know what that necklace meant to Thalia. The amulet the chain held contains a lock of Thalia's brother's hair. Thalia was never without the necklace. She and her brother were very close. I don't believe she would have risked losing that amulet if this were some ploy to manipulate your grandson."

"I'll call Hugh. We can't lose Clay."

"You're making the right decision."

Julie inhaled deeply. Her colour was returning and when she stood and squared her shoulders, she was herself again. "Hugh and I will face them together, and we'll do what's necessary," she said. "The idea of capitulating to that little bitch makes me sick, but I'll bide my time." Julie's eyes narrowed. "There's more than one way to skin a cat, Joanne. Just watch me."

After Julie left, I sank into my chair, stared at the fire and marvelled at the amazing resilience of Julie Evanson Gallagher Fairbairn. In less than an hour she had moved from the shattered figure of defeat to a warrior with a plan that would begin with capitulation but end in victory. Once again, Julie's universe was unfolding as it should.

* * *

Zack called at five to say he was finished for the day, and if I wasn't busy, he'd welcome a ride home. When I picked him up outside the glass tower that houses the Falconer Shreve offices, he looked exhausted. After he'd transferred his body to the passenger seat, collapsed his wheelchair and stowed it in the space behind us, I leaned across and kissed him. "I won't ask you about your day if you don't ask me about mine," I said.

His smile was weary. "Deal," he said.

And we didn't exchange another word till Zack poured the martinis and we'd had our first sip. "I'll go first," Zack said, "because, although it was a lousy day, I have some news that I think will please you.

"Maisie and I have talked this through. I told her you and I were counting on some time at the lake, and Maisie and I have decided that the work that needs to be done now can be done from Lawyers Bay. She has to be in court tomorrow, but she talked to Pete, and they're planning to bring the twins out to the lake Wednesday morning and stay until Sunday after lunch."

"That does please me," I said. "But won't you need to be closer to your client?"

"Thanks to Warren Weber, that's exactly where we will be. Debbie Haczkewicz took one look at the number of stitches on Mike Braeden's face and started asking questions. On the advice of counsel, Mike answered Debbie's questions honestly. At that point, of course, Debbie had questions of her own, but they're questions for the forensic pathologist to answer."

"You said Mike found Patti in bed, face down on her pillow."

"He did. The bedroom is on the second floor, so I was SOL about getting a first-hand look, but the police photographers were still working when I got there, and I was able to see pictures. There was an almost empty bottle of Southern Comfort on the nightstand and an open prescription pill bottle in Patti's hand. The pills had spilled onto the bed, and the photographer said the duvet reeked of alcohol. There was no suicide note, but considering the stew of alcohol and drugs that must have been in Patti's bloodstream, I guess that's not surprising."

"How's Mike doing?"

Zach shrugged. "He's holding up, but it must have been a hell of a scene to walk in on."

"And the police are looking into the possibility that Mike didn't simply walk in on the scene?"

Zack nodded. "You know Debbie. She keeps her options open, but Mike hasn't been charged, and when Warren laid the situation out for Debbie, she didn't object when he proposed to take Mike out to their place on the lake. Debbie's a good cop, but she's also a decent human being. Earlier in the week, Mike suffered a physical trauma from which he is still recovering, and now this.

"The Webers are able to offer him care and comfort, and if Debbie decides she needs to crack the whip, they can have Mike at headquarters on Osler Street in forty-five minutes. It's a sensible decision. What a change from the guy whom Debbie replaced as head of Major Crimes. He was a major asshole, and it would have been a real kick in the head for him to make things as miserable as possible for everyone concerned."

"What happened to Debbie's predecessor?"

"What always happens to people like that," Zack said. "Shit floats. He's now chief of police in a very large city that shall remain nameless."

I smiled. "Well, I'm grateful we have Debbie. Zack, I know you hate it when I worry about you, but I do worry, and I know the drill. Even if your client hasn't been charged, you have to gather all the facts, lay the groundwork and that means twelve-hour days."

Zack took my hand. "But not for me. Not this time out. Maisie is taking the lead, and Falconer Shreve is a large firm. When it comes to legal talent, we have a deep bench. Expense is not a concern for this client, and I've already spoken to Bob Colby. Colby and Associates are the best private investigators in western Canada, and they'll be following through on everything we learn from our client about what happened. They'll also be looking into our client's life and the victim's life."

"So, this can be a working holiday for you and Maisie."

"It can, and Jo, I know that Taylor's fine, but I also know *Sisters and Strangers* starts showing this Friday. Vale's all over the media. It will be good for our daughter to have her family around. And — breaking news — Maisie says the twins are already talking about learning how to drive the big boat."

"Time to hand over the captain's hat?" I said. "I've been relieved of one of my duties too. Colin can now make his own PB&J sandwiches, and he insists I step aside while he works. You and I are becoming redundant."

Zack squeezed my hand. "Not to each other," he said. "And, as far as work is concerned, Maisie and I have talked about this. We won't be spending all our time staring at our laptops. We can do everything that needs to be dealt with immediately from the lake and still have time to prepare for the eventuality that Mike Braeden may be charged.

"The police will be working on this 24/7 — interviewing possible witnesses, checking into alibis, establishing timelines, looking into the personal lives of the principals involved. We have to run our own parallel investigation. Analyze the collected facts of the case and create a theory of defence that presents our client's version of the story and answers any questions or doubts the Crown will likely raise at trial.

"We need a team approach for that, so Maisie and I are going through the files on our associates to select the ones strongest in knowledge of case law, and the ones with a gift for coming up with effective outside-the-box strategies that will help us develop a theory of defence. That's job one."

"What's job two?"

"Getting to know our client, and he'll be staying right across the lake in Warren and Annie's guest house."

"That's a lot of preliminary work, Zack. It sounds as if you and Maisie think there's a good chance Mike *is* going to be charged with this."

"Mike has been determined to keep the problems in his marriage to Patti private, but Warren told me today that Mike has spent most of the last year extricating his wife from bad dates and other situations involving risky behaviour. Those incidents are all going to come to light. Maisie and I have to be ready to deal with them. Being together at Lawyers Bay will give us the time we need to prepare." Zack took a large sip from his drink. "So, all in all, a satisfactory outcome. Your turn now. Was the outcome of your day satisfactory?"

"That depends on whether your money is on Julie Evanson Gallagher Fairbairn or Thalia Monk."

Zack's eyes widened. "Is there a cage match in the offing?"

"Your guess is as good as mine. Julie was here." I gave him the full rundown. "I suggested she and Hugh talk it out with Clay and Thalia."

"That sounds reasonable."

"I thought so, and, surprisingly, Julie seized on the idea of a meeting. She saw it as a blueprint to victory because although the idea of capitulating to 'that little bitch' made her sick, she could bide her time. Julie's exit line was a chiller. 'There's more than one way to skin a cat,' she said. 'Just watch me.'"

Zack shuddered. "The hair on the back of my neck just stood on end."

"Mine too," I said. "Let's split what's left in the martini pitcher and do our best to mellow out."

CHAPTER SIXTEEN

Zack was still asleep when Pantera, Esme and I left for our run. The fresh morning air was invigorating, but the days were undeniably getting shorter. The dogs and I now started out and returned in darkness. It was not a pathetic fallacy I welcomed.

My dreams the night before had been a collage of sharp-edged fragments: two-year-old Clay in his pumpkin suit spinning in front of the mirror as his mother, Lori, sang "He is the potter. We are the clay" in her sweet, musical voice. Then in the fractured logic of dreams, it was Thalia Monk standing in front of the mirror. She was holding two-year-old Clay and spinning with him, singing "I am the potter, you are the clay." Then Clay was sitting on the floor playing with a knot of wires and cords very much like the one he had pushed into Alison Janvier's path the day of the picnic. Julie's image appeared in the mirror, Thalia sang "I am the potter" and Clay stood, picked up the ball of wires he had been playing with, hurled it at Julie's reflection and the mirror shattered.

Heart pounding, I had woken up, grateful to be in the familiar safe world, but that morning as the dogs and I ran through the unending darkness the memories of the night stayed with me. When we got back to the house, Zack was at the breakfast table in his robe; coffee was perking, and the porridge was bubbling.

Pantera's ardour for Zack had never cooled. Our bullmastiff jammed his 185-pound self against Zack's side of the bed every night when we turned in and remained there until he heard me rattle his leash in the morning. That morning, he and Zack had been apart for a little over an hour, but when Zack turned his chair to face us, Pantera lunged at his master as if they'd been separated for eons.

After Pantera finally loped over to his water dish, Zack picked up his napkin, wiped the slobber off his cheek and turned to me. "How was your run?"

"It was okay, but I hate running in the dark, and there are months of that ahead."

"We have a big yard," Zack said. "You could put the dogs out; they could chase each other around to their hearts' content, and you could have a swim in our soon-to-be renovated pool."

"And you could swim with me," I said.

Zack chortled. "I walked right into that one, didn't I?"

"You did," I said, "but I'll let it pass. But good news on that front. I had a text from McCudden and Co., and they're ready to start work tomorrow, and we'll be out of the way." I took the juice out of the refrigerator and poured us both a glass. When I took my first sip, I raised my glass to Zack. "This is fresh squeezed," I said. "You've been busy."

"I'm not the only one. Warren called. He and Annie are at the lake. They'd like to see us as soon as we have some time."

"Both of us?" I said. "So it's not about Mike Braeden?"

"Warren said 'both of us,' and that makes sense," Zack said. "Mike Braeden says he's ready to talk to me, and Warren and Annie's picture of what's been going on at MediaNation is far from complete. You can fill them in."

"How about early afternoon?" I said. "Once we're at Lawyers Bay, we just need time to unpack the groceries. Today's special at Pacific Fish is arctic char, and that's an easy dinner."

"And one of Taylor's favourites," Zack said.

"I'm aware of that," I said, "and when we unpack the groceries, you'll see that we have enough arctic char for three, even if one of the three is Taylor, who is a trencherwoman when arctic char is on the menu."

Zack grinned. "You do know that Taylor will catch on to your nefarious plan."

"I do," I said, "but I also know that when we sit down for dinner, our daughter will be in her old place at the table."

"Well done," Zack said. "And Warren has an idea that I think will appeal to you. He suggested we take the boat over, so we can get a lakeside view of that new addition they've built before the snow flies."

"It seems our impromptu getaway is off to a good start," I said.

"And it hasn't even begun," Zack said.

* * *

Not long after Zack left the house, Mieka called. She didn't bother with preamble. "I've taken the plunge, but now I'm having second thoughts."

"Is this news I should sit down for?"

My daughter's laugh was short and rueful. "No, you can stay standing. I'm being overly dramatic. Today is the first day of autumn, and at breakfast Madeleine and Lena were talking about inviting some of their BFFs by after school to rake leaves into piles and jump in them."

"I'm surprised," I said. "I thought the young women might have said goodbye to all that now that Madeleine's in grade eight and Lena's just a year behind."

"Pete and I were jumping into leaf piles when we were in high school, and if Jill was around, she'd jump in with us. She had more fun than we did, but she was always strict about us raking up and bagging the leaves when we were through." Mieka paused. "I've been trying to come up with a way to reach out to Jill that didn't seem too freighted with significance, so after the girls got on the bus, I picked up the phone, called Jill and reminded her that today is the first day of fall, and I thought it might be fun to get together and remember jumping in the leaves. Lame, huh?"

"Not lame at all," I said. "I think it struck just the right note."

"It did for Jill. Anyway, the upshot of all is that at ten o'clock, I'm meeting Jill for coffee at the MediaNation cafeteria and I'm bringing Des. Mum, I don't know if I'm ready. Could you come with me?"

"Of course. Do you want me to pick you up?"

"No. I need to do at least part of this on my own."

"Okay, in that case, I'll see you, Des and Jill at MediaNation at ten."

* * *

I arrived at the stroke of ten, but Jill and Mieka were already sitting at a table by the window, and Jill was holding our youngest grandson. When she turned to greet me, Jill's face was soft with pleasure. "Mieka said that she hadn't had a truly hot cup of coffee since Desmond was born, so I volunteered."

I leaned over to peek at our grandson. "Des seems absolutely content," I said.

"I'm content too," Mieka said. "I'd forgotten how good coffee tastes when it hasn't been sitting around, getting cold for twenty minutes." She looked up at me. "Join the party, Mum. Jill and Des and I are just getting started."

Our talk that morning was rambling, inconsequential and deeply satisfying. When I checked my watch and saw that it was almost eleven, I picked up my sweater. "I'm going to have to take off. Maisie and Zack have a case they need to work on, and Charlie and Colin have decided it's time they learned to drive the big boat, so we're going to spend a few days at the lake."

Mieka raised her hand. "Videos, please."

"The twins will be in the company of five adults with phones," I said. "You may regret that request. Now, I'd better make tracks. I have grocery shopping to do, and I have a special list from Taylor. She has decided to start making the food for her cats."

"That's impressive," Jill said.

"I agree," I said, "but Taylor says, and I quote, 'If I'm destined to be a spinster with three cats, I'd better learn to do everything right.'"

Jill and Mieka exchanged looks of disbelief. "Taylor's twenty-one," Mieka said. "I don't believe her destiny is already written in stone."

"Agreed," Jill said. "Also, does anybody actually use the word 'spinster' these days?"

"Taylor does," I said. I leaned over and kissed Des's forehead. "You change every day," I murmured. "You just keep getting better and better."

Mieka stood and hugged me. "Call me when you get there."

"I always do," I said. I touched Jill's shoulder. "It's good to see you."

"We're going to do this again," Mieka said. "But let's include Madeleine and Lena next time."

***

One of my husband's many gifts is his ability to sleep anywhere at any time. Knowing he was facing a tough row to
hoe, I was in the driver's seat. Zack was asleep before we
passed the city limits, and he didn't awaken until we pulled
through the gates at Lawyers Bay. As always, he awoke fresh
as the proverbial daisy, and after we unloaded the car, we
went straight to the boathouse.

The lake was choppy, but the view of the late September
landscape was worth twenty minutes of rock and roll. Zack
had told the Webers we'd be at their place around two
o'clock, and they were waiting when Zack steered the *Amicus*
smoothly beside the dock.

Warren was natty in light tan slacks and a pumpkin cashmere pullover, and as always, Annie had coordinated her
outfit to complement her husband's. Her long sweater was
taupe but her leggings were a tapestry of autumn colours:
cranberry, wheat gold and saffron.

The original Weber cottage was set back from the lake,
but the addition — a single very large, very handsome
room — faced the water, and the view was dynamite. The
room's decor was starkly modern, but it was humanized by
a wood-burning fireplace and furniture from the old Weber
farmhouse. Much of the furniture had been in storage for
decades, but Annie had rescued the lovely old pieces and
had them restored to their former glory.

Zack was impressed. "You've done a great job with this,
Annie."

"Warren wants us to move our bed out here, so we never have to leave this room." Annie's smile was mischievous. "I'm for that. And look at the view we have of the foliage around your place, Zack. I told Warren I was sure Joanne chose those trees because she knew they'd be spectacular well into October."

"They're Amur maples," I said. "And you're right about their staying power, but those trees were planted long before I was on the scene. The landscaper made certain there would be something lovely to look at all year long."

Annie sighed with pleasure. "Like your forsythia and that copse of lilac bushes north of your dining room in spring. Warren and I are planning to do some landscaping, and we're open to suggestions."

"I'll unearth the landscaper's notes and keep them handy, so you can pick them up the next time you're at our place. I know the priority for the foreseeable future is Mike Braeden, but I imagine the time will come when Mike will appreciate a visit across the lake too."

"That's what Annie and I want to talk to you and Zack about," Warren said. "But let us bring you some refreshments first."

The Webers left and when they returned, Annie was carrying a tray with four heavy monogrammed glasses, four ecru monogrammed napkins and a plate of goodies, and Warren was carrying a bottle of Old Pulteney in one hand and a bottle of non-alcoholic ginger beer in the other. As Warren was pouring the drinks, Annie offered the cookies. "This is Scottish cheddar shortbread," she said. "Warren told me he always looked forward to this shortbread when he was a boy, and his parents had a party."

"No Old Pulteney for them," Warren said. "My parents were strict teetotallers, but the shortbread goes well with ginger beer, so Annie doesn't miss out."

The Old Pulteney and the shortbread were indeed a sublime pairing, and as soon as he was certain Zack and I were taken care of, Warren waded into the subject at hand. "Zack, in all the chaos yesterday morning, I didn't have a chance to thank you for the fact that you and your daughter-in-law have agreed to represent Mike Braeden. I'm relieved and I'm grateful. Falconer Shreve is the best firm in the province, you and Maisie are two of its top trial lawyers and Mike is innocent."

"You sound very certain," Zack said.

Warren's voice was as steady as his gaze. "I am certain."

"Then our task is clear," Zack said. "I articled with a lawyer who taught me that if there's a turtle on top of a fence post, it didn't just get there. Somebody put it there."

Warren chuckled. "My father used to say something similar. We believe Mike Braeden is innocent, so it's up to us to learn what happened to Patti Morgan in the hours before she died."

Zack turned his chair towards the door. "Joanne and I made notes on some of the people and events we felt Colby and Associates should look into. We made copies for you and Annie. Jo thinks it might be useful to go through what we know with you. You may see a pattern we're not picking up on."

"Let's hope," Annie said. "Mike is bearing up, but this is getting to him."

"Tell Mike this is going to work out," I said.

Zack shot me a questioning look. "Do you know something I don't know?"

"No, but look at the team Mike has backing him: Colby and Associates, Maisie, you, Falconer Shreve's best and brightest, the Webers and me."

Zack's grin was sardonic. "Piece of cake," he said, and with that he was gone.

When the door closed behind him, Annie said, "That was a nice send-off. Are you really that certain?"

"No," I said. "So, let's get to work." I took out my copy of the notes. "I'd like to start with Thalia Monk because Thalia and the people closest to her seem to be at the centre of all the unsettling events that have happened in the past four and a half months."

"Mike is determined to keep Thalia out of this," Warren said. "I don't see how that's possible. She's clearly a very troubled young woman."

"The first time I saw Thalia was that day when we were at the Scarth Club with you," I said. "She was wearing that white eyelet dress and an *Alice in Wonderland* ribbon that held her hair off her face. She seemed so young and so fragile. Watching her being ripped apart by that farce with the cake, the candles and the servers singing 'Happy Birthday,' was sickening. I realize Patti Morgan was drunk that day, and I understand she was in her own private hell, but I remember thinking that she wasn't drunk when she ordered that cake.

Patti must have known that celebrating the birthday Thalia shared with her brother would break Thalia, but Patti went ahead with her plan."

"That struck me too," Annie said. "What Patti did to her daughter was unforgivable. But that day when I drove her home, Patti was as broken as her daughter. She couldn't stop talking about Nicholas — 'her glowing child,' as she called him. She kept saying that Thalia had taken Nicholas from her and somehow led him to the path that ended in his suicide."

"Did she express any concern about Thalia?" I asked.

Annie's tone was uncharacteristically harsh. "No. Except for blaming Thalia for Nicholas's death, Patti didn't mention her daughter at all."

Warren had been listening intently. "Joanne, I'm sure you remember that line of poetry Thalia quoted, before she ran out of the Scarth Club that day."

"I do," I said. "'For nothing now can ever come to any good.'"

"It's a line that goes straight to the heart," Warren said. "I knew I'd heard the line before, but I couldn't remember the source. When Annie and I arrived home that day, I looked it up. The line is from the last stanza of W.H. Auden's 'Funeral Blues.'

The stars are not wanted now; put out every one,
Pack up the moon and dismantle the sun,
Pour away the ocean and sweep up the wood;
For nothing now can ever come to any good.

"Those lines seem strangely prophetic now, don't they?"

"They do," I said. "And, as Zack said, someone put the turtle on that fence. There've been a number of strange and damaging occurrences, and all of them seem to have a connection, however tangential, to MediaNation.

"Thalia Monk is the daughter of MediaNation's head of human resources and Patti Morgan, who for twelve years was an on-air personality at MediaNation. Thalia was one of the company's four summer interns. The other three, like Thalia, are members of a tightly knit group called the University Park Road Gang."

"That's our street," Annie said.

"It is," I said. "And all the members of the group live on it. I'm sure you and Warren know their families. Clay Fairbairn is Hugh and Julie Fairbairn's grandson; Austin Brinkmann is the son of Graham and Nancy Brinkmann. Ronan Farquhar, like Clay, is being raised by his grandparents."

"Lionel and Mercedes Farquhar, our next-door neighbours," Warren said. "Ronan couldn't have been more than seven when he came to live with Lionel and Mercedes. He was a dear little boy but fearful. Not surprising because the first seven years of his life were not easy. The Farquhars' daughter, Ronan's mother, had a drug problem, and there was never any mention of Ronan's father." Warren leaned forward. "Joanne, you said those young people were all part of a *gang*. To me, that word connotes lawlessness. I realize there's a several generation gap between me and Thalia Monk and those young men, but I can't imagine any of them breaking laws."

"As far as we know, they haven't," I said. "They all attended Luther College High School, the school Thalia transferred to when she moved back to Regina in grade eleven. Taylor went to Luther too, as did one of her best friends, Gracie Falconer. Taylor was a year younger than the kids from University Park Road, but Gracie was in their year. According to Gracie, before Thalia arrived, the boys in the group were just some very smart kids who lacked social skills and who all lived in the same neighbourhood."

"But Thalia Monk changed them," Annie said.

"According to Gracie, in the summer between grades eleven and twelve, Thalia transformed the boys, physically and emotionally. When they started grade twelve, they saw themselves as a 'cohort'; they dressed well, they took pains with their appearance and Thalia convinced them that they were superior beings who could make their own rules."

"They certainly sound obnoxious," Annie said. "But isn't it possible they're just compensating for all their nerd years?"

"I know what you're saying, Annie, and you're right. At that age, kids do go through phases; they try on identities until they figure out who they are. But this is different. Gracie Falconer is one of the most sensible and generous people I know, but she says that when the members of the cohort were together, they emanated a darkness that she could feel."

Warren leaned against the back of his chair and closed his eyes. "Do you believe the cohort is at the centre of all this?"

"I don't know," I said, "but the problems did start when the interns began their tenure at the beginning of May. They got off to a bad start and the exit letter the interns submitted collaboratively at the end of the summer puts the blame squarely on Rosemary Morrissey, the former executive producer for programming. Warren, the letter is the first item in the folder we brought. Would you mind reading it aloud?"

"Not at all," Warren said, and he put on his wire-rimmed reading glasses and began. When he'd finished, he shook his head. "That's a powerful indictment of MediaNation's treatment of their interns. Is it true?"

"Yes," I said. "I talked to the producer of Charlie D's show, and he says everything in that letter is factually true, but he feels the interns' interpretation of what happened is wrong."

"That's not a convincing argument," Warren said. "Facts are facts. The letter says that Rosemary Morrissey suffered a breakdown and left MediaNation. Where is she now?"

"No one knows. The head of HR in Toronto asked the one hundred and fifteen people in Rosemary's unit to write individual letters assessing her ability to do her job. They did. Joseph Monk delivered the verdict of her co-workers to Rosemary. That was towards the end of June. That day, Rosemary cleared out her office, put her house and cottage up for sale and no one has heard from her since."

"That is so unfair to everyone," Annie said. "Ms. Morrissey's colleagues had to tell the truth, but they must have felt sick about what they were doing. And why did the head of HR feel compelled to tell Ms. Morrissey that all her co-workers sent letters saying she was no longer capable of doing her job?"

"Zack's reading of the situation is that Joseph Monk is a sadistic son of a bitch," I said. "That's as good an explanation as any. And Rosemary was only the first casualty.

"At the end of August, Joseph Monk told Ellen Exton, the producer of Charlie D's show, that the company had received a sexually explicit video of her with an extortion threat. Ellen told Charlie she'd sent several relatively innocuous videos via an online dating site, but Joseph Monk refused to hear her out.

"Monk gave Ellen Exton two options: sign a non-disclosure agreement and resign with a generous severance package and a glowing reference — or be fired."

Warren made no attempt to hide his disbelief and disgust. "MediaNation must have a legal department," he said. "Monk must have known the options he gave Ms. Exton left the corporation open to a charge of wrongful dismissal. Why did he go rogue and handle Ms. Exton's case alone?"

"Because Joseph Monk was the one who engineered the Jared Delio debacle."

Annie's eyes widened. "I remember that. Three women accused Jared Delio of forcible sex offences. The MediaNation spokesperson defended Delio until tapes surfaced proving what the women said was true, and Delio was fired."

"Joseph Monk engineered that debacle," I said. "But that's history. This summer Monk has treated situations with two loyal long-serving employees in ways that were both ham-handed and cruel."

As I described Joseph Monk's handling of the situations with Rosemary Morrissey and Ellen Exton, Annie made no attempt to hide her disgust. "And he still has a job? Joseph Monk must have something career-ending on somebody."

"Or, as Zack always says, 'shit floats.'"

Annie smiled. "True enough," she said, then her smile faded. "Where's Ellen Exton now?"

"Nobody knows," I said. "Everything happened very quickly. A MediaNation employee appeared. He was charged with making certain Ellen Exton cleared out her desk and did not take any of the company's property with her. Ellen got in touch with Charlie. He'd already gone home for the day, but he came back and offered to help her in any way he could. Charlie said she was dazed. She just wanted to get out of the building, so he helped her carry out her things, drove her to her house, and when all the boxes were carried in, she thanked him and he left. No one has seen or heard from Ellen since. Unlike Rosemary Morrissey, Ellen did not set her house in order before she left. She simply vanished, leaving her two much-loved cats behind."

Annie's brow furrowed. "Joanne, where have the police been in all this? Surely when no one could reach Ellen Exton, the police were alerted."

"They were," I said. "But Ellen is an adult. There was no evidence of wrongdoing at her house, so the police waited. Over forty-eight hours passed before they started investigating. They've been pursuing the case diligently, but nothing has come to light. Kam Chau, who took over producing Charlie's show, was a friend of Ellen's. Her cats are now with him. He's still hoping, but I'm sure he's convinced that Ellen's dead."

"Two women working for the same company disappear within a month and a half of each other after being treated abysmally by management." Warren picked up the folder we'd brought. "Is there anything in here suggesting a connection between what happened to Ms. Morrissey and Ms. Exton?"

"No, but there are extensive notes on what Zack, Maisie, Jill and I know about other troubling matters. Some of the information, like Clay Fairbairn's attack on Alison Janvier at the Real Prairie Picnic, will be old news to you, but that, at least, is documented. The cohort's not-so-veiled attempts to make public the circumstances behind the conception of Alison's son, Harper, are not well known, but Maisie gathered enough concrete evidence about Ronan Farquhar's involvement in that particular venture to prove the cohort is behind it. Much of the rest is pure conjecture, but we've included copies of two fragments of paper in the folder. Neither of them conveys a coherent message, but we believe they're significant. Kam Chau found the first one under a script on his desk the morning after Rosemary Morrissey left MediaNation for the last time."

Annie stared at the words and then spoke them aloud: "I am warning you not to be fooled. This person is young, charismatic, narcissistic and capable of . . ." She looked at me questioningly.

"Kam is certain that Rosemary Morrissey wrote those words," I said. "She always used a fountain pen and black ink, and her handwriting was strong and distinctive. He believes this scribble reflects Rosemary's state of mind — that she was attempting to warn him, but at the last minute changed her mind and ripped off the words that would have completed her thought."

"The second piece is a photograph the police took of a Post-it Note on Ellen Exton's refrigerator door. 'It's not enough!'"

Warren's headshake reflected the frustration we all felt. "Those three words would seem to describe the weight of the information we have at the moment," he said. "What we have is suggestive, but it's not enough."

* * *

When Zack returned, his expression was unreadable.

"How did it go?" I said.

"It went well," Zack said. "But since Mike is now my client, that's about all I can volunteer. Any Roman candles go off here while you were looking through the folder?"

Annie shook her head. "No, but aren't Roman candles the fireworks that ignite in stages? Give us a little time." As she looked at her husband, Annie's smile was wicked. "We always manage to ignite, don't we, Warren?"

Zack and I exchanged glances. "I believe that's our cue to leave," I said. Annie started to protest, but I waved her off. "Taylor's at Lawyers Bay, and she'll be eager to hear about our visit with you."

Annie jumped up. "Give me a second, and I'll box some shortbread for her. Is Vale with her?"

"No, she's not." I swallowed hard. "I'm still not used to saying these words, but Taylor and Vale are no longer a couple."

Annie's face fell. "I'm so sorry."

Warren put his arm around his wife's shoulders. "I'm sorry too. Annie and I had a long talk with Vale and Taylor at the Falconer Shreve Canada Day party. They seemed to have a bright future ahead of them."

"They'll still have bright futures," I said. "Just not together."

The Webers walked us to the dock. When Zack and I had our life jackets on, Annie handed me the box of shortbread for Taylor.

"Taylor will appreciate this," I said. "Thanks for thinking of her."

"And thanks for being there for Mike," Zack said. "He's going through hell. It's a relief for me professionally and personally to know that you two are close by."

Warren's gaze was piercing as he looked first at Zack, then at me. "Mike Braeden is a good and ethical man. He would never knowingly harm another human being. Hang on to that, and we'll all come through this just fine."

CHAPTER SEVENTEEN

When Zack and I were married, he purchased his late partner Chris Altieri's cottage at Lawyers Bay for our family to use when they joined us at the lake. It was a perfect arrangement: we were able to be together, but we were also able to be apart. Our grown children were responsible for getting their family's breakfast and lunch, but every night we all sat down at our place for dinner in the sunroom overlooking Lawyers Bay.

Wednesday afternoon, Pete called to say that Maisie was in court, so we should expect them a little later than planned. They were picking up takeout from the East Indian place in Fort Qu'Appelle. According to our oldest son, the Crawford-Kilbourn order was heavy on dumplings, and the boys were crazy excited about eating dumplings, sleeping over, seeing Taylor and the dogs and learning how to drive the big boat. When I passed the message along to Zack, he beamed. "Sounds like the days will be jam-packed," he said.

All the adults who sat down at the partners table that evening brought heavy thoughts with them, but we kept to our rule about sticking to light conversational topics during meals — a commitment made easier by the fact that, in a developmental spurt that children on the brink of turning four are prone to, both Charlie and Colin had suddenly become loquacious. The Rocky Mountain Play Structure was proving to be the neighbourhood kid magnet. The twins had tales to tell about their new friends and, between mouthfuls of tiger shrimp and vegetable samosas, Charlie and Colin filled us in. Charlie was voluble, but it turned out that Colin, the quiet observer, was the boy who delivered the telling detail. I was sitting next to Colin, and after he'd polished off his third naan, he turned to me. "Before he goes down the big slide, Cole Potter always does this," he said, touching his forehead, his lower chest, his left upper arm and then his right.

"Cole's making the sign of the cross," I said. "The way we do in church."

Colin's smile was patient. It was obvious I didn't get it. "No, you do it so you don't turn back. Cole says if you're too scared to go down the big slide, you just do this," Colin made the sign of the cross, "you won't be scared. So now all kids do that, and nobody ever turns back."

I knew that many of the children the twins played with came from Muslim or Jewish homes, but when I asked Colin if all their parents were okay with their children making the sign of the cross, he was clearly puzzled. "Mimi, nobody wants their kid to turn back. They just want their kid to go down the big slide." I left the table knowing that I had just learned a life lesson. What that lesson was was anybody's guess.

After we'd cleared away the dishes, Zack called Bob Colby and asked him to have his investigators look into Thalia Monk's relationships with her brother, mother and father. Then he and Maisie drove to the Webers' to meet with Mike Braeden, while Pete, Taylor and I took Charlie and Colin up to the guest cottage to get them ready for bed.

Taylor volunteered to read the boys Michael Kusugak's stories about Allashua, a young Inuit girl whose curiosity leads to hair-raising adventures with the mythical creatures who live beneath the sea ice. The books had been among Taylor's and then Madeleine and Lena's favourites, and the illustrations of inuksuit, the stone landmarks built by Inuit as signposts, had inspired Taylor, Gracie Falconer and Isobel Wainberg to build their own inuksuit around the horseshoe shore of Lawyers Bay. As an incentive to get the boys to be still so they could fall asleep, Taylor promised to take Colin and Charlie around the shore the next day. Together, they would inspect the inuksuit, so the boys could help make any necessary repairs before winter set in.

Less than two hours after they left for the Webers', Zack and Maisie were back at Lawyers Bay. Their interview with Mike Braeden hadn't been lengthy, but I could tell it had disturbed Zack. The creases that bracketed his mouth like parentheses had deepened — always a sign of stress. As soon as he came in the door, I rubbed my husband's arm and said, "Time to turn in."

Zack didn't put up a fight, and he was preoccupied as we readied ourselves for bed.

"Do you want to talk about it?" I said.

"Not much," he said. "Mike Braeden is innocent. A prof of mine at law school said the trial lawyer's greatest fear is having an innocent client. If your client's guilty, you give the case your best shot, and if you lose, you know that justice has probably been served. If you have an innocent client and your gut tells you that you can't save him, you want to put your fist through a window fifteen times a day."

"I know you can't give me details, but did you learn something tonight that made you question your ability to get Mike off?"

"No. It wasn't that. Jo, you and I both know that Mike Braeden's life would have been better if he'd never set eyes on Patti Morgan, but all Mike could talk about tonight was Patti's daughter. He's worried sick about her. He asked our advice about calling Thalia just to reassure himself that she was all right. Of course, Maisie and I nixed that. We have no idea what Thalia believes happened, and the police regard Mike as a person of interest. The optics of Mike calling Thalia would raise suspicions.

"He accepted our advice, but he was insistent that somehow we make sure that Thalia is not in a situation that will exacerbate what she experienced. I told him Thalia is staying with Hugh and Julie Fairbairn and suggested Clay Fairbairn as a possible go-between. Mike was content with that and then he said, 'I've never seen a human being suffer as cruelly as Thalia has. Patti never missed a chance to turn the knife. I married Patti because I thought I could give them both a stable home and a good life, but I failed.'

"And now," Zack said, "Mike is determined to save Thalia at any cost."

"That's why you want to put your fist through a window," I said. "Well, don't do it here. This cottage has premium PVC windows — guaranteed to withstand Saskatchewan winter blasts. If you tried to put your first through one of these, you'd just bruise your knuckles."

Zack harrumphed. "Spoilsport."

"Just saving you from yourself. Speaking of which, that leg spasm you had today wasn't the first one this week. Time for some leg exercises." I knelt beside my husband, placed one hand under his knee and the other around his ankle and extended the leg by lifting the ankle up until it was parallel to the floor.

"You don't have to do that," Zack said.

"I know, but I like doing it. For the same reason you like putting lotion on the parts of my back I can't reach. We like taking care of each other. And after we're through here, we're going to continue taking care of each other by going to bed early. You and Pete promised to teach the boys the rudiments of driving the boat. Colin and Charlie will be raring to go before the sun comes up, and you'll need to be in fighting trim."

Zack and I are early risers, and on Thursday morning, we were dressed and clearing away the breakfast dishes when there was a spirited knocking on our front door. I glanced at my watch. "It's six twenty-one," I said. "I believe your grandsons are here for their lesson in driving the Chris-Craft."

Once in a while, I'm prescient. When I opened the door, the twins in matching, hooded, fire-engine red rain slickers were standing on our porch. Behind them, smiling sheepishly, were their parents.

"They woke up at four," Maisie said. "We coaxed them into staying in their beds and playing quietly for another hour, but Pete and I are no match for the lure of the lake."

"Would you like coffee?" I said. "Taylor's going to crew with Pete, and she'll be here at seven."

Before Charlie and Colin had a chance to cloud up at news of the delay, Zack wheeled over to them. "I went online to the Chris-Craft store and got us each a manual," he said. "A manual is a book that shows you how to do something like drive a boat. On the big table in the sunroom, there are three manuals: one for each of us. We have to go through them carefully before we go down to the lake."

Colin nodded sagely. "The manual keeps us from making mistakes," he said.

Zack beamed. "And you've just learned the first lesson."

Taylor arrived on the dot of seven. The manuals had been a hit, and we hadn't heard a peep from the boys or their grandfather since they'd gone out to the sunroom. When they emerged, the boys were clutching their manuals and looking determined.

"So, did you guys have fun?" Maisie said.

Charlie narrowed his eyes. "No," he said. "We were learning."

Maisie ran her fingers through her thick copper curls. "I stand corrected. Everybody take a pee and then we'll go down to the dock, and you guys can show us what you learned."

* * *

Except for the screech of the gulls and the lap of the waves against the hull of *Amicus*, the morning was quiet. Maisie held the boat manuals as Pete and Taylor tied the boys' red life jackets. Zack had a device that allowed him to lower himself into the boat. The mechanism was sophisticated structurally, and it depended solely on dexterity and strength. Zack was heavy-set, and I was struck again by the power his arms must have to hoist his body from land to boat. The manoeuvre took time, and the boys didn't move a muscle until Zack was in his place behind the controls.

As I watched Zack do a shoulder check to make sure everybody was ready, images of another ride in *Amicus* flashed through my mind. When I met Zack, he habitually left his life jacket on the floor of the launch when he drove. The first time we took out the boat after we'd made love, he put on his life jacket. I was relieved, but I'd tried to keep the moment light. "Decided to leave your inner rebel behind?" I said.

He took my hand. "Just aware that I now have something I don't want to lose."

Remembering that moment, my eyes filled. I reached over and took the boys' manuals from Maisie. "I'll run these down to the twins," I said. I squatted next to the launch, handed the boys their manuals and then rested my hand on Zack's shoulder and leaned in to kiss him. It was a serious kiss, and he was clearly surprised but pleased. "What was that for?" he said.

"For wearing your life jacket," I said. Then I swallowed hard and went back and stood with Maisie, watching until *Amicus* disappeared from view.

* * *

I'd had no part in decorating the house at Lawyers Bay. Like the landscaping, the colour scheme and furnishings had been in place long before Zack and I met. But from the day I first walked through the front door, I'd been at ease in our home's cool, uncluttered, light-filled spaces.

With one exception, the furnishings were tasteful, and remarkable only for their clean lines and fine craftsmanship. The exception was a treasure that Zack's decorator found at a local auction: a gleaming oak partners' table from a long-defunct law firm. The table came with twenty-four oak chairs upholstered in leather the colour of the fine port that I imagined the partners sipping on Friday afternoons.

Zack's speculation about the early life of the partners' table was less romantic than mine. Any law firm that had twenty-four partners was obviously a major player in early twentieth-century western Canada, but Zack had had no luck chasing down the names of the lawyers who had thundered and bellowed in the chairs where our granddaughters now drew pictures of girls with spiky purple hair and saucer eyes.

* * *

Maisie wasted no time getting down to business when we returned to the cottage. Her briefcase and laptop were already on the partners' table, and she sat down, opened her laptop and glanced at the screen. "Looks like Colby and Associates are living up to their reputation," she said. "Information about Thalia's relationship with her brother and her parents was a trickle when I checked at four a.m., and now it's pouring in. Bob Colby says they're still nailing down precise dates, but what they have is certainly enough for now."

Maisie kept her eyes on the screen as she gave me a running commentary of Colby's report. "By the time Joseph Monk left for Toronto, he and Patti had been separated for several years, but they lived in the same condominium block, and apparently Nicholas and Thalia moved easily between their parents' respective homes. Nicholas was six and Thalia was five when Joseph Monk was offered the job in Toronto. They were already enrolled in the neighbourhood school in Regina, so Joseph and Patti decided their children should stay there. Joseph Monk had generous visitation rights, and he exercised them. The children were with him for holidays and for one month in the summer.

"When Nicholas was twelve and Thalia was eleven, they moved to Toronto to live with their father. Patti was amenable to the decision. By that point, she'd sensed her career here was going nowhere, and she'd been applying elsewhere. Joseph Monk was settled in Toronto, so the children moved in with him. From everything Colby and Co. have picked up, it seems the life of the Monk family was harmonious. The children seemed to be thriving, doing brilliantly at school, never in any trouble.

"Then out of nowhere in the middle of a school year, Joseph Monk yanks his sixteen-year-old daughter out of the school where she's been an exemplary grade eleven student and sends her halfway across the country to Regina. The day after Thalia was sent away, seventeen-year-old Nicholas Monk jumped from the roof garden of their condominium to the courtyard below — a twenty-seven-storey drop."

Nicholas's death was not news to me, but hearing the words had the force of a punch in the stomach. "That fits with everything we know," I said. "Where did Colby's people get their information?"

"From a snitch at MediaNation. Colby's people have sources in all the right places. They really are good." Maisie shifted her focus from the screen to me. "Do you know what the motto of Colby and Associates is? 'The truth will come to light.'"

"Comforting words from *The Merchant of Venice*," I said.

"Words that take me back," Maisie said. "We did what our teacher called a stage reading of *The Merchant of Venice* in grade eleven. I loved that line: 'The truth will come to light.

Murder cannot be hid long.' I was Portia, but that's not her line. It's Launcelot's, and the boy who read Launcelot played it for laughs. I was furious."

"It should have been your line," I said.

Maisie's eyes were blazing. "Damn straight." She took a deep breath. "Okay, I'm over it. Back to work."

"So, Colby's people know what happened," I said. "Do they have any theories about why it happened?"

Maisie shook her head. "No. That is still a matter for conjecture. What's your conjecture, Jo?"

"From all accounts, Joseph Monk was devoted to his children. He must have known that separating them would be devastating for them both."

"And yet he carried through with a decision that destroyed them. Why did he separate Thalia and Nicholas?"

"Because he had no choice," I said. "The alternative was unthinkable."

The silence between my daughter-in-law and me was fraught. Neither of us wanted to put into words what we knew must be the truth.

Finally, Maisie said, "Colby's people sent photos of Nicholas and Thalia from their yearbook the last year they were in school together." Maisie pulled her chair closer to mine and adjusted her laptop so we could both see the screen. "As soon as I saw their photos side by side, I knew what must have happened between them."

Nicholas's and Thalia's likeness to each other was breathtaking as was their physical beauty. Their eyes were the same stunning shade of sapphire blue; their ash-blond hair, centre-parted, fell in brush strokes around their fine-boned faces; even their mouths were identical: expressive lips curled in a sardonic half smile.

I couldn't take my eyes off them. "Siegmund and Sieglinde," I said.

Maisie's look was quizzical.

"Siegmund and Sieglinde are characters in Richard Wagner's opera cycle, *The Ring of the Nibelung*," I said. "They're twins, separated at birth, unknown to each other. They meet, realize they're brother and sister, but they still fall in love. Sieglinde becomes pregnant with their child and gives birth to Siegfried, who is the hero in another opera, but that's as far as memory takes me."

"That's far enough," Maisie said dryly. "Nicholas and Thalia knew they were brother and sister, and became lovers anyway. And that is not a problem covered by Dr. Spock."

"No, it isn't. I've heard nothing good about Joseph Monk, but no parent should be faced with a situation that heart-rending."

"I've dealt with cases of incest more often than I care to remember," Maisie said. "But Jo, this isn't a drunk father violating his daughter, or an uncle forcing himself on his niece. This looks consensual. Look at them. Apparently, he was as brilliant as she is. They're certainly both beautiful."

"And they thought of themselves as superior to their peers in every way," I said. "Maisie, something Gracie Falconer mentioned is nagging me. She told me that Thalia and the other members of the University Park Road cohort all carried around copies of *Thus Spake Zarathustra*."

Maisie closed her eyes and massaged her temples. "Nietzsche," she said. "I read *Thus Spake Zarathustra* when I was seventeen. My sister and I went to a high school where most of the students, like us, were farm kids. A lot of them were smart, but Lee and I were always at the top of our class. Lee was more grounded than I was. She said there were many different kinds of intelligence — ours was just the kind that was rewarded at school."

"But you didn't agree," I said.

Maisie's smile was rueful. "No. Unlike my sister, I did not see the larger picture. I just saw me, and when I came upon Nietzsche's concept of the Übermensch, I fell for it hook, line and sinker."

"The idea that superior beings can create their own morality because they're beyond the morality dictated by society is seductive," I said. "And Nicholas and Thalia were both at an age where hormones play a large role in choices."

Maisie was pensive. "The incest taboo is one of the most widespread in all cultures."

"Nicholas and Thalia obviously felt their love for each other transcended the taboo," I said.

Maisie sighed. "This case is going to bring a world of grief to people who have already suffered far too much."

"There's a possibility we could be way off the mark about the relationship between Nicholas and Thalia," I said. "Even if we're not, Nicholas committed suicide almost five years ago. I can't see how it's relevant to the Patti Morgan case."

"Let's hope you're right," Maisie said. "It's inevitable that the media will dig up Nicholas's suicide, but I don't see them using it. And it won't affect the Crown's case or ours. Maybe we'll catch a break, and everyone will see that his death is a tragedy that is best left alone."

"I wonder," I said. "Five years ago would have been around the time *Sunny Side Up* was phased out. Suddenly Patti had no job and no prospects; her beloved son had committed suicide, and the daughter whom Patti had always seen as her rival was suddenly her responsibility. That's a heavy burden; she must have confided in somebody."

Maisie scrolled through the information from Colby and Associates. "The only friends listed here are Rosemary Morrissey, whom Colby's people describe as 'mentor and colleague.' Ellen Exton, 'casual friend and colleague,' and Kam Chau who produced *Sunny Side Up* its last year on the air, 'good working relationship.' Joanne, do you think Patti had any inkling that the relationship between Nicholas and Thalia was sexual?"

"I'm sure she didn't — at least not at first. I don't think she would have agreed to having Thalia live with her if she'd known."

Maisie rubbed her temples. "And what you and I have is just conjecture. We may be way out in left field with this, Jo."

"I hope to God we are," I said. "But we can't dismiss the possibility. This has been gnawing at me, Maisie. We may not have anything concrete, but we do have a timeline that could be a red flag. Warren told Zack that just before Christmas something happened to Patti Morgan. At that point she and Mike had been married three years. Mike told Warren that he had hoped the marriage would lift Patti out of her depression and give Thalia a stable life. That hadn't happened, but Patti was making an effort. She'd volunteered for a couple of charities; they'd begun to entertain some of Mike's friends, and Patti was getting to know their neighbours."

"Mike was optimistic, then everything changed," Maisie said. "The Braedens had planned to have a celebratory holiday meal at the Scarth Club with another couple. According to Mike, Patti arrived very late and drunk, and that was the beginning of the end. Since then, Mike has been extricating Patti from ugly situations with men Patti picked up when she was drinking and people who Patti believed had been condescending or insulting."

"And the pattern culminated in Patti's attack on Mike with the broken liquor bottle," I said.

Maisie raised an eyebrow. "You do understand that I can't say anything more about that."

"I do, but I can say more. The morning after she attacked Mike, Patti showed up at MediaNation. Kam Chau said she hadn't been in the building since *Sunny Side Up* went off the air. He also said her behaviour was unnerving.

"Kam came to Lawyers Bay because he knew Zack was Mike's lawyer. He was aware of Patti's attack on Mike the night before, and he was afraid Patti might strike out at Mike again. Kam said Patti was obsessed by the fear that Mike would spread ugly lies about her son and that he was going through her things trying to find something about Nicholas that a therapist could use against her."

"Zack and I have talked about this," Maisie said.

"I know that subject is off the table," I said. "But it seems to me the picture might be clearer if we knew what happened to Patti in the period just before Christmas, when her behaviour changed so radically."

Maisie raked her curls with her fingers. "Okay," she said. "We may have something to go on here. It's time Zack and I leaned harder on Mike. If he knows what sent Patti off the rails before Christmas, we'll at least have a starting point."

"And there's something else," I said. "Jill Oziowy mentioned that Thalia had always been her father's favourite. Why didn't Joseph Monk send Nicholas to Patti and keep Thalia with him? Warren says Thalia blames her father for Nicholas's suicide."

Maisie shuddered. "So, Thalia lost her brother and was sent away by her father. The only family she had left was a mother who hated her."

"According to the Colby notes, Joseph Monk suffered too. The MediaNation snitch said Monk went through hell after Nicholas died, but he came out of it determined to salvage what was left of his family, and that meant getting his daughter back.

"Patti Morgan worked at MediaNation for twelve years. There must have been someone besides Rosemary Morrissey with whom Patti was close. I'll call Jill Oziowy." I picked up my phone and speed-dialled. My call went straight to voice-mail, and I left a message.

* * *

At noon, the mariners returned, rosy-cheeked from the wind on the lake and hungry. Maisie and I prepared the perennial favourites for a crisp fall day: tomato soup, grilled cheese sandwiches and Maisie's chocolate chip cookies — by her own admission the only recipe she'd never managed to screw up.

By the time they'd polished off their milk and cookies, Charlie and Colin's eyelids were beginning to droop, and so were Zack's. We all had busy afternoons ahead, so the Crawford-Kilbourns, Chris-Craft manuals in hand, headed for their cottage; Taylor headed for her studio, and Zack and I headed for our bedroom.

Zack was buoyant as he related the highlights of the twins' boat-driving lesson, and I didn't darken his mood by sharing Maisie's and my theory about the relationship between Nicholas and Thalia. The exhilarating adventure on the water with his grandsons, his daughter and his son-in-law had erased the worry lines from Zack's face, and our ninety-minute nap restored us both. Zack was facing an afternoon of heavy slogging, but dressed in khakis and a blue cashmere pullover I was particularly fond of, he appeared up to the task.

"You look as if you're ready to take on the world," I said.

Zack wheeled closer to me. "We live in hope," he said. "Now, give me a quick smooch to get me through the afternoon."

* * *

As soon as we left the cottage, Taylor, Charlie, Colin and the dogs ran ahead of Peter and me, eager to start their tour of inspection. It was a great day to be outdoors. The sun was bright, the air was clear and the sky was the shade of cerulean that makes September on the prairies such a heart-stopper. These days, Pete and I seldom spent time alone together, so we were content to move at a leisurely pace and savour the pleasure of talking about nothing in particular. Pete had inherited the Kilbourn men's good looks: wavy black hair, pale complexion, chiselled features, but his temperament was closer to mine than to Ian's. My eldest son was not ambitious. His aspirations were within reach: a degree in veterinary medicine, a family, a quiet life, and he had been willing to make concessions along the way to make his dream a reality.

"I'm always sad to see summer go," I said. "But autumn is glorious at Lawyers Bay. As are winter and spring. It doesn't matter what month we're in, it's always a wrench for me to leave the lake. Zack says if I want to sell the house in town and move here permanently, I should just say the word."

"And?" Pete said.

"A thousand years ago when I took Psych 101 at university, I learned about approach-approach conflict," I said. "I love being here, but I also love being a brisk ten-minute walk from you, your sister and your families when we're in the city. Now, you and I better step it up. We don't want to miss Taylor's lecture on how to build an inuksuk."

"When did Taylor, Gracie and Isobel decide to build the inuksuit?" Pete asked.

"The summer before Zack and I were married — so, seven years ago."

"And they dug up all those rocks from the land around the cottages?"

"It wasn't that simple," I said. "Every rock except those saved for ornamental groupings had been removed from Lawyers Bay before the girls were born. We had to go into Fort Qu'Appelle to a business called Peter's Rocks to get what they needed. The weather was miserable that day: cold and windy with rain that seemed to be coming down in sheets, but the girls were determined to choose the perfect rocks. It took them at least an hour to make their selection."

Pete gave me a quick admiring head nod. "You're a trooper, Mum."

"It wasn't that bad," I said. "I got to explore the collection of lawn ornaments Peter offered his customers, and the ladies and I all enjoyed watching the buff young guy in the tight jeans load the rocks onto his pickup."

Pete laughed. "Are those magic moments included in *Sisters and Strangers*?"

"No," I said. "I've had more than my share of joy, but the great parts of my life get short shrift in *Sisters and Strangers*."

"Are you disappointed in the way the series turned out?"

"No. Not at all. Telling the truth about Sally's life and mine mattered to me, and now the truth will be out there."

"MediaNation is certainly pulling out all the stops to make sure viewers know when and where to tune in."

"No complaints on that score," I said. "The corporation's been behind the series from the beginning, and their publicity department has been in overdrive since Canada Day."

"Mum, does it bother you that starting tomorrow night, millions of people are going to be watching your life unfold?"

"No, I've made my peace with that. It's Taylor I'm concerned about," I said. "Zack and I could have seen the final version of *Sisters and Strangers*, but we decided to wait. Even in the rough cut, Vale's performance as the young Sally Love is astounding. Unless she stumbles — and Vale never stumbles — she's destined for a long and very successful career."

"Maisie and I caught an interview with Vale on one of the late shows last week. She's certainly a charmer, and the host was obviously smitten. After they showed a clip from *Sisters and Strangers*, he said that when he was prepping for the interview, he'd only planned to look at a few scenes from the series, but once he started to watch, he couldn't stop until he'd seen all six episodes. He told Vale her performance as Sally was flawless, and that it brought him to tears."

"MediaNation will be jumping for joy," I said.

"No doubt," Pete said. "Mum, I'm not sure you'll be jumping for joy when you hear how Vale responded to the host's compliment. She said that Sally Love's sister, Joanne Shreve, and her daughter, Taylor, had been invaluable in helping her discover the key to Sally's character, and she would always be grateful to them both for welcoming her into their lives."

Suddenly I felt weary. "Taylor is hoping that now that she and Vale are no longer together, her private life will be private again. Zack and I are hoping for that too."

"So are Maisie and I," Pete said. "But I think you and Taylor should be ready for an onslaught of media interest at least for a while."

"As long as we're here, we're safe. This is a gated community. Nobody in our family is on Twitter, and we can monitor texts and email."

Peter's expression was grave. "I wish this wasn't happening," he said.

I took his arm. "So do I, but it is happening, and we're lucky we have options."

CHAPTER EIGHTEEN

I awoke Friday morning with my stomach in knots. When I told Peter that I'd made my peace with the production of *Sisters and Strangers*, it was the truth. The genesis of the series was an anecdote I'd told writer Roy Brodnitz about the story behind Sally Love's painting, *Flying Blue Horses*. Through a sequence of events that could be viewed as either purely coincidental or fated, Roy Brodnitz had received incontrovertible evidence that my biological father was not Dr. Douglas Ellard, the physician who I'd grown up believing was my father, but his closest friend, Desmond Love, the visual artist and the father of my lifelong best friend, Sally.

Roy had come to our home to tell me the news in person, but before we'd talked, he'd noticed a painting of Sally's on the wall facing the door. Sally had been twelve when she made the painting, and it captured a moment of magic that she and Desmond Love had shared. He had taken her to the Saugeen First Nation reserve on Lake Huron to see the workmanship on the decorative boxes the women there made out of birchbark and porcupine quills.

One of the women suggested that Des and Sally climb to a place where they could take in the beauty of the land and the water. They'd been sitting on a hillside overlooking the lake when a band of wild horses streaked down the hill, heading for the water. The horses were only a few metres away from them. Sally said their hooves barely touched the ground, and their coats were so black they were almost blue.

When I told Roy that Sally and Des had brought me back a birchbark box with a pattern of a loon family on the lid, a fleeting shadow crossed his face, but as I showed him the art Taylor had made as she was growing up and talked about my years with her, his expression of concern faded. As he was leaving, Roy said that when he heard that Des had taken Sally to a place where they saw flying blue horses but brought me back only a token gift, he was concerned that I might feel life had cheated me, but that when he saw my face as I talked about Taylor, he knew that the sister left behind was the lucky one.

Working with the writer on the scripts for *Sisters and Strangers* had been painful but cathartic for me. Many lies had been told about Sally's life and about Izaak Levin's relationship with her. Now their stories and the stories of the tangled relationships between the two families who shared our island on McLeod Lake would be told honestly. The sister left behind had been the lucky one, and she was grateful she'd been given the chance to redress the balance and tear away the veil of rumours and falsehoods that had clouded Sally's life and Izaak's.

That said, I was glad that there was plenty to distract me in the hours before *Sisters and Strangers* aired. Taylor was working in her studio, but the rest of us spent a lazy morning wandering along the shoreline skipping stones, throwing sticks for the dogs and testing the water periodically to see if it was warm enough for a quick dip. It never was, but like every child before them, Colin and Charlie wheedled an agreement from their parents that they could roll up their pants and walk out till the water was knee-deep. Also, like every child before them, both boys accidentally tripped, so the wishes for quick dips had been granted.

At noon, Zack and Maisie took a plate of sandwiches and a thermos of tea into the sunroom where they would be working on eventualities if Mike Braeden was charged, and Pete, Taylor and I took the boys over to Standing Buffalo for an adventure.

Friday was a day of firsts for Colin and Charlie. Rose Lavallee, who had lived with the Falconers and raised Gracie since the day she came home from the hospital, was a member of the Standing Buffalo Dakota Nation, and Gracie, whose mother was also from Standing Buffalo, had often stayed with Rose in her house on the reserve. Taylor had been a frequent guest there too, so when Rose and her sister Betty invited us to attend Mass with them at the historic and beautiful Sacred Heart Church in Lebret and go back to Betty's for a lunch of venison and corn that the boys could pick from the sisters' shared garden and then shuck themselves, we didn't have to be asked twice.

Betty loved to entertain, and that afternoon as she greeted us, fragrant with her favourite Elizabeth Taylor White Diamonds cologne, and stunning in her newest stilettos and a scoop-necked red satin dress that hugged her curvaceous body, we knew she was pulling out all the stops. As always, Rose was trim in ironed blue jeans and a crisp cotton shirt, and she welcomed each of us with a firm handshake and the hint of a smile.

The sisters were very different women, but they both loved and were great with children, so Colin and Charlie were in their element. After lunch, Taylor drove Pete, the twins and me over to the house on the hill where Ol' Man Pilger, a tall, lanky scarecrow of a man, shared his home with the distressing number of animals that had been abandoned at the end of summer by cottagers who believed their pets, like the Muskoka chairs Taylor had reclaimed, had no part in their real lives back in the city.

I wasn't surprised when Peter, a veterinarian, talked privately with Ol' Man Pilger about bringing the twins out in a week or two to check over the animals' health and talk further about placement. After an hour with the pups and the cats, we went back to the Lavallees' to help Rose dig potatoes.

The afternoon was as close to heaven as an afternoon could be for the twins. When we returned to Lawyers Bay, Charlie and Colin, muddy but blissful, were each carrying a sack of potatoes they had dug themselves. The afternoon had been tonic for Taylor too. Her smile was once again coming easily, and her laughter was unforced. Our daughter was starting to look like her old self again, but Vale's words haunted me. I knew when Vale said she was grateful to us for welcoming her into our lives, the words came from her heart, but a tie that Taylor believed had been severed had been publicly acknowledged. It seemed that particular chapter wasn't closed after all.

Zack and Maisie came out to greet us. They both looked careworn, but when Colin and Charlie barrelled towards them, spilling potatoes as they ran, and held out their now depleted potato sacks for approval, Zack and Maisie rose to the occasion. They each grabbed a muddy boy and demanded to hear every detail of the afternoon. When the boys began to fade, Pete said, "We've got to get these guys cleaned up, fed and into bed ASAP. If they fall asleep now, they'll be bouncing off the walls when *Sisters and Strangers* starts, and nobody wants that."

I squeezed Zack's shoulder. "This is where the advantage of being a grandparent kicks in. Getting those two rapscallions clean, fed and into bed is a parental responsibility; you and I get to go home and have a martini."

* * *

Taylor had decided not to watch *Sisters and Strangers* with us. It was the right decision for her, and that night as Zack and I moved along the path towards the guest cottage, I wondered whether watching it would still be the right decision for me.

Zack sensed my hesitation and stopped. "We don't have to watch this with Pete and Maisie," he said, and his voice was deep and comforting. "In fact, we don't have to watch it at all."

I shook my head. "We promised, and if we back out now, Pete and Maisie will be worried that I'm falling apart."

"Are you?"

"No," I said.

Zack held out his arms. "How about a smooch for courage?"

The smooch was lovely, but as it turned out, it wasn't necessary. During the pre-production stage, I had attended table meetings — gatherings where the heads of all the departments met for what was essentially a session of show and tell, discussing and showing sketches or mock-ups of what each of their respective departments was planning.

Before I went into my first table meeting, I was approached by a towering broad-shouldered man with dark eyes, a mellow brown complexion, a shaved head and a winning smile. He introduced himself as Hal Dupuis, the costume designer for the series, and he thanked me for sharing the home movies that recorded our summers in the years between my birth and my sixteenth birthday.

I was taken aback. I had given the movies to Roy Brodnitz who was writing the script, but I hadn't realized they'd be distributed to other departments. Hal Dupuis picked up on my apprehension and apologized. "Once you see the ways in which we've used what you've given us, perhaps you'll forgive us," he said.

That meeting had been a revelation for me. There were twenty-five departments represented, and as each department presented, I realized that the elements of my life had been parcelled out and, in Hal's word, "used" to make something that was not my life, but the starting point for a piece of art that the people around the table would co-create. Georgie Shepherd, who ultimately replaced Roy as writer and who became my friend, alerted me to the fact that everyone at the table felt intimately connected with my family and Sally's, but for them, we were all characters to be dressed or lighted or moved in and out of a scene. Then she'd laughed and said that even if this was the story of my life, I shouldn't take what was said personally.

At the meeting that day, there'd been a discussion about whether the music in the series would be used to foster a mood, evoke an era or as a Greek chorus with lyrics commenting on the story. The question was still unresolved when the rough cuts were made, and the music used was generic.

That night, when Pete turned off the lights, and I heard Joni Mitchell's shimmering, vibrato-laden, mezzo-soprano singing "Circle Game," I knew the music director had gone for music that would not only foster a mood and evoke an era, but would also throw into sharp relief the truth driving the series: that we can't go back; we can only look behind at where we've come from.

When I was on the cusp of adolescence, I had tried to impress Desmond Love once by saying that I knew his paintings were abstracts, but I wanted to know what they were "about." His answer was thoughtful. He told me his work was about the magic of paint. He said, "I start with a blank canvas, and then gradually where there was nothing, there's colour and movement and life."

There had been a blank page, and for over a year, everyone connected with *Sisters and Strangers* had worked towards filling the emptiness with colour and movement and life. As soon as I heard Joni Mitchell's sweet voice hitting the pristine high notes, I knew the stories in *Sisters and Strangers* had been shaped by capable and caring hands, and I relaxed.

Ainsley Blair had convinced MediaNation to show the first two episodes in a block. In the final scene of the second episode, Joanne is standing alone on the dock. She has watched as Izaak Levin carries the Loves, one by one, down to the motorboat and now she is listening numbly as her father tells her that Des is dead and that he is uncertain of Nina's and Sally's chances of living.

As Douglas Ellard readies himself to start the motor, there is silence, and then the quiet of the early evening is shattered by the roar of the outboard motor, and the boat, low in the water from its terrible cargo, begins to move across the lake into the brilliant gold of the sunset. Joanne is watching intently, and even as the boat disappears from sight, she continues to watch and watch and watch.

When the credits began to roll, Peter came over to me. "Mum, was that the way it really happened?"

"Yes, that's exactly the way it happened."

Zack moved his chair closer to mine, and Maisie joined Peter. "How did you ever get over it?" she said.

"I didn't," I said. "But that was forty-six years ago. There've been a thousand other memories since then. Most of them have been good, but good or not good, that night at McLeod Lake will always be the figured bass that runs beneath them all, the bass note that anchors them and gives them context."

I glanced at Maisie. I knew that the death of Maisie's twin sister four years earlier was never far from my daughter-in-law's mind. "I'll never get there," she said tightly.

"You will," I said. "I was watching your face this afternoon when the potato farmers came home with their bounty. You're on your way, Maisie. Just give it time."

* * *

The next morning as soon as I left the house, I heard Taylor calling me. She was standing in front of her cottage. "Want some company on your walk?" she shouted.

"Love some."

Taylor's cottage was a fair distance from ours, and she was pink-cheeked and breathless from running when she joined me. The day was cool, and like me, our daughter was wearing a windbreaker over her shirt.

"Thanks for texting us last night," I said. "When your dad and I walked past your place, there were no lights on, and we didn't want to disturb you."

The sound Taylor made was somewhere between a moan and a chuckle. "No worries on that count," she said. "Vale phoned as soon as *Sisters and Strangers* was over, and I took the call, so I was already disturbed." Taylor didn't elaborate, and we continued to walk, her eyes remained firmly on the path ahead. I waited. "Vale wants us to get back together," she said finally. "She pushed all the right buttons, and she knows my vulnerabilities. When we were a couple, there were times when I believed she knew me better than I knew myself. That might have been true then, but last night I realized it wasn't true anymore. Ever since I came home, I've been thinking about myself 24/7. That sounds awful, but I needed to do it, and I'm glad I did, because last night when I told Vale that we didn't have a future together, I knew it was true."

"You sound very sure."

"I am sure. I was hurt and confused about Vale's affair with Etienne, but I've had time to think about that and some other issues." My daughter took my hand, the way she had when she was very young. "I understand now that when Vale said having sex with Etienne didn't mean anything more to her than sitting in the makeup chair for three hours in the morning, she was telling the truth. Vale had sex with Etienne because she knew she wasn't getting the balance between Sally and Izaak right. It was something she had to correct to get her performance right, and she corrected it."

Taylor fell silent, her eyes fixed again on the path ahead. The dogs had been ambling along twenty metres away, still in our line of vision. Suddenly she turned to me. "Esme's got a squirrel," she said, and she grabbed one of the leashes I was holding and took off. Esme had already headed down the hill towards the beach, but Pantera hadn't moved. When I called his name, Pantera looked around, then lumbered towards me. My lucky day.

Bouviers are gentle, but they have problems with anything that comes at them suddenly from above. This wouldn't be Esme's first squirrel, but she never knew what to do with them, and Bouviers have a soft bite. If we got to her in time, she'd drop the squirrel; the squirrel would scamper back up the tree, shoot Esme a look of triumph and disappear into the foliage. When Taylor and Esme reappeared on the path, I felt a wash of relief. Esme was on the leash, and she was squirrel-less. Seemingly our luck had held.

When Taylor returned, I greeted her like the hero she was and then I looked her over. "Are you okay?"

"I'm fine," she said, "but Esme wrecked my big moment — the moment when I was about to share my life-changing insight." Taylor's lips twitched into an endearingly crooked smile. "I hate when that happens. Don't you?"

"It's the worst," I agreed. "But the dogs are leashed now, so if you want to take another shot at it, I'm here."

"Remember telling me how Roy Brodnitz's relationship with an actor ended because the actor was in rehearsal for a play and he felt living with Roy was interfering with his clarity of thought about the character he was playing?"

I nodded. "I also remember that Roy's husband, Lev-Aaron, explained that while Roy's ex seemed ruthless, he was simply desperate. He'd put all his eggs in one basket, and he had to do whatever it took to protect the basket." I paused. "Taylor, do you think that's why Vale didn't understand that you'd be wounded if she had sex with Etienne Simard?"

"I know that's why." Our daughter's voice was calm and assured. "Vale has an incredible talent, but she's invested everything in it, so she has to protect it. The only way our relationship could survive is if we both lived Vale's life, and I need to live my own life." A tang of skunk wafted by.

"Mother Nature appears to be out in full force today," I said.

Taylor's focus was elsewhere. "Jo, do you think I'm making a mistake?"

"No. You made the right choice. When you said you didn't make any art during the year you were travelling, I knew you had to find your own way. Now, let's go home and tell your dad about Esme's great escape. After that, Pete, you and I will take the twins to the farmers' market, and they can have one of those huge cookies with the neon icing that you always loved."

Taylor cocked her head. "I wouldn't mind one of those cookies myself."

"You saved a squirrel's life today," I said. "The cookie's on me."

CHAPTER NINETEEN

Charlie and Colin loaded up on pumpkins at the farmers' market. Although both boys had gifts, wrapped and ready for the birthday party they were attending, they were both determined to take the birthday girl a pumpkin. The twins' own birthdays were three days away, and the boys chose small pumpkins for all their birthday-party guests and then a pumpkin each for their cousins and a medium-sized pumpkin for me because the 29th was also my birthday and a large pumpkin for Zack, so he wouldn't feel left out. Zack's pumpkin and mine were warty. We both noticed the warts, but fearing the answer, neither of us asked why. When the Crawford-Kilbourn station wagon pulled away, its cargo area was a sea of orange — the change of season was now official.

It had been a great visit, but keeping up with Charlie and Colin was exhausting, and I was in bed before the sun went down. I slept well, and the next morning when I put on my running clothes and came into the kitchen, Zack was already at the breakfast table. "You look chipper," he said.

I kissed the top of his head. "Ten hours of uninterrupted sleep will do that."

A pitcher of orange juice was on the table, and Zack poured me a glass. "Fresh squeezed, again," I said. "You spoil me."

"Just trying to cushion the blow," he said. "Jo, we're going to have to go back to the city after breakfast."

I pulled out the chair next to my husband. "What's up?"

"Maisie called after you went to bed last night. A flaming shit bag has been thrown at our case."

I grimaced. "A graphic image but I get the point. To save your case, you and Maisie have to stomp on a shit bag — not a pleasant prospect. So, what's happened?"

"Some low-life Patti had been dating got in touch with Maisie and told her that 'on numerous occasions' Patti said she was afraid of Mike Braeden. The low-life was prepared to forget Patti's words if we slipped him five thousand dollars."

"I take it that no money changed hands," I said.

"Our daughter-in-law doesn't like to be jerked around," Zack said. "She gave the guy directions to the cop shop on Osler Street and thanked him for his time."

"And he called Maisie's bluff and went to the police," I said.

"Maisie did the right thing, but now we're going to have to establish the context of Patti's words, and that means doing exactly what our client did not want us to do."

"Bring Mike Braeden's relationship with Patti and her daughter into this."

"Warren, Annie and Maisie are going to meet us at our house later this morning to discuss next steps." Zack had been watching my face carefully. "Jo, if you want to opt out . . ."

"No. We've been together on this from the day Charlie told us how shamefully Ellen Exton had been treated. I was furious about what had been done to Ellen, and I'm still furious about not having any answers — not just about what's happened to Ellen, but also about what happened to Rosemary Morrissey and about who's behind the Concerned Friend messages to our daughter. I want answers as much as you do. If I seem reluctant, it's only because I'm worried about leaving Taylor here alone when she's still finding her way to a future that does not include Vale."

"You can put that worry to bed," Zack said. "After I talked to Maisie last night, I called Noah Wainberg. He, Rose and Jacob are coming to Lawyers Bay this afternoon. Noah said they have a number of winterizing chores that are three-person jobs, so with Taylor around, he and Rose can get started."

Knowing Noah Wainberg would be with our daughter lifted the weight of worry from my shoulders. Noah, a gentle giant of a man, was the husband of Zack's late law partner, Delia Wainberg, and the father of Isobel, the third member of Taylor's trio of best friends. The Wainbergs had been a part of Taylor's life since Zack and I met. With the help of Rose Lavallee, Noah was now raising his grandson Jacob, a winning six-year-old, whom Taylor had known and adored since he became part of the Wainberg family.

"You chose the perfect company for our daughter," I said. "So much has changed in Taylor's life; she needs a reminder that the people she values and who value her are still here."

"Not all of them are still here," Zack said, and the silence that suddenly enveloped us was heavy with my husband's grief and the heart-stab I felt at knowing there was nothing I could do to allay it. Delia Wainberg had been only eighteen when she joined the study group that Zack and three other students formed in their first year at law school. Ultimately, the five friends became the founding partners of Falconer Shreve Altieri Wainberg and Hynd. For over twenty-five years, they had been more than colleagues; they had been family — living in houses that were within blocks of one another in the city and spending weekends and holidays in their summer homes at Lawyers Bay. Zack, who was at home with a serious case of the flu on the grey November day of the tragedy, was the sole surviving member of the Winners' Circle, and he had never forgiven himself for that.

That morning, I did what I always did when the darkness swallowed Zack. I went over, stood behind his chair and embraced him. Zack remained silent, but he reached up to stroke my arm. After a long while, I kissed him and said, "I'm going to eat something, give Esme and Pantera a quick run, then we can load them up and head back to the city."

* * *

By the time we were ready to leave Lawyers Bay, Zack was quiet, but he no longer seemed unreachable, so as we drove towards the highway, I massaged the back of his neck and waited.

When Zack was working on a case, I left it to him to decide how much, if at all, he could talk about what was going on. As we drove towards Regina that morning, my husband was in need of a sounding board, and he knew I'd give him straight answers about the validity of the strategies he was considering.

"We have anecdotal material for establishing that Mike did everything he could to protect Patti from herself," Zack said. "Warren told Maisie he could come up with a dozen people who saw Mike step into situations where Patti was risking her reputation and her safety."

"Make that a baker's dozen," I said. "I told you how sensitively Mike handled that incident at the firm's Christmas party when Patti had been drinking and her breast slipped out of her dress. I know Mike doesn't want to publicly shame Patti, and neither do you, but if the need arises . . ."

"I don't think it will," Zack said. "When I went to the Webers' the night Patti attacked Mike with the broken bottle, I thought an acrimonious divorce might be in the offing, so I made recordings of both Mike and Warren recounting what happened and I took photos of Mike's hospital discharge papers and close-ups of his face."

"What would we do without smartphones?" I said.

"We'd rely on Bob Colby's guys whose hourly rate is just about the same as mine."

"But you're not charging Mike Braeden."

"No, if it gets to a place where the firm is formally involved, Maisie and I will have to charge, but we're not there yet."

"When Kam Chau told us about Patti's meltdown at MediaNation, he said that Patti accused Mike of going through her personal things, searching for something incriminating about Nicholas that he could use to force her to see a therapist. Did Mike mention Patti making that specific accusation on the recording?"

"He did. Mike also said Patti and Thalia had both suffered enough, and he didn't want anything made public unless it was absolutely necessary."

"And now it is absolutely necessary. Zack, I think we may have been too quick to dismiss what Patti believed was going on."

Zack turned to me abruptly. "Surely you don't believe Mike was rummaging in Patti's things looking for something he could use against her?"

"No. Not for a minute. But it's possible Patti possesses or did possess something that, in her words, could 'taint' her son's memory. Kam told us that when he was trying to soothe Patti, he told her that no one was going to say anything about Nicholas because he'd been dead for six years and what happened was in the past, and Patti said, 'People always leave something behind.'

"What if Nicholas really did leave something behind that could damage his memory? You and I agree that Mike Braeden wouldn't have been looking for something he could use to force Patti into therapy. But it's possible that Thalia believed that her mother had something that might cast a shadow over Nicholas's reputation. Given what everyone says about how close Nicholas and Thalia were, if Thalia thought her mother had something that reflected badly on her brother, she would have searched for it."

Zack shifted in his seat, an unconscious gesture to protect his skin against pressure ulcers. "Jo, you know I can't raise that possibility with Mike."

"I realize that. I think we have to work from the premise that when Patti said she was afraid of Mike, she wasn't afraid he would harm her physically; she was afraid he'd find something he could use to force her to go to a therapist."

"Who would give her a drug that would make her reveal something incriminating about Nicholas. Mike did tell Maisie and me that's what Patti feared."

"A truth serum," I said. "I remember seeing characters being given that on old TV shows. Did a truth serum ever really exist?"

"It did. It was called sodium pentothal, and I don't think psychiatrists have used that since the early '60s. It shuts off higher brain functions. The theory behind it is that telling a lie is a more complex behaviour than telling the truth, so administering sodium pentothal should induce people to tell the truth."

"But it didn't work?"

"The problem wasn't with the drug itself; it was with how the drug had to be administered. Subjects were offered too much information, and they were smart enough to pick out the answer that worked best for them. The results of the tests were unreliable, and since certainty was what sodium pentothal was supposed to produce, psychiatrists just stopped using it."

"So, Patti was driven over the edge by her fear of something that could never have happened."

"Looks like," Zack said. "Patti created a paper tiger and her fear of it killed her."

"That is so sad. I remember Kam saying that *Sunny Side Up*, the title Patti gave her program, reflected the way she approached life: she approached everything she did as if she were experiencing it for the first time. And now she's dead, and that is probably a mercy because there was nothing good ahead for her."

* * *

The twins weren't the only ones who'd been seduced by fall vegetables at the farmers' market. Des Love had had a garden on the island, and the gourds he grew always added the perfect seasonal touch to our cottages when we came up for Thanksgiving. It was a nice tradition, and as I filled our old wooden dough bowl with gourds and placed it at the centre of the kitchen table, I smiled at the memory.

The Webers and Maisie arrived almost simultaneously at noon. Given Mike Braeden's determination to keep both Patti's and Thalia's name out of any plans his lawyers made for his defence, Zack and I had been prepared for opposition from the Webers, but after we settled around the table, Warren cleared his throat and said, "Annie and I have an announcement that should shorten this meeting considerably. Thalia Monk has urged us to use whatever means necessary to clear Mike Braeden of suspicion in Patti Morgan's death."

Maisie and Zack exchanged a glance. "What dark magic did you work to bring that about?" Maisie said.

"No dark magic," Annie said. "It was Thalia Monk's doing."

"Okay," Zack said. "Time to rewind the tape. What happened?"

Warren picked up a gourd with the fingertips of both hands and turned it so he was able to examine it from all sides. "Amazing," he said under his breath. Then his focus shifted to Zack. "After you and I spoke, I knew we had to convince Mike to rethink his refusal to let Thalia explain what she knew of her mother's relationship with him.

"Hugh Fairbairn had always been close to Mike," Warren continued. "So, I suggested to Annie that we try to enlist Hugh's support. Hugh still prefers the landline, so when I called their house, their grandson answered. I said Annie and I wanted to drop by, and Clay said to come ahead."

"Both Hugh's and Julie's cars were in the driveway," Annie said. "I crossed my fingers that Julie wouldn't be the one to answer the door."

The smile Warren gave his wife was impish. "And your crossed fingers did the job," he said. "Julie did not answer the door."

"Right," Annie said. "Thalia Monk answered the door, and I was gobsmacked, but Thalia made it clear from the outset that she was exactly where she needed to be, and that she had the situation well in hand. She guided Warren and me into the living room, indicated the chairs we should sit in, pulled an ottoman close to where we were sitting and said, 'Here's what needs to be done.'

"And then," Warren said, "cool as a cucumber, that young woman laid out the steps she was prepared to take. She suggested that I ask Maisie and Zack to arrange for her to give a statement to Inspector Debbie Haczkewicz. Her statement would describe in detail Patti Morgan's irrational fears and risky behaviours. As well, Thalia would attest to the fact that, despite Patti Morgan's innumerable provocations, Mike Braeden was always an exemplary husband to Patti and stepfather to Thalia. She would give Inspector Haczkewicz a list of people who had witnessed Patti's irrationality and provocative behaviour and who would swear under oath to the truth of their statements."

"And then," Annie said, "Thalia asked if we had any questions. At first, Warren and I were both too taken aback to say anything. Then Warren asked if Hugh was home, and Thalia said Hugh and his wife were upstairs, but they'd agreed to let her handle the situation and they supported her decision."

"I wonder how Thalia pulled that off?" I said. "Julie must have been . . ."

"Muzzled?" Annie said brightly.

I laughed. "I was going to say 'apoplectic' but 'muzzled' is better."

"Whether she was apoplectic or muzzled, we didn't hear a peep out of Julie, and Thalia didn't need assistance. When she'd decided our meeting was over, she stood and gently but firmly showed us to the door." Annie shook her head in amazement. "We weren't there for more than five minutes."

Warren and Annie wanted to deliver the news about Thalia's support to Mike Braeden in person. He was still staying in the Webers' guest house, so they were driving back to the lake. Zack and Maisie headed to Falconer Shreve to draft a statement for Thalia to send to Debbie Haczkewicz and run through the personnel files of prospective members of their dream team if the worst should happen and Mike was charged with his wife's death.

As soon as everyone left, Cindy Hock, our next-door neighbour came by with her three teenage kids. All were carrying floral arrangements and packages that had been sent to me on the day after *Sisters and Strangers* had its premiere. We were away, so Cindy had signed for the deliveries. It was quite a haul, and I knew dealing with the deliveries must have taken a chunk out of her day. Cindy waved off my apologies; we discussed where donations of floral arrangements would be most appreciated and then Cindy said that she and her family would deliver the flowers, but that they were all counting on a dinner invitation the next time Zack barbecued rolled prime rib.

Being back in the world of good neighbours and simple problems easily solved was balm to my raw nerves. So was the prospect of dealing with a routine and mindless task. I'd just begun sorting through the gift cards that came with the flowers when our landline rang. I picked up, waiting for a blast from Julie Fairbairn, but my caller was Thalia Monk. She was parked outside our house and needed to talk to Taylor.

Thalia clearly had an agenda, but there was something a little off about her call. The request was simple, but Thalia had not sounded like herself. Her low husky voice lacked the assurance I'd heard in it at the stew and bannock luncheon or the forcefulness Warren and Annie had experienced the night before. Curious but wary, I told her I'd meet her at the front door.

Thalia was dressed casually but fashionably in slim-fit black leather pants and a soft-blue, cropped leather jacket. Her cornsilk hair was smooth and shining, but her eyes were downcast. "May I come in?" she said.

I stood aside. "Of course."

She stepped into the hall. "I need to apologize to your daughter."

"Taylor's not here," I said.

Thalia seemed stricken. "It wasn't easy for me to come to your house today . . ."

"I could pass along a message," I said.

She nodded. "Could I please have a glass of water?"

"I'll get you one. Come inside with me. It's chilly out here."

When I headed for the kitchen, Thalia followed me. I poured us each a glass of water and then we sat down at the table.

"I watched *Sisters and Strangers* today," Thalia said. "All of it. Is it true?"

"Not every detail, but yes, the story is true."

"So, Taylor's mother, Sally, never wanted her, and after Sally died, you adopted her."

I leaned across the table. "Thalia, if you saw all the episodes, you know that Sally was a complex woman with a

340

difficult life. There were no easy choices for her. But yes, after Sally died, I adopted Taylor."

Thalia sipped her water. "I never knew any of that," she said. "Would it have mattered?"

"Yes." She raised her head so that her extraordinary sapphire eyes met mine. "If I'd known, I wouldn't have needed to hurt her."

The awareness was a jolt, but the words came slowly. "You're Concerned Friend," I said.

Thalia's nod of assent was almost imperceptible.

"Why did you want to hurt Taylor?"

"Because life seemed so easy for her. I hadn't even noticed Taylor until Ronan Farquhar invited her to grad, and she turned him down. Ronan was one of the few friends I had at school, and Taylor's rejection hurt him.

"I started tracking her. Social media makes everything so easy. She had it all: a family that wasn't broken, talent, friends and then finally a romantic relationship with a woman who was as gifted and beautiful as she was. Everyone was happy for Taylor and Vale. Everyone wanted them to have a brilliant future together, and that's exactly what would have happened. Taylor would have had everything she ever wanted, and that would have been unfair."

"Because everything you ever wanted had been taken from you," I said.

Thalia ignored my words. "It's too hot in here," she said. She glanced down at her jacket and when she spied the front zipper she seemed surprised, and then she pulled the zipper down. She was wearing a white scoop neck T-shirt. When her jacket was open, I saw a chain of small red abrasions around her neck. They appeared to be very like the abrasions Clay Fairbairn said Thalia suffered when she was attacked and her grief amulet was stolen. Thalia ran her index finger carefully over the tiny wounds.

"Your necklace was never returned to you?" I asked.

"No," she said. "But touching these reminds me of how much I've lost."

I walked Thalia to the door. Her eyes seemed slightly unfocused. "Are you all right to drive?" I asked.

"Yes," she said. "There's just been too much."

"You're right," I said. "There has been too much."

As soon as Thalia's car pulled away, I called Taylor. My call went straight to voicemail; I left a message asking her to call and then I called Zack.

After I told him about Thalia Monk's visit and her confession, Zack said, "What a lousy life that girl has had. I'm starting to understand why Mike has been so protective of her." His focus shifted to our daughter. "Have you talked to Taylor yet?"

"No. When she's working, she turns her phone off, so we still have that hurdle to clear."

"How do you think she'll take this?"

"Honestly, I think she'll be fine. You and I have talked about Taylor's clarity about why she and Vale could never have had a future together. Learning that Thalia Monk is Concerned Friend will be a shock, but when Taylor hears Thalia's rationale for needing to hurt her, she'll realize how damaged Thalia is, and I think she'll pity her."

Zack's voice was deep and intimate. "Is that how you feel?"

"It is, and if you'd seen Thalia today, you would have pitied her too. Zack, she's so broken. It seems that story she told Clay Fairbairn about being attacked was the truth." I told him about the marks I'd seen around her neck. "Thalia said that touching the cuts reminded her of how much she had lost."

Zack's sigh was audible. "This just gets worse and worse, doesn't it?"

"Seemingly, but the day after tomorrow the twins and I are celebrating our birthdays. Maybe by then the cosmos will have taken a gentle tip."

CHAPTER TWENTY

Two weeks earlier when Zack assured me that he was planning a day of surprises for me on my sixty-second birthday, I reminded him that I don't like surprises, I'm not crazy about parties and the only birthday parties I truly enjoy are his and those of our kids and grandkids.

My husband was sanguine. "Your preferences have been taken into account," he said. "Charlie and Colin's party is at four o'clock on the big day, and Maisie tells me that although the boys' choice of a theme changes daily, they seem to have settled on a pirate party. Apart from that, it will just be you and me doing the things you enjoy most. No more questions. All will be revealed on the 29th, when you come back from your run with the dogs."

Zack was true to his word. When the dogs and I returned

from our run on the 29th, the coffee was perking, and a schedule handwritten on elegant cardstock with a hint of a shimmer had been placed on my breakfast plate. The schedule touched all the bases.

6:00 a.m. to ???? — Great sex.

When you're ready–8:00 a.m. — Breakfast, all your favourites.

8:00–8:30 a.m. — Highly personal pedicure. Shade of polish: Russet Red (Taylor assures me this is *the* shade for autumn).

8:30–10:45 a.m. — Listen to Oscar Peterson and read. Outdoors or indoors, your choice, but my presence is non-negotiable.

10:45 a.m.–2:00 p.m. — SURPRISE.

2:15–3:30 p.m. — Nap/greater sex.

4:00–6:30 p.m. — Pirate themed bday party with family.

7:00 p.m. to ???? — Nightcap of choice. Even greater sex.

???? — Sleep.

Zack had been watching my face as I perused the schedule. "Sound okay?"

"Sounds perfect," I said. "But there's a lot of ground for us to cover. We should get started."

* * *

On my sixth birthday, I decided I would never again spend my birthday reading a book I hadn't read before. I'd been given a chapter book that seemed promising but did not deliver, and I'd fought tears of frustration all day.

Lesson learned. I was spending my sixty-second birthday rereading A.S. Byatt's *The Children's Story*. The day was bright and still, but it was too chilly to sit outdoors, and Zack and I had opted for the family room. Zack was reading William Deverell's *Needles*, and when the Oscar Peterson Trio began playing "You Look Good to Me" and my husband chuckled over something he'd just read, I knew I had never been happier than I was at that moment.

At ten forty-five, Zack slid a bookmark into *Needles* and said, "Time to change."

"Are we going somewhere?"

"We are."

"How dressy is this place?"

"I've never been there, but probably not very. You always look great in that dark green sweater Taylor gave you. Can't go wrong with that."

Ten minutes later, Zack and I were on the Trans-Canada

Highway travelling west; I was wearing my dark-green sweater, and there had been no mention of our destination.

When we passed Grand Coulee, I said, "Are you going to tell me where we're going?"

"Nope. Just kick back, listen to Oscar, Ray and Niels-Henning and ponder what you'd like to order for your birthday lunch."

"Pickerel," I said.

Zack didn't comment, so I pressed on. "Does the restaurant we're going to serve pickerel?"

My husband raised an eyebrow. "A clever ruse, but not clever enough. Yes, they will have pickerel. That's all the information you're getting."

There are many fine restaurants in Moose Jaw, and I was surprised when we passed the city without turning off. Forty-five minutes later when we were still on the road, I said, "I'm getting hungry."

"There's an A&W not far from here."

"I like their onion rings," I said.

"I do too," Zack said, "but this is where we leave the highway."

I checked for a road sign. There was a small one, but it answered all my questions. "Mortlach," I said. "We're going to the Little Red Market Café. I've wanted to go there since it opened, but that was at least five years ago. I'd almost forgotten."

"I hadn't forgotten," Zack said. "And they do have Lac La Ronge pickerel, fried and served on a bed of red beans and rice. It's one of their signature Cajun and Creole dishes."

"Zack, this is really a thoughtful surprise," I said.

"I like pleasing you, and the list of things you love to do is modest. At the risk of sounding smug, if we count hearing Oscar Peterson's trio playing 'You Look Good to Me,' you will have experienced five of your passions by midday."

I began to count on my fingers. "Running with the dogs. Having sex with you. Reading. Listening to 'You Look Good to Me.' And eating fried pickerel." I moved closer to him. "Well done. You really hit the ball out of the park. Thank you."

"You're welcome, but there's more to come."

The Little Red Market Café offered everything necessary for a peerless birthday lunch: an intimate and welcoming atmosphere, discreetly attentive service, and food and wine that were beyond sublime. We left the restaurant with warm memories, a box containing two pieces of homemade pecan pie and a solid commitment to the owner that we would return to Mortlach before the snow began to fly.

When we approached Moose Jaw, Zack said, "Decision time. I checked out the Moose Jaw Art Gallery and their current exhibition is of prairie vernacular folk and contemporary art. It's something you'd really enjoy, but if we see it now, we'll cut the time allotted for our next activity. The show's on for another three weeks, so that can be a pleasure deferred. Your choice."

I stretched and yawned. "I've had a deeply satisfying lunch, two glasses of Pinot Noir, and you made a promise that I want you to keep. Let's stay on the highway."

Zack reached over and stroked my leg. "I was hoping you'd choose that option."

When we turned onto our street, Taylor's car was in our driveway. "Looks like our day of surprises just spawned another surprise," I said.

Zack shook his head. "It's always a joy to see our daughter," he said, "but her timing could have been better."

"It could have been worse," I said. "Taylor could have arrived half an hour from now, and it's still her house. She never knocks."

Taylor came running out to meet us. "I saw you pull up," she said. "Where've you guys been?"

"Mortlach," Zack said.

Her eyes sparkled. "You went to the Little Red Market Café," she said. "A group of us went there for dinner one night during the *Sisters and Strangers* shoot. There was a problem with the lighting, and all the actors and peripheral people like me got off early. One of the grips suggested we have dinner in Mortlach. It was snowing like crazy that night, but the Cajun food was worth the white-knuckle drive."

"I'm sure it was," I said.

Taylor slapped her forehead with the palm of her hand. "And of course, you went there because it's your birthday, and all I've done is ramble on about me. Happy birthday. I love you. I love you too, Dad." She hugged us both. "I didn't forget your birthday, Jo. Your birthday is why I'm here. I have a surprise gift that can't be a surprise because I'm going to be working on it for at least a week — as soon as the McCudden crew finishes the reno of the swimming pool room, and I get the commission I'm working on out of the way. So, what do you think?"

Zack grinned. "Your mother and I could probably give you a more informed opinion if we knew what you were talking about."

Taylor rolled her eyes. "Angus always said I was a space cadet. Looks like he was right. I'm going to make some art on the walls in the swimming pool room. That white paint is bleak, and Dad, you know you'll use that as an excuse to get out of swimming." Taylor lowered her voice into a whining bass. "I know I should do twenty laps, but it's like a fucking *morgue* in there."

Zack and I were both laughing, but Taylor carried on. "Anyway, I've worked out what I want to do, and today I've been taking measurements and photos. The twins' birthday party doesn't start till four. That gives me two hours to get the supplies I need. So if you don't mind, I'm going to take off now and I'll meet you at the party."

Our daughter kissed us again, and then like the whirlwind she had become that afternoon, she was gone.

Zack widened his eyes and shrugged. "When everything breaks your way, don't ask questions, seize the moment." He turned his chair towards the hall to our bedroom. "Ready when you are," he said.

* * *

Zack and I arrived at the Crawford-Kilbourn house ten minutes before party time. Mieka, Madeleine and Lena were already at work transforming the twins' backyard into the world of pirates. Mieka had owned and managed UpSlideDown for over a decade, and she estimated that in that time she had hosted over a thousand birthday parties. The girls had often helped her, and, as a family, they had decided that their present to the twins would be a pirate party, complete with decorations, games, food and pirate talk.

Mieka had picked up Madeleine and Lena from school early, and the three of them had hit the ground running. Pete and the twins had joined Charlie and Des at their house, so the party planners were distraction-free, and they had worked wonders.

Skull and crossbones flags flew from the flagpoles on the garage and the Rocky Mountain Play Structure and Clubhouse; plastic palm trees flanked signs bright with illustrations for non-readers, marking the locations of Pirates Rock, Crocodile Beach, Shark Cove, Lost Lagoon, Sea Monster Swamp and the starting point for all the fun: the Pirates' Clubhouse. Vinyl tablecloths, decorated with maps alerting the unwary to the perils of a pirate's life, covered the picnic tables, and twelve treasure chests were lined up on a low table at the edge of the patio.

When Mieka and the girls saw us, they raced over. After a round of hugs and happy birthdays, Mieka said, "We've been trying to call you guys all day. Where've you been?"

"We went to Mortlach for lunch," I said.

Madeleine nodded approval. "That sounds nice. What else did you do?"

"That was about it," Zack said. "Mimi and I had a lazy morning and then we had a nap before we came here."

Lena was incredulous. "It was Mimi's birthday, and all

you did was have lunch and a nap. Granddad, that's not much of a birthday."

"It's what I wanted," I said.

Madeleine, a born mediator, attempted to explain. "Lena, what you want to do on your birthday changes. When you're growing up, you want parties; older people want naps."

Mieka, trying unsuccessfully to suppress a laugh, snorted. Fortunately, Lena had already lost interest in the discussion. "Hey, look!" she said. "Uncle Pete, Charlie and the boys just came through the side gate."

They might have come through the side gate, but as soon as the twins spotted the pirate decorations, they took off, and they were now on the move. After a brief exchange, Pete took Des from Charlie; Charlie sprinted after the boys, and Pete joined Zack and me.

"Charlie's riding herd on the dynamic duo," he said. "I wanted to talk to you two."

Mieka gave her brother a sisterly shoulder pat. "Time for the ladies and me to get back to work."

"Okay, so what's up?" I asked.

My older son had always gone straight to the point. "I invited Jill to come today," he said.

"Wow! That's a surprise," I said. Zack shot me a worried glance. "But it's a good one," I added quickly. Reassured, Zack's focus shifted back to the baby in his arms.

"Mieka said you'd be pleased," Pete said. "She sent me the Kintsugi video about repairing broken pieces of pottery with lacquer and powdered gold."

"The art of precious scars," I said. "It's a beautiful idea. Kintsugi helped me find my way with Jill too."

"So far I've just talked to her on the phone," Pete said. "This will be our first face-to-face, and I've never been great at social situations. I don't want to blow it, Mum."

"You won't," I said. "You have a good heart, and in a few minutes we're going to be attacked by twelve pirates under the age of six. You have nothing to worry about. I guarantee the pirates will break the ice for you and Jill."

Pete gave me a smile of goofy relief. "Thanks. Now, I should rescue Charlie from the twins." He flashed Zack a victory sign. "Des was not a happy boy on his way here in his car seat, but you've got the magic touch, big guy."

"He does, indeed," I said. This time it was Zack's turn to give me a goofy smile.

*　*　*

Jill came to the party alone. For a few moments, she stood just inside the gate looking around. She seemed unsure, but Pete must have been watching for her, because he was at her side almost immediately. Some of the parents of the children at the party had lingered after delivering their child, and Pete introduced Jill and stayed with her chatting until the parents left, and he and Jill both went over to join Mieka.

Taylor arrived at the party with Noah Wainberg and his grandson Jacob, who bore an uncanny physical resemblance to Noah's late wife, Delia.

Jacob and his cat, Toast, were frequent visitors to our cottage when we were at the lake, and that day, as always, Jacob was happy to see us. He was interested in Des, whom he was seeing for the first time, but a three-week-old baby was no match for the allure of the growing number of young pirates who were gathering at the clubhouse, and when Taylor offered to help Jacob find the pirate chest with his name on it, the two of them were gone in a flash.

Charlie D had helped his namesake and Colin dress in the striped jerseys and bandanas that were in the treasure chests labelled with their names, and the boys were already in the thick of the action. Zack was not ready to relinquish Des, so Charlie D, still a boy at heart, ran off to join the pirates.

Noah, Zack and I mulled aloud over Thanksgiving plans. Isobel Wainberg was studying at Johns Hopkins in Baltimore and, since American Thanksgiving wasn't until November, she wouldn't be home then. Taylor and Gracie would be here for the long weekend, but they were moving Taylor into Gracie's condo on Monday. Des was being baptized that Sunday, so our family was having Thanksgiving dinner in Regina on Saturday with the Wainbergs, Rose, Betty and whoever else was eager to take a place at the table.

There were always extra guests, but we had agreed that a 12.8-kilogram turkey, a large bone-in ham and a vegetarian option should be sufficient, when Zack asked if I could take Des while he made a pit stop. Noah brought over two lawn chairs, and we settled in.

As he watched Zack wheel towards the house, Noah said, "Zack's in good form."

"He loves being a grandfather."

"I do too," Noah said. "When Jacob and Toast come barrelling down the hall and jump into bed with me in the morning, the odds that I'll make it through the day turn in my favour."

"That's good to hear," I said.

"It is, but then an hour later, or a day later or a week later, something will trigger a memory and just like that, I'm standing on the lip of the chasm again."

"That's the way it is for Zack too. He'll be fine for weeks and then seemingly out of nowhere, the darkness hits."

"What do you do?"

"I wait," I said. "That's all I can do. Zack won't talk about it."

"This project I've been working on with Taylor is helping me," Noah said. "She's hoping it will help Zack too."

"What project?" I said. "I didn't know you and Taylor were working on something together."

Noah groaned. "And you weren't supposed to know. Can we just forget the last thirty seconds of our conversation?"

Des seemed to frown; his face grew red and then relaxed. Noah and I waited for a minute or two, and then he said, "I think it may be time for a diaper change."

"I think you may be right," I said. "And a diaper change takes precedence over everything, including whatever it was we were talking about a minute ago." I stood. "I'm going to take this guy into the house and clean him up. Maisie and Mieka seem to be conferring, so I think the games are going to start. I'll catch up with you and Zack when Des and I are less pungent."

When I came back out, Zack and Noah were with Charlie and Pete. Des was clean but hungry, so Charlie took his son to Mieka and rejoined us. "All's well with mother and child," he said. "And Mieka assures me that everything is under control." He took in the scene and shook his head. "Could have fooled me."

At UpSlideDown, Mieka had adopted my rule for the number of guests at children's birthday parties: the child's age plus two. I had no idea where the equation originated, but it had served me well. Now my daughter-in law, who was herself a twin, had adapted the equation for her sons. A guest for each year of the child's age plus one extra guest per twin.

On paper, two hosts and ten birthday guests was an eminently manageable number, but when the numbers became children — each of whom was six years old or younger, pumped for a party in a large backyard with a Rocky Mountain Play Structure and Clubhouse that had been transformed into a pirate's paradise — there was bedlam.

Kids that age are as quick and agile as cats. Determined to experience everything, they are constantly on the move, and in the first moments of the party, it seemed that the hosts and the original ten guests had morphed into a small but anarchic army. Mieka and Maisie were standing with Madeleine and Lena. All wore black leggings, and black-and-white striped pirates' jerseys. Mieka and her daughters had tied brightly coloured scarves pirate-style around their hair; Maisie was bare-headed. Despite the chaos they seemed unperturbed.

Then, after a brief exchange, Maisie reached into the large black duffle bag on the ground beside her, removed a lanyard, which she slipped around her neck, and a black tricorne, trimmed with gold braid and three scarlet feathers. She jammed the tricorne over her thick copper curls and then strode towards the play structure. She effortlessly scaled the rope to the second level, stood for a moment surveying the scene and then took the bosun's whistle hanging on the lanyard, placed it between her lips and blew two notes.

The sound of a bosun's whistle is shrill, piercing and loud enough to be heard by every seaman aboard a ship in the middle of a storm-tossed sea. When Maisie sounded the two-note blast, the effect was electric. The twins and their guests moved towards her as if they were under a spell.

Maisie has a strong, carrying voice, and she didn't have to raise it. The children were silent as they stood in a ragged line looking up at the woman in the tricorne. Maisie held out her whistle. "This is called a bosun's whistle," she said. "Pirate ships at sea are noisy places, especially during storms. Commands have to be given so that everyone knows what they should do to keep the ship afloat, but the pirates are all too far apart to hear each other.

"The bosun blows this whistle so that everyone on board the ship knows exactly what they should be doing. That long low pitch I blew before means *pay attention*. When the pirates hear that sound, they know the next sounds the whistle makes will tell them what to do." Maisie blew a high pitch note and then a low pitch note. "This bosun blast means *all hands on deck*, and that means all the pirates should come up on deck and stand together, so they'll know what to do next. Here's the third bosun blast." Maisie blew a warbling sound, like the song of a canary. "That blast tells the pirates that another ship is about to pass them. If it's a friendly ship, the bosun blows this whistle to let the other ship know there won't be any trouble. Finally, when the other ship has passed, the bosun makes this canary sound with his whistle." Maisie blew some warbling notes. "This bosun blast means *stand down* and that means each pirate can go back to what he was doing before.

"We're going to start the activities now. So, listen to the whistle blasts and do what they tell you to do. Whistle blast number one means *listen up*. Whistle blast number two means *all hands on deck* — that means you all come together. After whistle blast number three — the canary sound — we'll tell you what activity you're going to do. Whistle blast number four means the activity's over and it's time to listen for whistle number one. Got it?"

Charlie and Colin had obviously been practising with their mother and they shouted, "Got it." When Maisie repeated the question, all the kids shouted, "Got it." The party had officially begun.

For the next hour the bosun's whistle blew to signal the beginning and ending of each activity, and Colin, Charlie and their guests went on a treasure hunt, walked the plank, divided into teams for a race in which the members of the team who crossed the finish line first with a bagel on their foam swords each won a plastic parrot. This being the Age of Participation, there were also parrots for the team that finished last, for the team that dropped the bagel most often and for the team that dropped the bagel least often. And finally all engaged in a game of a mutiny where kids paired up to chase Captain Maisie and her crew, First Mate Mieka back on duty, and her underlings, Pirates in Training Madeleine and Lena, were all captured and wrapped in toilet paper by the rebellious pirates.

My single criterion for a successful birthday party is one where neither the birthday child nor a guest cries. By that criterion Charlie and Colin's party was a triumph. The guests who sat down at the pirate picnic tables were scrubbed clean, exercised, happy and hungry.

They mowed through the menu of pirate food: Goldfish; pretzel peg legs; cannon balls (mini-meatballs); seaweed (green linguine); gold doubloons (chicken nuggets); pirate's teeth (pigs in blankets); three watermelons fitted out as pirate ships, one carrying cubes of cheese, one carrying cut-up veggies and one carrying cut-up fruit; and two pirate birthday cakes for dessert — all washed down with pirate grogs (healthy smoothies that no kid turned their nose up at).

We were sitting at the adults' table with Pete, Maisie, Mieka, Charlie, Jill and Taylor. We all enjoyed the meal, and none of us felt the need for conversation. It was pleasure enough simply to listen to the piping voices of kids discussing their lives and times. As he washed down his last pirate tooth with pirate grog, Zack sighed contentedly and took my hand. "I hope you've had as much fun today as I did."

"I couldn't have asked for anything more," I said. "Maisie, unless you need help with clean-up, I think Zack and I are about ready to take off."

"No cleaning up on your birthday," Maisie said.

"The clean-up is part of the Kilbourn-Dowhanuik deluxe birthday party package," Mieka added. "We've got this, Mum."

"In that case, we'll wait till Jill comes back, hug the birthday boys and head for home."

Jill had been buoyant throughout the party. Everything delighted her; most of all, I think, she was simply delighted to be there. With her smart gamine haircut, caramel cashmere tunic and matching slacks, Jill was a far cry from the girl with the untamed carrot-red hair and fierce loyalty to the women's clothing racks at Value Village she had once been, but that afternoon she sparkled with the joie de vivre that three decades earlier made being with her a delight.

When she returned from taking her call, the sparkle was gone. Jill was pale and stricken, drained of life. Charlie D went to her. "What's wrong?"

Jill hugged herself as if she was suddenly very cold. "A farmer found Ellen Exton's body this afternoon. A blocked culvert was causing some flooding. He had trouble finding a tool with a long enough reach to clear out the blockage." Jill's eyes were blank, and she seemed to sway. Charlie steadied her and guided her to sit down at our picnic table.

Jill sat on the edge of the bench. "That's all we know," she said. There was a half-empty glass of pirate's grog on the table. Jill picked it up and drained it. The grog did the job. The colour returned to Jill's face, and her eyes lost their three-mile stare. She turned to Charlie. "Kam's at the station, putting together a tribute to Ellen. We should be there to give him a hand."

Charlie D looked over to Mieka. "Go," she said. "We're fine." Our daughter gave Zack and me an assessing look. "Zack, Charlie told me you'd offered to handle Ellen's case gratis, and that you went with him to the police station to report that Ellen was missing. You did everything you could, and Mum, it's your birthday. Salvage what you can of what's left of the day."

CHAPTER TWENTY-ONE

As soon as we came through our front door, Zack took my hand. "I know you're feeling shitty, but I have a thought. We still have that bottle of George Dickel. What would you say to three fingers of bourbon?"

"I'd say that I'm glad you have big fingers."

Zack chuckled. "I'll get the drinks. Let's go into the family room and put on the fireplace."

When Zack came back with the drinks and handed me mine, he said, "So, what do we drink to?"

"To Ellen," I said. "The woman we never knew."

I breathed in the old-wood scent of the bourbon and then sipped. Warmed by the bourbon and the heat from the fireplace, we were quiet for a long while. Finally, I broke the silence. "Zack, do you want to talk about Ellen?'

When he didn't respond, I thought I'd hit another brick wall, but my husband surprised me. "Let's talk," he said, "because this has knocked me off base, and I don't understand why. God knows you and I have both experienced loss, but we knew the ones we lost. We knew their past, and we had ideas about what their futures might hold if they were lucky. But we never knew Ellen Exton. All we have is her name and some random facts. Nothing. But, Jo, this has really gutted me."

"Robertson Davies has a line in one of his novels," I said. "'When one human creature dies, a whole world of hope and memory and feeling dies with him.'"

Zack sipped his bourbon. "And all we have to connect us to Ellen's world of hope and memory and feeling are the names of her cats."

I smiled. "Mary and Mr. Grant."

"Named after characters in a TV show that aired fifty years ago, but offered Ellen the pattern for a meaningful life." Zack had a beautiful mouth, full-lipped and sensual, but at that moment his lips were twisted with pain. "And she almost made it," he said. "She almost had the life she'd dreamed of, but someone decided to stop her."

"We don't know that Ellen never had the life she dreamed of," I said. "According to Charlie and Kam, she was a terrific producer, and her colleagues respected her. They say she wasn't gregarious, but she had good friends like Rosemary and Kam. Ellen seems to have chosen a path that took her exactly where she wanted to be." I gave him a sidelong glance. "Not everybody wants to live a big life."

Zack grimaced. "Ouch — a palpable hit from the woman I love."

"It wasn't a dig, just a comment. You were born to live a big life, but not everyone is." I sipped my bourbon. "I don't suppose you ever watched *The Mary Tyler Moore Show*."

"No, was it good?"

"It was very good: smart and funny, but most importantly, it showed a single woman who loved her work having a fulfilling life that was just the right size for her. When Mary Tyler Moore died a few years ago, I was astounded at the number of women who said that her character of Mary Richards freed them to live the lives they wanted to live."

Zack seemed pensive. "You know, I never really thought about what women wanted until I met you, and then you wanted me, so I knew all I needed to know."

I laughed. "You really are incorrigible."

"Maybe, but I made you laugh."

"Let's keep that good vibe going and watch a couple of episodes of *The Mary Tyler Moore Show*. They're only about twenty-four minutes each, but they'll help you understand Ellen Exton, and they'll make us both laugh." As we watched the first episode in which Mary moves to Minneapolis and is interviewed by Lou Grant for a job in the newsroom, I could feel Zack relax. When it was over, I said. "Are you up for another one?"

He shrugged. "Why not? I don't know whether it's the George Dickel or Mary and Lou, but I'm starting to feel human again."

After we'd watched the classic "Chuckles Bites the Dust," Zack said, "Okay, I'm hooked."

"Me too," I said. "But let's get into our robes, and I'll make us some tea and toast."

We'd just finished watching a fifth episode when our landline rang. Only our children and close friends used the landline, so I picked up. It was Mieka.

"I wanted to make sure you two were okay. You looked a little wiped when you left the party."

"We *were* wiped. I think we all realized that Ellen was probably dead, but hearing the words was a body blow. We're doing better now."

"So, what are you up to?"

"We're in the family room with our robes on, having tea and toast and watching reruns of *The Mary Tyler Moore Show*."

"Maddy will be happy to hear that you're engaging in age-appropriate behaviour," Mieka said. Her voice grew serious. "It's going to be a rough week, but we'll hang in there, Mum."

"You bet."

"Charlie wants to talk to you both, so I'm putting you on speakerphone."

Our son-in-law's normally soothing dark honey voice was jagged with emotion. "Not much news really. I just wanted you to know that the final twelve minutes of tomorrow's show will be a tribute to Ellen. Kam, Jill and I put something together that feels right. All that's left is finding the right sign-off music."

"What kind of music did Ellen like?" I asked.

"Another sin of omission for me," Charlie said. "I haven't a clue about Ellen's taste in music. But Kam remembered that on the first *Charlie D in the Morning* show, Ellen gave me a five-minute primer on What Not to Do on Live Radio."

Zack was surprised. "You'd had your own call-in show in Toronto for what — thirteen years?"

"And MediaNation had publicized that heavily in the announcement that I was taking over the late unlamented Jared Delio's spot, but the bit Ellen and I did was light-hearted: stuff like treat every mic as a live mic and don't sit too close to it or you'll pop your Ps. I was surprised at how much fun it was. Ellen had a pleasing radio voice and, as you'll hear tomorrow, a surprisingly sly wit. The chemistry between us on-air was good, and when Jill asked why the show hadn't used Ellen and me together more, I didn't have an answer.

"I should have pushed for it, and Ellen would have loved it, but I didn't. And she would have loved hearing the tributes we've taped from her colleagues. I think she would have been surprised at how much she meant to people."

"Realizing that you'll never have a chance to say all the things you should have said is like water torture," Zack said. "Drip, drip, drip, and it never ends."

I took his hand and mouthed the word "Don't."

Zack nodded acknowledgement. "Jo just gave me the 'put a sock in it' look, so moving right along. Jo told me that Ellen saw the character of Mary Richards in *The Mary Tyler Moore Show* as a role model. We've been watching reruns tonight, and the show's theme music might work for the tribute to Ellen."

"I'll check that out," Charlie said. "I never figured you for an MTM fan, Zack, but you're a man of surprises. I'll be in touch."

CHAPTER TWENTY-TWO

Despite the tragedy, Zack and I knew our only option was to keep on keeping on. He had a case coming to trial in November, so after breakfast, he headed for Falconer Shreve, and I headed for our dining room to tackle the gifts that had arrived after the debut of *Sisters and Strangers* and were still unopened.

My friend and *Sisters and Strangers* co-writer Georgie Shepherd had alerted me to a tradition of theatre that Rosamond Burke, who had been a stage actor for over seven decades, carried over to the work she did before the camera. The tradition of cast and behind-the-scenes colleagues exchanging gifts on opening night was a lovely one, and as the writers who had finished the script for the series, Georgie and I had taken our responsibility for choosing exactly the right gift seriously.

In the course of the series, the painting of the flying blue horses that Sally made after seeing the wild horses on Saugeen First Nation reserve with her father and the hand-made birchbark box decorated with porcupine quills she and Des brought back for me had become emblematic of Sally's life and mine. Sally was the sister who saw the magic, and I was the one who stayed home and found another kind of joy.

Taylor had etched images of the flying blue horses into a zinc plate, and a printing company had produced numbered prints of the piece bearing Taylor's signature. We had purchased birchbark porcupine quill boxes from Saugeen women to complete the gift.

These gifts would bring back memories of a time that was special for us all, and as I unwrapped the gifts from the people with whom we had worked, I was glad we'd made the effort.

The gift of the director, Ainsley Blair, was a handsomely bound copy of the scripts for the six episodes of the series, complete with director's notes. The other gifts all seemed like companion pieces to Ainsley's. Edie Gunn, the locations manager, sent an album of stunning photographs of the cabin and the virgin forest in Northern Saskatchewan where the exterior scenes were shot; the musical director, David McIntyre, gave a copy of the score for the series and a CD of the music; Hal Dupuis's gift was a slender polished leather briefcase containing copies of the sketches he had made of the costumes. Mine was inscribed with the initials "JES" because he always thought of me as Joanne Ellard. His gift had a special resonance for me because Hal had based his designs on the photographs and home movies I'd provided. The costumes, accurate down to the last pearl button on Nina Love's opera gloves, replicated clothing that had been worn either by me or someone close to me on the most joy-filled or pain-filled moments of my life. I wasn't ready yet to see them all again, so I slid the sketches back into the briefcase.

Rosamond Burke's gift was a DVD in a silver case embossed with the series' title and the dates of the shoot. Rosamond's calling card was included; on the back, she'd written the download link. Curiosity may have killed the cat, but it didn't stop me from going to our home office, picking up my laptop and keying in the link.

Throughout the shoot, Rosamond had a breathtakingly handsome young assistant named Narek at her beck and call. Someone said he was a filmmaker, but the exact nature of his duties was somewhat nebulous. He was never without his phone and he had dropped into the writers' room several times and asked Georgie and me for permission to film us as we talked about our work.

Georgie and I had assumed Narek was making a souvenir video for Rosamond, but as it turned out he really was a filmmaker and a skilled one. He'd edited the footage of each of us at work into a striking and revealing thirty-minute overview of the making of *Sisters and Strangers*, which included our informal comments about what working on the series meant to each of us. I was so absorbed in the video that it took me a moment to realize that someone was ringing the doorbell.

It was Alison Janvier, and her look was definitely uptown. Her shining black hair was twisted into a classic low chignon, and she was wearing a smart pinstripe business suit and black patent stilettos.

"Wow," I said. "Dressed to impress. Come in."

"Is this a bad time for you? I was driving past your street, and I thought I'd take a chance and see if you were home."

"I'm home and I'm glad to see you. Come in."

As soon as Ali was inside, she kicked off her stilettos and groaned with relief. "Why do people wear those things anyway?"

"Beats me," I said. "But they do look swank."

"I guess I wasn't born for swank," she said. "Could we please sit down somewhere?"

"Come into the dining room. I was just unwrapping packages from people who worked on *Sisters and Strangers*. It's a tradition on opening night."

Ali sank into one the chairs gratefully. "I watched the show Friday night," she said. "Joanne, it was so moving. I watched it again with Harper on Saturday. I know you were involved with the writing. You must be very proud."

"Proud and also relieved. It was a story that needed to be told, but it was painful watching my life become public."

Alison's laugh was short and dry. "I may be facing that problem myself. Remember those questions during my Q&A sessions about why I didn't have an abortion when I got pregnant at sixteen?"

"Of course, but I thought that ended when Maisie put the fear of God into Ronan Farquhar and told him to tell his cohort that they were on her radar. Has the gang resurfaced?"

"No. Thalia Monk and Clay Fairbairn are working on their podcast about our campaign, and they seem genuinely committed to the idea of getting people in their generation involved in social activism and politics."

"Then where's the threat coming from?'"

"There've been rumours about the circumstances around my pregnancy for weeks. My guess is that the University Park Road Gang put the rumours out there, and that despite the fact that the cohort dropped it, the rumours have developed a life of their own."

"That happens," I said. "But when rumours run out of oxygen, they die. I guess you'll just have to wait it out."

"My major concern in all this is Harper. He doesn't know the truth about how he was conceived. I made a mistake by not telling him. I know that now, but I've come to dread the Q&A sessions, waiting for someone to ask my opinion about abortion in the case of rape."

"If the question hasn't arisen by now, it's not going to," I said. "Until your campaign began, you and the man who raped you were the only people who knew what happened, and the number of people who know now can be counted on the fingers of one hand."

"It's not that simple." Alison had placed her messenger bag on the floor beside her. She picked up the bag, pulled out a brown mailing envelope and removed two high school yearbooks. "This envelope was in a tray we have for mail at the campaign office," she said. "The yearbooks are proof that something I kept secret for nineteen years is no longer a secret."

She opened the 2001 yearbook and turned it to the page of teachers' photos. The picture of Dylan K. Beveridge was circled in black Sharpie. Ali opened the second yearbook to the page of teachers' photos and handed it to me. The 2020 yearbook was from a high school in a town two hundred kilometres west of Saskatoon, and the photo of a teacher named Dylan Kyle had also been circled in black Sharpie. Dylan Kyle was twenty years older than Dylan K. Beveridge, but he was indisputably the same man, the man I presumed had raped Ali.

"There was no note?" I said.

Ali shook her head. "Just the yearbooks, but Joanne, they were enough to convey the message loud and clear."

"What message did they convey?"

"That the sender knows the truth," she said, and for the first time since I'd met her, she sounded defeated.

"I understand why seeing those yearbooks is chilling," I said, "but Ali, there's no indication that whoever sent the yearbooks is planning to do anything further with what they've learned. There are no threats or demands.

"I don't know what game the person who sent this is playing. But I do know the only weapon they have against you is the threat to tell Harper the truth about his conception — and the fact his biological father is alive and living four hours from here. If you tell Harper everything, the game will be over."

Ali leaned back in her chair and stretched her arms towards the ceiling. "I'm starting to unknot and it feels so good. Thanks for listening, Joanne, and thanks putting the situation into perspective."

"You're welcome, but you would have worked this out yourself. I just saved you some time. Speaking of . . ." I glanced at my watch. "*Charlie D in the Morning* is having a tribute to Ellen Exton. It's going to be on in about two minutes, and I'd like to hear it."

"So would I," Alison said. "Would you mind some company?"

"I'd welcome it," I said.

Charlie had said that he, Kam and Jill had put together something for Ellen that "felt right," and they'd been successful. The memories Ellen's colleagues shared about working with her were never mawkish, but their sense of what they had lost was palpable. Ellen's five-minute primer with Charlie on What Not to Do on Live Radio was a lot of fun. Her voice, low and alive with genuine interest in the conversation, was compelling. When Charlie said the show had missed a beat by not taking full advantage of Ellen's warm on-air presence, he'd tapped into the bottomless well of regret that comes with the knowledge that there will be no second chances.

Charlie had taken Zack's suggestion that the farewell to Ellen include the musical theme of *The Mary Tyler Moore Show*, the program that had so powerfully informed Ellen's life. The song hints subtly that Mary Richards's past was not all sunshine and roses, but is resolutely upbeat and ends with a statement of faith in the future: "You're gonna make it after all."

When I turned off my laptop, I had to swallow hard before I turned back to Ali.

She too was visibly moved. "That is so sad," she said. "But

Ellen would have known what she was doing. She obviously decided the story she was working on was worth the risk."

"I don't understand," I said. "Ellen was the producer of a national morning radio show. There was no risk in that."

Alison did not suffer fools gladly, even if the fool was a friend, and at that moment, she was unable to hide her frustration at my obtuseness. "Ellen was murdered, Joanne. Clearly there *was* a risk. I didn't know Ellen well, but my parents did, and they respected her for her ethics and for the fact that she was a journalist who believed it was her obligation to discover the truth and make it public no matter what the cost."

"Obviously there's some history here that I don't know about," I said.

Ali unknotted her chignon and shook her hair loose. She looked very young. "I'm sorry I snapped at you, Joanne. That tribute to Ellen Exton brought back memories.

"Nationtv used to have a station in La Ronge. It wasn't much — a couple of rooms over a store and one full-time employee — a jack or jill of all trades who acted as host. producer, newsreader, interviewer, roving reporter, plus a part-time cameraperson and a couple of kids from the high school who learned about working in media and kept the floors swept and the bathroom clean."

"Ellen was the only full-time employee," I said.

"It was an entry-level job," Ali said. "The guy Ellen replaced did the minimum, and everybody was happy. He covered the softball games and hobby shows and he still had plenty of time to fish and hunt with the locals."

"But Ellen took the job seriously."

"She did, and it was a big mistake. A man named Grant Timberlake owned a number of businesses in the north, nothing big — some restaurants, two hotels, a small factory that made knock-offs of traditional Indigenous crafts, an auto repair shop, that kind of thing. Nothing spectacular but it added up. Grant was doing very well for himself."

"And Ellen found something out?"

"She found out what everyone knew. Grant was, in my father's words, 'as crooked as a dog's hind leg,' but no one cared. A lot of people worked for him, and he was a generous donor to the right political campaigns. Favours were asked for and favours were granted."

"And everyone looked the other way but Ellen."

"She said there was no higher law in journalism than to tell the truth and shame the devil. So, she followed the money. She was dogged and meticulous, and she got the goods on Grant Timberlake. She had copies of receipts, cancelled cheques, complaints about health and safety regulations that had been swept under the carpet and blatant tax fraud."

"Let me guess — it was the tax fraud that got him."

"Yep. Like Ellen, the Canada Revenue Agency believes in telling the truth and shaming the devil. Grant served time, and he paid a whack of back taxes." Her smile faded. "But Ellen paid a price too. When it became known that she was looking into Timberlake's businesses, Ellen was ostracized and threatened, and a petition to have her fired was sent to Nationtv."

"But the company *did* back her up," I said.

Ali snorted. "Of course not. Once Nationtv received the petition, Ellen was on the next plane out of La Ronge, but the powers that be were smart enough to keep her on staff. Joanne, my point is that Ellen was aware that she was jeopardizing her relationships in the community, her reputation and her job, but that didn't stop her from doing what she felt compelled to do as a journalist. I have no idea what injustice Ellen was pursuing when she died, but I hope the police will pick up the cudgels and finish the investigation Ellen Exton risked her life for."

* * *

Alison Janvier's visit had shaken me. We had misread Ellen Exton's character. We had made false assumptions, and we had failed to ask the right questions. And now Ellen was dead. I was confused and unsure about the next steps. I needed a sounding board, and it was Zack's turn. When he got home, we could thrash this through together. In the meantime, there was a task I was confident I could handle, and it was one that I knew would soothe and restore me.

Harper Janvier's delight at receiving a handwritten letter of apology from Clay Fairbairn had resonated with me. The sincerity of Clay's apology was questionable, but Harper's enthusiasm had inspired me to pay a visit to the Paper Umbrella, where I spent far too much on some irresistible ecru cotton notecards. I'd been planning to save them for a special occasion, and now I realized that expressing my gratitude to people who had sent me gifts I knew I would treasure was occasion enough. I made myself a pot of Constant Comment, cleared a place at the end of the dining room table and began.

Remembering the pleasure I'd taken in writing the script with Georgie Shepherd and the thrill of watching talented people bring our words to life was absorbing, and when Zack called, I was surprised to see that it was already four o'clock.

"I'm on my way home," he said. "And none too soon."

"Tough day?"

"Actually it was pretty good. Our client is a yutz who thinks he knows how to argue his own case, but this afternoon I showed him the number of billable hours he's racked up so far, and that gave him pause. He has now agreed to limit his role in the trial to looking contrite, so we should breeze through this. Anything I should bring home with me?"

"I haven't done anything about dinner," I said. "How about Italian Star sandwiches and some of that fennel and olive salad they make?"

"Sounds good to me. Should I get a sandwich for Taylor?"

"Yes. She's having supper at Mieka and Charlie's, storing up time with Des and the girls before she moves to Saskatoon, but she loves Italian Star and she'll have the sandwich for breakfast.

"Got it. I'll be home at the usual time."

"And I'll be waiting with open arms and a very dry martini in each hand."

I'd left all the gifts we'd received on the dining room table for Zack to look at, so I set the table in the kitchen, made the martinis and returned to my thank-you notes.

By the time Zack wheeled through the front door, I had a stack of stamped, addressed thank-you notes and a sense of satisfaction that bordered on smugness. The aroma of the sandwiches from Italian Star was seductive. Dinner was taken care of, so free of responsibility, Zack and I took our drinks into the family room and settled in front of the fireplace.

"So, how was your day?" I asked.

Zack sipped his drink. "It was fine, but we need a fairer way to determine who gets to report first. Remember that routine you and Georgie had when you were writing a script?"

"We'd vote on whoever we thought had the best idea in the room and then we went with their idea."

"I never understood how you made that work. Didn't you ever just vote for yourselves?"

"Only if we really thought we had the best idea, and most of the time, we knew whose idea was better."

"What if you voted for each other?"

"Then we'd each explain why we voted the way we had and take it from there."

Zack shook his head in amazement. "There's no arguing with that logic. You go first."

The day of a Real Prairie Picnic, I'd told Lena that her grandfather was one of the best listeners I knew. As Zack and I sipped our drinks and watched the flames flicker in the fireplace, that assessment was born out. Zack listened attentively and without interruption when I told him how Alison had discovered the yearbooks in her mail folder at campaign headquarters that morning. When I'd finished, Zack was as baffled as I'd been at the fact that there'd been no explanations, no demands, no threats.

"This is a new one on me," Zack said. "Someone sets up an elaborate and time-consuming plan to either shake or shake down Alison Janvier, then apparently has a change of heart and just steps away."

"It makes no sense, but in case whoever is behind this has another change of heart, I suggested that she tell Harper everything."

"Good advice," Zack said. "Whoever sent those yearbooks to Alison wasn't acting on a whim. They'd done some serious digging — first to figure out the identity of the man who raped Alison and then to discover where he is today."

"Then after all that, they leave Alison with a simple solution to the problem. If she tells Harper the truth, she strips the yearbooks of their power."

Zack's lip curled. "Of course, before Alison's benefactor disappeared, they did make certain Alison knew what *could* have happened." Zack stared at the fire for a long while before he turned to me. "Jo, who do you think engineered this?"

I hesitated before I spoke. "This afternoon, I made a deliberate effort not to dwell on the significance of what Alison told me, but I couldn't stop thinking about those yearbooks and the skill with which they'd been used. Of course, that led me down the rabbit hole to revisit all the horrors that have happened this summer: Rosemary Morrissey's disintegration and her dismissal; Ellen Exton's abrupt termination; Clay Fairbairn's assault on Alison at the picnic; Patti Morgan's increasingly irrational behaviour, including attacking her husband with a broken liquor bottle; Thalia Monk's persistent attempts as Concerned Friend to destroy the relationship between Taylor and Vale; Patti's untimely death, and the dark spoor it's spreading over Mike Braeden's life and reputation. And now the final horror: the discovery of Ellen Exton's body in a culvert within easy driving distance of the city. It's a real chamber of horrors, and everything that's happened is connected, if only tangentially, with Thalia Monk's tenure as a summer intern at MediaNation."

Zack shifted his weight in his chair. "You said that Thalia appeared to be genuinely shaken by what she'd done to Taylor. It's possible that only dropping off the yearbooks is simply further proof that Thalia is committed to changing her life."

"I really want to believe that," I said. "But Thalia *is* manipulative. The Webers' account of their visit to Hugh and Julie Fairbairn's proves that. I'm still amazed that Thalia managed to keep Julie upstairs during the Webers' visit."

"It's possible Clay intervened," Zack said. "Hugh and Julie are his grandparents. More significantly, they're his ticket to a golden future."

"True, but Julie says Thalia has Clay dancing on a string."

"I suspect Ms. Fairbairn is not taking that situation well."

"She's livid," I said. "If Clay is going to dance on a string, Julie wants to be the puppeteer. That said, Thalia does know how to take control of a situation. I saw that myself at the stew and bannock lunch."

Suddenly I felt drained. "Zack, I want to believe that the broken girl we saw at the Scarth Club on her birthday *has* changed — that all that anger and pain has gone, but I just can't."

"People do change, Jo." Zack's voice was low and gentle. "Sometimes there really is that road to Damascus moment when a person realizes that the way they've been living their life is self-defeating, and they change course." He paused. "To be fair to Thalia, something does seem to be driving her to make amends. She gave that statement to Debbie Haczkewicz detailing Patti's irrational fears and risky behaviours and attesting that Mike Braeden is an exemplary husband and stepfather."

"Coming to our house to apologize to Taylor was painful for her, but she came, and I believe she was genuinely contrite."

Zack moved his chair closer. "You're really struggling with this, aren't you?"

"I am," I said. "I know you're right. People do change, and the last five years of Thalia's life have been a nightmare that was not of her making. I understand her need to take control of what she can."

Zack took my hand. "Let's give her the benefit of the doubt, Jo. After all, if Thalia was the person who sent the yearbooks to Alison, she deserves some credit for not pulling the pin out of the grenade."

"She does. But that raises another question. If, hypothetically, we accept the fact that the yearbooks were Thalia's project and that she did the right thing by removing the danger before anyone was harmed, what could have happened? If, before her epiphany about changing her life, Thalia had already set her plan in motion, Harper would have received the yearbooks and her explanation of the role Dylan Kyle Beveridge played in his conception. Harper would carry the knowledge that his father was a rapist and that his mother had been the victim of that rape forever and, despite her change of heart, Thalia would have been powerless to undo what she had done."

Zack's face was grave. "We're no longer about the yearbooks, are we?"

"No. We're talking about Rosemary Morrissey's disintegration and disappearance, and the possibility that both Patti Morgan and Ellen Exton were murdered."

Zack was clearly troubled. "Jo, where's this coming from?"

"I don't know," I said. My voice sounded as uncertain and frightened as I felt. "I'm just wondering if we're not seeing the whole situation clearly. Alison told me something this morning that made me realize you and I had misread Ellen's character."

Zack's eyes never left mine as I told him about how, years ago in La Ronge, a young woman had risked her career and her reputation by taking on Grant Timberlake. I was careful to include every detail in Alison's account because it was essential for Zack to realize what I now realized: that Ellen Exton had been far more than a quietly efficient radio producer with cats named after characters in an old television show. Ellen *was* that person, but she was also a journalist who believed her duty was to discover the truth, no matter the cost, to see that the truth was told and the devil was shamed.

Zack finished his drink. "Mary and Mr. Grant threw us off," he said quietly.

I nodded. "We seized on one detail and believed it revealed everything there was to know about Ellen. All we saw was, in Taylor's memorable description of her future self, 'a spinster with cats.' Zack, neither of us ever set eyes on Ellen. The first we knew of her was when Charlie told us that MediaNation had just given her the Hobson's choice of either signing a NDA agreement, picking up a generous severance package and walking away or being fired and walking away empty-handed.

"We made assumptions. I remember that you asked Charlie if there was any reason other than the extortion threat for MediaNation's senior management to want Ellen Exton gone. Charlie said the legal department had told all employees not to discuss the conditions under which Ellen left."

"But Jo, when I pressed him, he did tell us what happened, and he raised the possibility that there might be a connection between Rosemary's disappearance and Ellen Exton's termination. Somehow, I left that hanging."

When it came to his work, Zack was always his own harshest critic. I tried to remove the sting. "We were all flying blind."

"Jo, I'm a trial lawyer, and one of the cardinal rules of trial law is never leave anything hanging. I should have pushed harder, dug more deeply into why a corporation the size of MediaNation would terminate the contract of an experienced producer who, at the last minute, had been forced to assume a large role in ensuring the successful launch of an ambitious slate of fall programming and was handling the added burden of those duties well."

"If we're ever going to understand what's behind all this, finding the answer to why management felt the need to get rid of Ellen Exton will be a significant step."

"Do you have any idea what it might have been?"

"Not yet, but I think the problem began with what happened to Rosemary Morrissey."

"We know that Thalia was angry at Rosemary's dismissal of her ability to understand *Thus Spake Zarathustra*," Zack said.

"There had to be more to it than that," I said. "Charlie told us that after Rosemary's rebuke, all the summer interns started carrying copies of Nietzsche around. That's exactly the level of revenge I'd expect from student interns."

"Smartass but no harm done," Zack said. "You're right. But the torture that culminated in Joseph Monk's edict telling everyone working in Rosemary's unit to write a letter assessing her ability to carry out her responsibilities did start about that time. Given Ellen Exton's murder, I'm sure Major Crimes is already taking a hard look at what happened to Rosemary and asking some probing questions."

"Given what we've just learned about Ellen, I'm sure she was asking questions too," I said. "Remember the Post-it Note on the door of her refrigerator — 'It's not enough'? Kam Chau told me that Rosemary took Patti Morgan under her wing from the day Patti started at MediaNation. In the months before she died, Patti was deeply troubled. It's possible that she confided in Rosemary, and that when Ellen was investigating her friend's disappearance, she learned that same something, which put her in jeopardy."

Zack rubbed his temples. "And, of course, now there's no way of learning what Ellen discovered."

"Because she's dead, and in all likelihood, Rosemary is dead too," I said. We were both silent for a moment, as if acknowledging that fact. Then I said, "So, you and I are in exactly the position Ellen Exton was in when she slapped that Post-it on her fridge door. We know more than we did before, but what we know is still not enough. Have you learned anything new about Ellen Exton's death?"

"I did, and none of it's pleasant, so I'll keep it brief. The forensics people have a saying, 'The body always tells a story, especially when the heart stops beating.' Ellen had been dead five weeks and a day when her body was discovered. The tests show the body had been outdoors in the culvert for all but a fraction of that time. There's a lot of weather in five weeks. But the forensic pathologist was able to determine that death was caused by manual strangulation. It would have been over quickly for her."

"I guess we can file that under 'Thank heaven for small mercies,'" I said, and I was surprised at the bitterness in my voice.

Zack seldom left his chair during the day, but he wheeled over and transferred his body from his chair to the place next to me on the couch. He took me in his arms, and we held each other for a very long time. Finally, he said, "Are you ready to carry on?"

"I am," I said. "We need to stay close tonight."

"That was my plan," he said.

CHAPTER TWENTY-THREE

On the morning of Ellen Exton's funeral, I knew it was raining before I opened my eyes. The air that came through our bedroom window smelled of wet leaves and cold. Pantera was flattened on the floor outside Zack's bathroom door, but Esme stayed put until I was in my running clothes. When I came out of my bathroom, Zack was in his robe looking out at the rain through the open patio door. The sky was grey, and the wind had picked up.

"Winter is icummen in / Lhude sing Goddamm," I said. "Raineth drop and staineth slop, / and how the wind doth ramm! Sing Goddamm."

Zack chuckled. "Good lord, what is that?"

"A poem by Ezra Pound. The title is 'Ancient Music,' and I'm reciting it because I know how you hate winter. Do you want to hear the rest?"

"Absolutely," Zack said, "but I want to watch your performance." He closed the patio door and turned his chair to face me. "Showtime," he said.

"And I'm ready."

After I recited the rest of 'Ancient Music,' Zack opened his arms to me. "Thank you," he said, "for giving us a brave start to what we both know is going to be a grim day. How are you doing?"

"I'm okay," I said. "I'll be glad when the day's over, and we're home again, but going to Saskatoon for the funeral is the right thing to do for Ellen, for her parents and for us."

"Agreed," Zack said. "So, we're picking up Charlie D and Kam Chau at noon, and the funeral is at three thirty. We should be fine for time."

"Pantera, Esme and I better get going, but it's going to be a short run. The dogs and I are getting older, and we crave comfort."

"I'm not going to the office this morning, so we can take our time over breakfast. If I put macadamia nuts and dried cranberries in the porridge, will you teach me 'Lhude sing Goddamm'?"

"Deal," I said. I kissed the top of his head.

* * *

That morning, Zack and I worked across from each other at Sally Love's old work table in our home office. We often chose separate spaces for work at home, but this was a time when we needed to be together.

Saying that Ellen had always loved the months of September and October with their promise of new beginnings, her parents had asked that none of those attending the funeral wear black; Zack and I were both in the rich autumnal shades that always evoked harvest and Thanksgiving for me. But Ellen Exton's funeral would mark a bitter harvest for a life cut short, and I was dreading it.

When we left the house, the rain had stopped, but the wind had picked up, and the air carried the pungent zing of ozone. More rain ahead. As we made our way to our Volvo, I knew Zack's heart, like mine, was heavy.

Then, seemingly out of nowhere, the sky was suddenly black with geese, hundreds and then thousands of them on the great migration south for the winter. Their cries filled the air, and, like a tuning fork, my spirit resonated. I took Zack's hand in mine, and we watched until the last of the geese, the stragglers, flew out of sight. Neither of us spoke. We had experienced a pure and shining reminder that we are part of a timeless mystery, and there were no words.

* * *

When I entered the MediaNation galleria, Mark Evanson was sitting behind the reception desk. As always, he rose and greeted me with a smile of indescribable sweetness.

"Charlie and Kam told me you were coming," he said. "They'll be upstairs in just a very few minutes."

"Good," I said. "That gives you and me a chance to visit."

Mark's smile grew wider. "I'd like that." Then remembering the gravity of the situation, his face grew sombre. "This is such a sad day. Ellen was always kind to me, and to Lori. Every two weeks, Lori and I have lunch together at the cafeteria. Lori heard on TV that it's important to have dates even when you're married because you have to keep the romance alive. So, that's what Lori and I do." Mark lowered his voice and blushed. "It works," he said.

"My husband and I have dates too," I said. "And Lori's right. It is important to keep the romance alive when you're married."

Mark nodded. "I'll tell Lori you said that. She tries hard to do the right thing."

"Obviously you're both doing the right thing," I said. "After we ran into you that day at the picnic, Zack remarked on what a happy couple you are."

"We are happy. We just wish . . ." When his sentence trailed off, Mark seemed at a loss about how to pick up the thread of our conversation. The silence between us was lengthening into awkwardness when Mark saw something on his desk that saved the day. "Lori made a card for Ellen's parents. Would you mind giving it to them after the service?"

"I'd be glad to."

"And there's something else Ellen's parents should have." He reached beneath his desk and brought out a gift box with a lid covered in pictures of cats. "Islande, who does the night cleaning, found this when she started her six o'clock shift the day Ellen left MediaNation.

"Ellen had to clean out her desk, and management said I had to be there to make sure she didn't take anything that belonged to the company. She would never have done that, but I guess nobody in management knew the kind of person she was.

"I offered to help, but Ellen said she was okay, and everything seemed fine until she couldn't find her key and then she just fell apart. She dumped her purse and her messenger bag out on the desk, and we went through everything, but we couldn't find the key. When I asked her what the key was for, she said her desk had a file drawer that locked and she needed what was inside. I offered to go down to maintenance to see if they had another key. She started to cry. Ellen never cries. I didn't know what to do, and then Charlie D came, and they finished packing Ellen's things into boxes, said goodbye to me and carried everything down the hall to the elevator.

"I thought Ellen and Charlie D had settled the problem with the file drawer, so I didn't think about it again. The next morning when I started my shift, this box was in the space under my desk where, for twenty-four hours, I keep items people have left behind so they can pick it up before it goes into Lost and Found.

"There was a note from Islande taped to the box saying that one of the other cleaners had told her everything was supposed to have been cleared out of Ellen's desk, and if there was anything left there, we'd all get heck. When Islande found the locked drawer, she went to maintenance, got a key, unlocked the drawer and found this box.

"I tried a hundred times to call Ellen. Lori and I talked it over, and we thought that since the box mattered so much to Ellen, she'd want her parents to decide who should see what was inside it." Mark's eyes were troubled. "Mrs. Shreve — Joanne — did we do the wrong thing?"

"No," I said. "You and Lori didn't do the wrong thing. This is a very difficult situation, Mark. None of us knows what the right thing is. I'll make sure Ellen's parents get the box, so they can decide."

I looked towards the door from the studios downstairs. "Charlie and Kam are here, so I have to go. Mark, I really enjoyed our talk."

"So did I," he said. "Joanne, I know saying goodbye to people we've cared for is hard. John 1:5 will help you. 'The light shines in the darkness, and the darkness has not over-come the light.'"

"I'll hold on to that," I said. "Right now, there's just so much darkness."

Mark's voice was patient. "The light's always there, Joanne. Sometimes, you just have to wait awhile before you see it."

"Sorry for the delay," Charlie said. "Kam and I had to change out of our jeans and sweats into something more appropriate, and neither of us could remember how to tie a Windsor knot."

I checked both ties and made a small adjustment on Charlie's. "Perfect," I said. "And while you were getting spiffed up, Mark and I had a chance to have a good talk."

Charlie winked at Mark. "This is a good man to talk to," Charlie said.

"He is indeed," Kam added.

When we left the galleria, Mark was beaming.

The rain had started again, and as we left the building to run to the car, I tucked Ellen's box under my jacket. After we were all belted in, I handed the box back to Charlie. "You guys have more room back there than we do."

"No problem," Charlie said. "What's the story with this?"

After I'd finished relating Mark Evanson's account, Zack said, "Do you think it's wise to hand this over to Ellen's parents without knowing what's inside? If it's connected to whatever Ellen was investigating, it may contain evidence, and it belongs with the police."

"Good point," I said. "And even if it's not evidence, there was that exchange of explicit photos with the online creep. Ellen wouldn't want her parents to see those. I'm with Zack on this. I think you have to open the box."

Charlie shook his head. "Nope, not us. Kam and I worked with Ellen, and we're on our way to her funeral. If there's something in that box that she'd prefer we didn't see, I think we'd prefer that too. But I do agree that someone should look inside the box before we hand it over to Ellen's parents."

"Fair enough," I said. "I'll take it."

The shiver of trepidation I felt as I opened the box evaporated as soon as I saw what was inside. "Nothing to worry about," I said. "The box is full of pictures of Mary and Mr. Grant. And they're dressed up for the holidays — Christmas, Valentine's, St. Patrick's Day. I wonder how Ellen got those costumes on them."

Kam laughed. "As a cat owner, I can assure you those costumes didn't stay on them long."

I continued sifting through the pictures. "These are fun though. And — bonus — there's an envelope at the bottom of the box. I suspect these are the cats' more formal portraits."

When I saw the first photo — a professional quality black-and-white picture of a naked beautiful adolescent and his equally beautiful lover — my pulse raced. They were so young and so wholly involved in each other. Bodies pressed together, limbs tangled, eyes closed, oblivious to everything except the sliding scale of pleasure carrying them headlong towards the ecstasy of release, they were the embodiment of carnal joy. A breath-stopping embodiment of that moment of abandonment that, for the lucky among us, is part of the human experience.

But I knew that the boy in the picture was seventeen years old, and the girl was sixteen, and they were brother and sister.

I sifted through the photos. All were of Thalia and Nicholas Monk exploring the complexities and joys of physical intimacy. The photographs were as breathtaking as their subjects, and I was overwhelmed.

"Zack, there's a public rest area somewhere along here," I said. "Could you pull in?"

He gave me a quick grin. "Sure. Never say no to a pit stop."

"It's not that. Zack, there were some other photos in the box, and I think they may be significant." When I handed the photos back to Charlie and Kam, there was silence for a moment and then Charlie breathed, "Holy shit."

After we pulled over, Kam handed the photos to Zack. He looked at them carefully and shook his head. "Not quite the smoking gun," he said. "But close."

"They're so young," Charlie said. "And those pictures don't leave any room for misinterpretation. This is going to blow everything sky high."

"It will," I said. "Maisie and I talked about the possibility of incest just after she and Zack received information about the Monk family from Colby and Associates. Joseph Monk's decision to separate his children in the middle of the school year puzzled us both. From the information Colby had gathered, it seemed that Thalia and Nicholas were both thriving, and that Joseph Monk was a devoted and caring father. He must have known what separating his children would do to them, and yet he separated them."

"Because he had no alternative," Zack said, and his voice was ineffably sad. He handed the photos back to me.

"That's pretty much how Maisie and I saw it," I said, "but we had no proof that the relationship between Nicholas and Thalia was sexual. There was something chilling about the school photographs Colby and Associates sent of them their last year at school together. Maisie felt the chill too. She and I talked a little about the possibility that Nicholas and Thalia had a Siegmund and Sieglinde relationship, but we let it drop. All we had was conjecture, and as the headmistress at Bishop Lambeth said many times, 'Girls, when speculation has done its worst, two and two still make four.' Now we have those photographs, and they raise their own questions. Those photographs are not pornography; they're art. Who took them?"

"An answer to that question will have to wait," Zack said. "We need to hit the road."

As we headed back onto the highway, Kam leaned forward in his seat directly behind me. "I can shed some light on the question of who took the pictures. Nicholas and Thalia were both avid photographers, and at the farewell party for Patti after the last show of *Sunny Side Up,* it was clear that their interest was solely in photographing each other."

"Kam told me about that party," I said. "It was seven years ago, so Thalia would have been thirteen and Nicholas, fourteen. They were living in Toronto, but they'd flown out to surprise Patti."

"I take it the surprise did not go well," Zack said.

"It was a disaster," Kam said flatly. "The farewell show was supposed to be a trip down memory lane with former employees showing up to wish Patti well, interspersed with highlights from *Sunny Side Up* over the years: good moments, goofy moments, sentimental moments — the usual. But Thalia's and Nicholas's presence threw Patti off."

"Why?" Charlie said. "They'd lived with her before they moved to Toronto, and from what Ellen told me, there'd been no drama behind the move; it was just a practical decision. Patti was concerned that her show might be cancelled and she'd have to move to a different city and uproot the kids, and Joseph Monk's job was secure."

"Something must have happened in the interim," Kam said. "Because there were definitely tension that day. Nicholas and Thalia arrived dressed almost identically: black slim-fit slacks, lace-up boots and tailored white cotton shirts. They had the same haircut, very short with a long side bang. And, of course, they both had those amazing sapphire eyes.

"Nicholas and Thalia made no attempt to mingle. They both had camera bags slung over their shoulders. When they were approached, they were polite, but they made it clear they were fine on their own. Not long after they arrived, they took out their cameras — top of the line Leicas — and began taking close-ups of each other from different angles. They were wholly absorbed in what they were doing. It was as if the rest of the room didn't exist. People got the message and respected their space, but Patti was livid. Finally, she went over, took Nicholas by the hand and said, in a voice clearly intended to be overheard, 'Come on, Nicky, time to let your mother show off her pride and joy.' When she attempted to pull him after her, Nicholas didn't miss a beat; he extended his hand to Thalia. The dynamic shifted, and suddenly their mother was stuck with two pride and joys."

"Patti looked stricken, and she just wandered off. Nicholas and Thalia moved closer together, looked into each other's eyes and exchanged a private smile. The connection between them was electric. I'm an opera buff too, Joanne, and I remember thinking, 'Siegmund and Sieglinde.'"

"Charlie and I obviously had misspent youths," Zack said. "Could one of you explain who Siegmund and Sieglinde are?"

"They're characters in Wagner's opera *Die Walküre*," I said. "They're twins, separated at birth. Neither knows of the other's identity, but later in life they meet and fall in love. They discover they're brother and sister, but their love is too great for separation. They have a child together named Siegmund, but that's another opera.

"That's also a very pedestrian account of a really stunning work," I added. "The music when Siegmund and Sieglinde become lovers absolutely shimmers."

"So does Sieglinde's speech when she explains to her twin brother how she fell in love with him at first sight," Kam said. "'I saw my own image in a stream, and now it is given to me again; / Just as it came up out of the water / You offer my own image to me now!' and Siegmund replies, 'You are the image I harbor in me!'"

"My knowledge of opera may be lacking," Zack said, "but I am familiar with the myth of Narcissus."

Kam laughed. "You're not the only one. There's enough scholarly work on the connection between narcissism and incestuous love to fill a good-sized library. In essence, the argument is that the narcissist transfers their erotic energy to the object most like themself — the sibling."

"And the photos of the Monk siblings were in a locked file drawer in Ellen Exton's desk," Zack said. "I imagine Debbie Haczkewicz will see that as a compelling motive for murder." He paused for a moment. "Come to think of it, so do I."

CHAPTER TWENTY-FOUR

By the time we hit Davidson, an hour away from Saskatoon, there was a marked improvement in both the weather and our spirits. The sky was cloudless; the sun was shining, and the pavement was dry. It was a perfect October day.

Even more significantly, we had agreed on the next step and taken it. The discovery and disposition of the photographs of Nicholas and Thalia called for legal advice. Fortunately we had a lawyer behind the wheel. The four of us floated possibilities and settled on one that covered the legal bases and protected Thalia.

I sent Maisie a picture of one of the photos that had been in the filing cabinet of Ellen's desk. Maisie called back almost immediately and said she would track down Thalia Monk, explain the circumstances in which the photos were discovered and make certain Thalia had a lawyer. Maisie said she'd check with Mike first, but she was certain that's what he would want. At that point, with Thalia's consent, either Maisie or Thalia's lawyer would forward the photo and the information we'd given her to Debbie Haczkewicz.

Maisie called just as we entered the city to say that she had found Thalia, told her that the photos had been discovered and suggested that the next step would be finding a lawyer to be with Thalia when she was questioned by the police.

Thalia recognized that she needed a lawyer, and Maisie introduced her to Katina Posaluko-Chapman, a trial lawyer with the empathy Thalia would need and the intelligence necessary to earn her respect. Maisie had just left the two women alone so they could talk.

In her short life, Thalia Monk had already suffered more than her share of pain, and there was more grief coming her way, but she would not be alone, and that was as much consolation as we could hope for. So, we returned our focus to Ellen Exton and the service ahead.

Few places are more beautiful and more filled with promise than a college campus before the newness has worn off and students are not burdened by work and worries. On that early October day, the grass was still green; the brown-gold leaves were still clinging to trees; students were sitting outside, reading or just chatting; and St. Thomas More College was almost as lovely as its brochure photos.

Many years ago, I had taught a senior class in the contemporary politics of our province at the University of Saskatchewan while I finished research on a book I was writing. At that point in my life, I was a widow at home with two children in university and a teenager, so I treasured moments of quiet reflection, and I'd always found those moments in the chapel here, where the Mass of Resurrection for Ellen Exton would take place. She had completed her undergraduate sixty credit hours prerequisite for admission to the B.A. in journalism at Saint Thomas More (STM).

We were early, but the chapel was filling quickly. Zack always bristled at being escorted to the special seating reserved for the handicapped, but space was at a premium. Zack and I had not known Ellen Exton, but in that hackneyed phrase, we were attending her funeral to find closure, and that meant knowing what we'd lost.

The simple teak box containing Ellen's ashes was already on a small table on the altar. Beside it was a watercolour of Ellen, painted when she was an undergraduate here. The artist had captured her vibrancy: the intelligence in her deep-set grey eyes and the determination in the set of her generous lips. The watercolour did what all good art does — conveyed in a few moments the essence of the subject and left those who saw the piece with a deeper understanding of what it means to be alive.

Father Gary Ariano was the celebrant of the mass. Sally Love had frequently attended the five o'clock Mass in the months before her death. She had questions about faith, and she and Gary had grown close as they worked together towards answers. Not long before her death, Sally had been baptized and confirmed. By default, I had had the responsibility for Sally's funeral, and Gary had been, as they say, a godsend in helping me arrange a Catholic funeral. Over the years, we had kept in touch, and as he followed the servers up the aisle with Ellen's family members close behind, I knew the service would be a comforting one for them.

Anyone who has been involved in electoral politics has attended plenty of funerals, and I was familiar with the Mass of Resurrection. I found solace in the ritual of the confession, the prayers and the Bible readings. Seemingly, Zack, Kam and Charlie were soothed by them too. Gary Ariano read the Gospel — "No one who is alive and has faith in me shall ever die" — with reassuring conviction in his voice, and Zack squeezed my hand.

Charlie was sitting on the other side of me, eyes on the altar. Suddenly his body shot forward in the pew, and he half rose. "Jesus Christ," he said. Kam too had straightened, his face slack with shock. His voice was a whisper. "It's Rosemary."

A tall, very thin woman with shoulder-length greying hair and the long narrow face and elongated ivory neck of a figure painted by Modigliani had stepped to the lectern.

I leaned towards Zack. "The woman about to deliver the eulogy is Rosemary Morrissey."

Zack's eyes widened. "I thought she was dead."

"We all did," I said. "It seems we were mistaken."

Rosemary was wearing one of the vibrantly coloured, hand-sewn tunics she favoured. This one was black with cerise and lime trim. She was tanned and clearly in robust good health.

"I treasure all my memories of Ellen Exton," Rosemary said, and hearing her deep and assured voice again sent a shiver up my spine. Rosemary's stories about Ellen were warm and affectionate — stories of on-air disasters triumphantly averted; of covering nail-bitingly close all-night election results; of reporting heartbreaking family tragedies; of interviews where subjects suddenly revealed a self that seemed a surprise even to them. Rosemary ended the eulogy with an account of how, despite verbal and physical threats and community condemnation, Ellen had investigated Grant Timberlake's financial and ethical malfeasance and brought him to justice. In her closing remarks, Rosemary refuted Rudyard Kipling's reference to journalism as the "dark art" and said that Ellen Exton's life was proof that "in the hands of a person who loved her craft, journalism could be a shining thing."

The eulogy was beautifully crafted and beautifully delivered, and as Rosemary stepped from the lectern and returned to her place in the congregation, Charlie said, "What just happened?"

Kam drew a deep breath. "A miracle?"

After that, the Mass of Resurrection continued: the kiss of peace, the celebration of the eucharist, the incensing of the altar and ashes, the post communion prayers and the final prayer for Ellen Exton. "May the angels lead you into paradise." The mass was over, and the party of mourners followed the servers and Father Ariano back down the centre aisle.

Charlie was quick off the mark. "Kam and I have to talk to Rosemary. We'll catch up with you and Zack at the reception." With that, he and Kam streaked down a side aisle that opened into the hall outside the chapel and disappeared.

Zack looked up at me. "Remind me again why there are receptions after funerals," he said.

"The reception is intended to reconnect mourners with the world of the living."

"Even if the mourners don't want to reconnect?" he said.

"Especially if they don't want to reconnect. Remember how it was for you that November after your partners were murdered."

"I remember. Jo, there's something I've been meaning to ask you, because I've never been sure if it really happened or it was just a fever dream. After Debbie told me they were all dead, did you lay down beside me and say, 'I love you so much, but I don't know what to do'?"

"That really did happen," I said. "You had a temperature of 104, and you'd just been hit by news that severed you from the life you'd known for almost three decades. I was so frightened."

"But you were there. Every time I woke up you were there, and later when the truth about what had happened was finally sinking in, you and Taylor were always there, and that made all the difference." Zack turned his wheelchair into the aisle that Kam and Charlie had used. "My turn to return the favour," he said. "Let's go."

* * *

We had no trouble finding the reception. The crowd who'd attended the funeral were all headed in one direction. When the scent of good coffee drifted down the hall, we knew we were close, and when I saw Father Gary Ariano waiting for us in the hall, I knew we'd arrived.

Gary and I were in early middle age when we met, but Sally had been dead for seventeen years, and Gary and I were both visibly older. His dark hair was now shot through with grey, and the laugh lines around his eyes had deepened, but he still moved with the easy grace of the star basketball player he and his brother, Lou, had both been in college, and he still had a great smile.

After we greeted each other and I introduced Zack, Gary plunged right in. "I spotted you in the chapel, Joanne. I was looking forward to getting caught up, but first I have a question. Is your friend, the man who was sitting next to you, all right? He seemed disturbed."

"Actually, Charlie's not just a friend; he's our son-in-law. I take it you heard his outburst."

Gary's eyes were amused. "People are always surprised at how much we can hear from up there. When your friend said 'Jesus Christ,' I thought he might have been having a spiritual awakening."

Zack's reply was thoughtful. "That might be a valid interpretation," he said. "When we came into the chapel today, Joanne, Charlie, our friend Kam and I all believed that Rosemary Morrissey was dead. Seeing her step up to the lectern to deliver the eulogy did seem miraculous."

"I imagine it did," Gary said. "I take it there's a story there."

"There is," I said. "But it's a long one, best saved for another time, and judging by the expectant looks aimed in our direction, I think people are waiting for you to say a prayer, so they can eat."

Gary glanced around him. "And you're right," he said. "Are you going to be in Saskatoon for a while?"

"No, we're going back to Regina later this afternoon."

"I'm sorry. I was hoping we would have a chance to get together."

"There'll be plenty of chances in the future," I said. "Our daughter Taylor is moving to Saskatoon Thanksgiving weekend. And — you'll like this — she's moving into Sally's old studio across the river."

Gary brightened. "Ten minutes away on my bike. Please give Taylor my contact information. If she needs help with anything, I'm here."

"That's reassuring," Zack said.

"I'm a hopeful guy," Gary said. "Taylor's birth mother was a friend, and the mother who raised Taylor is a friend. I'm hoping there's a place somewhere in Taylor's orbit for me."

"Knowing our daughter, I'm sure Taylor will find that place," Zack said. "After seeing you in action today, Father Ariano, nothing could please me more."

The men shook hands, Gary smiled, touched my arm and went back to work.

Zack was pensive as Gary walked away. "Sometime I'd like to hear his story," he said.

"I bet he'd like to hear your story too," I said. "That's what the future's for."

Zack looked around the room. "In the meantime, there are a couple of young lawyers I'd like to get your opinion on."

"Why?"

"The firm is going gangbusters. I've been mulling over the possibilities of opening a branch in Saskatoon."

"Exactly how long have you been mulling?"

Zack checked his watch. "About ten minutes."

Ellen Exton's parents had a group of mourners with them and more waiting, so Zack and I introduced ourselves to the young lawyers, who were pleased as punch to have the senior partner of Falconer Shreve seek them out, and to some people I knew from the old days when I was doing the political panel for Nationtv.

When it was time for us to move on yet again to other conversational partners, Zack said, "I don't know about you, but it's been a long day, and I'd like to get on the road."

"So would I," I said. "But we can't leave without Kam and Charlie, and they and Rosemary obviously have a lot of unfinished business to deal with. I guess we'll just have to find ourselves some other hapless soul to glom on to and wait."

We didn't have long to wait. Ten minutes later, Charlie, Kam and Rosemary Morrissey came through the entrance to the reception area. They seemed at ease with one another; apparently, whatever fences needed mending had been mended.

Rosemary and I greeted each other cordially. She looked healthy, rested and at peace. "It's good to see you again, Joanne. It's been a few years." As I'd noticed during the eulogy, Rosemary's voice had lost none of its deep, rich resonance.

"It has," I agreed. "You're looking well."

"As are you," she said, "And I understand congratulations are in order to both you and Zack on your marriage."

"Joanne and I have been married for a while now," Zack said, "but congratulations are always welcome. It's nice to see you again, Rosemary. I was on a show you produced a few years back, and it was a lot of fun."

Charlie raised his hands, palms out. "Enough tripping down memory lane," he said. "There is much to discuss, and Rosemary has a plane to catch. I thought we'd find an empty classroom and make the most of the time we have."

"Let's not waste time roaming the halls in search of an empty classroom," I said. "I'll ask Gary Ariano. He teaches at STM, and he's standing right over there. Hang tight."

Once again, Gary proved to be a godsend. Within minutes we were in an elevator headed for the priests' common room on the third floor.

"I think you'll find this more congenial than a classroom," Gary said, as he unlocked the door. "Joanne's been here before, so she can show you where everything is. The bar is well stocked, and there's always something to eat. Help yourselves. I'll leave the key with Joanne. When you're finished, come back to the reception, so I can introduce you to Ellen's parents, and we can say our goodbyes."

When Gary closed the door, I turned to the others. "I don't know about the rest of you, but I would really like a drink."

Zack wheeled towards the bar. "What can I get everybody?"

"I'll have a scotch on the rocks," Rosemary said. "And please make it a good one. A friend of the Extons is driving me to the airport, so I won't be getting behind the wheel."

"Speaking of getting behind the wheel," Kam said. "Unless somebody else wants to, I'm happy to drive back to Regina."

"You're my hero," I said. "Zack, I'll have what Rosemary's having."

"I'll have an IPA," Charlie said. "And Kam's my hero too."

"I'm on it," Zack said.

The priests' common room had a wall of windows with an enviable view of the campus. Apart from that, the ambience was strictly 1960s recreation room: a worn but comfortable leather couch, three lounge chairs, four easy chairs arranged around a round coffee table, an oversized TV, a very large aquarium and a wet bar.

While Zack got the drinks, I emptied a box of Goldfish crackers into a bowl and placed it on the table with some napkins and coasters. After we'd picked up our beverage of choice, we took our places around the coffee table. I noticed Zack had positioned his chair to face Rosemary.

"Our time is limited, and I don't know what you three covered before you came to the reception, so I have one question for Rosemary, and we'll take it from there," Zack began. "Rosemary, are you aware there are police investigations into the murders of Patti Morgan and Ellen Exton?"

"I am."

"Do I have your permission to tape our conversation and hand it over to the police if necessary?"

"You have my permission."

Zack smiled. "Good, that will simplify matters. Could you state your contact information please?"

Rosemary gave Zack her street address, the address of her place of employment, her cellphone number and her work number. All were in Winnipeg.

She was working for the local station of a private media company that was a rival of MediaNation's. Her responsibilities were essentially the same as those she'd had in her position at MediaNation, but they were on a smaller scale for a smaller salary. She added that she was content and optimistic about the future.

"We're all glad to hear that," Zack said, "especially because we are all aware of the ordeal you endured during your last weeks at MediaNation. I know it will be painful, but could you describe what happened during that time?"

Rosemary took a large sip of scotch. "I'll describe what happened, but with the caveat that I'm still unsure about exactly what did happen."

Zack's voice was encouraging. "Just do your best."

"In that case, I have to start by saying that what I *believed* was happening then is not what I'm now relatively certain actually happened, so I'm going to begin at the ending.

"Kam and Charlie have been filling me in on events here. They tell me that when I disappeared after the termination, everyone assumed I was travelling. And that was true. I was in terrible shape, physically and emotionally. I couldn't seem to hold a thought. It was as if my brain had fragmented. I seriously considered suicide and then I decided to give myself a month, and if nothing had changed . . ." She shrugged. "Well, you can fill in the blank.

"In the spring I'd purchased a ticket to Bequia. I was planning a holiday after our new slate of programs was safely launched in the fall. After I was terminated, I needed a quick and easy way out, so I simply changed the date of my flight.

"Bequia is part of Saint Vincent and the Grenadines in the Caribbean. It's a small island, seven square miles with a population of around five thousand and it is beautiful.

"I have very little memory of what I did to pass my days and nights there, but one day I was lying on the beach and I realized that I was better — not wholly better, but I could feel the fragments starting to come together, coalescing.

"When the month was over, I called a friend in Winnipeg and explained my situation. She worked for the company that employs me now, and she arranged for me to have a trial period in my current position. I was on my way back.

"My friend was my salvation. She made an appointment for me with her doctor. He asked me a number of questions and arranged for tests. He concluded that I had indeed suffered a stroke on the May long weekend when I was at the cottage. The blanks in my memory and my confusion would have righted themselves if I had sought treatment, but by that time my paranoia — and that's what it was — had advanced to the point where I didn't trust anybody.

"I really believed the summer interns were out to get me, to punish me for the condescension I'd shown Thalia when I saw her carrying *Thus Spake Zarathustra*. Instead of getting medical treatment, I self-medicated on a stew of antidepressants, painkillers and anti-anxiety medications. You know the rest. It got worse: the slurred speech; the outbursts of temper, the denials, the hostility and then finally the call from Joseph Monk in Toronto telling me he'd received one hundred and fifteen separate letters from employees in my unit saying that I was no longer capable of carrying out my responsibilities.

"That's when I hit bottom," Rosemary said. "And I accept full responsibility for everything that happened. The blame is solely mine."

"I know how difficult reliving that time was for you, but you did it," Zack said. "You're doing remarkably well, but Rosemary, there's another difficult subject facing us. How would you characterize the nature of the relationship between Thalia Monk and her brother, Nicholas?"

"So you know," Rosemary said, and her entire body seemed to relax as if a burden had been lifted.

"Yes," I said. "We know."

"The relationship was incestuous," she acknowledged.

"Just three more questions," Zack said. "We're almost finished, Rosemary. Are you aware that Ellen Exton possessed a series of photographs of Thalia and Nicholas Monk having sexual relations?"

"I am."

"Do you know how she came to have them in her possession?"

"I gave them to her the day MediaNation terminated me. I told her they were her insurance policy."

"Meaning?"

"Meaning that if Joseph Monk attempted to do to her what he'd done to me, she could threaten to make the photos public." Rosemary lowered her head and said, "It was a terrible thing to do, and I'm deeply ashamed."

"We all do things of which we're ashamed," Zack said gently. "How did you get the photographs?"

"Patti Morgan gave them to me."

"Do you remember when?"

"Just before last Christmas. Patti found the pictures in Thalia's room. She called Joseph Monk, and he said that he wasn't aware of the photographs but that he had come home early from work one afternoon and heard his son and daughter in Nicholas's bedroom. He confronted them, and Thalia was on the next flight to Regina.

"And Nicholas decided to end his life," Rosemary said. "I'm able to see the tragedy of what happened now, but on the day I left MediaNation, I simply wanted to hurt Thalia Monk because I believed she had plotted against me. I knew Patti had been unbelievably cruel to that girl, but that didn't stop me from compounding the cruelty." Rosemary paused. "I was hoping Thalia would be here today, so I could apologize to her."

Zack finished his drink, and leaned back in his chair. "Unless anyone else has something we should discuss, I think we're finished here."

When Charlie, Kam and I remained silent, Zack wheeled his chair to where Rosemary was sitting. "Thank you," he said. "I hope you know that we all wish you the best."

"I believe that," Rosemary said, in her thrilling voice. "And I'm grateful I had a chance to say what needed to be said."

And with that, it was over. We washed and dried the glasses, wiped the table and when the others were in the hall, waiting for the elevator, I locked the door to the priests' common room. It was time to go downstairs, meet Ellen Exton's parents, say our goodbyes and return to a world that we knew was about to be strafed by pain.

CHAPTER TWENTY-FIVE

It was close to nine o'clock when we dropped off Charlie and Kam. Fifteen minutes later, we pulled into our driveway. Zack turned to me. "I can't remember ever being this tired."

"Neither can I," I said.

Those were the last words we exchanged until eight o'clock the next morning, when Pantera and Esme decided enough was enough and nudged and whined until Zack and I faced the inevitable and started the day.

It was past nine when the dogs and I returned from our run. Taylor was already at work on the mural in the swimming pool room, and Zack had breakfast ready to go. After I showered and changed, we sat down to juice, coffee, bagels, cream cheese and lox.

Zack smeared cream cheese on his bagel, covered the cream cheese with slices of smoked salmon, then carefully topped the salmon with a spoonful of capers. "You know what you and I need?" he said.

"I assume that's a rhetorical question."

"It is," Zack said. "Remember the mental health days Taylor used to take?"

"I do," I said. "Two mental health days per term. Mieka, Peter and Angus had them too. Peter and Angus always used one for American Thanksgiving, so they could stay home and watch football without having to fake a mysterious short-term illness. Having a day in which you have no obligation to do anything but recharge your batteries is a gift."

"It's a gift you and I could use today," Zack said. "What do you think the odds are?"

"Not good," I said. "You sent Debbie Haczkewicz the tape of Rosemary Morrissey's interview. I expect Debbie will be joining us very soon."

Right on cue, the doorbell rang, and as I had anticipated, it was Debbie. She was a tall, large-boned woman who favoured trouser suits and wore them well. That day she was wearing a sand herringbone tweed that was particularly flattering, but she was uncharacteristically curt with me, so I swallowed the compliment on the tip of my tongue and led her into the kitchen.

At a dinner where Zack had been the guest of honour, Debbie had used a graceful simile to describe the relationship between Zack and her. She said that like the orca and the great white shark, police officers and trial lawyers were natural enemies, and that although Zack would always be a great white shark and she would always be an orca, they had learned to cherish the times when they were able to swim side by side.

Clearly that morning was not one of those times. Zack felt the chill but waded in. "So, how's it going, Deb?"

"It's been better," she said.

"I sent you an audio file last night. Did you get it?"

"I did. It was kind of you to remember that there is a police department here in Regina working 24/7 on a murder case. In all likelihood, Ms. Morrissey had information that could have been pivotal to that case. The file is useful, but knowing that Ms. Morrissey was alive and within range for an interview would have been even more useful."

Zack sliced his bagel in two, slid one half onto a plate and pushed the plate towards Debbie. "Peace offering," he said. "I didn't know Rosemary Morrissey was alive until she strolled to the lectern in the St. Thomas More chapel and delivered Ellen Exton's eulogy. She was in Saskatoon for the funeral only. She had a plane to catch. She's in a probationary period with her new job, and she didn't want to miss a day's work. You have all her contact information, and you have a recording of everything she said during our hastily arranged interview. I'm not holding anything back."

"He really isn't holding anything back," I said. "We were with our son-in-law, Charlie Dowhanuik, and Kam Chau, who took over as producer of Charlie's show after Ellen disappeared. All of us walked into that chapel believing

Rosemary Morrissey was dead. As Zack said, seeing her alive was a shock, and our time with her was limited. Zack did the best he could under the circumstances, and he sent you everything he had."

"I believe you," Debbie said. "And I apologize. But Zack, I know you and I know how you operate. When I listened to that interview, I couldn't understand why you didn't push Rosemary Morrissey harder. There were a dozen questions you could have asked, starting with whether she and Ellen Exton stayed in touch after Rosemary left town.

"If we knew they had, we could have a real sense of Ellen's life in the weeks before she died, and that would have given us leads into how Ellen Exton apparently vanished into thin air until her body turned up weeks later in a farmer's culvert. As it stands, we don't know enough to ask the right people the right questions. I'm tired of banging my head against brick walls. Why didn't you do what you always do with a witness: keep pummelling until they break?"

Zack drew a deep breath. "Because Rosemary was already broken," he said. "You heard the interview. She'd suffered a total breakdown, and she is now just beginning to put the pieces together again."

Debbie was unconvinced. "Rosemary Morrissey was totally in possession of herself. Her answers were precise and economical."

"They were," Zack agreed. "But her fingernails were bitten down to the quick. She's been through enough, Deb, and she'd just endured the funeral of a dear friend. If you have questions, all you have to do is call and ask."

"I'll wait a day or two," Debbie said. "Thanks for the bagel. May I pour myself a cup of coffee to go with it?"

"I'll get it," I said.

Debbie had just taken her first bite when her phone rang. She glanced at the screen. "Work," she said and picked up. She listened without comment for several minutes until her caller had finished. When she responded, her voice was even, but I was grateful I wasn't the person on the other end of the call. "Tell me how this could have happened," she said. "We did a grid search of the area around the culvert. Seven experienced officers examined every square inch of that area twice. And suddenly a cellphone turns up?"

Zack and I exchanged a quick glance. Whatever information Debbie's caller had passed along was worth listening in on. As she processed what she was hearing, Debbie was intent, but the tension in her face lessened. "I'll be right there," she said and ended the call. And then, surprisingly, she smiled — a genuine smile, broad and open.

"A break in the case?" Zack said.

Debbie nodded. "And it could be a big one." She took a sip of coffee. "From my end of the conversation, I'm sure you were able to piece together part of the story. As soon as the body was found, we did a grid search: every square inch around the culvert was searched, and there was nothing. Suddenly it turns out there *was* something: a cellphone."

"What happened to it?" I said.

"A seven-year-old boy named William Duncan had found it weeks ago. The boy spotted the phone when he was out in the field gopher hunting just before he went back to school in September. So we have a time frame. There'd been a rain-storm, and the phone wasn't working, but William helps his grandfather when something around the place needs to be fixed, and he knows his stuff.

"Long story short: William carried the phone back to the house; took it apart; used his magnifying glass to make certain no part had any moisture on it; replaced the parts; added a new battery; and the phone worked."

"Why didn't the parents tell the police?"

"They didn't know. William had been wanting a cellphone for a while, and his parents believed he was too young to have one. William didn't want them to take it away from him."

"That poor kid," Zack said.

Debbie raised an eyebrow. "Maybe save your pity for the person who owns that phone because they're in big trouble." She wrapped her bagel in a napkin. "Mind if I take this with me? It looks like I'm not going to be able to eat for a while."

"I can make you a fresh one," I said.

"Thanks, this'll be fine. When we find out who owns the phone, I'll let you know."

"Please do," I said. "Deb, I noticed when you were hauling Zack over the ashes, you said the police were investigating a murder case, not two cases. Was that just a slip?"

She grimaced, then shook her head as if to clear it. "This case is making me sloppy. One of the reasons I came over here this morning was to tell Zack that his client, Mike Braeden, is off the hook. There is no concrete evidence connecting Mike Braeden with Patti Morgan's death, and we've interviewed at least two dozen people who say Mr. Braeden is a salt of the earth guy with the patience of a saint. There's no reason to suspect him except for the facts that he and Patti Morgan had a bad marriage and he found the body. We were watching someone else for a while, but that blew up in our face last night."

My pulse quickened. "Was Thalia Monk the person you were watching?"

Debbie leaned forward. "How did you know that?"

"Just conjecture."

"I guess it doesn't matter now," she said. "We had an anonymous tip that on the early morning of the day Patti Morgan was killed, Thalia was seen without a necklace that apparently she was never without. There were marks around her neck suggesting that the necklace had been forcibly taken from her. Our anonymous tipster said we should check into Thalia's story."

"When we questioned Thalia, she said that she'd been mugged in Wascana Park on her morning run, and her assailant had ripped the necklace off her neck. Her story was corroborated by a person who was with her shortly after the incident. Thalia left a description of her necklace with the police in case someone found it and turned it in.

"That would have been the end of it, but when we learned that the relationship between Ms. Monk and her mother was troubled, to say the least, Ms. Monk became a question mark. Last night the man who assaulted Thalia Monk attacked another woman. A bystander witnessed the incident, called us, and the man was brought in for questioning.

"A lucky break for us and for Ms. Monk. This guy is a collector. When we checked out his apartment, we discovered a cache of trophies he'd taken from women he attacked. Among them was the amulet that Thalia Monk described." Debbie paused. "The officer who returned it to her this morning said Thalia wept when he handed it to her."

"That amulet contained a lock of her dead brother's hair," I said. "It was the only link she had with him."

"I'm glad we were able to return it to her," Debbie said. "At any rate, Mike Braeden and Thalia Monk were our only possibilities. The coroner says there's a fifty-fifty chance that Patti Morgan suffocated because of the combination of alcohol and drugs in her system rendered her incapable of turning her head to breathe. Our investigation turned up nothing to disprove that, so the case is closed."

After Debbie left, Zack said, "Do you realize it's only ten thirty in the morning? Whatever we do after this will be anticlimactic."

"Where's your spirit of adventure?"

Zack gave a satyr's smile. "Why don't we go back to bed and see if we can discover it?"

"Let me get these dishes in the dishwasher and I'll be right there."

At that point, Taylor bounced into the kitchen. She was wearing cut-offs and a button-up shirt. She had paint in her hair; her feet were bare and she was ebullient. "This mural is going to be amazing. I can't wait for you to see it."

"How long do we have to wait?" Zack said.

"I've been thinking about that," Taylor said. "With Thanksgiving and the baptism, this weekend will be a zoo, and I want there to be a time for just a few of us to see it together. I thought maybe we could look at it on Saturday afternoon before everyone arrives for dinner."

"That's settled then," I said.

But Taylor's attention had already wandered to the kitchen table. "Bagels, cream cheese, lox and capers. I am so hungry."

"Go for it," I said. "When you're through, you and I can straighten up the kitchen together."

Taylor was already slicing a bagel. "I can clean up the kitchen," she said. "You and dad just go ahead with whatever it was you were planning to do."

Zack held his arms out to me, and I reached in. "Rain check?" he whispered.

"You bet," I said.

Zack turned his wheelchair towards the hall. "In that case," he said, "I'm going to the office to check in with Maisie about the latest. Debbie didn't say anything about telling Mike Braeden he was in the clear, did she?"

"No," I said. "You should probably make certain he knows."

"Will do," Zack said. "The news will be an immense relief to Mike and to the Webers."

As Zack chose his clothes for the office, and I made the bed, I thought of someone else who would welcome the news.

"The fact that Mike Braden is no longer a suspect will be a relief to Thalia too," I said. "Mike Braeden never stopped caring about her. Sylvie always said no matter what happens in the future, a child will remember that there was someone who never walked away."

"And Thalia picked up on that," Zack said. "When push came to shove, she was as eager to protect Mike as he was to protect her. She deserves to know all's well."

"She does," I said, "and when I talk to her, I'll be sure to mention the role the anonymous tipster played in getting Thalia's amulet back to her."

Zack chortled. "You do that, and tell Thalia you and I are both pulling for her. She really has had a helluva life."

When I called Thalia, I got her voicemail. I left a message asking her to call me and added that the news I had for her was good. Then because there was nothing on my calendar and because thirteen years at Bishop Lambeth School had taught me that idle hands are the devil's workshop, I decided to tackle a job I'd been avoiding.

Desmond Zackary Dowhanuik was being baptized wearing the ivory muslin christening dress with Ayrshire whitework that generations of Maisie's family, the Crawfords, had been christened in. The dress was an heirloom, and it was fragile. Maisie had called all over town in search of a dry cleaner or laundry service that would clean the gown. No one would risk it. I had looked online, and the directions for washing a delicate baptismal gown seemed simple enough, so I volunteered.

The baptism was five days away, and I was free until Zack came home. I picked up my phone and called Mieka. After we'd exchanged news, I said, "I'm calling to tell you that I'm just about to wash Desmond's gown for the baptism. Now that I've told you what I'm going to do, I can't back out."

"Mum, if it's such a big job, I'll do it."

"No, you won't. It's not a big job; I'm just being dramatic. I'll bring the dress over when I'm finished. That'll probably be around the time the school bus drops off the ladies, so I'll be able to get the lowdown on what's happening at Pius X."

The process turned out to be simple but messy. It involved a lot of time bent over a bathtub filled with a combination of lukewarm water and pre-dissolved Woolite and then rinsing the gown under a very gentle shower until it was soap-free. I was finishing phase three — flattening the dress on a thick towel in a sunny place until it dried — when the doorbell rang.

I was wearing shorts and a T-shirt, and both were soaked, but when the doorbell rang again, I answered it. Thalia was on the front porch. "I've caught you at a bad time," she said. "I tried to call but . . ."

"I turned my phone off," I said. "I was doing something that demanded my complete attention, but I'm finished now. Come in, and I'll show you what I was doing."

Thalia followed me into the living room where the gown was drying. As we examined the dress, I described the process. She was intrigued. "It was worth the effort," she said. "That really is beautiful. Is that lace?"

"It's called whitework, and it's a kind of embroidery that involves drawing the thread from the material of the piece of clothing the sewer is working on through the material itself. I just looked that up earlier this afternoon, so it may not be wholly accurate."

"No, that was a good explanation. I think I understand," Thalia said, and I was struck again by the vulnerability in her low husky voice. "It must have taken the people who did that work forever to complete all those tiny stitches."

"I'm sure it did, and I'm sure the people doing the white-work were women," I said. "I read once that girls in almost every culture are set tasks like needlework to teach them the patience they'll need for the tedium of raising children and running a household."

After we both laughed, Thalia said, "There's so much I need to tell you. On the way over, I was trying to think of the right words, and here we are laughing together about women's work. I didn't expect that."

"Neither did I," I said. "Let me just change into some dry clothes. I'll make us tea, and we can talk some more."

When I came back to the kitchen, Thalia was looking at the photos of the grandkids on the refrigerator door.

"So, this is real life," she said.

It was a curious comment, and I was taken aback. "It's *my* real life," I said. "There are other options."

Thalia nodded. "I'm beginning to understand that."

"Let me make the tea, and we can sit down and wait 'till it has colour,' as an old friend of mine used to say."

Thalia smiled. "I wanted to thank you and your husband and daughter-in-law for arranging for Katina Posaluko-Chapman to be with me when I talked to the police about the photographs."

"You needed support, and Katina's an excellent lawyer and a fine person."

"She is, and I was very grateful to have her by my side. Knowing others were seeing the photographs was difficult, but I'd already prepared myself. During one of the many times Patti was castigating me for being a whore who ruined Nicholas's life, she told me she'd given the photos to Rosemary Morrissey. The idea that Rosemary had seen those photos made me sick. I was afraid that other people might see them. Then I realized that the worst thing that I could imagine happening to me had already happened: Nicholas was dead. There was nothing to be afraid of anymore."

"Thalia, you don't have to answer this if you don't want to, but were the other summer interns — the young men who were your friends in the cohort — aware that you were no longer afraid of the photos coming to light?"

For the first time since we'd begun talking, Thalia was visibly shaken. "They never knew about the photographs," she said. "They never knew that Nicholas and I were lovers."

Thalia's candour surprised me. When I had opened the front door and saw her on our porch, I knew whatever had brought Thalia to our house would involve discussing her relationship with Nicholas. I anticipated that we would both find a circumspect way of referring to another kind of love that, in Lord Alfred Douglas's words, "dared not speak its name," but Thalia hadn't shied away from speaking the truth. Her statement was direct, and it was a relief to realize that whatever else had happened, Thalia would not lie to deny a truth that had informed her life.

"Could anyone else have told the members of the cohort about the photos of you and Nicholas together?"

"Obviously Patti knew," Thalia said, "but Patti was terrified that something would stain Nicholas's memory. I have no idea what she was thinking when she gave the photographs to Rosemary. I know now that Rosemary gave them to Ellen Exton, but there would have been no reason for Ellen to tell Clay or Ronan about them. If they had found out something, they would have told me. But whatever, the cohort is no more. We'd all outgrown it, so I decided the time had come to disband."

"And the others accepted that?"

"They had to," she said simply. She paused. "You said you had some good news?"

"I do. The police are no longer investigating Mike Braeden. They've closed your mother's case. They're accepting the coroner's opinion that there's a likelihood that Patti brought about her own death."

Thalia exhaled slowly. "I guess I should feel something about that, but I don't." Her face became animated again. "But I am very happy that the police are no longer investigating Mike. He was never anything but kind and concerned about me. More often than I can tell you, when Patti started one of her tirades about me being a whore who ruined Nicholas's life, Mike would try to calm her down. If she didn't stop, he'd take her into another room or even out of the house for a walk.

"I've thought about this a lot, Joanne, and I've come to realize that if it hadn't been for Mike Braeden, I would have accepted my mother's evaluation of me. He's a good man who tried to help a woman at the lowest point in her life and her daughter who was confused, angry and making nothing but bad choices. He was heroic. And his reward was getting his face slashed and watching the life and reputation he'd spent years building ripped out from under him. It was so unjust, and yet he never once blamed me."

"Thalia, no one who knows the truth blames you."

"I blame me," she said. "What I did to Taylor was mean and small and destructive. All I can hope is that the damage I did to her life can somehow be repaired."

I thought of Taylor bounding into the kitchen that morning, barefoot, paint-smeared and exuberant. "Taylor's fine. She's finding her way to a life that will fulfill her," I said. "How about you? Have you thought about what you're going to do next?"

"I don't know. I've pretty well screwed up my life."

"You're twenty-one years old, Thalia. You have at least sixty more years to screw up."

Her eyes widened, and she started to laugh. "That's right, isn't it. The rest of my life is a tabula rasa, and I'm the one who will decide what message I want my life to convey."

"That's exactly right. You have a blank slate and all the time in the world to figure out how you're going to fill it."

Thalia looked around the kitchen as if she were seeing it for the first time. "I didn't want to come here today, but I'm so glad I did."

"I'm glad you came too," I said. "Thalia, I couldn't help noticing that you're not wearing your amulet."

"I have to move on," she said, and her voice was small and tentative.

"How's that working for you?"

"Not very well, but I'm trying," she said. She reached into her purse, pulled out a small clutch evening bag, opened it and took out the necklace. "It helps to keep it close."

"I understand," I said. "Mike gave you that evening bag, didn't he?"

Thalia nodded. "It was his wife Sylvie's. When I called to tell Mike the police found my necklace, I told him I would try to break myself of the habit of always wearing it. Not long after that, he came by the Fairbairns with this lovely little purse. He said Sylvie would want me to have it as a reminder that life gets better."

"That's exactly what Sylvie would have said." I touched her hand. "Thalia, keep that thought close."

* * *

My plan for the rest of the day was ambitious. I would put up my feet and read until the baptismal dress had dried and then I would wrap the gown in tissue, place it in a box and deliver it to Mieka's, where I would play with Des until the ladies' school bus arrived, get caught up on the news from Pius X and come home, make the martinis and wait for Zack.

With a few minor adjustments, everything went according to plan. The muslin dried quickly, and as I wrapped the baptismal gown in tissue paper and slipped it into the box, I thought of our newest grandson, snug in his godparents' arms at the font in the cathedral.

Des was sleeping so I missed playtime, but Mieka and I talked about the lunch we would be having at their place after the service. She and Charlie had invited Jill and Kam Chau to join the party. "Are you playing matchmaker?" I said.

"Nope. I've tried before, but the results have always been disastrous. I think Jill and Kam are destined to be good friends and that will be enough. Jill offered to bring dessert on Sunday, and Kam offered to bring a special dessert for the kids, so the invitation has already paid off."

After the school bus dropped them off, Madeleine and Lena raced up the front walk, breathless with news. "There was a lockdown at the school today."

Mieka had inherited my penchant for catastrophic thinking. "Did someone inside the school have a gun?"

The girls frowned. "Of course not," Madeleine said. "You know our principal would never allow that."

Mieka tried a laugh. "Of course he wouldn't. Mo St. Amand has been at Pius since you two were tadpoles, and he's super vigilant."

"So, what did happen?" I said.

"The teachers always call the roll after lunch and when the grade one teacher called the roll, one of her pupils — a boy — was missing," Madeleine said. "They locked all the doors to the outside, and everybody looked for him.

"The grade eights," she added proudly, "were sent out to check the playground. The boy was not there. Mo called his house, but no one was home. So, they called the parents' work numbers. They're both nurses, and they were both in surgery.

430

So, Mo called the police. When the police went to the boy's house and knocked at the door, there was no answer."

Lena's impatience had worn thin. "Then the police went in the backyard, and there was the boy sitting on the swing eating a sandwich."

Madeleine glared at her sister. "Let me finish the story, Lena. The boy said he'd had too much school, so he went home."

"That's a great story," I said. I stood. "And you know what? I've had a day like that myself, and I think it's time for me to do what that boy did and give you all a hug and head for home."

CHAPTER TWENTY-SIX

When Zack came through the front door at five o'clock, the martinis were made; the casserole of boeuf bourguignon Mieka had given us was in the oven; the table was set; and I was looking forward to a long evening filled with nothing much at all.

I helped Zack off with his jacket. "Something smells amazing," he said.

"Mieka gave us a casserole of boeuf bourguignon as a reward for washing Des's baptismal gown."

"Sound like we came out ahead on that deal."

I remembered waiting for the Woolite to dissolve in boiling water. "It was a fair exchange," I said. "Taylor's still working on the mural, so we have plenty of time before dinner. Why don't you turn on the fireplace, and I'll get the drinks?"

"Another fair exchange," Zack said.

When we'd settled in the family room and taken our first sips, Zack said, "I have news."

"Those are not words I want to hear."

"Well, gulp your martini because you're not going to like these words either. The cellphone the enterprising young William Duncan found belongs to Clay Fairbairn. I only got the broad strokes from Debbie, but I gather the cellphone is a gold mine of information about what the cohort has been up to lately."

"The cohort has disbanded," I said. "Thalia Monk was here this afternoon. She said she'd realized it was time. When I asked her if the other members of the group accepted her decision, she said they had no choice."

"She was wrong," Zack said. "The three remaining members of the University Park Road Gang were determined to keep the band together, and they had a plan."

"Zack, I don't like the direction in which this is heading."

"I don't either, but we can't change the direction. It's a *fait accompli*. Apparently, the late Patti Morgan told the young men that Ellen Exton had photographs of Thalia that Thalia wouldn't want made public. Patti told them if they could get their hands on those photos, Thalia would do anything they wanted her to do to keep the pictures from being made public."

"That's not good," I said.

"MediaNation has a gym for its employees. Clay Fairbairn works out there frequently. As does Kam Chau. Clay was aware that Kam had a key to Ellen Exton's house to check on her cats on the weekends she was away. Clay took the key from Kam's locker, had a copy made and returned the key. He, Ronan and Austin were in Ellen's house the day she was fired. Her habit was to have dinner in the cafeteria, go back to her desk and work an hour or so longer and leave around seven.

"But the day she was fired, she left early. The cohort members were in her bedroom, going through her drawers when they heard Charlie and Ellen come in. Obviously there are still a lot of gaps to be filled in, but Deb's theory is that when Charlie left, the cohort boys demanded Ellen give them the photos. Deb thinks that when Ellen said she didn't have them, Clay didn't believe her. Apparently, at some point, Ellen started to scream, and that's when Clay choked her.

"Oh, God, no."

"It doesn't get better," Zack said. "Jo, this is just conjecture, but it's Debbie's conjecture, so I guess it deserves some credence. Debbie thinks that as soon as it was dark, Ronan and Austin carried Ellen's body out and buried her in the culvert."

There was an afghan beside me on the couch, and I pulled it around me. "This story has a real Alfred Hitchcock ending," I said. "When Thalia was here, we talked about the photos. She knew that Patti had given them to Rosemary. She said that at first the idea of the photos becoming public terrified her and then she realized that her worst fear — that something would happen to her brother — had already been realized. And that's when she knew there was nothing more to be afraid of."

"So, the photographs were no longer a weapon to keep Thalia in line."

"No, Ellen Exton's death served no purpose, and somehow that makes everything that's happened even worse."

For a long while we just sat, staring at the fireplace and trying to get our bearings.

Finally, Zack said, "Okay, time for us to get a grip. It's almost six, and our daughter will soon be joining us for dinner. Next week, she's moving to Saskatoon. Let's make this evening as good as we can make it."

Zack and I did our best to keep the mood upbeat, but Taylor knew us well, and when she asked what was troubling us, we told her the truth. She seldom drank, but that night when Zack offered to pour her a glass of burgundy because Mieka's boeuf bourguignon deserved a perfect pairing, Taylor accepted.

Processing our account of what happened took her awhile. Like us, she was overwhelmed by the horror and futility of Ellen Exton's death. Finally, she said, "It's hard to conceive of people you actually know killing another human being. And just because a little group they'd created to make themselves feel worthwhile was in danger of losing its leader."

"And it was all for nothing," I said. "Even if Ellen had been able to give them the photos, nothing would have changed. Thalia was through with the cohort. She'd outgrown it. No matter what the University Park Road boys did, Thalia would have walked away." I turned to Zack. "Another paper tiger in this tragedy."

Taylor looked quizzical. "What's a paper tiger?"

"It's a person or a thing that appears to be threatening, but is really no threat at all," Zack said. "The example your mum and I were referring to was Patti Morgan's obsessive fear that if Mike Braeden found proof that the relationship between Thalia and her brother Nicholas was unnatural, he'd make what he'd learned public and sully Nicholas Monk's reputation. Patti was convinced that Mike would force her to go to a therapist, and the therapist would give her a truth serum that would make her tell everything she knew about Nicholas and Thalia."

"The 'truth serum' was Patti Morgan's paper tiger. Her fear of the serum drove all of her erratic and destructive behaviour, and it posed no threat to her at all. In the early '60s, the so-called truth serum was found to be unreliable, and therapists haven't used it since then."

"So, Patti Morgan created a paper tiger, and her fear of it killed her." Taylor was thoughtful.

"Why did Patti Morgan think the photos of Thalia and her brother were so damaging that Thalia would have done anything to avoid having them made public?"

Zack turned to me. Clearly the ball was in my court.

"Thalia and her brother were lovers, and the photos were of them having sex."

"Were the photos pornographic?"

"No. Taylor, you're familiar with Robert Mapplethorpe's photography."

"Of course. Those black-and-white photos he took in the 1980s were sexual, but they were also incredibly beautiful and powerful. They're art."

"The photographs of Nicholas and Thalia were beautiful and powerful too. But they're photos of a brother and sister."

"Incest," Taylor said. "Thalia was only sixteen when she came to Luther. All that happened to her when she was so young. Jo, do you think she'll ever be all right?"

"Honestly, I don't know," I said. "She was here today. One of the reasons she came was to make certain you were all right."

"I hope you told her I was."

"I did. I told her you were fine now, and you would be better."

"I am," Taylor said. "And, Jo, I hope that will be true for Thalia too."

"So do I," I said.

* * *

The days before the Thanksgiving weekend were a mix of firming up comforting domestic plans and dealing with the dark spoor of tragedy that Ellen Exton's murder had left in its wake.

The texts on Clay Fairbairn's phone were incriminating enough to have charges pressed against the three young men. Jill had told me Hugh Fairbairn was a hard-ass except when it came to his grandson, and she was right on both counts. Jill said that Hugh was broken-hearted about Clay's situation, but he was clear-eyed in evaluating what Clay was up against legally, and he immediately hired the lawyer who had successfully defended Jared Delio to represent Clay.

Zack had followed the Delio trial carefully, and he had been impressed with the stunning performance of Delio's lawyer. She was a preternaturally cool combatant who never revealed a flash of temper or distaste for the misery she was about to inflict upon a witness with information that might be damning for her client, and she maintained her laser focus until the job was done. Zack made no bones about the fact that he was looking forward to sitting front and centre at Clay's trial.

Ronan and Austin were represented by local lawyers. Zack said both were good, but Ronan's was young and unseasoned, and Austin's was past his best-before date. However, both Ronan and Austin were accessories, and typically punishment for a convicted accessory is not as severe as for the perpetrator.

All my news about life in the Fairbairn household continued to come from Jill. After a night of vitriol largely focused on Thalia, Julie Evanson Gallagher Fairbairn had, like the dowager in a Victorian novel, taken to her bed. Mark and Lori Evanson were at their son's side for as long as he wanted them there and, again surprisingly, Clay seemed to welcome their company. I was hopeful, but Zack said Clay's boutique lawyer had undoubtedly suggested Clay would be smart to establish a pattern of remorse and repentance before the trial opened. Whatever Clay's motivation, I was grateful that Mark and Lori were finally able to be accepted by their son.

Thalia too had spent time with Clay. Hugh told Jill that Clay hadn't discussed the specifics of what Thalia and he talked about, but he had been strengthened by her willingness to accept responsibility for urging the University Park Road group to accept a philosophy that until recently she herself had not fully understood. Clay had also been impressed by the example Thalia set by sending Alison Janvier the yearbooks that revealed the identity of Harper's father and allowing Alison to decide whether or not to destroy them.

On the Friday before Thanksgiving, Thalia flew to Toronto to spend the weekend with her father. She stopped by our house on her way to the airport. Dressed for travel in a smart charcoal zip-up soft hoodie, skinny jeans and zebra-patterned runners, Thalia was the epitome of casual chic, but when I met her at the door, she said, "I'm here for reassurance. I want you to have my number in Toronto, and I want you to tell me I can call you whenever I need advice about how not to screw up my next sixty years."

I smiled. "You're not going to let me forget about that, are you?"

"No, because it made me laugh. It also made me realize that I can still make good choices about my future. My father and I are going to spend the weekend trying to figure out how we can salvage our relationship. He's always taken pride in the way he conducts his professional life, but I made him compromise his reputation by giving me everything I needed in my campaign to hurt Taylor, especially the footage of Vale and Etienne Simard from the filming of *Sisters and Strangers*. I will never stop being ashamed of what I did to your daughter or why I did it.

"Joanne, I have no idea what I'm going to do next. All I know is that I'm going to try to do better, and I'm going to try to be better." Thalia reached into her grey leather tote and took out Sylvie's evening bag. "Still carrying this," she said. "It's a hard habit to break. I'm so scared." She stepped close to me. "Could you . . . ?"

"I could," I said. When I took Thalia in my arms, I was surprised at how insubstantial, how bird-light, her body was. I could feel her heart beating against mine. As I stood watching the taxi that would take her to the airport waiting with its meter ticking, I found myself hoping against hope that Sylvie's wish would come true, that in the not-too-distant future, Thalia Monk's life *would* get better.

* * *

At four-thirty Saturday afternoon, Zack and I were doing a last-minute check of our readiness for Thanksgiving dinner. We were planning to eat at six. Taylor had worked her artist's magic setting the two tables we were using; Gracie had proven to be a deft hand at making salads. When I complimented her on the astonishingly thin, lucent slices of cucumber she was cutting, she grinned. "I'm planning to be an orthopedic surgeon. Cucumbers are good practice." The potatoes were mashed; the turkey was ready to come out of the oven; the ham was waiting to be carved; the side dishes were ready for their finishing touches; and the pies were on the sideboard.

There would be seventeen of us at the table: Mieka and Charlie and their family; Maisie Peter and the twins; Noah Wainberg and Jacob; Rose and Betty Lavallee and Gracie; Taylor, Zack and me. A small number by our usual standards, but it felt right.

Angus and Leah Drache, his first love and, in my opinion, his best, were spending the weekend with Leah's family in Saskatoon; Jill and Kam were with Kam's family in Indian

Head; and Alison Janvier and Harper were in La Ronge visiting with the Janviers and doing some last-minute politicking.

We were ready, but we had promised an event of pre-dinner excitement: the unveiling of Taylor's mural and the newly renovated swimming pool room. Taylor had been insistent that Zack and I see the mural with only Gracie and her, before anyone else arrived, and time was growing short.

At twenty-five to five, Zack turned to me. "Did I get my wires crossed? I thought we were supposed to have a private viewing before everyone got here."

"You didn't get your wires crossed," I said. "And Taylor and Gracie are still in the dining room, perfecting the fan of the napkins at the place settings. Let's ask them if we're ready to go."

All week Taylor had been fired up about us seeing the mural. She said she was counting the hours before the big moment. Now when Zack asked her if we were ready for lift-off, she looked stricken. "I'm having second thoughts about this, Dad. It may be too much. Before you look at the mural, I want you to know that I can change it. Tell me the truth. I won't be hurt."

Zack was clearly baffled. "Taylor, you know I'll love it. I love everything you make. Besides, this is your mum's gift."

When Taylor looked at me, she was close to tears. "This *is* your gift, Jo. And I thought about what I could paint that would make you the happiest, and I knew that what would make you the happiest was something that would make Dad stop hurting so much. I'm sorry I can't explain. Just come and look at the mural and tell me if you want me to change it because I will."

As soon as I saw the mural, I understood.

It was a painting of Lawyers Bay on a perfect high summer day. Our houses were all there; the trees and bushes were in full leaf. Everything was as it was now except for the people. The only people in the painting were Zack and his law partners as they were during their first summer at the lake.

I had seen the picture hundreds of times. Each of the partners had a copy of it. Kevin's was framed in birch and set on a rustic end table, with birch-log legs, that had been in the cottage since he was a kid. Delia's, in a starkly modern metal frame, had had a place of honour on the mantle of the Wainbergs' fireplace until that terrible November day when, like so much else, it seemed to disappear. Blake Falconer's copy was framed in cherrywood and it was kept on the credenza in the den of the house where Pete and Maisie and their family now lived. Chris's copy had been hung on a wall in the main reception area at Falconer Shreve. But, like Zack's copy that until that November day had always been in a chased silver frame on his dresser, Chris's copy of the photo was gone.

Taken during the partners' first summer at Lawyers Bay, the photo showed the new lawyers, dressed in jeans and T-shirts, up to their thighs in the lake. Zack was in the middle: on one side of him were Delia and Chris; on the other, Blake and Kevin. Almost two-thirds of Zack's chair was submerged. It was a tender photo filled with the light of the sun bouncing off the water and the joy of five young people alive on a summer day with the future shining before them.

The figures were full-sized, and Taylor's painting had captured everything about that long-ago morning so filled with hope. For a time that seemed endless, Zack simply stared at the painting and then he wheeled close and reached out with his forefinger and touched the young faces of each of his partners. "We really were something," he said. His voice was ragged with emotion, and I knew the words were not directed at us.

"Dad, it was a mistake," Taylor said. "I can fix it. I'll change it tonight."

"No, don't," Zack said. "Taylor, it's exactly right. I'm just . . . at a loss. Tonight after everyone leaves, I'll probably come in here, look at the mural and cry. Joanne will come with me because she always does, but right now I'm just so grateful to remember that, for all those years, Blake, Delia, Kevin and Chris were part of my life, and now I have all of you."

It was a poignant moment, but it didn't last long. The glass wall of the swimming pool room faced the side lawn. Gracie pointed to the wall. "Look," she said. A small face was pressed flat against the glass, followed within seconds by another small and identical face and then Pete and Maisie appeared, looking embarrassed but waving. And then seemingly out of nowhere, Jacob Wainberg had joined the twins and pressed his face against the glass, and Noah, Rose and Betty were standing with Pete and Maisie.

Gracie went to Zack, kissed the top of the head. "Time to straighten up and fly right, Zack. The rest of our family is here."

"So they are," Zack said and turned his chair and wheeled towards Taylor and me. He took my hand. "Gracie's right," he said. "It's time to join the rest of our family."

We didn't get far. As it turned out, the rest of the family had decided to join us. The next half hour was a kaleidoscope of ever-shifting moments. The twins barrelling down the hall towards us, followed by everybody else who was joining us for dinner.

Taylor's mural was met first with stunned silence and then with extravagant but wholly justified praise. It was a piercingly beautiful piece of art and deeply personal to each of us in the room. And then, as we all moved closer to examine the details, we began to whisper as people always seem to do in art galleries.

The hush didn't last long. Charlie and Colin had voices that carried, and their words rang out loud and clear. "Where. Are. We?" It was, I think, the question that was in the back of all our minds, but mercifully Gracie had the answer. "I'm glad you asked that question," she said. "See that big-screen TV on the wall, pull up a beanbag and you'll see where you are."

The big flat screen TV had been there when we bought the house. We seldom used it, and when we were planning the renovations, I'd suggested removing it all together, but the contractor said, "You might as well leave it. It's not in the way, and who knows, someday it might come in handy."

Seemingly that day had come. The boys had chosen their beanbags, and Gracie was sitting beside them with her laptop. "Here's where you come in," she said, and the screen was filled with the images and sounds of the summer just passed.

The adults gathered round, and the room was filled with the exclamations, laughter and groans of people watching home movies. We were all there. Mieka, vastly pregnant with Des. The twins hurtling through life, always with Madeleine, Lena or an adult close behind. Betty and Rose teaching Jacob how to swim. Taylor diving off the high tower as Vale cheered her on. Peter rubbing sunblock on Maisie and leaning in to kiss the back of her neck. Noah lifting the canoe into the water, so Madeleine and Lena could paddle over to the next shore to follow up on the rumour that a new family had bought a cottage, and they had sons who were just about the same ages as Lena and Madeleine.

It was a lot of fun, but when the twins and Jacob became restless, we knew it was time for a change of venue. Time for the kids to throw a ball around in the backyard for a while and burn off some energy, and time for the adults to get dinner on the table.

Before we left, Gracie had a final announcement. "You know that Dr. Seuss poem, 'Today Was Fun / Today Is Done / Tomorrow Is Another One'? Thanks to Noah, Rose and Betty, our family has a movie for every summer since the summer in Taylor's painting. When Taylor had the idea for this mural, Noah, Betty and Rose decided to put together all our old snapshots and home movies. Now, any time you want to watch yourself grow up or Maisie and Peter want to watch themselves get married or the girls painting their toenails three different shades or making an inuksuk, or see Jo and Zack smooching when they think nobody's watching, or remember one of the people in the mural who is no longer with us, just make a bowl of popcorn and choose a movie, and you can see how we've all become the people we are."

When Gracie's speech was met with a round of applause, I nudged Taylor. "Look at your dad's face."

Our daughter knew Zack's every expression. "He's on his way back," she said.

I squeezed her shoulder. "He is," I said, "and I think *that* may just be the best present ever."

ACKNOWLEDGEMENTS

Thanks to:

The late Jean Spurgeon for her support of the Joanne Kilbourn Shreve series from the beginning and for her commitment to READsaskatoon and all its learners.

Emily Shultz, my editor who, like Maxwell Perkins, realizes that writers need coddling but they also need to write the best book they can write, and that the editor's job is to make certain they do.

Crissy Calhoun, who gracefully extricated me from a whopper of an error and who gave the manuscript the necessary final polish.

Anita Ragunathan, a consummate professional at marketing and sales, and a poetry lover who swoons at the same shimmering lines as I do.

Jessica Albert, Digital and Art Director, who supported my passion for the stunning photograph on the cover of *An Image in the Lake*.

Hildy Bowen and Brett Bell, who were always cheerful and loving as they helped me deal with my endless technological challenges.

Max and Carrie Bowen, for their love and support.

Our grandchildren: Kai Langen, Brittany Scheelhaase, Madeleine Bowen-Diaz, Lena Bowen-Diaz, Chesney Langen-Bell, Ben Bowen-Bell, Peyton Bowen and Lexi Bowen, who bring light and laughter to our lives.

Najma Kazmi, MD, for her professionalism and her many kindnesses.

Wayne Chau, BSP, for his endless patience and good humour.

Lynne Bell, Joanne Bonneville and Margaret Wigmore for being dear and supportive friends.

Ron and Cindy, our loving and generous neighbours.

Ollie, the cat, who has brought our family so much joy.